D0492790

The Loveday Secrets

Also by Kate Tremayne

Adam Loveday
The Loveday Fortunes
The Loveday Trials
The Loveday Scandals
The Loveday Honour
The Loveday Pride
The Loveday Loyalty
The Loveday Revenge

The Loveday Secrets

Kate Tremayne

headline

First published in 2008
by HEADLINE PUBLISHING GROUP

1

Cataloguing in Publication Data is available from the British Library

ISBN 978 0 7553 3352 3

Typeset in Bembo by Avon DataSet Ltd,
Bidford-on-Avon, Warwickshire

Printed and bound in Great Britain by
Mackays of Chatham plc, Chatham, Kent

Headline's policy is to use papers that are natural, renewable and recyclable
products and made from wood grown in sustainable forests. The logging and
manufacturing processes are expected to conform to the environmental
regulations of the country of origin.

HEADLINE PUBLISHING GROUP
An Hachette Livre UK Company
338 Euston Road
London NW1 3BH

www.headline.co.uk
www.hachettelivre.co.uk

To Alison, Stuart and Tanya, Jasmine, Dan, Noah and Megan for the sheer joy you bring to our lives. To my dear friend and fellow Piscean, Karen, who never forgets my birthday. Many happy returns.

And, as ever, to my rock and inspiration – Chris.

Acknowledgements

Writing can be a solitary experience and I have to thank the Lovedays who have become my extended family and given me so many enjoyable adventures.

I have also been blessed with a wonderful, supportive team: Teresa Chris, Jane Morpeth, Sherise Hobbs, Jo Matthews, Jane Selley, Nancy Webber and everyone at Headline; all my friends and family who patiently listen to me trying to resolve a Loveday character's personal dilemma and, of course, all Loveday fans who so kindly take the trouble to write and email me.

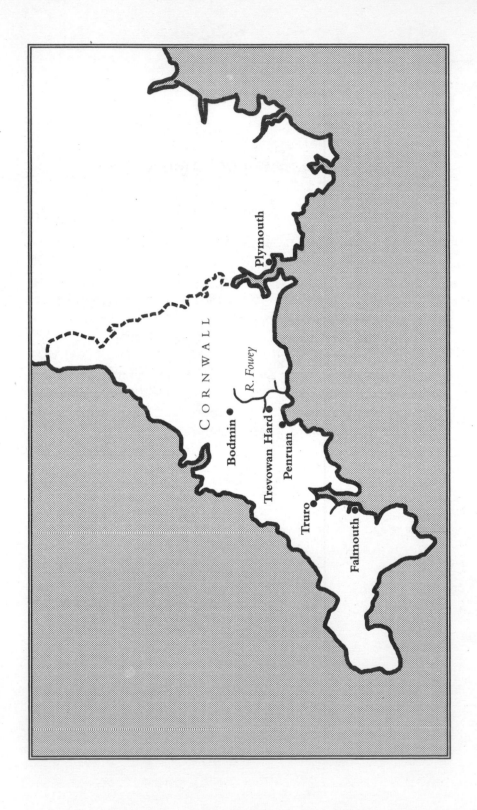

THE LOVEDAY FAMILY

Arthur St John Loveday **m.** Anne Penhaligan
b. 1679   b. 1691
d. 1742   d. 1733

George Loveday **m.** Joan Trelawny
b. 1711   b. 1722
d. 1785   d. 1764

Margaret   Elspeth   St John   Edward *(twins)*   Rowena   Joshua   Hubert   William
b. 1736 –   b. 1738 –   b. 1740   b. 1743 –   b. 1743   b. 1745 –   b. 1746   b. 1747 –
m. Charles Mercer   d. 1744   d. 1794   d. 1743   **m.** Cecily Truscott   d. 1777   d. 1794
b. 1726   (1) **m.** Marie Lenoir   b. 1749 –   **m.** Lisette
d. 1791   b. 1747   Marquise
Thomas   d. 1767   de Gramont
b. 1758 –   (2) Amelia Allbright   (*née* Riviere)
m. Georganna Lascalles   b. 1759 –   b. 1771
b. 1768 –   d. 1794

                                                 Tamasine   Richard Allbright Japhet   Hannah   Peter
                                                 b. 1778 –   b. 1781 –   b. 1763 –   b. 1768 –   b. 1771 –
                                                 m. Maximillian Deverell   **m.** Gwendolyn Druce (1) **m.** Oswald Rabson **m.** Bridie Polglase
                                                 b. 1770 –   b. 1764 –   b. 1763   b. 1777 –
                                                                                                               d. 1796
Adam   Rafe   Joan   Druce   (2) **m.** Sam Deighton   Michael
b. 1767 –   b. 1791 – b. 1794 –   b. 1798 –   b. 1764 –   b. 1798 –
m. Senara Polglase   d. 1796   Japhet Edward
b. 1768 –   b. 1794 –   Charlie Deighton
                                                                                                                 b. 1792 –
St John *(twins)*   Nathan   Joel *(twins)* Rhianne   Sara
b. 1767 –   b. 1792 – b. 1794 –   b. 1794 –   b. 1796 –   Davey   Abigail   Florence   Luke
(1) **m.** Meriel Sawle   b. 1787 – b. 1789 –   b. 1790 –   b. 1792 –
b. 1771   b. 1792 –
d. 1796
(2) **m.** Felicity Barrett
b. 1772 –

Rowena   Thea   Charlotte Barrett
b. 1788 –   b. 1799 –   b. 1792 –

Chapter One

1801

A full moon lit the earth of the track. St John Loveday was weary from his long ride and still suffering from a hangover, which had delayed his departure from Truro. The meal of fatty, overcooked beef in thick onion gravy that he had eaten at an inn on the road sat uncomfortably in his stomach. What should have been a week of entertainment and enjoying the company of old friends had gone disastrously wrong, and he could not shrug off a sickening feeling of guilt. He had lost the equivalent of an entire year's income from his estate during the gaming session in Truro. Felicity would never let the matter rest when she learned of his misfortune.

He had been the guest of the Honourable Percy Fetherington. He shook his head to clear his befuddled thoughts and corrected himself: Lord Fetherington – his friend Percy had inherited the title when his father died last winter. Lucky old Percy was now so rich he could afford to gamble to his heart's content. Some people had all the luck. St John scowled, his handsome face saturnine in the moonlight, and rubbed his hand over the dark stubble forming on his jaw. Depressed at his losses, he had not shaved for two days and his clothes were crumpled from having slept in them last night at the inn. Something else his wife would upbraid him for. The woman was fast turning into a shrew. She would not regard the gambling losses as bad luck, but would berate him for a wastrel to risk their security and livelihood on the turn of a card. The rest of the family were bound to take her side, and this time there would be no way he could hide his debt from them.

Close by, a vixen called to her cubs, and overhead, bats darted below the overhanging hawthorn and elder trees in the hedgerow. Pulling a hip flask from the pocket of his greatcoat, St John gulped its contents. The brandy settled the churning of his stomach. He was about a half-hour's ride from the crossroads where he would turn off towards the coast and his home at Trevowan. At least he would arrive home after his wife, aunt and stepmother had retired to their beds. There was no joy awaiting him in a house full of strong-minded women with strict moral judgements on anything a red-blooded male would find enjoyable. Was it any wonder that he frequently escaped their vigilance to spend time with his friends?

Home was no longer the sanctuary he had once relished. The Loveday women were a formidable and condemning brood and he was shackled to their company. One would think that they would be more appreciative that he housed and supported them. The drink and the guilt made him view his current life with disfavour.

He cursed the day he had wed Felicity. He had been in debt then and thought the young widow a wealthy prize. He had not learned the truth about her paltry fortune until after they were married. Then, after a year of marriage, she had presented him with another daughter instead of the son he longed for, and he had begun to find her company even more irksome. But at least she was again with child and her confinement would end before Christmas. This time it must be a son. Celebrating the news of the forthcoming birth had been his excuse for this latest session of gambling.

Suddenly there was a low rumbling like thunder behind him. St John's horse reared with fright. He barely had time to pull it out of the way before a coach sped past at a reckless pace, missing St John and his mount by less than a hand's breadth. He caught a glimpse of straining horses white-flecked with sweat and heard the wheels creaking as the coach lurched over the rocky path. Was the driver drunk or a madman? St John watched the coach sway dangerously as it rattled round a bend.

'Confounded idiot! You could have killed me.' His shout was lost in the night, his mood turning even bleaker.

It took some moments to calm his horse and it continued to snort and quiver in terror. He had been lucky not to be severely injured. Downing the last of the brandy, which swirled warmly

2

through his veins, he felt its calming effect. Not so many years ago, in his early twenties, he had regularly diced with death. Perhaps his guilt was making him paint too black a picture of his current life. Trevowan had been free of debt for a year, and that at least had enabled him to mortgage the estate as security for the loan he needed to settle his gaming accounts. He had overcome financial losses before and he could do so again. He did not know why gaming always took such a hold upon him and made him take risks with the security of his home. Yet undoubtedly the excitement of the turn of a card, the throw of a dice, or a wager on a horse race, was something his blood craved beyond caution or reason.

The quantity of brandy he had drunk and the steady clop of his gelding's gait after what had been a long day in the saddle began to take their toll. The breeze whipped the last of the May blossom from its branches so that it fell like snow upon his shoulders, and the air was sweet with the scent of bluebells. He pulled the collar of his coat around his ears against the chill in the night air. His eyes drooped and he slackened his hold on the reins. In the distance he heard the clock in the tower of Penruan church strike nine. Not far to ride now. The horse would find its own way to the comfort of its stable. As his head began to nod, he allowed his body to be lulled by the rhythm of his mount.

Abruptly, he was jolted awake. His horse snorted in alarm and reared on its hind legs, and for a moment he was in danger of being unseated. Ahead of him, St John saw the dead and mangled body of a large stag on the track, its blood still fresh and glistening silver in the moonlight. The smell of it had unnerved the young horse that had never been used for hunting. Engrossed in the task of calming his mount, St John did not immediately notice a vaster dark shape blocking the road ahead. Belatedly he realised it was an overturned coach. There was no sign of the horses. Or of life . . .

The narrow lane had widened into an open space with tracks leading off in three directions. St John dismounted and tied his gelding to the broken wheel of the vehicle. He shook his head to clear it of the cloying effects of the brandy and stared blearily at the wreckage. The coach's axle was broken and some of the luggage was scattered on the ground. The shaft the horses were harnessed to had been sheared off and no doubt the animals had bolted.

Or had they been taken by the occupants of the vehicle to continue their journey? he wondered. Surely, though, they would not have left so many of their possessions behind? He rubbed his temple, forcing his mind to function more rationally. As he stared at the scattered objects, he realised belatedly that one of them was human in shape. His step weaved precariously as he advanced on the figure. It was the coachman, who, before releasing the reins, had been dragged some distance along the earth by the terrified horses. The man was on his stomach, and his legs, twisted out at odd angles, were clearly broken.

St John stooped to ascertain if he was still alive. The sight of the damaged and bloodied skull lying against a small boulder was evidence enough that the man was dead. St John stumbled over to the vehicle, frantically trying to shake off the effects of the brandy. The coach must be the one that had almost run him down earlier. He needed to check whether there were injured passengers on board.

For a moment dizziness made him cling to the vehicle, then he grabbed the side of the window and hauled himself up. When the scene before him stopped revolving, the moonlight revealed more carnage: the bloodied body of an attractive woman in her thirties, her eyes staring sightlessly back at him. Even in the poor light there was no mistaking the expensive lace on her bodice and the glitter of gems on an exposed wrist. She was also beyond his help. There was no one else inside the coach.

A rush of nausea made him turn away. What a waste of two lives. Why had the vehicle been driven at such a reckless pace? From her clothing the woman was a person of position. Such a dangerous pace suggested a desperate flight born of fear. Yet from whom had she been fleeing?

It was a question that stayed with him. Over the top of the drystone wall he scanned the undulating countryside. At so late an hour, no candlelight lit the windows of the scattered farmsteads, and it was several miles to the nearest inland hamlet. The fishing village of Penruan was no closer than Trevowan. He doubted anyone else would be on the road this late, unless they were smugglers or vagabonds. They would strip the woman of her finery and steal anything of value.

He strained to listen for some sound of an approaching traveller. There was nothing but the song of a nightingale and the croak of toads in the nearby dewpond. He turned at a scuffling in the hedgerow, and a family of badgers, the white stripes on their faces clear in the moonlight, scurried across his path. It was a reminder that hungry foxes would gnaw on a corpse if left in the open and that by dawn carrion birds would also be feasting. Clearly he could not leave the woman's body here, but it would not be easy hauling her out of the carriage. For some moments he stared at the scattered luggage. There was a trunk on the road near the wheels that was large enough for him to stand on.

Several minutes later he was sweating and weary as he struggled to lift the woman from the coach. Her arm flopped against the handle of the open door and the glittering bracelet she had been wearing fell to the ground. The clasp was broken, and guessing that the diamonds were worth several hundred pounds, St John absently stashed it in his pocket for safe keeping. There were also diamond drops in her ears, which he pocketed too lest they were dislodged and lost. The woman was heavier than he expected and it took all his strength to haul her over his shoulder, stagger to his horse and heave her across the saddle. Pausing to recover his breath, he wiped the blood from her face with the corner of her cloak. She was dark-haired and olive-skinned, and had been beautiful in a rather exotic way. He knew all the gentry in this part of the county, and this woman was a stranger to him.

It was then he heard a low groan. It was human and had certainly not come from the woman or the driver. Infuriatingly, a long, narrow strip of cloud had covered the moon and plunged the track into almost total darkness, and he could see no sign of another figure. Then, as he strained to listen, the groan came again from near some elder bushes. Moving towards the sound, he stumbled over an unseen casket and crashed to his knees. As he pushed himself up from the ground, his hand encountered a slim leg partly hidden by the wayside ferns. He ran his palm along the limb clad in breeches, and the moon, again free of its veiling cover, revealed a youth of about ten. There was blood on his head and his pale velvet jacket. His eyelids flickered briefly.

'Mama,' he gasped, and then went limp in St John's arms.

'Poor motherless child,' sighed St John. 'Let's get you home and a doctor to tend you. Then we'll have to find out who you are.'

St John lifted the lad, and as he walked towards his horse, his foot struck the casket that had earlier tripped him. Its lock had broken and its contents were spilled on the ground. His throat dried and a hot rush of sweat coated his body. He could not believe his eyes. This was the answer to his prayers, the resolution of all his problems. It was riches beyond his dreams. But they were not his.

Yet who would know? whispered in his head an insidious voice. The owner of these jewels and gold coins was dead, and so was her driver.

Temptation had always been St John's weakness. He closed his eyes and swallowed. He despised himself for allowing the spread of riches to lure him, even for a moment, into considering something so dishonourable.

He drew a shuddering breath. He had made some foolish mistakes in the past and suffered the shame of his lapses from grace. He was now older, wiser . . .

As he hoisted the boy on to his already laden gelding and took the reins to lead the horse, the clock at Penruan struck ten. The hour was later than he expected. He had no idea of the seriousness of the boy's condition, but since the lad remained unconscious, he suspected it was grave. Leading his horse, it would take him over an hour to reach his home, and then a physician would need to be summoned, which would take another hour. The boy could be dead by then. His twin's estate at Boscabel was closer than Trevowan, and Adam's wife Senara had skill with herbs and had treated many of the injuries of the shipwrights' families who worked in the Loveday shipyard.

His aching body called out for the comfort of his own bed, but the boy should be tended as soon as possible. He led his horse around the corpse of the coachman. Hopefully the foxes would not get him before servants were sent to retrieve his body. Also, the coach could not be left blocking the track and the luggage must be saved from thieves and searched for clues of the lad's identity.

The Tudor house at Boscabel was in darkness when he arrived and banged on the door. A young serving boy, who slept by the fire in the kitchen, rubbed the sleep from his eyes as he answered his demand for entrance. St John pushed past him carrying the injured lad.

'Fetch your master and mistress,' he ordered. 'There has been an accident on the road. This boy's mother was killed and he needs immediate attention.' He strode up the stairs towards the bedrooms.

Woken by the raised voices, Adam appeared from the master bedchamber in a long velvet night robe and carrying a candle. The feeble light elongated his shadow on the wooden panelling covering the walls. Senara was wrapping a robe over her nightgown a few paces behind him.

'Did I hear you say there had been an accident?' Adam queried. He showed no surprise that the shorter, stockier figure of his twin, with the same dark hair as himself, had appeared in the dead of night. They led far from conventional lives and took the unexpected in their stride.

'A coach overturned. The driver is dead and so is a female passenger. Her body is outside on my horse.' St John was breathing heavily from his exertions. 'This boy was unconscious when I found him, which was about an hour ago, and has not stirred since.'

'Put him on the bed in here.' Senara led the way to a guest chamber and threw back the embroidered covers of a tester bed. 'I shall need more candles to examine him, and the fire lit.' She turned to the hovering servant lad. 'Rouse a maid to assist me.'

'You'll need to send men to collect what possessions there are from the coach and set it upright,' St John told his brother. 'I doubt it can be moved. The axle was broken and one of the wheels.'

Adam called after the disappearing serving lad. 'Wake Eli Rudge and Billy Brown, then hitch up the farm wagon.'

Senara had bent over the boy and was expertly running her hands over his body to discover if there were any broken bones or internal injuries. 'I do not like the look of that cut to his head. His pulse is very weak and he is starting a fever. You did right to bring him here, St John. If a fever takes hold, it could kill him.'

Feeling his duty was done, St John backed out of the sickroom, accompanied by Adam. St John said, 'There's the woman's body. It could be his mother. She'll need burying. I'll send word to Uncle Joshua tomorrow.'

'That is for her family to deal with,' Adam stated.

'Unless there are papers in the coach, I've no idea who she is,' St John snapped. His headache lingered and he was bone weary from his exertions. 'The lad will tell us when he regains consciousness. I still have to ride back to Trevowan.'

'Why not stay here? Or is Felicity expecting you? The hour is very late. Are you not interested to learn the boy's family?'

St John shrugged, infuriatingly indifferent, and did not meet Adam's gaze. 'I have done all I can for the lad. You can deal with his family. And my wife will expect me when she sees me.'

The callousness of his twin's remarks did not surprise Adam. His brother was indolent by nature and had never liked added burdens. The responsibility of a sick, possibly orphaned boy, whose family had to be found and notified, was not something St John would wish to undertake. Though Adam was disturbed that his words also showed that his brother was discontent in his marriage.

As they passed the carved stone fireplace in the entrance hall, the thickset figure of Adam's bailiff, Eli Rudge, appeared. The shorter figure of Billy Brown, who managed the livestock, sleepily rubbed his eyes. Adam explained the night's events, then added, 'Take the wagon to collect all luggage from the coach and bring it here. If you find the horses, they should also be stabled.'

St John had slumped down on a wooden settle and leaned his head back against the oak panelling, his eyes closing. He mumbled brief instructions where to find the coach. When the servants left, Adam put a hand on his brother's shoulder and insisted, 'Sleep tonight in the chamber above the porch. We will decide what to do about the woman in the morning.'

'Do what you think best.' St John yawned and rose unsteadily to reclimb the stairs. 'Send a maid up with a bottle of claret, there's a good fellow. It has been a long day.'

Adam suspected that his own day, after working ten hours in the shipyard and another two on the estate farm, was far from over. He carried the dead woman into the old hall and laid her on the long Jacobean table. St John was right in saying she was a stranger. Her clothing was expensive, and, apart from a wedding band, her only jewellery was a simple gold pendant containing a miniature of a handsome blond man and a lock of blond hair. It was a mourning locket often worn by widows. So the boy upstairs could indeed be an orphan.

Adam did not like mysteries and there were so many surrounding this night's events. When later he looked in on Senara, who had bathed the lad's head wound and fashioned a splint for his wrist, the candlelight showed the boy's face crimson with fever.

His wife's face was drawn with worry as she regarded Adam from across the bed. She had braided her dark hair into a plait, which hung over her shoulder to her waist. 'I shall stay with him all night. You need your sleep, my love.'

'I cannot rest. Though I passed St John's door and he is snoring loudly.' He grinned. 'Anyone would think he had a clear conscience. He looked rather sheepish this evening. He's probably been gambling again and lost, or he would have been bragging of his winnings. He's ducked his responsibility by bringing the lad here. He could have summoned Dr Chegwidden to tend the boy at Trevowan.'

'Do not condemn him so harshly,' Senara replied. 'His actions may have saved the lad's life.'

Adam placed a hand lovingly on his wife's shoulder. 'You have duties enough with our four children and the village and shipyard patients. One of the maids can watch over him. They will call you if he gets worse.'

She shook her head. 'He has lost so much this night. He will need love and comforting when he comes round.'

He knew he would never dissuade her. 'I will work on estate business until Rudge and Brown return. Then I shall go through the lad's belongings to discover his identity and where his family can be contacted.'

Two hours later, Rudge stood uneasily inside the door of Adam's study. 'We found the coach and the dead driver, Cap'n Loveday. But that were all. There was no sign of any luggage or possessions. Nothing inside the coach either.' He finished ominously, 'Someone got there afore us. There were fresh horse tracks. Looks to me like some smugglers got an extra haul this night.'

'In the morning I want those tracks followed.' Adam gave vent to his rage. 'Those goods may be all that lad has in the world.'

'Won't do no good, Cap'n. I followed them some ways and they

9

were headed to the moor. There be no way anything of value will be found. They'll be hidden in a secret place with the contraband.'

Adam knew the bailiff was right. 'But there may be important papers the boy will need. And his family could be witless with worry over what could have happened to him if he and his mother fail to return to their home. The woman must be buried in a day or so. The family need to be notified. We must hope the lad recovers quickly to give us the information we need. What about the driver? Was there any identification on him?'

Rudge shook his head. ''Twere an outrage. They'd stripped him of his clothes. Bain't right taking the clothes off the back of the dead and leaving 'im naked and indecent.'

'I'll have one of the carpenters in the yard measure them both for coffins. Gilly Brown will lay them out and they'll be interred at Trewenna church tomorrow.'

Adam had an uncomfortable feeling about the incident. He did not begrudge the boy the hospitality of his home, but there was a pressing need to discover the identity of his family, if the woman was not to lie in an unmarked grave.

Chapter Two

'So there you have the whole sorry tale of the boy, Uncle.' Adam was in Joshua Loveday's study at Trewenna rectory the next morning, needing advice from his relation, who was both spiritual and titular head of the family. 'He is still unconscious. I have notified the *Sherborne Mercury* so they can report the accident, but it is too soon to receive replies. We cannot in decency delay burying the woman any longer. Though I dislike the thought of an unmarked grave.'

'And I of having the poor creature disinterred when her family learn of the accident.' Joshua frowned. He was not wearing his Geneva bands or his cleric's wig, and his short grey hair was rapidly thinning. With advancing years Joshua had become more portly, although he looked ten years younger than his middle fifties. He hooked his thumbs into the silver-embroidered black waistcoat of his suit and breeches, which broke from the traditional reverend's attire. 'I will perform a funeral service tomorrow morning. There is space for the woman's coffin within the crypt. That may be the best solution for now.'

Adam nodded agreement. The parlour was small and cramped with furniture smelling of beeswax, and on this overcast morning little light penetrated the thick bottle panes in the window. The room faced north and was always cold. Despite its being June, a log fire had been lit in the grate, but it was burning sluggishly and giving little heat.

'How is the lad?' Joshua asked, moving to clear a chair piled with old sermons for Adam to be seated.

11

'Still gravely ill. Senara refuses to leave his side. The fever had not abated this morning.'

'If he lives, he owes his life to St John,' Joshua stated. 'It is good that he is taking his responsibilities more seriously. Felicity is a sobering influence on his more selfish ways.'

'He is regarded at Trevowan by our womenfolk as quite a hero.' Adam grinned. 'Aunt Elspeth and Amelia are praising his actions.'

Joshua crossed to the hearth and prodded a smouldering log with the toe of his brass-buckled shoe, sending a puff of smoke into the room. 'That should please St John. My sister usually mixes bitter aloes and not honey with her words, and your stepmother has also been harsh on your twin in the past. She is too fond of comparing him to Edward.'

'No one could step easily into our late father's shoes.'

For a moment Joshua was lost in reflection, his face saddened by memories of his brother. He turned to warm his back at the feeble flames and cleared his throat before replying. 'St John has his failings, and though I suspect he is far from a reformed character, this last year he has been a better master of Trevowan than I expected.'

Adam spied a London news-sheet lying open on the table. He was amused to see that the venerable preacher had been studying the account of the last race meeting at Newmarket. Hanging on the plain limewashed wall above the desk was a wooden Celtic cross carved with intricate swirls, and by the inkwell was a gilded crucifix on a stand. Joshua was no fire-and-brimstone preacher, and as well as his interest in church architecture, he was fascinated by the pagan ancient stones and circles spread across their country. He was not blinkered by his religion, and that gave him a compassionate and open mind.

'St John still spends more time with his friends than is responsible,' Adam commented. 'He has stayed another week in Truro.'

There was a tightening of his uncle's lips. 'Did I speak too soon? Was he gambling again?'

'He spoke of fortune smiling on him, so I suppose the cards were favourable this time.' Adam shrugged. There had been a smugness about his brother's manner before he left for his home this morning. Adam knew him well enough to discern when his twin was lying

– and he had been lying then. But St John had always been evasive and the family were often too quick to condemn him. Before leaving Boscabel, St John had called in upon the sickroom and demanded that he be informed as soon as the youth regained consciousness. 'St John finds the company of so many women at Trevowan onerous,' Adam charitably defended his twin. 'Elspeth, Amelia and Felicity are never slow to speak their minds and criticise. He adores Rowena, but his daughter will soon be a young woman and is too like her mother with her demands for attention. And his stepdaughter idolises Rowena and emulates her actions.'

'Charlotte is but nine. Felicity should be stricter with Rowena. She needs a sensible woman's guiding hand.'

'That is not easy when St John indulges Rowena's every whim. The minx resents any control Felicity would exercise over her and I fear Elspeth also spoils her niece. Amelia at least will take no nonsense from her.' Adam did not envy his brother in a household of formidable women. They were quick to judge St John, often rightly so.

He frowned as he recalled his twin's manner that day. He had not expected St John to be interested in the boy's health, having relinquished his responsibility by handing him over to Adam. It was a pity that St John did not overly trouble himself about the welfare of their younger half-brother Rafe, who was three years younger than Rowena and with no other male company unless Amelia brought him to play with Adam's sons. It was out of character for his twin to trouble himself over the recovery of the boy he had rescued. Also St John's anger on learning that the passengers' possessions had been stolen had been less than the outrage Adam would have expected. Though in his defence his brother had been nursing a hangover at the time: a rather too frequent occurrence in recent months, to Adam's mind. His brother was on the road to becoming a drunkard. Yet he had ceased trying to fathom the workings of St John's mind years ago. They might be twins but their personalities and looks were not similar, except in that they were like all the Loveday men, above average height and dark-haired. Adam curbed his judgement on his brother. Since childhood there had been fierce rivalry between them, which had threatened to tear the family apart. Now in their thirties, an uneasy truce had existed between them for two years. It was indeed time that they were older and wiser and accepted each other's failings or differences of nature.

A commotion at the rectory door drew the men's attention. The homely figure of Aunt Cecily bustled in from the street, her arms raised as she removed her bonnet. Her short, plump figure was breathless from hurrying home after visiting a sick parishioner. She smiled a welcome at Adam that brought a dimple to her apple-red cheeks.

'Young Olive Wibbley would speak with you, husband,' she said to Joshua. 'She wishes to ask when it would be convenient for her newborn child to be baptised and herself churched after the birth.'

'I will keep you no longer from your duties, Uncle.' Adam picked up the riding crop he had laid beside the news-sheet.

'Will you attend the interment?' Joshua queried.

'It would not seem right to have the woman laid to rest without mourners. I will send word to St John.' He bowed to Cecily. 'I trust you are well, Aunt.'

'I am in vigorous health, thank you, nephew.'

Adam made his farewells to his uncle and aunt and rode back to Boscabel, sending word to St John that the coffin would be laid in the crypt at Trewenna church the next day. A half-hour after Adam returned to the house, their servant Carrie Jensen informed him that the boy had recovered consciousness.

When Adam entered the sickroom, he found the youth looking wildly around the room and struggling violently as Senara and the nursery maid, Lucy, held his arms to stop him from getting out of bed. Senara was speaking soothingly, and the two slim women needed all their strength to restrain him.

'There is nothing to fear,' Adam's wife was saying. 'You had an accident and were brought here. You are safe. No one will harm you. Please do not fight us, or you will injure yourself further. You have been very ill and unconscious since last night. Truly we mean you no harm.'

The boy stared at her, wide-eyed and terrified as a trapped fawn. As Senara continued in the soft voice she used to tend injured animals, his rigid body gradually relaxed and for a moment he stopped fighting. His blond hair was dark with sweat and pasted to his skull; his cheeks flamed with the residue of fever. He studied the women warily. Then he saw Adam filling the doorway and the wildness returned to his eyes, and despite his face being white and clenched with pain, he kicked frantically in his attempt to escape.

'You had better wait outside.' Senara addressed her husband. 'A man's presence clearly disturbs him.'

Adam hesitated, concerned that Senara would in some way be hurt by the lad's surprising strength. Besides his concussion the boy was covered in livid bruises and welts that could not be explained by the way he had been thrown from the coach. Adam had seen the youth's body after Senara had bathed it and he had obviously been severely thrashed with a whip. There had also been a lot of bruises and lash marks on the woman's body. Was their wild flight because both their lives were in danger from someone?

'Please leave, Adam,' Senara added as she continued to wrestle with her charge. 'The lad will then quieten. He knows I mean him no harm.'

'Neither do I!' Adam did not raise his voice but it carried the weight of command to cut through the boy's fear. 'God grant him a speedy recovery. I shall leave him in your tender care, wife.'

When Adam stepped outside the room he paused by the open door and heard Senara continue to reassure the boy, who had remained strangely silent throughout his struggles. Within minutes the lad appeared to grow calm, and Adam went to his own bedchamber to change into his work clothes. The coffin was already placed on the estate cart ready to be driven to Trewenna.

Senara joined him as he was pulling on his work boots.

'How is the lad?' he asked.

'I have given him a sedative. He will sleep now.'

'Who is he? Did he say?'

'He has not spoken a word. Not to cry out in pain at his discomfort or even to ask after the woman.' Her eyes were clouded with concern. 'He is still dazed and confused. He needs to recover his strength and not be upset by a barrage of questions. He would not even give me his name.'

'He looked terrified. He may fear whoever thrashed him

discovering he is here.' Adam stamped his foot down into his boot and straightened to pull down the cuffs of his shirt.

'He has obviously suffered cruelly at the hands of someone,' Senara observed. 'He may be wary of strangers.'

'Is it not strange that the lad did not speak or cry out in his fear? He is presenting us with a mystery that has sinister and unpalatable undertones.'

Senara picked some fluff from the shoulder of her husband's navy jacket and gazed thoughtfully up into his face. His countenance was not without the marks of his adventurous life. There was an old crescent scar on his cheek. Another more recent one on his temple was from his last fight with an old enemy, Harry Sawle, when the smuggler was apprehended. Thankfully Sawle had been taken for trial and hanged for his crimes.

'The boy was lucky to survive the accident,' she said. 'His head wound was serious. Sometimes the mind is slower to heal than the body. We must be patient. I would not like him to fall into the hands of whoever has beaten him.'

'We cannot keep him from his family when they come forward.'

'I would like to tell the fortune of the sick-minded bully who would beat anyone to that extent.' Senara's eyes flashed dangerously.

Adam rubbed his thumbs along her cheeks, aware of her distress and anger at her patient's treatment. Whilst sympathising with his wife's sentiments, he noted the stubborn tilting of her chin. 'I despise bullies as much as you. We must save our judgement until we learn more from our guest. We can make his stay here as pleasant as possible.'

She nodded and covered his hand with her own. 'And what will we do if his family does not come forward and his memory does not return? An orphanage is a miserable place. And he clearly comes from a good family.'

Adam smiled reassuringly. 'We will cross that bridge when we come to it. I can see you are taken with the tragedy surrounding this boy. He will not stay silent for ever.'

'I am sure you are right. It is too soon to be sure whether his memory has been affected. But if, as St John described, they were fleeing from something, or someone, at a dangerously fast pace, he may find the events of whatever led up to that flight too terrible to want to remember. Memory can lock unpleasant incidents into a deep, dark vault within the mind.'

The funeral services at Trewenna church were short. A persistent drizzle had accompanied their journey to the church. The sky was oppressive and dense with leaden clouds and the air had turned cold. There was little Joshua could say about two people who were strangers to them. The driver had been buried in the churchyard the previous afternoon, and if they ever learned his identity, then his family would be notified. Adam offered a prayer for the woman's soul and for the protection of the boy, who may or may not have been her son.

When the flagstone was placed over the opening of the crypt, Joshua concluded, 'May her soul rest in peace.'

'Amen,' Adam said with feeling, unable to shake the unease he felt over the accident.

'So you have not been able to get any information from the boy?' St John asked as they walked out of the church. The rain had stopped but the sky remained overcast. 'Rum do, all this affair.'

'He is a long way from recovery. Senara says that whatever trauma caused their wild flight may have affected his mind,' Adam replied.

'You mean he may actually not remember anything?' St John took his father's hunter watch from his waistcoat pocket and studied the time as though unconcerned, but there was a tightness to his shoulders that made Adam study him more closely. His twin seemed on edge about the rescue.

Adam suspected that his answer meant more to St John than he was prepared to show. 'Why is his lack of memory important to you, St John?'

'It has no importance to me whatsoever, other than as a curiosity as to who he is,' he answered with unwarranted defensiveness. 'I did save his life. But I have no intention of making my heroic deed into a full-time responsibility.'

'No one would expect you to,' Joshua interceded.

'The boy is welcome to remain with us at Boscabel for as long as is necessary.' Adam curbed a more heated retort at his twin's selfishness.

'You are welcome to him.' St John had stiffened with affront and he marched towards his waiting horse without further comment.

Joshua sighed. 'Why must you two be at each other's throats? St John did save the lad's life.'

'He usually does nothing without profit to himself.'

'You are too harsh, Adam. You would be the first to give another the benefit of the doubt. Why not your brother? He would not have left a child to die of his wounds even had he been a beggar.'

Adam rubbed his temple, admitting that he had been justly upbraided. If they were to put the old rivalry behind them then he must trust St John more. 'You are right, of course, Uncle. It is just that he can be sly and secretive at times, which too often means that he is up to no good. There is something he is not telling us, I am certain of it.'

Joshua regarded him indulgently. 'When have any of us been saints? Most likely St John has been gambling in Truro and probably lost more than he could afford. He would be evasive about that. There is also talk amongst the villagers that he is not happy in his marriage. His absences from home feed such gossip.'

'Felicity deserves better from him,' Adam observed.

'Yes, she does, but . . .' Joshua paused before adding more heavily, 'Clearly, he resents that you have two sons while he has only daughters. No woman can inherit Trevowan. He will be more content when Felicity gives him an heir. He told me before you arrived that his wife was again with child. I pray that will encourage him to spend more time at home.'

'Strange, he said nothing to me of Felicity's condition.' Adam watched his brother ride through the village. St John was usually quick to gloat and remind Adam on any occasion that he would never inherit the family home.

Joshua patted his shoulder and there was sympathy and understanding in his sharp stare. 'It is early days. It could explain why you felt he was being secretive.'

Adam nodded. He had been delayed from the shipyard too long and there was no time for him to return to Boscabel to change.

'I must bid you leave, Uncle. You will have your parish duties to attend. Give my regards to Aunt Cecily and beg my pardon for not calling upon her.'

★

18

The conversation stayed with Adam as he rode to Trevowan Hard. In the past there had been too much distrust between the twins. He had been quick to condemn his brother, and yet had they not resolved to put the old rivalry behind them? A divided family was only as strong as each individual, whereas if they were united they were all but invincible, and that had been proved in overcoming enemies in the past. Even so, he was disgruntled that St John had not shared the news of Felicity's condition, if only to gloat. Why must his brother make a contest out of everything, even the birth of a child? But the answer was simple. St John had always been jealous of Adam and regarded him as a rival for their father's affection. And Adam, as the younger son, had always resented that St John was the heir to Trevowan, the home he adored but would never possess. Even if St John did not produce a son, the entailed estate would not become Adam's. He had forfeited that right when he had married against his father's wishes. His half-brother Rafe was St John's heir. Although it had been painful to accept, Adam did not begrudge Rafe his chance to inherit; however, there would always be a deep sadness in his heart that he would never be master of Trevowan.

In fairness to his father, Edward had forgiven him for disobeying his wishes and they had been reconciled before Edward's death. If Adam could not have Trevowan, he at least had the Loveday shipyard. In the past the two had always been bound together. St John had never shown any aptitude or interest in shipbuilding and had grudgingly tended to yard business. Adam had won the yard by his love of ships, passion for shipbuilding and ability to design vessels that had made the business one of the most prestigious in the county. Its future should have been secured, but the war with France had made merchants nervous about investing in new ships. Even with talk of a truce between the countries this year, nothing had changed. French privateers had captured too many ships, and hostilities could flare up at any time. The need to fill the books was always a headache for Adam. At the moment three ships were being worked on in the yard. The merchantman *Good Fortune*, built to one of Adam's designs, had been launched and was moored in the deeper waters of the inlet of the River Fowey, while the carpenters installed its internal fitments before its completion due at the end of July. Last month one of the Falmouth packet ships had been brought in for repair, having been damaged by enemy fire on its return from New York.

This was the first packet ship Adam had repaired. With two masts, the vessel was narrower and smaller than his own design for a brigantine, but it had been developed for carrying mail and not cargo. Such ships had to be fast, and although armed in times of war, they were under orders from the packet agents to run from any enemy. If they could not escape they were to fight, and if in danger of defeat the mailbags were to be sunk before the ship surrendered. Most of the vessels were privately owned and hired by the Post Office on contract. All mail from England was taken overseas from Falmouth. Although their routes were usually Barbados and Jamaica, Halifax in Canada, New York and Lisbon, as the war continued some were used by the army to carry pay to their troops fighting the upstart Corsican who for over a year had ruled France as its First Consul. As a consequence, more of the ships were returning damaged, and Adam was determined that this first contract would not be his last.

Shipbuilding was not the only enterprise Adam was engaged in. Two of the ships he had built – *Pegasus*, his first ever design and owned by himself, and the larger merchantman *Pride of the Sea* – had both sailed to the new colony in New South Wales carrying convicts and trading goods for the growing number of settlers. *Pride of the Sea* was owned by a group of investors, himself included, and most of his capital had been risked in that enterprise. The profits from those voyages could be immense, but to achieve such riches he had recklessly gambled the security of the yard and estate at Boscabel, against the hazards of a ship spending eighteen months at sea on the round voyage.

Perhaps he was more of a gambler that he had believed and he was wrong to judge St John. Even so, his unease remained that St John had not been completely honest about the accident for reasons of his own. Adam hoped his twin's secrecy would have no consequences for his family.

Chapter Three

Trevowan Hard was approached down a tree-lined lane leading off from the crossroads on the main track from Penruan to Fowey. As Adam drew near to the shipyard, the squawking of gulls descending upon the river inlet all but drowned out the sound of hammering and sawing from the work sheds. When the trees opened out there was revealed a score of limewashed thatched cottages inhabited by the shipwrights and their families.

As Adam rode past, two women drawing water from the well bobbed a curtsey to him and another group of women outside the Ship kiddley paused in their gossip to acknowledge his presence. There was a chorus of excited young voices from the children playing in the schoolyard, released from their morning lessons. One or two of the youths, who would soon be old enough to start as apprentices, eyed his progress warily, having clearly been up to some mischief. He bit down on his lower lip to suppress a grin, and to his amusement the youths scampered back to the schoolhouse just as his sister-in-law Bridie appeared ringing the brass hand bell to summon the children back inside for their next lesson. She raised a hand in greeting to Adam, which he returned.

The familiarity of the sights around him brought a stab of pride to his chest. He breathed in the air laden with the smells of freshly cut wood, pitch from a recent caulking of the repaired decking of the packet ship and weathered hemp from the ratlines. His mount sidestepped the coils of ropes, which had been delivered by the ropemaker that morning and were being hauled into the rope shed by four of the apprentices as they ribbed each other as to who was the strongest. The tang of heated iron and smoke from the furnace drifted across the yard from the busy forge, and permeating everything was the scent of salt water and mud from the river. The noises that greeted him were as melodious as birdsong to his experienced ear: the rhythmic rasp of the long two-handled saw in the sawpit, the scrape of adzes emerging from the carpentry shed and the steady thud of hammers.

The tide was full and the merchantman *Good Fortune* bobbed gently at its moorings, the men labouring on her deck and rigging singing a shanty as they worked. Other carpenters hoisted planks on the deck of the packet ship, their deep voices chanting, 'Heave!' before every haul on the pulley rope. There was also the occasional raised voice giving orders.

Adam handed the reins of his gelding Solomon to the stable lad and noted that the two shire horses were today hitched to the yard wagon. They were to deliver a figurehead to a shipyard in Charlestown. The carved form was of a woman wearing a knight's helmet with visor raised and carrying a shield and a lance. She was brightly painted with golden hair and a red gown. It was a striking emblem of a sea goddess protecting her ship and crew. Adam's master carpenter, Seth Wakely, was renowned for his figureheads and it had been a profitable venture for them to supply other local yards. The stocky, bearded figure of Seth hobbled around the wagon on his peg leg, shouting instructions to lash the figure tightly.

When a lad slackened his hold on the rope he was pulling and the carving toppled dangerously over the side of the wagon, Seth clipped the apprentice on the ear and roared, 'Damned clodpate! That be two months' work. You want I carve the next figurehead from out of your hide? I will if you damage her.'

The apprentice paled and worked industriously to placate Seth, but when the master carpenter turned away, the lad pulled a face behind his back, which made his companions grin. Then he saw Adam watching him and ducked his head, worried that he would receive a further rebuke.

Closer to the river, away from the main work sheds, Adam observed half a dozen men wielding long, curved blades, scraping barnacles from the keel of a schooner in the dry dock.

Outwardly the yard looked busy and prosperous, but Adam was

aware of the outlay and cost of each stage of the work being carried out, and how easily a late payment from a customer could imperil the financial status of the yard. He had faced ruin too often in the past to ever be complacent.

'Cap'n Loveday!' He was hailed by the barrel-chested figure of Ben Mumford, his overseer. A felt cap covered Mumford's bald head and a white beard crusted his square jaw. 'There be that lawyer fellow from Dartmouth awaiting you. He be taking a meal in the kiddley.'

Adam grimaced. 'Has Mr Heathcote been waiting long? I was not expecting him.'

'Long enough to down a couple quarts of ale and a huge plate of Pru Jensen's eel pie,' Mumford chuckled. 'He be a man who likes his food.'

Adam entered the two-storey building created by knocking two adjoining cottages into one. The kiddley served the yard as both alehouse and general store and was also owned by him. He paused inside, taking a moment for his eyes to adjust to the dark interior of the taproom after the bright sunlight. The air was ripe with the smell of stale ale and wood smoke, overlaid with the aroma of freshly baked bread, pies and pasties. Pru Jensen paused in her counting of eggs brought in by one of the local farmer's wives to be sold in the store.

'Morning to you, Cap'n.' The young wife regarded Adam's hand-some figure with more boldness than her marriage vows permitted. She was attractively plump, with rosy cheeks and a saucy sparkle in her eyes. A toddler with a grimy face was swinging on her skirts.

Adam nodded briefly and politely returned her greeting, but his attention was drawn to the lawyer sprawled on a bench by the inglenook fireplace. It would have been hard to miss him, for Heathcote was twice the size of most men. He filled the two-seater settle, his embroidered waistcoat strained over his walrus stomach and his thighs were solid as water barrels. Within the pendulous folds of his face, gimlet eyes gleamed brightly, and a shock of silvery curls covered his pumpkin-shaped head.

'Your servant, Heathcote.' Adam smoothed from his voice any irritation that the unannounced visit was at an inconvenient time. 'This is an unexpected pleasure. I trust you have been well served. I was called away on family business.'

'I am staying with my daughter in Fowey for a week or so,' clipped Heathcote, gravy dribbling from his full mouth. 'Thought I would see how the merchant ship was progressing for my client.'

Adam was glad now there had been no time to change into his work clothes, for he frequently worked alongside the shipwrights if a vessel had fallen behind schedule. The mysterious customer who had commissioned *Good Fortune* had saved him from laying off half the shipwrights when orders had been sparse. Yet however grateful he was for the contract, it irked him that Heathcote's client's identity still had not been revealed to him. He was a man who prized integrity and did not like secrets, especially in business. There was always the uncomfortable feeling that they could one day rebound on him. Smugglers used too many ships and their owners were the most ruthless of men. Had not one such man, until Adam's kinsmen brought him to justice over a year ago, almost destroyed his family? Adam wanted no dealings with his like again.

Mr Heathcote had assured him that the vessel was not to be used for illegal gain. He had to be satisfied with that, and since the customer had honoured the conditions of the contract and all payments were made on time, he had no cause for complaint. Was that not more important than solving the mystery of the owner's identity? He sought to convince himself.

'Can't 'bide to eat alone, Captain Loveday.' The lawyer's three chins wobbled appreciatively as he continued to devour half a chicken and a mound of buttered mashed potatoes in a thick onion gravy. 'We can discuss our business as we eat.'

Adam saw Pru watching them, having paid the farmer's wife for her eggs. 'I'll have one of your excellent fish pies and a pint of ale, Pru.'

'Good choice, Captain.' Heathcote smacked his lips in appreciation. 'I had the pie as my first course. Most excellent. Most excellent indeed, as is this chicken.' He waved a knife at Pru. 'Another one of your eel pies would be most appreciated, Mistress Jensen, followed by your steamed pudding.' He forked a large portion of potato into his mouth and swallowed it before addressing Adam. 'So how progresses the work on *Good Fortune*? She looks almost finished to me.'

'Her rigging is nearly complete. You are welcome to inspect the internal fitments to the captain's cabin and galley. But she will not be ready to hand over to your client for another two months. Your last instructions were that she would carry passengers as well as cargo. Four of the cabins have yet to be fitted out. The customer also wished for more elaborate carvings and gilding upon the stern. Also the six cannon, which she will carry for protection, do not arrive from the foundry for another three weeks. Then she must undergo sea trials.'

'It is a sorry state of affairs that our trading vessels must be so armed.' The lawyer's teeth tore into the last shreds of chicken on the carcass, its juices running down his flaccid jowls.

'Six cannon are barely adequate. I advised another four and two swivel guns on her half-deck. *Pride of the Sea* is so armed.'

Heathcote soaked a large wedge of bread in the gravy remaining on his plate and scooped it into his mouth, then wiped his hand across his fleshy lips and pushed his empty plate aside. When Pru placed another pie in front on him, he eyed it greedily.

Adam had not touched his food and took a sip from his ale. The lawyer slurped noisily at his quart tankard before replying. '*Good Fortune* will sail on the American and Canadian trade routes. She will be in little danger from any French men–of–war.'

'It is the privateers you must safeguard against,' Adam patiently reminded him. 'Piracy still thrives in those waters. I strongly advise that you accordingly express my suggestion to the customer. The *Good Fortune* will be a grand prize for any privateer to attack. She could be lost for want of those cannon.'

'I will speak with my client.' The quart of ale was downed in several long gulps and the pie attacked with relish. 'Can they still be fitted? And how long will this work delay her completion?'

'If extra cannon are needed for her first voyage I must know this week. There are four such guns available, which have been salvaged from a wreck. They can be delivered ten days after the order is placed. New cannon will cause further delay. I will give your client an estimate of the cost before you leave. Has a captain been found for her?'

Heathcote rubbed a hand over his vast paunch and smothered a loud belch with his hand. 'You need not concern yourself with such matters, Loveday. The final payment for your work will be made once her sea trials have been satisfactorily completed and a captain and crew engaged.'

'The owner is welcome to be aboard to experience how she handles.'

'My client has faith in your work. Her captain will be appointed by then. He will represent the owner.'

'I dislike this secrecy,' Adam protested.

The lawyer grinned slyly and wagged a finger, fat as a sausage, patronisingly in front of Adam's face. 'My client has his reasons for not revealing his name and it is more than my reputation is worth to disclose it now.'

Adam stiffened with affront. Heathcote chuckled, taking a perverse pleasure in his discomfort, and added, 'Everything is legal and above board. Nothing for you to take exception to.'

The lawyer pushed his empty pie plate aside and snapped his fingers to gain Pru's attention. 'I will have half of one of your steamed jam puddings with cream, and another quart of ale.' He then sat back and regarded Adam, his manner more placating. 'You have a reputation for honesty and integrity. That is why your yard was chosen.' He leaned forward again and the settle creaked alarmingly beneath his shifting weight. 'Much will depend on the profits made by the *Good Fortune*. There may yet be a sister ship or two required in the future.'

Adam checked his irritation. This customer had been too important to the future of the yard to antagonise him now. He had to keep an eye towards future business.

Heathcote sighed with satisfaction when the steamed pudding covered with cream was placed in front of him. Adam found he had lost his appetite and pushed his half-eaten pie aside. For a moment he thought Heathcote was going to offer to finish it, but with a small sigh the lawyer dug his spoon into his pudding.

'Your discretion over this matter has been noted and appreciated, Captain Loveday.'

Disliking Heathcote's tone and manner, Adam again checked his sliding temper and rose to his feet. 'I will leave you to finish your meal, and will prepare the costing for the extra cannon for you to present to your client. When you are ready I will escort you to inspect the *Good Fortune*.'

The provocation behind the lawyer's final remark had fuelled rather than dampened his interest in the mysterious owner and made it hard for him to concentrate on the costing he needed to prepare. It was not the only comment that made Adam uneasy. After Heathcote had inspected and approved the works, the lawyer followed Adam into his office to collect the papers for the price of installing more cannon. The only seat that would accommodate his size was the sea chest where Adam stored the yard's ledgers. The walls of the office were covered in paintings of the ships the yard had built. On two shelves were also wooden models of all the classes of ships they had constructed.

The sturdy wooden box groaned in protest as the lawyer sank his weight upon it and accepted a glass of brandy. As Heathcote savoured the cognac, he remarked, 'You are acquainted with another client of mine, I believe, Captain Loveday. A Lieutenant Francis Beaumont.'

The sudden mention of an old adversary made Adam's blood run cold and he struggled to keep his voice neutral as he replied. 'We served together in the navy. It has been many years since I have heard of him. I believe he is no longer in these parts.'

'Some would say you were enemies. You were both cashiered from the navy after fighting a duel.'

'We were young and hot-headed and paid the price.'

'Yet your enmity did not stop there.' Heathcote placed his hands on his knees. The pressure from his haunch-of-venison-sized arms tested the skill of his tailor with the strain on his jacket seams. The man's black eyes had become cold and calculating as he accused, 'Did you not have cause to hate him?'

'Hate is too strong a word. I held him in low esteem,' Adam countered. From the first day he and Beaumont met there had been antagonism between them. Adam had been transferred to a new ship to serve as midshipman. He had been on board half an hour when he saw Lieutenant Beaumont thrashing the cabin boy Billy Brown, then a lad of nine, for some minor misdemeanour. The young lad was reeling and vomiting from the force of a brutal blow to his head. As a midshipman it was not Adam's place to question a superior officer. However, he could not abide unnecessary cruelty and stepped between the officer and his victim.

'I believe the lad has received ample punishment,' he had cautioned. 'He will be no good for duty if he is unconscious.'

Beaumont had rounded on Adam, his glare haughty as he noted his inferior rank. Adam had been twenty and Beaumont, who was four years older, had been but recently promoted from a midshipman and lost no opportunity to lord it over his subordinates.

'Who the devil are you, sir?' Beaumont had sneered. 'Some jumped-up midshipman who has not learned his place. You are a nobody on this ship. I'll have you court-martialled if you question my judgement.'

Adam had stood his ground. Beaumont was an arrogant, opinionated bully. 'I doubt that Captain Rawcliffe will view your conduct towards a cabin boy as becoming to an officer.'

'Rawcliffe is in awe of my grandfather, Admiral Beaumont. He will take my word against some upstart midshipman,' smirked Beaumont.

'Then we should approach the captain at once, Lieutenant,' Adam challenged. 'I had heard that Rawcliffe had a quick temper but that he was a fair man. He has given much honourable service to the navy. As did your grandfather, the Admiral, in his day. He has been retired for many years. Where is the honour in your treatment of a defenceless cabin boy?'

At Adam's audacity, the officer's face had turned from puce to parchment in rapid succession, and his close-set eyes had sparked with hatred. Their depths were also shadowed by fear that a subordinate officer had not been cowed by his threats. The man was gutless, a common trait in most bullies.

'On this occasion we will not trouble Captain Rawcliffe,' Beaumont had blustered. 'This is your first day on board. I am prepared to be lenient over this incident.'

It was the first of many confrontations between the two men, from which Adam had always emerged the victor. Beaumont was the worst kind of naval officer: pompous, with no true understanding or empathy with the sea, and a total disregard for the welfare of the common sailors. That they had duelled was an exaggeration. They had fought when Adam had discovered that Beaumont had pressganged Dan Holman, the halfwit son of a family living in a tied cottage at Trevowan. Holman was slow to understand commands and would be a danger to the lives of other seamen. Adam had explained the circumstances to Beaumont, but he had refused to release Dan. Adam lost his temper and they had crossed swords. They had both been cashiered. Adam had left the navy and been recruited by Squire Penwithick as a spy for the British government in the early days of the revolution in France. It was only after his marriage to Senara that he could pursue his passion for shipbuilding. Beaumont, after some intercession from his grandfather, had been appointed a revenue officer.

'Your enmity did not end with the duel, did it?' Heathcote's sharp tone jolted Adam from his reflections. The lawyer continued, his words now ringing with accusation, 'Wasn't Beaumont the excise officer in charge when illicit goods were found on Loveday land and your father was shot resisting arrest?'

Adam still mourned the death of Edward, and his anger at the revenue officer's actions burst to the surface. 'Sir, my father was a man of honour and a law-abiding citizen of impeccable character. He had been ordering the smugglers to remove the contraband, which had been hidden without his permission. He was not resisting arrest. He was shot because of Beaumont's incompetence.'

'Did your father not later die from those wounds?' Heathcote persisted. 'If you do not hate Beaumont, you must blame him for your father's untimely death.'

Adam did not answer, but his pain and fury blazed in his eyes. He turned his back on the lawyer to stare out of the window and bring his emotions under control. He grasped his hands behind his back, his slender body rigid with tension. Behind him he heard the sea chest creak as Heathcote shifted his weight to a more comfortable position.

'Beaumont is absent without leave from his excise duties,' the lawyer persisted. 'He has not been seen for several months.'

'He was a man who made enemies easily.' Adam voiced his disdain. 'Some years ago he fled these parts to avoid Harry Sawle, who had sworn to kill him.' Adam still did not turn to face the lawyer. 'He also abandoned his wife and child at that time. Perhaps another smuggler has threatened his life and he is in hiding.'

'Mrs Beaumont and her husband have long been estranged,' Heathcote clipped out.

Adam spun round. 'What are you implying? Clearly you have not raised this matter to indulge in common gossip. If your investigations on the status of the merchantman for your client are complete, I have other matters to attend this day, Mr Heathcote.'

'To protect his loved ones, a man must oft-times appear to act in so craven a fashion.' The lawyer showed no inclination to drop the subject.

'A man of honour would give his life to protect his family – not run away,' Adam declared.

'Few men would stay to face the vengeance of the smuggler Sawle. The man ruled by terror, and his reign as a gang-leader was littered with the corpses of any who dared to defy him. But then you were the one who brought him to justice when he turned upon your family. You are a brave and ruthless man where your enemies are concerned, Captain.'

At Adam's challenging glare, Heathcote conciliated with a benign smile. 'Sawle was hanged eighteen months ago. He is no longer a danger to Beaumont. Mrs Beaumont has engaged me to locate his whereabouts.'

Heathcote levered himself to rise and came to stand beside Adam. He scrutinised the shipbuilder's profile for some moments before stating, 'Mrs Beaumont wishes to ascertain whether her husband met with some accident. If she is a widow, she could remarry.'

'As I said, I have not seen Beaumont for some years. I cannot help you, Mr Heathcote.' Adam kept his spine ramrod straight. He faced the lawyer with all emotion levelled from his voice. 'Are there any other matters pertaining to the client of *Good Fortune*? If not, I am needed at Boscabel.'

'I will not keep you further, Captain Loveday.' Heathcote assumed a weary expression. 'Mrs Beaumont is not the only one interested in her husband's whereabouts. The excise office is always suspicious that murder has been committed when one of their officers disappears without trace.'

For a long time after Heathcote left, Adam stared out across the river, oblivious of the noise and activity in the yard. His hatred for Beaumont festered like a canker in his chest. They had been bitter enemies and he did blame him for his father's death. He had thought they were free of his malicious evil for good. These investigations into the officer's disappearance left him with a nagging sense of unease. He had not been entirely honest with the lawyer. There had been a more recent meeting with Beaumont – one that could have severe repercussions for his family.

Chapter Four

An hour later, Adam returned to Boscabel still unsettled by the visit from the lawyer. Since his last meeting with the excise officer he had not given Beaumont much thought, but with Sawle hanged and no longer a threat to Beaumont, it did now seem strange that he had not been seen patrolling these waters. Sawle had not been the only smuggler operating in the district.

Unwilling to upset Senara, Adam pushed his fears aside. His wife had enough worries with the arrival of the boy who had lost his memory. Yet it had never been easy keeping anything from her. She was incredibly perceptive at sensing a person's moods, her gypsy blood giving her an uncanny intuition concerning people and their future. Her premonitions had been proved right on too many occasions for him to doubt her ability. She had always feared Beaumont's vindictive nature, and had not the excise officer shot Edward Loveday when Beaumont had been in the pay of Harry Sawle?

Adam shuddered. He had thought the smuggler's death would have freed him from the sinister shadow the man had cast over their lives. Annoyed at the way his common sense had deserted him, he drew a sharp breath. He did not fear ghosts or any man alive. Yet he could have wished that his last meeting with Beaumont had been less acrimonious.

Beaumont had not been seen in the area for months when Adam had met him in a chance encounter close to his cousin Japhet's land. With Japhet out of the country, the farm had been rented to a tenant. Adam had been out returning from a visit to Sir Henry

Traherne, his neighbour and friend, and as it was a fine afternoon had taken a detour to ride past the farm and assure himself that all appeared in good order. Since a previous tenant had allowed contraband to be stored in the barn against the express instructions of the family, Adam kept a closer eye on his cousin's property. He had been alerted by a flash of light coming from a small coppice. It could only have been caused by sunlight glinting off metal or glass. He had dismounted and approached on foot to see a lone figure crouched behind a tree with a spyglass to his eye, watching the farm.

Across the fields the tenant's twelve-year-old daughter Millie was standing at the water pump. From the state of her bodice and skirt she had slipped over and landed in horse droppings. Her mother was berating her and pulling at her skirt and top as she stripped it from her to soak in the water from the pump. Millie was crying, and the water splashed over her petticoats, moulding the linen to her budding figure.

'Have you taken to spying on young girls?' Adam had sneered.

Beaumont snapped shut the spyglass and glowered at him. 'There was a landing on the coast last night. This farm has been used to store contraband in the past. I was checking whether anything looked suspicious. My men are searching other farms by the moor.'

'I warned you to stay off our land,' Adam challenged.

'As an officer of the crown I have my duty to perform. The Lovedays may proclaim their innocence, but you have been hand in glove with smugglers in the past. With Sawle as a brother-in-law, what else would we expect? You even built a ship for him so he could outrun the revenue cutter. For all we know, you are in partnership with him. It would not be the first time your land has been used.' Beaumont was a head shorter than Adam, and his thin face was now heavily scored with lines of debauchery and excess.

The insults plucked at Adam's pride, and his temper crashed through his reason like storm waves over a breakwater. 'Or that you have acted too hastily against us. I have not forgotten that you murdered my father.'

'I was doing my duty. He resisted arrest.' Even though he had to tip his head back to look up at Adam, Beaumont glared along his hooked nose with arrogant disdain.

'We both know that is a lie.' Adam had closed the space between them, his fists bunched as his anger ground through him. He could see sweat glistening on Beaumont's face.

'Lay a hand on me and I'll have you arrested for attacking an officer of the King about his duty,' Beaumont blustered and fumbled to draw his sword.

Despite being unarmed, Adam was defiant. 'It could be worth it.'

Beaumont was backing away to where his horse was tethered, his sword held ready to counter an attack. His boot tangled in the knee-high bracken and he stumbled. Adam leapt forward and, ducking the lunge of the blade, landed a punch on the officer's jaw. At the force of the blow Beaumont dropped the sword and Adam swiftly delivered two more blows to his head and body. Beaumont was knocked to the ground and covered his head with his hands.

Adam picked up the fallen sword and pointed it at his enemy.

'Don't kill me. I beg you. Don't kill me!' the officer pleaded.

His cowardice disgusted Adam. This knave had shot Edward Loveday in cold blood. He did not deserve to live. Yet where was the honour in killing such a coward?

Breathing heavily, Adam had controlled his anger and stood back. 'Any smuggler who uses our land to store their goods knows that we will summon the authorities.' His voice was thick with warning. 'Get on your way, Beaumont. This time I will not stain my hands with your craven blood. But if I ever catch you within a mile of our land again, I will know you are intent upon dishonouring our name and I will kill you.' He slashed the sword down on a granite boulder in the undergrowth; the steel snapped in two and he threw the hilt as far as he could.

Beaumont had staggered to his feet, holding his hand to his bleeding face. 'This assault and your threats will be reported to the authorities.'

Adam had turned from him and walked away. For some days afterwards he had expected the militia to arrest him. Nothing had happened and he assumed that Beaumont had slithered away to lick his wounds on the other side of the county. It was not until he remembered the incident now that he recalled that Beaumont had not been in his uniform. If he had not been on duty, what had he been doing in the area?

He had wasted enough time on Beaumont. The man was inconsequential. If he had intended to act against him he would have done so by now. No doubt scared of Harry Sawle's threats, he had fled the county. The incident had happened a few weeks before Sawle's arrest and had been so overshadowed by those events that Adam had given it little thought at the time.

Adam spent the rest of the day concentrating on the work being done on the estate. This spring two extra fields had been cleared and put to the plough, and he needed to select a site for a new barn. He would then draw up plans for its structure and a team of carpenters would be released from the yard to start the work as soon as possible. The house at Boscabel was set on the edge of a wood and its grounds stretched down to the river on one boundary and to the edge of the moor on another. The far fields were no use to agriculture, covering terrain surfaced by outcrops of granite rocks. It was often late morning before the night mist had dispersed and the grass was lush grazing for his livestock.

The tall brick chimneys of the stone Tudor house speared the sky above the high wall that surrounded the coach house and stables on the main drive to his home. At his approach a flock of doves flew in a wide circle before returning to the dovecote. As he rode under the archway set in the high wall, the tall oriel window at the front of the house reflected the cascading water from the dolphin fountain in the courtyard. The afternoon sun had turned the stonework of the residence to an amber hue. The water tumbling from the dolphin's mouth was a soothing refrain, and when he glanced at the regilded sundial above the entrance porch, it showed that the time was just after four. Even though Boscabel would never hold the same place in his heart as Trevowan, it was an impressive building. Adam had restored the roof and a great deal of its interior after he had purchased it as an abandoned ruin. His competitive nature was impatient for it to rise to its full glory and be greater than his old family home. Those dreams were frustrated. During the seven years since he had purchased the property, his income had been so straitened by the financial problems incurred at the shipyard that there had been no spare money for luxuries. Even now funds remained tight as he continued to use the profits from the crops and sale of livestock to improve the estate.

His own needs had never been excessive, and although Senara never complained, it troubled his conscience that she had not had a new dress for two years and possessed few jewels. In fairness to his wife, she would be the first to deny any wish for the trimmings of wealth. After her years of wandering with her gypsy family, she was content that her children were well fed with a roof over their heads. He also acknowledged that given the choice, she would have preferred to remain in their first home at Trevowan Hard. Her love and loyalty for him had made her accept that the wife and children of a successful shipbuilder must live in a house that proclaimed his status. Her love humbled him. He had never believed that her background would shame him in any manner. She had never disappointed him and had faced the challenges of her new life with grace and dignity to win the acceptance and respect of the gentry in their community. His love for her was stronger than ever and he was proud of her love and compassion towards those less fortunate than herself. She gave unstintingly of her time, caring for patients who sought her healing remedies when they could not afford a physician's fees. In return, the local villagers adored her.

He smiled when through an open window he heard her singing a nursery rhyme accompanied by their youngest child Sara. Their older daughter Rhianne and her twin Joel would still be attending lessons with the tutor engaged at Trevowan. Next year Joel would join his brother Nathan boarding at Sherborne school in Dorset. Adam was determined to give his sons the best education he could afford.

The open window was that of the room given to their injured guest. He had not heard Senara sing since the boy had been brought to them. The lad had not spoken since he regained consciousness and he still suffered bouts of fever and had been kept to his bed. Hopeful that he was much improved, Adam delayed his meeting with his bailiff, Rudge, and went to investigate. Senara sat in a rocking chair at the side of the bed holding Sara in her arms. The little girl had fallen asleep clutching her rag doll to her chest and the boy lay unmoving with his eyes closed. His complexion was pale and free of any flush of fever.

'I thought he was improving when I heard you singing.' There was a thread of disappointment in Adam's voice.

Sara opened her eyes and her face lit with pleasure at discovering her father had returned early from the shipyard. She wriggled to the floor and ran to him. Adam hoisted her in the air and planted a kiss on her soft cheek. 'Off you go to the nursery, sweeting. I would talk with your mama. I shall come and sit with you later while you take your supper.'

The girl skipped off and Adam gave his full attention to his wife. Senara smiled and tucked a tendril of hair behind her ear. 'There has been a change. He managed to take a little broth, though he did not speak even to say his name. I thought some familiar songs would make him feel less cast adrift in a strange world.'

'Is it not uncommon that he does not speak? He called for his mother, so he is not mute. Could he be deaf, do you think?'

'When he is awake he understands me, though the poor mite still seems very dazed. I explained that his coach had been in an accident and he was safe here, which he seemed to accept with indifference.' She reached to the bed and tenderly brushed a lock of freshly washed blond hair from the boy's brow. 'The mind can play tricks after such an injury. There may be some swelling to the brain, and he must be in pain. He is a brave fellow not to cry or whimper.'

At the sound of their voices, the boy stirred. Adam stepped closer as his lids flickered open. The eyes rounded in alarm.

'I will not hurt you,' Adam reassured, holding up his hands in supplication. 'Do you remember that your coach was in an accident? I am Captain Loveday and you are in my house in Cornwall.'

The boy stared at him, showing no sign of comprehension. Adam continued. 'This is my wife Senara, who has been tending you.'

The boy glanced at Senara and some of the tension left his body.

'What is your name?' Adam asked.

When the boy continued to stare at him without answering, he persisted. 'Do you remember being in a coach?'

Again there was no response.

'Where do you live?'

The boy's lip trembled and in his distress he turned to Senara. She sat on the side of the bed, took his hand and gently stroked his fingers. 'Can you remember your name, my dear?'

The trembling of his lips increased and his eyes darted from one to the other of them. When he began to shake, Senara leaned forward, her voice low and soothing. 'There, do not overset yourself. You are dazed and confused from your accident. Your memory will soon return. You are safe here. You are welcome in our home.'

There was a scraping at the door and Scamp, Adam's crossbreed spaniel, ambled into the room. His pace was slow and stiff with age. Adam was about to order the dog out when Scamp thrust his nose against the boy's hand lying on the edge of the counterpane and licked it. The boy stared at the dog, and as he lifted his hand to stroke the brown head, a single tear ran down his cheek.

'This is Scamp,' Senara said. 'Would you like him to stay?'

There was no answer, but the boy continued to stroke the dog. Senara took Adam's hand and drew him towards the door. Once outside she said, 'The lad needs time to heal.' She looked back through the opening of the door and saw that Scamp had clambered on to the bed and now lay stretched out beside the boy, who had put his arms around the dog. 'Animals have an unerring sense when someone is in need of unquestioning love. The boy has taken to him.'

'Scamp has an eye for a comfortable bed and extra fuss,' Adam jested. 'But the mutt will do no harm.'

Two days later the boy still had not spoken, and Dr Yeo was summoned from Fowey. The patient was sitting up in bed with Scamp a constant companion. After an extensive examination Dr Yeo straightened his stocky figure and declared, 'I can find nothing wrong with him. Mrs Loveday's tender ministrations have brought about a remarkable recovery. The trauma to his head could explain his inability to speak and it could have affected his memory.'

'It concerns me that his relatives will be worried that he is missing.' Senara voiced her anxiety. 'His description, plus that of the woman travelling with him in the coach, has been posted in several news-sheets, but no replies have been received.'

'He could of course be foreign and recently landed at Falmouth,' Dr Yeo suggested. 'He may not understand your questions.'

Adam shook his head. 'I have spoken to him in French, and I picked up a little Spanish, Italian and German in my travels. He does not respond to any.'

Senara interrupted. 'He is English, I am certain. He understands when I mention everyday objects.'

'Then you must be patient,' Dr Yeo advised. 'There was a similar case in my father's day. A young lad was found unconscious on a beach near St Mawes. An old hermit, who lived in a cave and made his living from the flotsam washed up from the sea, discovered him. The man tended him but the brain fever had affected the boy's mind. The hermit took him to a kindly fishwife who nursed him back to health. When his memory returned it was learned that he had been sold to a cruel sea captain to serve as cabin boy on a slave ship. The child had witnessed unimaginable horrors and was terrified of being sent back to sea.'

Adam solemnly regarded the doctor. 'The lad has no fever. How long could it take for his memory to return?'

'There is no easy answer to that,' Dr Yeo replied. 'It takes as long as the body and mind require.'

Adam digested this in silence. It was one more mystery in a week of unsolved secrets.

With his older brother Nathan away at school, Adam's son Joel was bored with the company of his sisters and frequently sneaked into the sickroom. A boy who did not speak and seemed to have no memory fascinated him. Today he had brought his fleet of wooden ships and lined them up on the floor. The boy was lying on the bed watching him. He was dressed in a shirt and breeches that belonged to Nathan.

'Do you want to play pirate ships?' Joel asked. 'It is much more fun playing pirates in the garden, but until you get well we must stay inside.'

The boy slid off the bed and propped himself on the floor, and Joel pushed three of the ships towards him. 'Those are yours. We'll have a battle. I'm Blackbeard, the most fearsome of all the pirates. You can be a Frenchie and I will blow you out of the water.'

The boy turned away and took the ships to the far side of the room. Joel studied him. 'So you don't want to be a Frenchie then?' He shrugged, his curiosity about the boy making him unusually complaisant. 'Or don't you like the idea of pirates? You can't be Admiral Nelson because he's the best. You could be Pellow; he's a good Cornishman. Or you could be Drake fighting pirates on the Spanish Main.'

His new friend nodded and lined up his ships. Although the sick boy was some years older than Joel, he seemed content for him to take the lead, and that suited the headstrong twin. As they played, Joel kept up a constant stream of chatter. 'My great-great-grandfather was a buccaneer. Papa's ship *Pegasus* fought the French. Papa was a privateer before Grandpapa died and Papa had to stay at home and work in the yard. Papa says that *Pegasus* sails to lands beyond the seas. She trades with the new convict colony in Botany Bay, or as Papa says they now call it, New South Wales. She is not the only ship my papa owns. He builds the best and fastest ships in England and some he sells to the preventive men and some he sells to smugglers. Not only is that good business, it is only fair. That way it gives the smugglers a fair chance of success in landing their cargo without being caught. It must be great fun to be a smuggler. They are daring and brave. When I grow up I'm going to be a smuggler, or a pirate, and have loads of adventures, and Papa will build me the fastest, bestest ship ever.'

Senara had come to check on the invalid, and hearing her son's excited chatter she paused outside the bedroom door. Her patient might be less inhibited with another boy, and after the way he had been beaten, he could have a natural suspicion of adults.

Joel continued with his animated prattle, which was interspersed with explosive noises whenever his ship fired a cannon. Then Senara was startled by a deeper voice shouting, '*Kerpow!* Got you. You're dead. Your ship has been blown out of the water. I win the battle.'

She held her breath. The boy had finally spoken. She curbed her urge to rush in and question him. She did not want her presence to make him withdraw into his shell like a mollusc.

'No, I'm not dead,' Joel shouted. 'That stupid shot missed my ship by a mile. I've got two ships firing broadsides. I win. I *win*.' His voice rose; he hated to be the loser in any game.

'No you don't,' the older boy protested. 'I sunk that ship.'

There was a squeal of fury and a thud. Senara sighed. It was the unmistakable sound of two boys rolling across the floor fighting. As she moved to the open doorway, she saw them locked in combat, arms and legs flailing. Joel, despite his lesser size and weight, had taken advantage of his opponent's weakened state and sat on his chest, his arms flailing like a windmill as he attempted to land a punch.

'Joel! That is no way to treat a guest.' Senara yanked her son to his feet and held his hands down to his sides. 'Your friend has barely recovered from his accident. He should be resting. Why must you always be so naughty and take your games too far?'

The boy he had been attacking jumped to his feet. 'Please, don't beat him, Mrs Loveday. It was my fault.'

Senara stopped struggling with the squirming figure of her younger son, but it was Joel who spoke first and his tone was indignant. 'Mama never hits me. Neither does Papa. Did your mama hit you?'

A mask dropped over the boy's features and he threw himself back on the bed and drew the cover over his head.

Joel groaned and pulled a face. 'Is he not going to play any more? He's not much fun. I wish Nathan was here.'

'I think there has been enough playing for now, Joel,' Senara said. 'Cook has made butter biscuits. Go and bring some from the kitchen and share them with your friend.'

When Joel ran out of the room, Senara sat on the edge of the bed. As she tried to lift the covers from the boy's head, they were jerked back in place and she could feel the mattress shaking with the force of his sobs.

'Do not cry, my lovely. I have no intention of hurting you. It was good to hear you speak. Do you feel strong enough to get up and share Joel's biscuits when he returns? My son misses his older brother and he can be a bit wild and unruly at times. I would not want him bothering you if you prefer to rest.'

Slowly the covers were lowered, but the boy continued to regard her warily. Senara smiled and with the edge of the sheet wiped the tears from his cheeks. 'It must be very frightening for you to find yourself in a strange house with strange people. We would like to help you. And it would be nice to know your name.'

The cover was jerked back over his head and his voice was cracked with fear. 'I don't know it. I don't know anything.'

'You do not know your name?' she prompted gently.

Beneath the covers there was a shake of his head, and a small, tormented voice said, 'No. Nor where I live. Or who my parents are. That's why I did not speak. I have no name, no home, no one.' He burst into renewed sobs.

Senara stroked his back. 'That must be very upsetting and scary indeed. But you have a home for now, my lovely. That is here. You do have someone. You have Joel, my husband and myself to take care of you. You are not alone.'

Her words calmed him and one eye peeked out from the cover. 'You will not beat me because I cannot give you my name, or tell you of my home?'

She shook her head. 'But you remember beatings, or so it would appear.'

His eyes shadowed. 'I hear shouting voices in my dreams but not what they are saying, and in those dreams I feel pain that is not there when I wake.'

'You were in a great deal of pain when you were thrown from the coach. And you hit your head very hard. That could have affected your memory. It will come back in time.'

Joel bounded into the room, his hands full of biscuits. 'They are still warm. Carrie said she'd bring some buttermilk for us.'

'Would you like buttermilk and biscuits?' Senara put her hand on the boy's shoulder.

For several moments he did not move, then he sat up and nodded. Carrie Jensen appeared carrying a tray with two horn beakers and two slices of fruit cake.

'Looks like you are to have a feast,' Senara laughed. 'I will leave you to enjoy it. And no fighting, Joel. Your friend is our guest.'

'But what do I call him?' puzzled Joel. 'You can't have a friend who has not got a name.'

'Then we must find a special name for him,' suggested Senara.

'Bryn,' Joel piped up.

Senara laughed. 'Last month you were pestering your father to buy you a deerhound from a pedlar. The dog's name was Bryn.'

'Papa said no to the deerhound and Bryn would have been my friend. Bryn's a proper name. It's not a dog's name, not like Scamp. Now I have a new friend who has no name. So a good name for him would be Bryn.'

There was no arguing with a child's logic. Senara smiled at the older boy. 'It is for our guest to choose his name.'

The lad shrugged. 'Bryn is as good a name as any, I suppose.'

'Then it shall be Bryn, until, that is, you remember your own name,' replied Senara.

Two weeks later there was still no improvement in Bryn's memory, and no one had replied to the notices in the news-sheets about a woman and child who were missing. Bryn did not speak of the accident and it worried Senara that when she asked him about the woman in the coach his memory remained blank. Adam, who was a natural artist, had sketched from memory a portrait of the woman in the coach. When Bryn looked at it he showed no emotion. Surely, if he had been travelling with his mother, grief would somehow have triggered some kind of memory. Since he became upset whenever the accident was mentioned, they had stopped referring to it.

Apart from his loss of memory, Bryn was now fully recovered from his wounds and accepted his role within the family. With Joel and Rhianne attending lessons at Trevowan, Senara was concerned about the boy's own education. His clothes on the night of the accident and his way of speaking proved he came from a family of good breeding, and he was also well educated. When he had first regained consciousness she had read him the first few chapters of *Robinson Crusoe*, and had returned one afternoon to find him propped up in bed reading it for himself.

He had stared at her in bewilderment and asked, 'Mrs Loveday, how is it I can remember the names of all the things in this room and outside the window, and I can read this book, but I cannot remember my own name?'

It was a heartrending question that deserved to be answered truthfully. 'I cannot answer that, but I think it is a good sign that your full memory will return.'

'I get so frightened in my dreams. What if something bad happened in my past, or I hated it? Will you send me back?'

'We are not your legal guardians, so we would have no choice. Why do you ask? Have you remembered something?'

Bryn shook his head. 'Except that I feel safe here and I am happy and it feels sort of strange.'

Her heart clenched with concern. The words had an ominous ring to them. Fleetingly it occurred to her that if he did remember something bad, or had been unhappy with his life, he might lie to conceal it. She studied his face. There was fear in his eyes, but it stemmed from the unknown and the not knowing, not from the need to conceal a past pain. All her instincts told her that he was being honest with her and none of his memory had returned.

His lower lip trembled slightly, revealing his vulnerability and the brave face he was showing to the world.

Senara was quick to reassure him. 'Possibly everything about our life here is very different from what you knew before; that is why it feels strange to you.'

His expression was grave as he digested her words. 'I like it here. What will you do if my memory does not return, or Captain Loveday does not discover the identity of my family?'

'You have a home here for as long as you need it, Bryn. We will cross the bridges of your future when it is necessary.'

Chapter Five

In the following weeks, life in Cornwall proceeded as normal, and with each day Bryn not only became part of the family, but was also accepted by the community as Adam's ward. Although notices were placed in several other counties' news-sheets and also in London, there were no replies. Bryn remained ignorant of his past, and with a child's resilience and a full return to health, he was happy to integrate seamlessly into the Loveday world.

Senara was taking a dish of tea with Amelia, Elspeth and Felicity in the orangery at Trevowan as she awaited the children finishing their lessons with their tutor. Baby Thea was asleep in the nursery. Adam's stepmother and St John's wife sat side by side at a large embroidery frame, working on an altar cloth for Trewenna church. Elspeth was still in her riding habit, intending to exercise another of her hunters that afternoon.

'Do you not find it odd that Bryn does not seem unduly disturbed or eager to be reunited with his family?' Amelia questioned. Her greying auburn head remained bent over her delicate work.

'I think he must have been a lonely child,' Senara answered. 'He takes great delight in playing with the children and never seems to mind when Joel becomes quarrelsome or would rule their games.'

Amelia broke off from her work, her frown showing that she thought proprieties should be maintained. Putting a hand to her heart, she gave a small shudder of horror. 'What if the boy has been abandoned by an evil guardian?'

Beside her, Felicity's pale blue eyes widened in distress and there was no colour in her face beneath her fair hair and brows. She looked almost ghostly in her white muslin gown. 'Or his inheritance stolen?'

'You read too many fanciful novels.' Elspeth tutted in exasperation and glared at them over the top of her pince-nez. She had been studying the bloodlines in an auction announcement of a forthcoming sale of thoroughbreds at Tattersalls. 'If the boy comes from a good family he has likely spent some years away at school. His parents could be abroad, his father serving as ambassador at some foreign court.'

'Apart from his reading, his tutor informs us that his education is lacking in languages, simple mathematics and geography,' Amelia reminded her sister-in-law with equal impatience. 'Clearly his education has been neglected. Felicity could have a point. A guardian may have wanted him dead to steal his inheritance. A young charge would be at the mercy of an unscrupulous elder. Is it not our duty to discover this?'

'What more can we do?' Senara responded, thinking they were being overdramatic, although it could be a possibility.

'We have done all we can.' Elspeth was firm. 'We can but keep him safe and rear him as a gentleman. If his parents are alive and abroad and return to find him missing, surely it will be in the news-sheets.'

'Not if they are told he is dead,' Amelia said with distress.

Felicity put her hands to her cheeks. 'It is too dreadful to consider. But is he the responsibility of our family?'

'It would be cruel to turn our backs on him.' Senara was appalled at her sister-in-law's lack of charity. 'I would not like to see him placed in an orphanage. He is a charming, well-mannered child. Fate has been cruel to him.'

'I think fate has been exceptionally kind to the lad, giving him you and Adam as his champions,' Elspeth snorted.

Felicity stopped her sewing and waved her fan vigorously to cool her agitated state. There was a mutinous glitter in her eye. 'This Bryn could be anyone – a by-blow even. There has been much gossip.'

'Would that matter?' Senara demanded.

'Of course it matters.' Amelia flushed with indignation. 'It is a stigma. He would be shunned by decent society.'

'As you would have shunned Tamasine?' Elspeth glared at her sister-in-law. She had removed her riding hat whilst studying the auction details and her greying hair was pulled back from her high brow and cheekbones and hidden by a black caul. In her exasperation she picked up her hat, gripping the stiffened brim with whitened knuckles. 'She was your husband's daughter and Edward was never ashamed of her.'

The two women locked stares and the atmosphere in the room chilled to frost. Felicity coughed and shifted uncomfortably. Elspeth brandished her hat in her ringless hands as though it was a cudgel to knock some sense into them. 'Tamasine was the daughter of a noblewoman, a woman Edward would have married had she been free,' she rapped out.

Amelia mumbled an apology to her sister-in-law. 'However, you cannot escape the fact that Bryn is the cause of much speculation. And what of the robbery? No trace of his possessions were found. What if we are accused of abducting the lad and stealing his property for our own ends?'

Elspeth gave an unladylike snort. 'Have your wits gone begging, madam? No one would dare accuse a Loveday of such despicable roguery. The robbery was reported, was it not?'

Felicity stood up. 'In my condition I have no strength for these virulent debates. I will lie down for an hour. I do not sleep well when St John is away.' She left the room with her nose pointing to the ceiling.

Elspeth exhaled sharply. 'Her tongue gets more acidic by the day. A little more tolerance would not go amiss. I'm going riding.' She banged her hat on her head.

Senara lowered her gaze. Elspeth certainly did not heed her own advice. To break the tension in the room she commented, 'I was not aware St John was from home.'

Elspeth tutted. 'Young Lord Fetherington is back on his estate and intent on gaming away his father's fortune, by all accounts. From his smug mood, St John seems to be enjoying a run of fortune with the cards. Though I doubt any good will come of it. He never knows to quit when he is ahead.' She rose stiffly and limped to the door, only the tight set of her mouth revealing the pain she endured from her hip, which had been injured in a riding accident. She muttered darkly as she passed Senara, 'No wonder St John escapes her censure whenever he can.'

Senara glanced at Amelia. 'Perhaps I should go to Felicity? She did not look well.'

'She is too quick to criticise her husband,' Amelia confided. 'Though St John needs a restraining hand when it comes to his gambling. Sit awhile, Senara. The children will finish their schooling soon.' She put aside the embroidery frame and sat back in her chair, her rigid spine held away from the upholstery. Not a single hair was out of place in her elaborately styled coiffure. She stared into space for some moments before she voiced the thoughts that were troubling her. 'There has been much speculation and gossip in recent years about the family. Tamasine's arrival was a difficult time for us all. Bryn's presence could make people again speculate about her parentage.'

'Tamasine was accepted as Edward's ward. Few guessed she was in fact his illegitimate daughter. He was an exceptional man not to turn his back on her when he learned of her existence so late in her life, and she made a good marriage and is happy with Max Deverell.'

'In the circumstances she made a remarkable marriage to Mr Deverell, a man of great wealth and influence and respected by society. Yet it could all unravel if awkward questions are ever raised.' Amelia twisted her wedding band around her finger, her brow creased as she stared unseeing at a vase of roses.

'It is not Tamasine who you fear for, is it?' Senara voiced her inner intuition. 'Max will protect her with his name and his reputation as a man of honour. Neither is Bryn your only concern, though obviously people are curious that the carriage conveying him was wrecked and the coachman and a woman passenger were killed. We have made no secret that his memory is lost and we have done everything in our power to find his family. What is really troubling you?'

Amelia sighed. 'Am I so transparent?'

Senara stayed silent, allowing Amelia the time to have the confidence to reveal her fears. Her words when they came were dragged up from the depths of her dainty satin slippers. 'It is the scandal and the speculation surrounding Edward being shot that is hardest to bear.'

'But that is long past!' Senara was astounded that Amelia should feel shame that Edward had been shot whilst defending his land from smugglers using it to store contraband.

'Is it? Then why is Beaumont's name again on everyone's lips? It was all the talk when I called upon Lady Traherne yesterday. Dr Chegwidden's haughty wife was there, and Lady Fetherington. They could talk of nothing else but Lieutenant Beaumont's mysterious disappearance. He has not been heard of for over a year. His estranged wife suspects foul play. She wants him declared dead so that she can remarry. There was no love lost in that marriage. He married her for her money.'

Senara had gone deathly cold at the mention of the revenue officer. He had been no friend to the Lovedays and had done all in his power to bring them to ruin.

Her heart was still beating with a frantic urgency when she returned to Boscabel to seek out her husband. She found Adam supervising four carpenters who were putting a new roof on a barn that had not been used for over half a century. Although she did not immediately speak of her distress, he knew her so well that her expression told him that all was far from well. He finished his instructions to the men and came to her side.

She glanced around, uneasy that they could be overheard. 'Let us walk to the wood. I would speak in private.'

They strolled to Senara's favourite place where a bench had been built by a low waterfall that was fed by a fast-flowing stream. Senara had named it the Emerald Glade. Many of the herbs she used in her medicines grew here, and for her it was a place of reverence to the old spirits of nature. As they approached, two does and their fawns raised their heads from drinking and moved with a silent majesty into the undergrowth. The trunks of the rowan trees were closely packed, and the sunlight was so densely filtered by their canopy of leaves that the granite boulders beneath were thickly coated in moss. In the sunshine, with the last of the sweet-scented bluebells fading, and above them the translucent green leaves sprouting in abundance, the glade shone with an emerald light, magical and uplifting. The tinkling passage of the water was a fanfare of fairy bells to Senara's ears, yet today even these failed to comfort her.

49

Adam drew her close and kissed her hair. 'What has made you fearful? I can feel you trembling.'

She tipped her head back to look up at him. What was in her mind was too awful to contemplate, let alone speak about. She gazed into his blue-green eyes, the colour of the Cornish sea in summer before it broke upon the dark headland rocks. The long, sweeping crescent of his eyelashes cast shadows on his cheeks, and her hand was drawn to the scar near his eye where he had been struck when he had saved her sister Bridie from being attacked by a gang of young thugs. She knew from memory every scar on his body; from his battles at sea, and sword and gunshot wounds sustained protecting his family honour. His full lips drew back in a teasing smile, but his eyes had darkened to a deeper shade of the sea before a storm.

'What could daunt your valiant spirit, my love? I have never known you afraid, even in our darkest hours.'

'Because I have never doubted my abilities before.' She wrenched out her anguish. 'I have always known that somehow right would prevail.' A shudder passed through her slender figure and he pulled her against his hard frame. The heat of his body spread through her clothing but it could not warm her, so deep was her dread. 'There is talk about Beaumont. Someone has been asking after him. Making it sound as though there is something sinister about his disappearance.'

'He knows he is not welcome in these parts. I made that clear when we fought at our last meeting.'

The stiffness that had entered her husband's figure filled her with dread. A cloud passed over the sun, and cast into sudden shadow, the temperature in the glade plummeted. She shivered, feeling the shadow of Beaumont's evil close by. Her voice was ragged with a deepening sense of fear. 'I thought that any harm he could bring us was long in the past.'

'And so it is.'

Senara shook her head. 'He stayed away because he feared Harry Sawle. The smuggler vowed to kill him. But Sawle has been dead – hanged – these fifteen months. Beaumont hated us. He vowed to destroy us and you have never hidden your loathing for him.'

'Beaumont knew he could not beat us.' Adam cupped Senara's

chin in his hands and smiled into her eyes. His love for her bathed her in its intensity. He was a man who had triumphed over many dangers and enemies. 'Do you doubt that I will protect you — protect all that is ours?'

'I do not doubt you. I never have.'

'Then you are foolish not to conquer these fears. They are so unlike you.' His expression sobered. 'Or have you had a premonition that some calamity will befall us?'

She shook her head, unwilling to burden him with this darkness that had touched her soul. He linked his arm through hers and said, 'My love, as usual you are doing too much and push yourself to exhaustion. It is making you see shadows where there are none. Come, we will return to the house.'

'I interrupted your work. I will stay here awhile and enjoy the quiet. I have been foolish.' She forced a light laugh. 'I had thought our enemies had all been defeated when Harry Sawle met his end.'

'Beaumont was never more than an irritating wasp in a jam pot compared to the smuggler,' Adam replied, dismissing his old antagonist.

When Adam left her, Senara ignored the bench and sank down on to the ground near the water, allowing her fingers to trail in its coolness. Her nagging unease continued. It was not Adam's ability to defend them but her own conscience that troubled her. Her husband knew nothing of her last encounter with Beaumont. It was the only secret she had ever kept from him because she had been appalled at her actions that day. She had been away for many hours attending upon a birth at a farm a mile from here, and was riding home in the afternoon. It had been a hot, balmy day when little stirred and even the birds were silent. Tired from her long hours of midwifery, she had allowed her mare to clop along at an unhurried pace. From behind an outcrop of rock she had heard a young voice cry out in fear.

'I beg you, no. Have mercy.'

A following scream was cut off as though by a smothering hand. A lone woman was often at peril in a lonely stretch of countryside. Senara was now protected by her status and name, but before she had met Adam she had twice been set upon by men intent upon rape and had only escaped by her fleetness of foot and quick wits. Both experiences had terrified her.

Urging her mount, Hera, over the rough ground, she was appalled to discover Beaumont with his breeches around his ankles forcing his loathsome advances on a young mother returning from the woods on the edge of the moor after collecting firewood. Although the woman's face was covered in blood, Senara recognised Evie Tregony, who lived near Trewenna. Her daughter, who Senara had delivered two years ago, was sitting on the grass by the bundle of faggots, sobbing in fear. A gash to her temple showed that the toddler must have been roughly thrown aside by the woman's attacker.

Outrage had ground through Senara. Heedless of any danger to herself, she pushed Hera forward. The mare was unsettled by the cries and the smell of blood. This was not the first time Senara had encountered Beaumont forcing his unwanted attentions upon a woman. Her appearance had stopped him compromising Gwendolyn Druce's reputation in a bid to force the heiress to marry him. That was before Gwendolyn had married Japhet Loveday. Senara's intervention that day had added to the hatred the officer had towards the Lovedays. This time he had been so intent upon ripping at the struggling woman's skirts and bodice that he had not heard Senara approach. Senara had drawn the small pistol that Adam had insisted she always carry, for at the time Sawle had still been on the loose.

'Get away from the woman or I will shoot,' Senara ordered, aiming the pistol at the lieutenant's back.

The sun was behind her and Beaumont cursed as her shadow fell upon him and the frantically struggling farmer's wife. He put up a hand to cut the sun's glare from his eyes and his reptilian countenance twisted in recognition and loathing. His face was swollen and bruised, and the darkness of the bruises showed that they were some hours old and not from the woman's struggles. She now knew they were the result of his fight with Adam.

'Release the woman, or I will shoot,' she had repeated.

'Perhaps you would prefer to take her place.' Beaumont scowled and continued to press the woman down into the heather.

Knowing that she had only the one bullet, Senara was reluctant to fire lest she missed and placed herself in danger. Revulsion at his actions shredded all the decorum she had learned in her role as a gentlewoman. The wildness of her gypsy blood thundered through her veins, and the need for vengeance for all the injustices that her sex and race had suffered at the hands of men such as this arrogant bully rose within her. She had been brought up by her gypsy grandmother to be a priestess of the old religion, and as her rage took possession of her reason, she was governed by the old feelings of persecution. Too often a man would callously rape a woman weaker than himself.

She had learned to ride bareback as a child, and now, gripping the mare's sides tight with her thighs, she brought down her riding crop upon Beaumont's fleshy bare buttocks, raising blood. He yelped in agony and released his hold on Evie enough for her to bring her knee up towards his groin. She missed her mark and he slammed his fist into her nose, crushing the bone.

'I said leave her,' Senara spat. She aimed the pistol, but at that moment he rolled away and snatched up the sobbing child, holding her by the throat.

'Get on your way, Loveday bitch, or the child dies.' His face was contorted by his thwarted lust. The child dangled in his hands, her arms and legs thrashing ineffectively. Her mother crawled on the ground towards their tormentor.

'Let her go. You can have me. Don't harm my child.'

Beaumont continued to shake the toddler. The child's hood had come off and her face was turning blue. He held her like a trophy before him. 'Back off, Loveday bitch. This is not your concern.'

'The safety of a defenceless woman and child will always be my concern.' Senara fired the pistol, but at that moment Hera pranced in fear and to her dismay the shot went wide. Beaumont's horse, which had been tethered loosely to a gorse bush, whinnied in alarm and broke away to bolt across the field. It would not stop until it reached its stable.

Beaumont cursed the fleeing horse, his expression dark with malice as he shook the toddler so violently she stopped her screams and her movements were stilled. He tossed her aside as carelessly as he would a gnawed chicken bone. 'You'll both pay for that. Nothing can save you now, Loveday bitch.'

Convinced that the child was dead, her life snuffed out without remorse on a whim of lust, fury gouged through Senara. So fierce was her outrage at such disregard for an innocent life that she was unaware that she had raised her hand to the sky and screamed at the officer in the tongue of her forefathers.

Beaumont backed away. One hand fumbled to hitch his breeches up from around his ankles. The other was raised with the thumb thrust between the first two fingers in a sign to ward off evil. Dimly Senara was also aware that Evie was hugging her daughter to her breast and frantically pressing kisses upon her face as though her love had the power to revive the child.

The officer continued to back away, straight into the path of several vipers sunning themselves on the sun-heated rocks. Spitting and hissing, they reared up, their barred fangs striking at the exposed calves of his legs. It was the officer who now screamed in terror as he fell to the ground and dragged himself away from the snakes. The vipers disappeared as unexpectedly as they had appeared. It must have been their presence that had spooked Hera.

Evie was keening with grief and Senara's heart ached with compassion. It was then that she saw one of the child's fingers move very slightly. She leapt from the horse and held out her arms to the girl.

'Evie, let me see her. I do not think she is dead.'

The woman stared at her with round eyes that mirrored her horror. Gently Senara prised the mother's rigid fingers from her child, her voice calming as breathing lavender oil. 'I may yet be able to save your daughter.'

Evie still hesitated. 'What was it you shouted? And those snakes! Satan appeared to Eve as a serpent, so they tell us in church. Did he come for his own?'

'The fool walked into a nest of vipers sunning themselves. Nothing more. They are a common enough sight.'

Evie was illiterate and superstitious. 'They say you saved your village at Trevowan Hard from the plague. They hail you an angel. Are you witch or angel, Mrs Loveday? My child's soul depends upon it.'

'I am neither.' She had stemmed her irritation at the woman's irrational fears. 'I am but a simple woman who learned the wisdom of herbal cures.' She reached for the girl and pressed a finger to her throat. There was a very faint pulse. She took Evie's hands and placed them on the same spot. 'Feel that. It means she lives, but she is in shock and her throat is badly bruised. Ride behind me to Boscabel, where I have herbs and a balm that will help her breathing. She will be running round as normal in a week.'

She mounted Hera and held out her hands to take the child. Evie continued to stare at her with superstitious horror. Senara said patiently, 'The villagers trusted me with their lives. Will you not do the same? Your daughter could die if we delay.'

The authority in Senara's voice was obeyed, and Evie mounted to sit stiff and awkward behind her, holding tight to her waist. Neither of them gave the officer a second look. They left him crawling along the ground after them, begging them not to leave him to die.

Within the hour the child had been given a restorative, and her neck anointed with a balm to lessen the swelling. Senara had also prepared a tincture of honey and feverfew to ease her throat. Evie's broken nose had also been tended and she had been given a mild sedative to calm the shock of her ordeal. They were to be driven back to their farm by Billy Brown.

'You saved our lives,' Evie wept before her departure.

'I did but right a wrong.'

'I would wish that monster dead, but we will be blamed if he dies.'

'No one saw us. No weapon or human force has harmed him.'

'But the snakes? We left him to die,' Evie wailed.

'He was a danger to us. How could we risk lingering when your daughter needed immediate attention?' When Evie continued to look afraid, Senara added, 'A single snakebite is not lethal to a grown man. And we do not know for certain that the vipers bit him. Return to your home and say nothing.'

By the time Evie and her daughter had left, Senara's anger had faded. Her conscience would not be stilled that she could have left a man to die. No matter how evil Beaumont had been, she could not live with herself if she did nothing to save him. Using the excuse that she had dropped her purse during her ride, she asked Eli Rudge to accompany her when she rode back over her tracks.

The sun was setting as they reached the outcrop of rock where the attack had taken place. The sky was crimson and bruised purple with heavy clouds, and an eerie mist was floating a few inches off the ground. There was a patch of flattened grass where Beaumont had forced himself upon Evie. Of the officer there was no sign, although they searched for half an hour. Clearly he had lived and somehow managed to get away from the scene of his crimes. Since that day Senara had locked the incident deep in a recess of her mind, telling no one but Bridie, appalled at the invocation she had chanted when she had called on the old gods to protect them. Snakes were an ancient symbol of the goddess of nature, and when called upon she would protect her acolytes.

Chapter Six

With the passage of another month, nothing had changed within the household at Boscabel. Bryn still showed no sign of recovering his memory. He was a good-natured youth, and while happy to follow the games led by Joel, he tolerated none of the younger boy's fits of temper and even curtailed the wilder exploits that had so frequently landed Joel in trouble. The gossip surrounding Beaumont's disappearance became old news and Senara told herself that she had over-reacted. If he had died the day of his attack upon Evie, his body would have been discovered months ago. The officer had transgressed too far that day by turning on the child. If word of his conduct had spread, he would have faced the highest authorities to answer to his crimes. Clearly he had run away, as he always fled the district when trouble snapped too close at his heels. The man was a coward and would be far away by now where no one knew his true nature.

Then came welcome news for the Lovedays. Invitations arrived from Tamasine in Dorset to the christening of her daughter Olivia the last week of July. The family, after attending the morning service at Trewenna church, had paused in the churchyard to discuss the forthcoming celebration.

'This is wonderful news,' Senara enthused. 'It is what we all need and it will be our first chance to visit Tamasine in her new home.'

Cecily and Joshua finished speaking with the last of the congregation leaving the church and joined them.

'It will not be possible for me to forgo my duties,' stated Joshua, 'and neither can Peter.'

'Tamasine will understand that your work for the parish cannot be neglected,' said Adam. Even so, he was concerned. He knew it was important to his half-sister to have her family around her, especially as she had been an outcast for so long in her youth when her birth had been kept secret even from Edward Loveday. 'Have you heard from Hannah if she will be attending, Uncle?'

Joshua shook his head. 'Since her marriage to Sam Deighton, my daughter has many responsibilities. There is not only her farm here to be managed but also her new husband's commitments to his ward Lord Eastley at Highcroft. They are in Devon hoping to resolve the legal disputes with Sam's family. I cannot see Hannah returning here for some months, or being able to visit Dorset.'

'Hannah would wish to be present,' Senara observed. 'Yet Sam, as Charlie's guardian, is bound by his uncle's wishes that his young lordship be brought up at Highcroft when he is not boarding at school. It is unjust to keep the lad from a natural life with his new family.'

'He has to learn the responsibilities of his title and estate,' Joshua placated. 'Though I consider that the late Lord Eastley was harsh in his conditions for his grandson's upbringing. Sam will be the first to admit that his family has been torn apart by family disputes. His own father has disinherited him and will not acknowledge Charlie as his brother's legal heir, or as his grandson.'

'Sam cannot risk breaching the terms of the late Lord Eastley's will, or Charlie will lose his inheritance.' Adam sympathised with the couple. He had great respect for Hannah and had liked Sam when he had worked for some years as her overseer while he sought to bring Charlie up alone. Although Sam had never spoken about his private life, Adam had warmed to his honesty and obvious loyalty to Hannah. When Sam had suddenly left the farm to settle a matter of family business, Adam had thought him just another labourer moving on. It had surprised them all when Sam had returned last year, proclaiming that his nephew was now Lord Eastley, and then asking for Hannah's hand in marriage. The family had been concerned that Sam's responsibility to raise Charlie in accordance with his grandfather's instructions would compromise the financial security of Hannah's children. As a widow, Hannah had efficiently run the farm that had been in her husband's family for several generations, and she was determined that it would pass to Davey, the eldest of her four children. Not every couple could successfully discharge such duties without some sacrifice upon their personal happiness. Yet Adam believed Hannah and Sam would not fail in their commitments and would be happy in their marriage.

Adam turned his attention to his twin. 'I trust you will attend the christening.'

'I am surprised Max has gone to such extravagance over the birth of a girl,' St John replied, his manner abstracted. From the puffiness of his eyes and face he looked to be suffering a major hangover. Lately he had been drinking excessively and his temper had been short and erratic.

His harsh tone made Felicity wince, then she reprimanded him haughtily. 'The birth of a child is always a joyous occasion. Max will be giving praise that his wife has also been safely delivered.'

Elspeth waved her walking cane in the older twin's direction, harsh in her incrimination. 'Your late father would expect you to support Tamasine.'

St John spread his hands as though bowing to her wisdom. 'Then I must do so, must I not?'

Elspeth sucked in her breath. Too late she realised that her nephew had every intention of attending and had been deliberately goading his wife for not producing a son. She had heard the couple quarrelling on several occasions since the invitation had arrived.

'It promises to be a grand occasion with a ball and a week of revelry.' Senara tried to defuse the tension between the couple. 'Tamasine hopes that we will stay a further week. She says that Aunt Margaret and Thomas and Georganna intend to stay longer before they come down to Trevowan for the summer.'

'Max knows how to entertain in style,' St John returned. 'I look forward to a break from the routine of the estate.'

Felicity looked displeased, and beneath her straw bonnet her complexion was pale. 'I am not sure that in my condition I should undertake such an arduous journey, and the harvest will soon be ready.'

'Stay at Trevowan if it pleases you. It pleases me to celebrate with my family,' St John snapped. He sauntered away to discuss the price of livestock with another farmer.

His wife's hurt gaze followed him. 'Will he love me if I give him a son this time?'

Elspeth gave a deprecating sniff and her stare challenged her nephew's wife. Next to Margaret, Elspeth was the oldest member of the Loveday family and had a tongue that could flay a gorgon's hide. She did not like being used by her nephew to castigate his wife. 'He loves you well enough. You are being foolish. And I am sure you would not want St John to slight his own sister.'

The younger woman's lips clamped into a disapproving line. 'My husband's place is at my side.'

'His place is where his family duty takes him,' Elspeth reminded her. 'Delighted as I am that Tamasine has been safely delivered of a daughter, I will remain at Trevowan. With Hannah in Devon, I promised I would keep an eye on this year's foals at the farm. Besides, I am too old for such junketing. It is for you younger ones to show family solidarity. Are you sure you cannot accompany your husband, Felicity? The child is not due for over four months. Hannah never allowed her condition to curb her duty.'

'My condition was but an excuse to keep St John from gambling. Gaming tables for the men will be set up as part of the entertainments. Since he is determined to attend, with or without me, I shall accompany him.'

'I am pleased to hear it.' Elspeth nodded and pinned Adam with her stare. 'What are your plans, nephew?'

'It has not exactly come at the best time for me to be away from the yard and estate.' Adam frowned. 'But if it is just for two weeks, I can be spared.'

'You work too hard,' Elspeth replied. 'A break from the yard will do you no harm.'

'I am glad you agree with me, Aunt,' Senara said with a playful laugh, but her eyes were bright with the first sparks of censure. 'Tamasine needs our support, and she deserves it. There has been speculation enough about her ancestry from Maximillian's family and his friends.'

Adam chuckled at his wife's defence of the young woman she had befriended. 'Max adores my sister and would cross swords with any man rash enough to impugn her honour.'

'Her illegitimacy has always plagued her,' Senara persisted with deeper feeling. 'It is the first time Tamasine will be hostess to such a large gathering of polite society. She will be nervous. Though perhaps I should remain behind. Nathan will be home from school by then. The twins and Sara are rather young to travel and the excitement would be too much for them. Also, Bryn still needs—'

'Enough of excuses,' cut in Elspeth. 'Both you and Adam must attend. Your father would expect you to support Tamasine. The children can stay at Trevowan, Bryn included. His family have so far been dilatory in seeking his whereabouts. I suspect the child is an orphan. Time enough to decide what must be done for him when you return.'

'Will it not be too much for you? You will also have Rowena and Charlotte at Trevowan,' said Felicity.

Amelia hastily intervened, having held back her opinion until now. 'I shall be there to keep your children entertained. Rafe will delight in their company and so will I. With Richard on the high seas fighting the French, I miss my eldest son and worry about him. The children will be a welcome diversion.'

'But surely you are also to attend?' queried Felicity.

Amelia shook her head. 'I would not leave Elspeth on her own at Trevowan.'

'Will not your absence cause Tamasine's guests to speculate? There are many who would question her past.'

Amelia had the grace to blush but remained adamant. 'Tamasine will understand. She is a sensible woman and knows that I have come to love her as Edward's daughter. Elspeth cannot cope with the foals and ensure the children do not run wild on her own. Besides, I have done with travelling great distances and no longer visit my property in London.'

'After all your talk of duty, I would have thought it important that you did attend,' Felicity accused.

Amelia regarded the new mistress of Trevowan with a cool stare. Much of the tension in her home since St John's marriage had been between the three women living under the same roof. Each in their time had run the household, and both Amelia and Elspeth found it difficult to relinquish the reins. 'Perhaps you would prefer that your mama supervise the children, my dear. Though Sophia would expect you to entertain her during a visit.'

Felicity stiffened. 'Mama prefers to spend all her time in London now. Her last letter spoke of a regular caller, a Brigadier Peabody, a widower and retired from the army on account of an old leg wound. She hints that there will be an announcement before the end of the summer. It will be a great relief if she is happily wed.'

St John had rejoined them, and hearing the last remark said tersely, 'It will be a relief to us all. The brigadier has an estate in Derbyshire. A goodly distance from Cornwall.'

The family exchanged pointed glances, which Felicity chose to ignore. In the first year of her marriage her mother had constantly embarrassed her by her bawdy and inebriated behaviour on her frequent uninvited visits to Trevowan. They had never been close, and whenever Sophia was engaged upon a new love affair, she had no time for her daughter.

A young voice eager with excitement cut in. 'I think it is a marvellous idea that as many of the family as possible attend the christening of Tamasine's daughter.' Rowena had sidled over to listen to the adults' conversation. The sun glinted off the golden curls that tumbled around her shoulders. She wore a new rose-pink dress, the high waist and slender style showing the softening curves of her adolescent figure. She was tall for her age and could pass for a young woman. Despite her fairness, her lashes and brows were dark and she had inherited the bold, coquettish stare of her mother.

'You will be staying at Trevowan, young miss,' Felicity sharply reminded her stepdaughter. 'It will be another three years before you may attend such entertainments as the Deverells have planned.'

'You are all so mean.' Rowena stamped her foot.

Felicity sighed and looked at Amelia for support. 'There is no controlling the child. I have told her a dozen times she must stay here with Charlotte.'

Amelia remonstrated. 'By that show of temper, young lady, you prove that you are too young to be in polite company. Would you abandon your sister?'

'Charlotte is still a child.' Rowena poured all her scorn for her stepsister's lack of years into her voice. 'She would be bored. I would find it entrancing. And I am sure Olivia will be delightful and Tamasine is my dearest aunt. She would not deny me.'

'I will not discuss this now.' Felicity flushed, discomfited by such a fervent confrontation.

Rowena placed a hand on her father's arm. She would not be turned from her resolve. She hated Amelia and Felicity for always bowing to convention and doing what was right. She was bored with the company of the younger children and she hated being treated as a child. St John had been ignoring the conversation between the women and was discussing the latest news of the war with France with his brother and uncle.

'Papa,' she wheedled in a honeyed voice. 'I may go to Tamasine, may I not? I have heard so much about her lovely house and estate. If Felicity would turn her back on supporting my dear aunt, I would not.'

'Very commendable, my dear, but you are far too young.'

'Papa, that is so unjust,' she continued to coerce. She was confident that she could bend her father to her will. He rarely refused her. The dress she wore was proof. Felicity had declared that it was much too grown-up a style for her; Rowena had wept prettily and begged St John, and he had agreed to her demands. And she resented her stepmother, regarding her as a rival to her father's affection and time he would have spent in her company. 'I miss dearest Tamasine so very much. I will be no trouble. I will stay quietly in my rooms during the dancing and formal entertainments.'

'When will that child learn decorum and respect for her elders?' Felicity snapped. 'You are too lenient with her, St John.'

His eyes narrowed at her criticism, but he did not want his headstrong daughter ruining his chances of spending time at the gaming tables. Without Felicity at Beaucombe to deny him his fun, he intended to spend his days gaming.

'Your stepmama is right. There will be no other children attending. Your place is at Trevowan. The time will come soon enough when you are of age for such entertainments.'

Rowena lowered her gaze to glare at the hem of Felicity's gown. Her rebellious stare was concealed from Amelia and Elspeth's sharp eyes. She hated her prissy stepmother. Her fists clenched into tight balls and she spun on her heel and marched across the churchyard. She was watched by a group of lads from the village a few years older than herself, and when Joey Gateley, the eldest son of a yeoman farmer, called out to her, she stuck her nose in the air, refusing to recognise the attention of a farmer's son, even if he was the most handsome of all the boys of her acquaintance.

Rowena scanned the congregation, who were chatting with acquaintances before leaving for their homes. It vexed her that the sons of the gentry who were of an age to merit her interest were all away at school. She was thirteen and had spent the Easter school break testing her wiles on the older boys. Every morning the Venetian looking-glass in her stepmother's chamber showed her that she was blossoming into a beautiful young maid. She had inherited the Loveday charm and her mother's looks, cunning and ambition. Meriel had used her beauty to rise from a tavern-keeper's daughter to snare St John. If Rowena could believe the rumours about her mother, of which there were plenty for her sharp ears to focus upon, Meriel had later caught the eye of an earl and run off with him.

Rowena thought her mother a fool and had no love for the woman, who had never been interested in her daughter. Yet Rowena had gleaned all the gossip concerning the trollop of Penruan, as she had heard her father refer to his first wife. In her opinion Meriel had sold herself too cheaply in marriage to a man she did not love. Though why St John had failed to dazzle her mother did puzzle Rowena. She adored her father and had learned from an early age how to twist him around her finger and to get her own way. If Meriel had wanted greater riches than Trevowan could give her, then she should have had more faith in her beauty and her wiles. Only a fool became a man's whore, even if that man was an earl. Meriel had soon lost the interest of her lover and to survive had become a courtesan in London. When her looks and health had failed her, she had crept back to Trevowan to die.

Rowena knew enough about gossip to be aware that she carried the stigma of her mother's reputation, but first and foremost she was a Loveday. She would not make the same mistakes as Meriel. Had not Tamasine proved that you could rise above your past to marry a handsome and wealthy man? Maximillian Deverell's estate at Beaucombe was grander than those owned by their neighbours Sir Henry Traherne and Lord Fetherington.

If Rowena had learned one thing from her mother, it was that if you intended to aim high, you must keep your virtue intact until the wedding. And she had already decided that she wanted not only a beautiful house and riches, but also a title. Her ruthless Sawle blood would allow her to accept nothing less.

Senara watched her niece flounce away and suppressed a sigh. That one was a little madam, and she did not envy St John trying to control her in a few years' time.

Chapter Seven

The christening of Olivia Loveday Deverell was to be marked with a grand ball and a week of entertainments at Beaucombe. No expense was to be spared to celebrate the arrival of Tamasine and Max's first child, and more than sixty people were expected to attend.

'I must have been insane to agree to so many guests. Sixty is an army – all to be fed, entertained and comfortably accommodated.' Tamasine pressed her hands to her cheeks and stared at her reflection in the dressing mirror. A rope of pearls was threaded through her dark curls worn à la Grecque and her gown was a shimmering sheath of pale blue silk that skimmed her slender hips and was embroidered with silver roses around its high waist and hem. Sapphires and diamonds sparkled in her ears and around her neck. She did not see the beautiful, sophisticated woman; only a pale face with large haunted eyes. 'I shall forget half their names and be an abysmal hostess, Max.'

Her husband's elegant image appeared at her side, and he stooped to kiss her neck. 'You will be perfect. Everyone will adore you, as I adore you.'

She closed her eyes and leaned back against the strength of his figure, drawing in the scent of his cologne. 'They do not all adore me. There are many who still question and would probe into my background. They sense a mystery surrounding my heritage. I could not bear that they will discover the truth and use it against you. Secrets are insidious. They lie just beneath the surface, dormant but never slayed, awaiting the moment of discovery to rise up to devour and destroy all in their path.'

'Motherhood has made you melodramatic, my love.' His laugh was rich and warm against her neck.

'It has made me fear that Olivia will be persecuted because of my birth.' His teasing could not sway Tamasine. 'It will hang over her, threatening her future happiness. Not all men are as honourable and forgiving as yourself, Max.'

'Your beauty and courage enslaved me.' He always made light of her anguish, his faith her greatest support. 'Never was a woman more worthy of my love.'

'Yet many men in your position might have wished to woo me and make me their mistress, for my bastardy would have disgusted them, and I would have been considered unfit to bear their name.'

'You must stop torturing yourself in this manner.' He squeezed her shoulders, checking his impatience at her fears. 'You are now a Deverell and as such your honour is impeccable. Come, sweetheart, it is time to welcome our guests. I hear the first of the carriages arriving.' He raised her to her feet and kissed her with barely restrained passion. 'There is none more worthy to be my wife; you proved that by your loyalty and courage. It is why I fell in love with you. There is no reason to fear for our daughter's future. Your fears are natural for a new mother, but they are groundless.'

Max had never lied to her, and she had been astounded how she had been accepted as an equal amongst his friends. Even his mother, the redoubtable Lady Clarissa, who never ceased to remind people that her family traced their lineage back to William the Conqueror, accepted her in public. Though when the two women were alone, Tamasine was never at ease in her mother-in-law's company, and probing questions about her childhood were often raised.

When she descended the wide, sweeping staircase of Beaucombe House, threads of anguish shivered through her veins. For the next week many judgemental eyes would be watching her every move. She must not fail Max. Before their betrothal, he had been told the truth of her parentage, though it had been glossed over to his mother and family. Tamasine knew she had enemies who had reason to revile her. Not least her own mother's legitimate children. After the death of her husband, her son, the young Lord Keyne, had shut his mother away to die alone. He had refused her any further meeting with the daughter she had borne Edward Loveday and hidden Tamasine away in a school for children who had been conceived in shame. Lord Keyne hated Tamasine and would see her dead before he admitted their kinship. It was Tamasine's constant fear that one day they would meet at a gathering of polite society and he would denounce her.

She shuddered and pushed her fears aside. She refused to be melodramatic. As a new mother and a matron of almost two-and-twenty, it was time she curbed her high-flown fancies. Lord Keyne had more important matters to concern him than troubling himself over her existence. She had not seen him for four years. Was it likely he would even recognise her? She was safe, loved and protected from the stigma of her birth. Those secrets were deeply buried. She squared her shoulders and tipped her chin at a defiant angle.

A male guest broke into song as she descended the stairs to walk into the grounds. Tamasine grinned. Not all secrets were bad. Some were delicious surprises. How her family would be delighted at the revelations she had for them.

'That must be Beaucombe House through the trees, Adam.' Senara gasped as she saw their destination through the window of the coach. 'I never realised Max Deverell possessed such a large property. Tamasine must have been aghast on her arrival. No wonder she was so apprehensive. Max must mix in very grand circles indeed.'

Adam glanced at his wife, her tone telling him of her own misgivings at attending such a prestigious gathering. Senara nervously touched her dark hair which was dressed in a simple chignon. There was no spare money to pay for a lady's maid, even if she would have accepted one. Her lovely face tightened as she continued. 'It must have been so daunting for Tamasine meeting Max's neighbours and friends after their marriage. After her betrothal we should have prepared her for a more genteel way of life. No wonder she was so eager for us to visit. She must have needed our support and we failed her.'

Adam did not share these misgivings. Tamasine's bright and vivacious personality would have captivated all she met with effortless ease. It was what had impressed him most when he had first met his half-sister. Yet the house and grounds were beyond anything he had expected and his own conscience tweaked that he had been unable to visit Tamasine before now. During the last two years he had been working hard to keep the Loveday shipyard from ruin. There had been no time for pleasure jaunts. Fortunately, the overriding message in all of Tamasine's letters was her happiness in her new life.

'We are here to support her now.' He nodded to his brother sitting opposite them with Felicity.

St John was staring disconsolately out of the window whilst Felicity dozed with her head resting on his shoulder. His wife had announced her intention to accompany them only a few hours before they were to depart, and there had been a strained atmosphere between the couple throughout the journey. They were the only members of the family from Cornwall to attend, though cousin Thomas, his wife Georganna and Aunt Margaret were travelling from their homes in London and would return with the twins for a month's stay in Cornwall.

When St John did not break off from his reflections and reply, Adam took Senara's hand and squeezed it. He understood that his wife was sensitive about status and acceptance. After ten years of marriage she still felt the insecurities of her gypsy blood. 'My love, you allow your own fears to influence your feelings. When will you accept how accomplished a mistress you are at Boscabel? Are you not adored and respected by our friends?'

'My life is simple compared to the social whirl that Tamasine must now be a part of. I know my place, and your love has always sustained me. Tamasine is similarly blessed with Max, but that will not allay her fears that her past will come back to haunt her. Also there is the wilder Loveday side of her nature that will never entirely be tamed. It has got her into trouble in the past.'

'She is a mother now. Maturity makes us all wiser. Do you not agree, St John?'

'Speak for yourself,' St John replied, clearly indifferent. 'It brings with it greater responsibility, which can be onerous at times. I look forward to the diversions this week will bring. It is a relief to be away from the pressures of Trevowan. I daresay my dear wife will not object if I spend an evening or two at the gaming tables. It will be expected.'

Since the main cause of the dissension within St John's marriage was his gambling, Adam hoped it would not get out of hand. In the past St John had lost more money than he could afford and had almost brought Trevowan to the brink of ruin with his extravagant wagers.

Felicity stirred and opened her eyes. 'Are we there? Oh, is that the house? It is magnificent. The children could have accompanied us. With so many rooms they would have been no inconvenience to the other guests. I do not like being away from Thea. She has just learned to walk and every day she does something new.'

'There are seven children between our two families alone. If everyone brought them the place would soon be overrun,' St John snapped. 'You pamper them too much, Felicity.' His expression sharpened with irritation. 'And you have changed your tune. You were outraged when Rowena wished to accompany us.'

'She was being deliberately provocative,' Felicity replied. For a moment it looked as though she intended to expand on her list of complaints about her stepdaughter, then she clamped her lips closed and when the carriage lurched over a small rut in the drive she groaned. 'When will this interminable journey be over? I have been constantly nauseous.'

'Then you should have stayed at Trevowan.' St John was brusque in his lack of sympathy.

Senara was uncomfortable at St John's disregard for his wife's comfort. She was also missing her own children, and, conscious that she had not been raised to such extravagance and splendour, she was nervous that she would in some way let her husband and his family down.

Adam stared at the house. It lay nestled in the valley of a long, winding coomb protected from the wind by the steep sides of the hills. It had been built after the Restoration. A double row of steps led up to the entrance, while Doric columns flanked the three-storey-high central pediment and a fourth storey of smaller dormer windows punctuated the roof. Standing sentinel above these were four large chimney stacks and in the centre an impressive octagonal cupola. Two symmetrical wings completed the design, and in front of these were impressive fountains with the figures of Poseidon and Aphrodite. The house was some four times larger than either Adam's own home, Boscabel, or the family residence at Trevowan. To the right of the building the sun glinted off a large lake.

He let out an admiring breath. 'Tamasine has done far better than anyone could have believed, even though she is beautiful, spirited and sharp-witted.'

'Tamasine is doubly blessed in her home and her husband's devotion,' Senara noted. 'Many grand living quarters have accommodated loveless marriages and brought misery to their occupants. Yet although the house is magnificent, she would never prize possessions above love. Maximillian Deverell is a worthy custodian and protector. Such wealth can draw sycophantic wasps like a honey pot, their stings poisoned with jealousy.'

Adam laughed aside her seriousness. 'Let us hope no such parasites blight this visit. Max is more than capable of detecting them and sending them speeding on their way.'

A man was striding across the lawn towards the lake, and there was something about his manner that made Adam study him more intently. He was hatless but dressed in the latest mode, and outwardly appeared to be a gentleman of wealth and position. Yet the way he walked in a bold, strutting manner and the set of his head pulled Adam's brow into a frown. There was something disturbingly familiar about him, but it must be his imagination. The figure was too far away now to see clearly. Even so the unease lingered until he told himself he must have been mistaken. It could not be who he had at first thought. Rumour had it that that knave had died after a duel some dozen years ago or more. And the world was well rid of the scoundrel.

Chapter Eight

With so many guests arriving at once, the Lovedays had been shown to their adjoining rooms to refresh themselves, and the maids allocated to them began to unpack their luggage. Adam and Senara were about to take a stroll in the grounds, but as Senara settled an Indian shawl around her shoulders there was an impatient knock on the door. At Adam's command to enter, Tamasine threw open the door and with a gurgle of delight ran into her brother's arms. He picked her up and spun her round, grinning.

'Has that husband of yours taught you nothing of decorum?' he teased.

'I am allowed to act the hoyden only in exceptional company.' She broke away from him to embrace Senara. 'I have missed you both so much.'

'Does this mean your husband ignores you?' Adam challenged. 'Or perhaps he has wearied of your wayward conduct. Must I call him to account for wilful neglect?'

For reply Tamasine rapped him playfully on his arm. 'You will do nothing of the kind. Max is the dearest and most adorable man. I have been so happy – happier than I ever thought possible. Yet strangely, brother mine, I miss your playful teasing. Max is more respectful of my dignity.'

Her cheeks were flushed with excitement that she was barely able to contain. Adam laughed. 'Thank the stars you have not changed. I did fear you would break with family tradition and become staid and conventional.'

'Heaven forfend!' she giggled. 'I warned Max I would not

change. Oh, Adam, life is so wonderful, I want to experience and enjoy every moment. Propriety would strip us of much of that pleasure.'

She intertwined her fingers and held them to her chest as though to calm some of her exhilaration. 'I must not forget my role as hostess. Have you everything you need? I long to hear news of the family. And the children must have grown so much. Is Joel still a little devil and Rhianne sweet as an angel? Nathan must be quite a young man now and away at school. You must miss him dreadfully, Senara. Does the yard prosper? And how are Bridie and little Michael?' The volley of questions was fired so rapidly that they were impossible to answer and Tamasine broke off with a laugh. 'I prattle like a halfwit, but there is so much news to catch up with.'

'We have plenty of time,' Adam reminded her.

As Tamasine paused to draw breath, Senara said quickly, 'And when do we get to see Olivia?'

The young woman's face softened with a radiant light of pride and love. 'She is so perfect. Such an angel. She is the sweetest, the most well-behaved of children.'

'Ah, she takes after Max then!' Adam laughed. 'Lead the way that we may pay our respects to this paragon.'

They were halfway down the corridor when Tamasine clapped her hand to her mouth. 'Oh, I should have greeted St John and Felicity. I would not have them think I slighted them, and Felicity was so brave to undergo the rigours of the journey in her condition.'

'Felicity intended to lie down and rest for an hour or so,' Adam remarked. 'And St John went to watch a game of bowls on the lawn immediately after our arrival. I have not heard him return to their chamber.'

'Then I will leave Felicity to rest and will greet St John soon enough.' If she considered her brother's abandonment of his wife strange, only the slightest frown creased her brow. 'I must get to know Felicity better. I have seen so little of her and St John since their marriage. Even St John is something of a stranger. I never felt we became close. He was in Virginia when I first came to Trevowan, and then rather distracted by the scandal he created when his fiancée arrived from America not knowing that he was still wed to Meriel.'

'Those are times best forgotten.' Adam dropped his voice to continue. 'He had no scruples trying to keep an American heiress tucked away while his wife was dying. Felicity is a much-needed sobering influence on him.'

'In a way you have to admire his audacity.' Tamasine seemed more impressed than condemning. 'It was a bold ploy and he was very much in love with the American woman. If she had not followed him to England, she would never have learned of his perfidy. Had the risk he took paid off, St John would be the master of a large tobacco plantation in Virginia. Would not our great-grandfather have done the same if he thought he could get away with it? He was something of a rogue. The risks we take and our faults are what make our family so interesting.'

'You have a romanticised view of our failings, sister,' Adam rebuked, but there was amusement in his voice.

They reached the nursery through a winding maze of corridors decorated with ornate plasterwork. The walls were all lined with portraits of Max's family in formal poses wearing the stiff and cumbersome fashion of the early Georgian, Stuart and Tudor times.

'Do you ever get lost?' Senara could not help remarking. 'I have no idea how to return to our rooms.'

'Like Theseus we should all be given balls of thread to guide our way through the labyrinth,' Adam chuckled.

Tamasine struck his arm with her hand, her tone indignant. 'That is mean. My beloved Max is no Minotaur.'

Adam grinned unabashed. 'Indeed he is a saint to suffer your wilful independence. That is no way for a lady to treat her guests. You have a very grand home. How many rooms are there?'

Tamasine's bright mood remained undimmed by his taunts. 'Far too many when they all have to be aired and cleaned. When we have no guests we only use a few rooms in this wing.' Then she cast a quizzing stare upon her brother. 'However, I would say that the reference to the Minotaur fits my mother-in-law. She still has the power to terrify me.'

She opened a door and stepped back for them to enter the nursery. Even this room was exceptionally grand. The crib was carved with cherubs and twice the size of any Senara had ever seen and it was draped with embroidered muslin. Two maids, a wet nurse and a nanny bobbed their curtseys, ready to pander to any of the needs of the infant.

'Mistress Olivia is asleep,' observed the nanny, who was a mountainous woman with the wisps of a moustache above her thin lips. She looked displeased that her routine had been interrupted.

'Then we shall be as quiet as church mice,' said Senara, and tiptoed to the cradle.

Adam stayed long enough to make the usual complimentary remarks about the baby, then left the nursery in search of his host. Senara lingered, reluctant to meet the guests, who would all be strangers to her. Tamasine was absorbed fussing over Olivia, who had woken and was smiling crookedly at her. She could not resist picking her up and handing her to Senara. Again she met with a look of disapproval from the nanny until with a sigh Tamasine took the baby from Senara and laid her back in the cradle. Olivia continued to smile and made no protest.

'The nanny is something of a dragon,' Tamasine whispered. 'Lady Clarissa appointed her and she last served in the household of a duke. I wish there were not so many guests, then I could spend all my time with you and Adam. I suppose I must go now and greet St John. And I forgot to mention to Adam that there is a surprise for him, well, for all the Lovedays. Actually, not exactly one surprise, but two . . .' She was deliberately enigmatic. 'Firstly, though, tomorrow Hannah and her new husband arrive. They did not know if they could get away from the estate at Highcroft, as there has been some trouble with Sam's father. The colonel still has not forgiven his son. Such a pity when Sam did so much to heal the family rift. At least it is not only our family that has so many skeletons in its cupboards.' She pulled a regretful face. 'Now I will show you back to the reception rooms. I have neglected my other guests.'

As they wove back through the maze of corridors, Senara breathed more easily knowing that cousin Hannah would be here. They had seen little of her since her marriage to Sam, as the couple spent much of their time away from Hannah's farm, leaving Mark Sawle as overseer in charge.

'It is four months since Hannah was in Cornwall,' Senara said. 'We all used to live within a few miles of each other and now we are spread over three counties. That is without considering London, which is Aunt Margaret and cousin Thomas and Georganna's home.'

'Papa said that Aunt Margaret moved there over forty years ago when she married the banker Charles Mercer.'

Senara nodded. 'But she has rarely missed a summer visiting her old home and still considers herself a Cornishwoman at heart.'

'I would not have met Max but for Aunt Margaret's matchmaking when I lived with her in London after Papa's death.' Tamasine smiled fondly. 'She was determined I would make a good match, and it so nearly went disastrously wrong.'

A flicker of pain in Tamasine's expressive eyes showed Senara that the scars of the young woman's illegitimacy had not healed. Although Edward had not learned of his daughter's existence until Tamasine's mother, the Lady Eleanour Keyne, was dying, he had accepted her into his family. Tamasine had then been sixteen, and had spent her childhood in a ladies' academy for the daughters of gentry born out of wedlock. Lady Eleanour had been in a loveless marriage. She had escaped it to live in Cornwall, leaving her husband to spend his days at court and his evenings with his current mistress. She had given him his heir and two daughters and considered her duty done. She had fallen in love with Edward Loveday, then a widower of many years. Their affair had ended when Lord Keyne had summoned her back to London, and she went carrying Edward's child.

On Edward's death, his sister Margaret had agreed that it would be best if her niece stayed in London and a suitable husband was found for her. No one had expected that Tamasine would fall in love with the man who was the new Lord Keyne's ward, and Tamasine had been heartbroken when her suitor married the woman chosen by his guardian. Perhaps Margaret Mercer had been too diligent in her wish to see her niece wed, but she could never resist matchmaking and her intentions had been for the young woman's good. Maximillian's father had been a friend and client of Charles Mercer, and when Thomas inherited the bank and Max's own father died, Max continued to use Mercer's Bank and often dined with the family. He had met Tamasine on several occasions when she had been besotted with her former suitor and had shown little interest in her. Eight years older than Tamasine, Max had been a handsome, enigmatic figure whom Tamasine had regarded as no more than a family friend. It was not until Margaret, at Amelia's insistence, was pushing for Tamasine to accept the proposal of a much older staid gentleman that Tamasine knew she could not marry a man she did not love and had run away.

When Max had been the one to rescue her from the unwanted attentions of a rake, he had not hesitated to show his anger at the young woman's disregard for her family name and her wilful nature. Tamasine had been sent home to Cornwall believing that Max must despise her above all women. Yet in the most romantic of endings he had journeyed to Cornwall and asked for her hand. He had courted her with such verve and diligence he had completely captivated her heart.

Senara had fallen quiet during her reflection. Misinterpreting her mood, Tamasine wanted to put her sister-in-law at her ease. 'It means a great deal to me to have you here. I know you do not like large gatherings, but the Deverells do everything on such a grand scale.'

'My pleasure is in seeing you so happy. You deserve it, Tamasine. We both have found good men who see us for who we truly are and were not influenced by our backgrounds. That is a rare blessing.'

Tamasine impetuously hugged Senara. 'You are the dearest of sisters to me. And you will be delighted to know that Aunt Margaret, Thomas and Georganna are here. They arrived an hour before you, and are in the rooms at the end of the corridor. Now I must attend to other guests who have arrived, or my mother-in-law will lecture me that I am failing in my duties as a hostess.'

'Does the Lady Clarissa make your life difficult? She has a high regard for her family lineage.'

'Max keeps her in line and he has satisfied her that my own background is impeccable.' Tamasine shrugged. 'I no longer care whether she is appalled at the truth. Max would never let her use it against me. Fortunately, she prefers to mix with her own set of friends and spends much of her time in her houses in London, Bath and Tunbridge Wells. She was disappointed that Olivia was not a son, her comment being, "We must hope she will advance the family by marrying well. Max should consider no less than a viscount for her." Dear Olivia was but a week old and already the old dragon was dictating her future.' There was outrage and rebellion in the young mother's eyes as she left to attend to her guests. Tamasine might be in awe of her redoubtable mother-in-law, but she certainly was not cowed by her or ever likely to allow that to happen.

Senara did not have to seek out her husband's cousin; she saw her in the corridor leading to their bedchambers. Georganna had her head down as she walked and had not noticed Senara approach. Senara's greeting froze on her lips. She had not seen the family in London since Tamasine's wedding and she was shocked by the older woman's appearance. Georganna had always been tall and maypole thin, but now her collarbone was prominent above her georgette fichu and her cheekbones angularly defined. Smudges of shadows accentuated the hollows of her eye sockets and cheeks, and there was a nervousness about the way her hands fluttered like restless butterflies. The saffron and black stripes of her silk gown emphasised her unhealthy colour.

At first Senara thought Thomas's wife must be suffering a debilitating malady and feared for her health. Then she sensed that the older woman's agitation stemmed from trying to conceal the state of her emotions. She looked deeply unhappy.

'Georganna, you are quite overset. What ails you?'

She jumped violently and her eyes widened in alarm. Then upon recognising Senara she let out a relieved sigh. 'You startled me, Senara. I am quite well. I keep losing myself in the maze of corridors. Silly, isn't it?' Her lips stretched into a welcoming smile, but there remained a haunted look behind her eyes.

It sparked Senara's intuition that all was far from well with her cousin. She was rarely wrong upon such matters and Adam often teased her for being a sorceress with her uncanny premonitions. Something was clearly disturbing Georganna, and Senara knew when she heard an excuse to evade unsettling questions. Clearly now was not the time to pursue the matter, although the fluttering of Georganna's hands continued to betray her distress.

'I am sure I shall lose my way. The house is very grand and

beautiful.' Senara cast her eye over the scrolls and leaf-patterned plasterwork adorning the corridor walls and ceiling. Dotted along the landing stood a patrol of half a dozen suits of armour complete with halberds. To soften the severity of the warlike figures, several marble pedestals displayed tall Japanese vases filled with fresh flowers that perfumed the air with their sweet fragrance. To lighten Georganna's mood, she remarked, 'I've just been to the nursery to see Olivia. She is beautiful. Tamasine said you had arrived before us. I was coming to find you.'

Georganna continued to look abstracted. 'Margaret is asleep. The long journey from London exhausted her. Thomas went to find Max two hours past. There are so many guests he must have been detained in conversation.'

Georganna was usually so honest and open that it was disconcerting when she did not meet Senara's gaze. Her glance darted everywhere but into her cousin's face. There had also been a tremor in her voice when she mentioned Thomas. Senara hoped the couple were not estranged. Their marriage was by no means orthodox and it would not be surprising if some cracks were appearing after eight years.

'I expect he is with Adam,' she felt the need to reassure. 'Did you need him?'

'No. Not at all.' She became even more flustered. 'He is with Lucien. Tamasine kindly included him in the invitation and has asked if he would give a reading of his poetry one evening.'

Lucien Greene had been Thomas's friend for many years before his marriage. He had encouraged the reluctant banker to pursue his passion for play-writing, and several of Thomas's works had been performed to great acclaim in the London playhouses.

Senara was becoming more concerned for her cousin, who had become so pale that she looked on the verge of fainting. 'I would rather not face a roomful of strangers just yet. Will you not come to my rooms so that we can talk? It has been so long since we have seen you.'

For a moment she thought Georganna would refuse, but when she opened the door to her bedchamber Thomas's wife followed her. She went straight to the window, which overlooked the grounds, and did not appear to hear Senara's first questions regarding her health. To get her attention, Senara poured a glass of Madeira from the decanter that had been placed in the room.

'Drink this. It will make you feel better. You look exhausted from the journey.'

Georganna took the glass and tossed the wine back as though it was water, then sank down on to a day bed by the window. Some of her colour returned and the tension eased from her shoulders. 'It has been a tiring day. I slept little at the inn where we stayed last night.'

Senara wondered if she had not imagined her cousin's distress and unhappiness. Georganna had always been very different from her. She was a bluestocking, and loved reading novels and plays. That was what had attracted her to Thomas in the first place. In her concern Senara continued to watch Georganna closely. The older woman seemed to be having a battle within herself. Then she drew a sharp breath and patted a stray tendril of hair into place. When her gaze locked with Senara's, she stretched her mouth into an unconvincing smile.

'Forgive me, I have not been quite myself. The journey was arduous. The coach broke a wheel . . .' She shrugged. 'You know how it can be.'

'There is no problem between you and Thomas?' Senara asked, prompted by her intuition.

'Good Lord, no!' The protest came too quickly and too loudly. 'Thomas is working on a new play and his responsibilities at the bank since Papa died have kept him from his love of the theatre.' She threw back her head and laughed, but it sounded false to Senara's ears. 'An offer has been made for the bank. He wishes to sell it and concentrate on his play-writing. But it has not been an easy decision.'

'Does Aunt Margaret not approve?'

Georganna fiddled with the pearl choker at her neck and Senara saw that her fingers were trembling.

'You know dear Margaret,' said Georganna. 'Loyal to the core. A typical Loveday. She wants what is best for Thomas but feels the bank is our heritage. The heritage of our children.' This time her laugh was shrill. 'Margaret will not accept that I cannot give Thomas a child.'

Senara went to her side and put her arms around the shaking woman. 'It must be hard for any woman to accept that she is regarded as barren.'

She felt Georganna stiffen and cursed her wayward tongue. 'I'm sorry, Georganna. It is not your fault, is it? And it cannot be easy for you to attend a christening.'

'You do not know the half of it.' It was said so softly Senara had to strain to catch the words. Yet they did not surprise her.

'There is no need to explain. Lucien Greene has been Thomas's friend for many years. They are inseparable, are they not?'

Georganna nodded. 'I do not complain. I married Thomas to be part of the theatre world. My father had turned his back on Lascalles Bank, of which he was co-owner with his brother. He became a sleeping partner. Papa, like Thomas, wanted only to be a playwright, and he had great success. He died while I was still a child and I inherited half of the bank. Thomas chose me as his bride to escape his mother's matchmaking. With our marriage the two banks merged and Thomas was happy to step down and allow my guardian to be in charge until his death, which suited my uncle. I care deeply for Thomas. I always will. I just wish Margaret would understand.'

A gong was rung announcing afternoon tea and the two women broke apart. Georganna drew another deep breath. 'Thank you for listening and not condemning.'

'What is there to condemn?' Senara replied. 'Many marriages within polite society are arranged for mutual benefit. And Thomas does care for you – you have so many shared interests.'

'Yes.' Georganna sounded brighter. 'You caught me at a weak moment when I was tired from the journey. Please, say nothing of this conversation. I love Thomas dearly. Now I will return to my room and splash my face with cold water before I meet the other guests. It will revive my flagging spirits. Go ahead of me. I will meet you below.'

Georganna sought the quiet of her chamber, and although she splashed her face with the water from the washing bowl on the stand, when she patted it dry with a towel she felt no better. She pressed a hand to her mouth to combat the sickly churning that continued to assail her. Remorse ploughed a relentless furrow through all she had once held dear. Until the last few months she had been happy in her marriage. Or had it been an illusion, paper-thin and ethereal? Recently there had been so many arguments between Thomas and herself. They had not been Thomas's fault. He had been honest and steadfast in his loyalty. He had not changed. It was her. And she had been such a fool.

Chapter Nine

Georganna stared at her image in the looking-glass. The thin, rather angular face was the same, yet within she had changed so drastically it seemed strange that there was no outer sign. Her hair was pulled back into a severe chignon, its colouring an unexciting shade of dormouse. The frizz of curls along her brow did little to conceal the large fawn-like eyes, which a less kind person would describe as myopic, a condition brought on by the hours she spent every day poring over books. Though not for her frivolous romances; rather the intellectual works of the great dramatists and philosophers. Her nose was straight and delicate but her mouth was too wide, although she had lost only one tooth and that was to the rear, and the others had retained their whiteness. She had never considered herself pretty. Her aunt and uncle who had brought her up had ridiculed her features throughout her childhood, destroying any confidence that she would win a husband by her looks, and had been adamant that her intellect would daunt any suitor.

She realised now that they had derided her to promote their own unattractive daughters. Since Georganna had inherited her father's fifty per cent share of the business, her uncle feared that once she married, he would lose his hold over the family bank. She had no illusions that Thomas had fallen for her looks. In fact she had been the one to approach him and offer her inheritance as a means of saving the reputation of Mercer's Bank after his father lost most of his investors' money in unwise investments and then took his own life. Yet Thomas had always been kind and had described her looks as striking in a far more memorable way than any established beauty of the day. He frequently proclaimed that she blossomed when she smiled or laughed, and that she was the best of wives and companions. But then Thomas had a winning way with words. His desire to succeed as a playwright had always been more important to him than his capability as a prominent banker. The plainness of her reflection mocked her husband's compliments. She had been compliant towards his friendship with Lucien because it suited her own wishes at the time, or so she had believed.

She dismissed the fine lines around her eyes and those touching the corner of her lips as carved by life and experience. Yet it was the eyes themselves that showed the greatest change. They were no longer bright, seeking new wonders upon the stage of a playhouse or reading poetry or a treatise. Now they were shadowed, barely concealing a growing sense of despair. Had Senara guessed her secret – her shame and mortification?

She smoothed her hands over her silk gown. The expensive material gave her no pleasure. Although her dress allowance was generous, as befitted the wife of the owner of one of London's leading banks, she had little interest in fashion. Her tall, reed-thin frame, with a waist that could be spanned by a man's hands, was in truth more mannish than feminine. There were no soft curves to her figure. Even so, she refused to resort to artifice and pad her petticoats at the hips or bosom, and if the striking colours she favoured were frowned upon as garish, what did she care? They expressed her need to be different, and she did not fear to stand out in a crowd. She found the current mode of pale muslin too insipid for her taste. Unfortunately, the bold saffron yellow of her attire, which was also reflected in the choker of thumbnail-size pearls around her throat, drained her complexion of all colour, as her soul had been leeched of its former vibrancy. How could anyone look at her and not know? Not see her sin and fear . . .

She turned away, despising the reflected apparition. It was a parody of all she believed to be good and true. She clutched her arms about her waist, hugging them tight to her figure. Torment gouged her, and her conscience flayed her treacherous flesh sharper than the barbs in a cat-o'-nine-tails. Her hand formed a fist and she beat against her aching heart, tears again forming in her eyes. She had never before felt this wretched, so incomplete as a woman.

Until this year Thomas had been all she wanted in a husband – a witty and intelligent companion who respected her views and opinions. She adored him still. She had never wanted children. The very thought of childbirth had been her greatest dread. At a young and vulnerable age she had witnessed her mother screaming for three days during a protracted labour. The child had been stillborn and her mother had bled slowly and insidiously for two days, her life's blood seeping through the mattress on to the floor until death finally claimed her ravaged body. She had believed her marriage to Thomas to be the perfect solution.

Yet gradually over the years it had not been enough. Although Thomas continued to show her every consideration, an empty bed was a lonely place to lie night upon night, year upon year. Married couples when they regarded her barren state were often commiserating in their glances upon Thomas, and pitying and sometimes accusing towards herself. They presumed that she had failed her husband in some way. She should be used to it after so many years, but it was so unjust.

There were too many nights when loneliness and an indeterminate longing left her discontent and restless. Had she failed not only Thomas but also herself by her fears of motherhood? Had her foolishness not denied her body its natural need for passion and fulfilment?

She swung round to regard the red-rimmed eyes in the mirror. Was she not more worthy than the barren state she had accepted? And was it not natural to want more than to lie in her virginal bed, never knowing the pleasure a man could bring her? She had married Thomas knowing that he would never lie with her. He had always been honest with her that it was men like Lucien Greene who would hold the greatest sway over his emotions.

Mentally, she cursed her wayward craving to experience so much more. She had never deemed herself motivated by base passion; always in the past, intellect had been her abiding stimulation. Regarded by most men as a bookish bluestocking, she was rarely pursued in a flirtatious manner. Also Thomas's reputation as an accomplished duellist would have deterred any but the most impassioned of seducers. That an admirer had found her attractive and been reckless and bold enough to pursue her had broken down all the barriers she had erected against such feelings. This swain had been zealous in his desire to breach her defences. At first she had been amused and her refusal had served to inflame his adulation. He had wooed her with verve and stealth until she could not help but be flattered. Yet it had all seemed a harmless game until a stolen kiss had plunged her into a maelstrom of sensation that had left her teetering on the edge of a precipice. Finally, a few weeks ago, she had known what it was truly like to be loved as a married woman should be loved.

If she closed her eyes, her body would glow with the memory of that wild consummation of her passion, which had ignited her blood. Then her heart would race until she was consumed by a wanton ache to experience everything that could be explored in the delights of surrendering to desire. Her lids flew open and she patted her flushed cheeks. Within such memories lay madness and danger. There had been no chance of repeating the experience. Yet the source of her downfall was so close, and her lover had vowed that with so many distractions and entertainments at Beaucombe, this would be the perfect time for them to meet in secret.

When she had begged him to make his excuses and not attend, he had laughed aside her fears.

Adam found Max escorting two elderly great-aunts to an outside table where they could watch a group of estate children dancing round a maypole. Further across the lawns a bowls match was taking place. St John was cheering on a competitor with such enthusiasm, Adam guessed he had placed a wager on the outcome. When Max finished settling the ladies, he came over to Adam and greeted him warmly.

'My pardon for being otherwise engaged when you arrived. Welcome to Beaucombe, my friend.'

'With so many guests you cannot be everywhere at once,' Adam replied. He gestured towards the dancing and the lake where three boats each with a man rowing a group of two or three ladies were enjoying the water. Others guests were strolling through the grounds calling out to old acquaintances or sitting in animated groups. 'There is much to occupy everyone.'

'I would have preferred that it not be on so grand a scale.' Max gave a shrug of resignation. His tall figure was relaxed, showing his confidence that all would go well. A lock of dark hair flopped over his brow. He was a handsome man with a natural reserve that sometimes made him seem aloof. That was before Adam had got to know him and discovered his warm and generous nature towards his family and friends. A humorous glint lightened Max's eyes as he went on, 'Mama was insistent Olivia be christened in style, and Tamasine wanted to show everyone that she is a competent hostess for Beaucombe.' Pride richened his voice. 'She has planned everything meticulously. This is very important to her.'

'Her desire is to be a worthy wife to you, Max.'

'She does not have to prove that to me, but you know Tamasine: nothing I say will convince her, she has to prove it to herself.'

As they walked, Max scanned the grounds to check that their guests were all content and were in no need of attention. 'Your cousin Tom arrived an hour or so before you. He's in the pavilion to the rear of the grounds. He agreed to bring a troupe of players to perform two of his plays during the week. He is checking the stage and props with Lucien. I believe Aunt Margaret was out here earlier conversing with an old acquaintance. I am not sure where Georganna could be.'

'I shall find them.'

A male guest with three other men companions hailed Max from across the lawn. He smiled apologetically. 'We will speak more later in the week when the other guests leave. I look forward to it.'

When they parted company, Adam went in the direction Max had indicated to find his cousin. As he neared the pavilion he was surprised to hear Lucien Greene's voice raised in anger, followed by an equally heated reply from Thomas.

'When I discover who the blackguard is, I'll run him through.'

Lucien's reply was softer, cajoling. 'You cannot solve this by a duel. It will only cause a scandal.'

'Honour demands it!'

The threat made Adam's blood run cold. He had never heard the two friends at loggerheads before. Lucien prided himself on never raising his voice during an argument, preferring instead to use a poisoned verbal barb as a set-down. Thomas was an accomplished swordsman and marksman and as a young man had earned a reputation for duelling. Adam had hoped that those days were now behind him. As the sole owner of Mercer and Lascalles, he had the reputation of his business to consider. None of his wealthy clients would use a bank where the owner put his life so carelessly at risk. If Thomas was mortally wounded it would cause havoc in the City.

Diplomatically, he called out his cousin's name before entering the pavilion. Thomas turned at the sound of his approach, his face showing the lethal depths of his anger. Lucien's handsome features were flushed a deep red beneath his short hair, which was elaborately curled to disguise the threads of silver that tarnished its flaxen brightness.

'Do I intrude?' Adam said, his alarm increasing at the charged atmosphere. 'And what is this talk of a duel? Surely not, Tom?'

At recognising Adam, the tension left Thomas's chiselled features. Consummate actor that he was, he looked his cousin straight in the eye. He did not want his family to know he suspected Georganna had taken a lover. 'My dear fellow, did you overhear us going through a scene of my new play?'

Lucien had also recovered his demeanour. He pulled a large lace handkerchief from his pocket to dab at his cheeks, careful not to disturb the dusting of powder that concealed the blemishes of his middle years. Adam also noted that his lips were effeminately reddened with carmine and that his dress was more extravagant and dandified than when last they had met. 'The emotion of the scene is quite debilitating.'

There remained a tightness in the two friends' shoulders, which alerted Adam that they were not being honest with him.

'What new play is this?'

'Just an idea,' Thomas said airily. His own blond hair had receded considerably in recent years, giving him a broad expanse of brow. Its natural waves were trimmed to fall over the edge of his high-collared cut-away coat. Although Thomas dressed in the height of fashion with an excess of ruffles at wrist and neck, his attire was never flamboyant. His eyes, which had always been heavy-lidded, were now hooded with cynicism, and his lips had tightened to a seam of disparagement. At forty-two he was not a man who had found peace within himself, and lines of dissatisfaction were etched around his mouth. 'I've no more than the first act. The plot is too thin. It lacks verve. I should be concentrating on the first play to be performed here. But when the muse strikes . . .' He shrugged as though Adam would understand how demanding was the strain to create the most memorable play to be performed on the London stage. 'Enough of my woes! The bank takes all my time and I get little opportunity to write. How are you and your family, Adam?'

'All of us are well. And how are Aunt Margaret and Georganna?'

Did he imagine it, or did a shadow momentarily darken his cousin's eyes at the mention of his wife?

'Mama puts us all to shame with her energy and has been in full matchmaking form all winter. There are four couples at least who owe their nuptial bliss to her machinations.' Thomas laughed. 'Give her another four or five years and she will be taking up residence in Cornwall with an aim to having your brood all settled. I think she already has her eye on a swain for Rowena.'

Adam gave a theatrical shudder. 'Heaven forfend when the time comes that there is another generation of Lovedays with their wild blood ignited by passion!'

There was a rustle of silk and an outburst of giggling behind them. 'Did I not say it was Lucien Greene?' A gushing matron pushed her three friends forward, oblivious that she was rudely interrupting their conversation. 'Mr Greene, will you recite something from one of your divine poems? We do adore them so.'

Lucien erased the flash of irritation that had appeared on his face. He gave a cursory bow. 'Dearest of ladies, I shall be enchanted when the occasion permits, which I believe is later this evening.'

'But could you not give us five minutes of your time?' the oldest of the four women simpered.

'Your pardon, but I am engaged in conversation with my friends.'

The woman let out a snort of indignation. 'I am a friend of Lady Clarissa, and Maximillian said we were to be entertained.'

Lucien bowed to them once more, and this time his voice had a chilling edge to it. 'And I am here as a guest and friend of Mrs Deverell and her family. My recitation this evening is given as a special favour to my friends. If you wish the paid help to amuse you, I suggest you watch the country dancing.'

The matron flushed an unbecoming shade of puce. 'Well, in all my born days I have never been so insulted. Do you know who I am?'

Before she could inform him, Lucien cut across her speech. 'You have just informed me that you are a guest of the Deverells, as are all of us here.'

The woman turned on her heel and flounced out of the pavilion, informing her companions in strident tones, 'Lady Clarissa will hear of this. My friend will be mortified that I have been so insulted by a common poet.'

'Was that not rather hasty, Lucien?' Adam was shocked by the older man's rudeness towards another guest, and a woman at that.

Lucien sighed. 'It was unforgivable of me. I shall apologise to the old harridan later, but such presumption that I will perform like an organ grinder's monkey is greatly vexing. Am I not allowed to relax and enjoy the company of friends without being so accosted?'

'My dear friend cannot go anywhere in London without being recognised,' Thomas explained. 'Complete strangers think they have the right to importune him.'

'It is vexing in the extreme, dear fellow. But alas, one should always be mindful of one's public.' Lucien rubbed his temple and cast a meaningful glance at Thomas. 'It has been an eventful week. We will work more on the new play later. Now I shall retire and write a glowing ode dedicated to the Lady Harridan so that she will be dough to be moulded in my hands.'

'She will as well,' Thomas said with a shake of his head. 'And you will be invited to her estate and be the toast of all her friends. You will be wined and dined and showered with expensive gifts.'

'I am doing this for Tamasine, not myself.' Lucien assumed a mortified air. 'Your sweet and innocent cousin does not deserve to fall foul of the Lady Clarissa because I was less than my usual charming self.'

He sauntered away to find a quiet place to compose his ode.

'You are busy, Tom,' Adam said. 'I will leave you to your work.'

Thomas waved a hand, dismissing his cousin's words. 'The play is not important. Your company is. It has been too long, cousin. There was a time when we never missed a summer reunion in Cornwall, but it has been difficult the last two years. Business can be onerous.

The bank takes too much of my time. I am considering selling it. But Mama is horrified at the thought. It was Papa's life.' He pinched his thumb and forefinger on the bridge of his nose, his expression now pained. 'It even killed him in the end. But I have no interest in the business. It is not as though I have a child to pass it on to.'

Adam nodded sadly. Although the subject was never mentioned, he had his suspicions about his cousin's married life. 'If you truly are not cut out to be a banker, then you should sell. I am fortunate that the shipyard was all I ever wanted. Aunt Margaret will understand if you tell her how you feel. Mercer and Lascalles is one of the most prestigious banks in the City. None of Georganna's cousins who inherited their father's share of the business have married bankers. You could live comfortably on the income from your and Georganna's shares in the bank once it is sold.'

'You make it sound so simple.' Thomas spread his hands as though in supplication that somehow this would be possible. 'But I feel I am letting my father down. Especially in the circumstances in which he died. The bank was everything to him.'

'Uncle Charles took his own life because he had failed his investors,' Adam gently reminded him. 'You are not Charles Mercer, and to your credit you saved the bank from ruin and by so doing saved your father's reputation. Play-writing is in your blood and you must honour the gift you have been given. The world would have been a bleaker place without the works of Shakespeare, Marlow, Wycherley and Sheridan. Your plays have been highly acclaimed.'

'I certainly have no wish to go on as I am,' Thomas confessed. He smiled, and much of the tension left his taut body as he prophesied, 'It is indeed time for change. Though for my sins I doubt it will come lightly.'

'And what sins would they be?' Adam challenged with a stab of unease.

His cousin gave a harsh laugh. 'That would be telling.'

No amount of questioning would draw Thomas further, and when Adam left him to change into evening dress, he could not shake the impression that Thomas had darker intentions than just selling the family business.

Chapter Ten

Lucien was true to his word. He charmed the woman he had offended, who turned out to be Lady Clarissa's cousin, the dowager Marchioness Myddleford. Not only did he dedicate an ode to her beauty, but also he had found out enough about the late marquis to write a tribute about his life and his political works to improve the conditions in orphanages and workhouses. Her ladyship was completely captivated by Lucien and could not stop singing his praises. Max had given him access to the family archives, and to appease Lady Clarissa, who Lucien knew frowned upon Tamasine's relationship with a playwright, he had promised to devise a saga extolling the valiant exploits of her illustrious family from the time of the Conqueror, which would be performed in a few days.

Clearly no expense was to be spared for the comfort and entertainment of the Deverells' family and friends. The christening took place in the church on the estate the next morning, followed by a banquet and Thomas's play and ending with a firework display. In the next week there was to be a cricket match, an excursion to Corfe Castle, a ballet, music recitals, charades, gaming and dancing. It would all end with a grand ball. There were enough entertainments to please the most discerning and jaded of palates and it should be a time of merriment and pleasure.

Yet within an hour of the end of the banquet Senara sensed ripples of disquiet amongst her family. Felicity was clinging to St John like a vine. He had had to be carried to his bed the previous evening, too drunk to climb the stairs, and she was determined he would not make such an exhibition of himself again. St John was growing surlier by the hour, unable to shake her vigilance. Felicity was insisting that they listen to the violin quartet playing in the music room.

'If you want to hear them play, then go with those ladies over there.' St John pointed to two spinster sisters who walked everywhere arm in arm. 'Or join Aunt Margaret, Georganna and Senara. They were walking by the lake.'

'I am tired. In my condition is it too much to expect a little courtesy and consideration from my husband?'

'You should have stayed at home if you want to sit around all day.' His ill humour exploded. 'I want more lively entertainment. Hannah must be about somewhere. Though she is not likely to be swooning and demanding Sam stick to her like molasses. She is in your condition and further along than yourself. She worked all day on the farm throughout her other pregnancies.'

'I am more delicate than Hannah. My nerves are not strong. I wish I had her vitality. Everyone adores her and wants to make her acquaintance. And Sam barely leaves her side.' Her jealousy made her more shrewish.

St John was scanning the guests, impatient to find more amenable company. 'Hannah is popular because you never hear her complain. Nothing I do pleases you, and only you could be discontent when so much has been done to entertain the guests.' St John strove to control his irritation and the boredom his wife roused in him. Felicity had proclaimed that she had been prey to her nerves ever since their daughter Thea had been born. Though St John suspected her nerves had nothing to do with her malaise. She merely wanted to spoil his enjoyment of the occasion. 'Hannah is vivacious and people flock to her because her company always brightens their mood. And Sam is not always at her side. She is happy for him to mix with the men and make new friends.'

Felicity pouted unattractively. 'You prefer to get drunk with your new friends than spend time with your loving wife.'

'Is that what you call loving? It is more like suffocating and cloying. You expect me to constantly dance attendance upon you.' He angrily shrugged her hand from his arm. 'You stifle me and I weary of your constant carping. Sometimes you sound just like Charlotte when she cannot get her way with Rowena.'

He marched away. Felicity saw several curious people watching her, and to cover her embarrassment she forced a bright smile. Inwardly she was fuming. She would seek Aunt Margaret's company. She knew the younger Loveday women were scornful of her complaining, and Margaret would be more sympathetic at St John's neglect.

Senara had been watching the couple. Even from a distance, the way St John stalked off and Felicity covered her lower face with her hand, it was obvious they had quarrelled again.

'I should go to Felicity,' she said to her aunt and cousin. 'She looks upset.'

'It will be no more than a lovers' tiff,' Margaret advised. 'Felicity is the strong woman St John needs to guide him, though it would be better if she were more diplomatic in her approach. Honeyed words will coerce a man faster than a shrew's tongue. She needs to give St John more rein.'

'And he will use it gambling,' Senara replied. 'It has become an obsession with him.'

Margaret sighed. 'Unfortunately, Felicity will not curb such habits by nagging. He needs diversion. It is a pity that Thomas is so wrapped up with his play at the moment. I suspect any advice from Adam will only goad his twin further.'

Margaret had been studying the groups of guests strolling in the late afternoon sun after the large feast. She was tall and had kept her slender figure; the only change in her appearance in recent years was that her dark hair, although it remained thick and luxurious, was now white as a barn owl's chest. Her sharp eyes were darting everywhere, taking in their companions, as she walked through a knot garden with Senara and Georganna.

'I always knew Tamasine and Max would make a perfect couple. I am rarely wrong,' she said with a contented sigh. Despite her three score years and five, she showed no sign of slowing down in her life. Although she had a passion for matchmaking, she had no interest in remarrying herself. Two years older than Elspeth, she had none of her sister's acerbic nature. Since Thomas and Georganna had brought their own home in Brook Street, she had sold the house in the Strand, where she had lived since her marriage. In recent years the Strand had become a crowded thoroughfare filled with carriages and sedan chairs, and many of the larger houses had been turned into shops. Margaret had been happy to buy a house in Grosvenor Square. As it was one of the most fashionable addresses in London, where many of the nobility had bought London homes, she had a full social life and was often called upon by the wives of wealthy businessmen and gentlemen to use her matchmaking skills.

She continued with barely a pause for breath. 'Lady Clarissa is holding court under the cedar tree. She was hoping for a match between the second Myddleford girl and her son-in-law Leo's brother, Eustace. I must find out if there is to be an announcement. If not, Eustace would be perfect for one of the St Blazey girls. Then I must find Hannah. I have not seen my niece to converse with since she arrived this morning. I understand she and Sam can only stay three days, and I have yet to meet Sam properly. They were in Dorset last summer when I came to Trevowan, and there was no time for us to come down from London for the wedding the previous Christmas, even had the roads not been too treacherous to travel in winter.'

Margaret opened her parasol and strode purposefully towards Lady Clarissa.

Georganna, who had also spent the last half-hour looking anxiously around her as though she expected to meet someone in particular, said rather breathlessly, 'There are so many people it is quite overwhelming. I am never adept at polite conversation unless it is to talk about the theatre or a novel. I never know what to say. I think I shall take my book and find a quiet place to read for an hour.'

She darted away before Senara could question her further. Georganna was unlike any woman Senara had met. She had no interest in clothes or children, but could recite pages of poetry by heart and had read many of the Greek philosophers in their original language. The older woman's behaviour continued to puzzle her. Georganna had always been at ease with Thomas's family. With them, at least, it was not like her to be more nervous than a cat trying to cross a large puddle and not get its paws wet. And usually she was a strong-minded and independent woman who had as little time for convention and proprieties as did most of the Loveday family. So why was she so ill at ease?

No doubt Georganna would eventually tell her. It was not Senara's way to pry into another's affairs. Even so, she remained worried that Felicity was so obviously unhappy.

Whenever she travelled, Senara carried her box of dried herbs and simple unguents, and she decided that she would prepare a tisane that would calm her sister-in-law's nerves. Later she would make a point of having a long talk with Georganna. Something was clearly troubling her and causing her distress.

Aware of the need for caution, Georganna had seen her lover watching her from the path by the corner of the house. It was the first time she had seen him among the guests. Tamasine had mentioned his arrival yesterday. She had been the one to introduce them but was unaware how their acquaintanceship had developed. To Georganna's surprise, Tamasine had sworn her to secrecy about his presence here, which she had been only too happy to comply with. The sight of him cast aside her usual common sense and she felt her heart flutter in both excitement and panic. She had feared this moment and yet been longing for it ever since her arrival, and she had to curb the impulse to pick up her skirts and run in the most unladylike manner towards him. At least he was being discreet and had not approached any member of her family. She dreaded such an encounter, afraid that somehow she would betray her guilt and desire. Yet it was inevitable that they would meet. Would the encounter go well, or would it be as disastrous as she feared? Her lover had been strangely enigmatic when she had mentioned Adam and St John Loveday of Trevowan. They obviously knew each other but he would not be drawn on the subject.

Once she had made her excuses to Senara, she forced herself to stroll at a leisurely pace. At her approach, he inclined his head in acknowledgement and moved languidly in the direction of a shrubbery.

Willing her pounding heart to slow its erratic pace, she glanced across the grounds, checking whether anyone might have seen them. Everyone seemed too occupied with their own amusement to be aware of others. Yet she remained terrified that she would be discovered and that guilt must be branded across her forehead for all to see. To recover her composure she drew a slim volume of poems from her reticule, and made herself walk slowly and steadily in the direction her lover had taken. She prayed that anyone who glanced in her direction would assume that she was absorbed in her book.

The shrubbery covered half an acre and there were winding lawn paths weaving through it. The bushes were thick and for a moment she feared that her procrastination had denied them the chance of a meeting.

'Over here!' A voice husky as wood-smoke sent a familiar shiver through her, and he stepped out from behind a laurel in the densest part of the shrubbery.

'We must be careful we are not seen,' Georganna began, but her words were cut short as he locked his arms around her and kissed her into silence.

When they parted she was gasping for air and her legs were so weak she could barely stand. 'That was madness! Anyone could come upon us.'

'That is what makes it all the more exciting.'

He kissed her again, but this time she was more composed and turned her face away and stepped back. 'I will not risk my reputation. And if you were a true gentleman neither would you.'

He grinned roguishly. 'If I were a true gentleman I would never have pursued you in the first place.' He traced the line of her cheek with his forefinger and allowed it to trail down her neck to the lace trimming her bodice. 'Then how dull would our lives have been. Is the risk not worth taking?'

She fought to control her need to again feel the touch of his lips hot and demanding upon her own. He stood so close she could smell his cologne and his hair oil. She was used to the darkly handsome Loveday looks, and Thomas, despite his blond hair, had his mother's bone structure and features. Her lover was attractive in a rugged, devil-may-care manner, and his riotous short brown curls were completely untameable. His aquiline nose was imperiously long, his lips decadently full, but his wickedly enticing smile was devastating. His dark eyes with their scandalously long lashes had a provocative twinkle that was impossible to resist. Their depths were as black as an abyss and could either reveal nothing of his emotions, or suck you in until you felt yourself devoured. Even though he was two fingers' breadth shorter than herself, his presence seemed to fill a room whenever he entered.

'I will come to you tonight.' His ardent gaze beguiled her. 'Which is your room? Your husband will be with his paramour, will he not?'

'Thomas shares my room. He would not shame me before his family.'

'Then we will sneak away while he is engaged with his play this evening. I cannot spend another day without you.'

The madness of his proposal left her breathless. Yet the insanity of it and his boldness held her in its seductive thrall. She clung to the last vestiges of her reason, gasping, 'I dare not. You must keep your distance. It is too dangerous. I could not bear it if Thomas called you out.'

'I do not fear your husband's or any man's reputation with a sword or pistol. And I have never backed down from a fight.' At her horrified expression, he laughed. 'Neither would I seek one. Besides, we will not be caught. You worry too much.' He chuckled softly and kissed her with a thoroughness that left her a slave to his will. When her arms bound him tighter, he whispered, 'Your husband does not deserve you.'

A sob burst from her throat. 'I have never felt like this before and I fear to lose it. But it is wrong. So very wrong.'

'How can this be wrong?' He again kissed her to silence until half swooning she had to cling to the lapels of his cut-away coat to stop herself from swooning. He laughed enticingly against her ear. 'You are a woman made for loving. If your husband fails you . . .'

'No, it is not Thomas. I am to blame.' She shook her head.

'How sweetly you defend him.' He smiled and ran his thumb along her trembling lip, sending darts of pleasure down her spine. 'He does not deserve such loyalty. He has neglected you. I worship you. Even a day when I cannot be with you is torture. Come to the Chinese folly behind the walled garden as soon as the play begins. Thomas will be too busy to notice you have slipped away.'

She struggled to resurrect her reason against the coercing

seduction he offered. 'That is when he will miss me most. I always sit at the side of the stage. I am the prompt who must remind an actor of their lines if they forget them.'

'Someone else can perform your task.'

'It is expected of me. I always prompt Thomas's plays. He says I bring him good luck.'

The handsome face before her was marred by a scowl. 'Then my love means nothing to you,' he flared. 'If you want a man who mopes like a lovelorn puppy for the merest crumb of your affection, then we have no future. Is it not painful enough that I must take such an inferior place in your life, never able to publicly claim you as my own? The agony of our constant partings threatens my reason.' He released his hold upon her and rubbed his hand over his face in his distress. 'You care nothing for me. I am but dust beneath your feet.' His voice cracked with pain as he wrenched out, 'I am your devoted servant. I would lay down my life for you, yet you crush me with each cruel word of rejection. Mayhap you merely toy with my affections to make your husband jealous. I thought better of you, madam.'

She had never been accomplished at coquetry or flirtation and was appalled at his reaction. This was the first man who had avowed such passionate love for her that she was completely discomposed. He had bared his soul and she had been so foolish and unworldly as to somehow deeply insult him. That was her last intent. Stricken with remorse, she delved into her reticule and pulled out a small packet wrapped in gold silk.

'My love, please accept this as a token of the highest affection in which I hold you. I was saving it until later but you must have it now.' She thrust the package into his hands.

'I cannot accept a gift from you, it would be most unfitting.' He hesitated.

'It is a token of my devotion. Keep it close to your heart and you need never doubt my affection.' She was desperate to make amends for the pain she had unwittingly caused.

He unfolded the silk, and a gold snuffbox, its lid edged with a row of diamonds, glinted in the sunlight that filtered through the foliage. He put a hand over his heart. 'Most revered and beloved lady, this is too much. I cannot accept it.'

She smiled and closed his long fingers over the gold box. 'Never doubt me again.'

He raised her hand to his lips. 'I am unworthy. This will be my greatest treasure. I shall indeed keep it close to my heart.'

She relaxed, but, aware of the laughter and voices that were never far away from them, said softly, 'I must return to my family.'

He bowed as deeply as though she were a queen. 'I live only for the times we can be together. Slip away tonight or I will have no choice but to challenge your husband. I would rather die than continue this torment.'

'You must never say that.' Georganna was light-headed at the force of his passion. 'I will not come during the play, but afterwards. Everyone will be taking refreshments before the firework display. I will not be missed then. I will come to the folly, I promise.'

'I shall count the minutes, my sweet love. Though each second we are apart will be another thorn thrust into my heart.'

Voices drifted to them from a path close by, and terrified of being caught, Georganna tore herself free of his hold. 'Until after the play, my darling.'

As he watched her hurry away, his expression hardened. With so much at stake, he had to tread carefully. He had been watching the Lovedays covertly since their arrival. How little they had changed in their arrogance and their weaknesses. The years rolled back, pierced by bitter memories. There could well be more than one explosive display this evening.

Chapter Eleven

The sun was stroking the top of the treetops at the end of the second act. It would not be dark until after the play ended. Now there was to be a short intermission. Liveried servants appeared carrying glasses of punch to refresh the guests. Hannah rose from her chair to stretch her legs. Before her marriage, this hour of the day would have been milking time, one of the busiest times on the farm. It still felt strange to spend this part of the evening at her leisure, and strangely, in her new life of grandeur, she missed the simpler existence on the farm.

She had never thought she could love another man as she had loved her first husband Oswald. After his death, she had mourned him deeply and found contentment in her children and running the farm that had been in Oswald's family for several generations. Yet through the difficult years of Oswald's illness and her mourning, Sam, as her overseer and friend, had been a rock she had relied upon. She was blissfully happy in her second marriage, although there were times she felt trapped at her new home at Highcroft and missed the freedom of the life she had led at the farm. Sam understood this, and though he was tied by the conditions of his uncle's will in bringing up his ward at Highcroft, he urged her to visit the farm and her family whenever possible. It made her love him even more and their partings were hard to bear. Fortunately at the end of the summer Charlie would attend Eton and they would then be able to spend more time on the farm in Cornwall.

It was at times like this that Hannah realised how much she

missed her family and the closeness that had bound them together. During the interval Senara joined her.

'We were worried you would not be able to attend. It is lovely to see you. How long are you able to stay?'

'Only three days.' Hannah's dark-winged brows drew down in a frown and a fierce fire ignited in her expressive eyes. 'Sam then has to visit the lawyer. There is to be another hearing over Charlie's inheritance in a few weeks. Sam still hopes it can be settled out of court. But the colonel, his father, stubbornly refuses to acknowledge Charlie as Lord Eastley's heir and continues to maintain that Highcroft should be his.'

'Is it greed or family pride that drives him?'

'Pride and a cantankerous nature, which are potent weapons.' Hannah groaned. 'Sam's older brother Robert has acknowledged Charlie as the heir, and he would have been next in line to the estate and title after the colonel.'

'Yet life seems to be treating you well. And I must congratulate you that you are again with child.' Senara eyed the sapphire-blue silk of her cousin's gown. In all her days as a farmer's wife Hannah had never worn silk.

Hannah plucked at the elegant gown. 'Sam spoils me. The wife of the guardian of Lord Eastley cannot appear as a drab. But I would happily give up all my fine clothes to see Sam reconciled with his father and Charlie accepted by his grandfather. I hope that this child,' she touched her stomach, 'will aid a reconciliation.'

'Is Colonel Sir Hugo Deighton as bad as Sam paints him?'

'He has a bark like a cannon's roar and the temper of ignited gunpowder. Quite the charmer, is he not?' Even caught up with such testing family troubles, Hannah's sense of humour had not dimmed. She shrugged, accepting the vagaries of fate. 'Sam blames his father's irascible temper on the head wound he received during the War of Independence in America. He was never the same man after he returned. He is arrogant, short-tempered and antagonistic as a wild boar, and he cannot abide having his will thwarted. He will see no one's side of a matter but his own. Rather like Grandfather George.'

'Time may yet mellow him,' Senara soothed.

'It did not George Loveday. The colonel has sworn he will

dispute the will until his last breath. That will make the lawyers very rich men.' Hannah rolled her eyes heavenwards. 'The old firebrand will not spoil my time here. I did not think I could miss my family so much. Pray tell me how Mama, Papa and Peter fare.'

'All are well and missing you. They are hoping you will be in Cornwall for the harvest.'

'If I am, I shall have to come without Sam. Davey will be home from school and needs to spend time learning how to run the farm that he will one day own. Florence and Abigail miss their cousins. Luke is happy, as he has Charlie's company all the time at the moment. They were always best friends.' Sadness momentarily shadowed her eyes. 'Unfortunately, that will change when they start school next year. Luke will join his brother at Winchester. The restrictions placed on us are most heartrending for Charlie. He begs Sam to allow him to be with my boys during the harvest, but how can we break the conditions of Lord Eastley's will? If we do, the estate reverts to the colonel and Charlie will get nothing.'

'Charlie is a likeable boy and will make many friends at his new school.' Senara said. 'And with yours and Sam's love he will come through it.'

'He has had so many upheavals in his young life.' Hannah smiled, her eyes sparkling with tenderness. She took Senara's hand. 'Now tell me, how are your children? And Adam mentioned you have a boy living with you who has lost his memory. And how is Bridie's little Michael? I worry he is not strong, and he had such a dreadful cough all last winter. I hope Elspeth is not doing too much in supervising the training of Japhet's mares that we bred on the farm.'

Senara answered the eager questions and ended by saying, 'Elspeth loves every moment working with the horses. They are her passion. She fusses over the mares and foals as if they were the children she never had.'

'Are we mad to keep the foals?' Another fear touched Hannah's eyes. 'Japhet has been away for so long. Will he ever return to these shores?'

'In all his letters he has said he will return from New South Wales once his fortune is made. If anyone can succeed in the new colony, Japhet will.'

'Yet when he learned that Oswald had died, he wrote to tell me to sell the mares.' Hannah's gaze searched her friend's face for reassurance.

Senara's answer was simple and truthful. 'That was only because he would consider you had enough work with the farm. He did not wish to burden you further. The horses were the dream he had for a new life in England after his marriage to Gwendolyn. You have kept that alive.'

'A dream cut tragically short by his arrest for a crime he did not commit. I still get angry at the injustice of it.'

A gong sounded to announce the second half of the play, and Sam returned to take his wife's arm and escort her to their seats. All traces of sadness and worry were erased from Hannah's face as she laughed at something her husband was saying. The sexual alchemy that crackled between them made Senara feel she should look away. She was grinning when Adam joined her.

'You look inordinately pleased. Has some handsome beau made an assignation with you, and should I be seized with a jealous rage?'

Used to his teasing, she sighed softly. 'Despite the problems she has to deal with, Hannah looks so happy. I am pleased for her. She was a widow for too long.'

There was a clash of cymbals and the actors appeared on the stage. The audience ceased their chattering as the play built to a tense and thrilling climax. The final applause was deafening. Tamasine sought out Adam and Senara before they could leave the pavilion.

'Come quickly, I have someone special to introduce you to.' In her excitement she grabbed her brother's arm and pulled him impatiently to the rear of the tent.

'Oh, now where have they gone? It is too vexing,' she groaned. 'Two days you have been here and the two of you are never to hand to meet.'

'Who is this mysterious guest?' Amused at her chagrin, Adam went along with her ruse. 'They must be very important.'

'It is my fault for insisting that I am present when you meet. I want to witness your delight.' Tamasine could not contain her impatience. 'The dear fellow must be spending his time in hiding, or else he is naturally elusive.'

'So this mysterious guest is a man,' Adam teased. 'That narrows it down to about half the people present.'

Tamasine clutched her hands together in agitation. 'I must find him. I promise you that you will meet him tonight. I cannot wait to see your reaction. You will be thrilled.'

Georganna was impatient to escape the pavilion as soon as the play ended. To her frustration Thomas had drawn her into a crowd of people praising his work. Once she would have been delighted to be thus included in his theatrical world. It was a rare occurrence nowadays, but tonight, in her agitation to meet her lover, she resented this untoward show of possessiveness by her husband. He linked his arm through hers as Lucien held court, praising the fine speeches that Thomas had written.

She could feel a line of moisture break out on her upper lip and her throat was arid as a desert. What if her lover became impatient and would not wait in the folly? This could be the one time they would be able to meet in private for days. Her smile was fragile as glass and threatened to shatter at any moment as the praise for her husband dragged on. It was impossible to stop her gaze seeking the exit.

Thomas gripped her arm tighter. 'You seem ill at ease, my dear. If I did not know you better, I would think you had a more pressing engagement. Is not a wife's place at her husband's side? Or did the play not please you?'

'The play was superb.' She managed to find her voice while her mind was frantically seeking a plausible excuse to leave. She had not missed the thread of warning in Thomas's voice. Did he suspect that she had made a tryst? The very thought filled her with alarm. The guests were now discussing the latest plays that had been performed in London that season and their merits and failings. Usually Georganna would have been animated in her opinions, but tonight she was struck dumb in her anxiety to leave.

'Your mind is elsewhere, wife. Do we keep you from an assignation?' Thomas's tone was light and teasing, but as she gasped and met his stare, she saw a hard glint in his eye. He knew, or at least had guessed. His honour was at stake and she doubted he would give her his blessing even though they had never lived as true man and wife. The injustice of it made her rebel. She had not condemned his love for Lucien. She was entitled to find her own happiness providing that she was discreet. But all she could hear in her mind was the lure of the promise of her lover to meet her; and it was his image, with its power to banish sane thought, that drove her to pay any price to be with him.

'I – I promised Felicity I would walk back to the house with her. St John has abandoned her again.'

'I saw her leave with Mama.'

'Oh!' She chewed her lip in agitation. 'Only she wanted to discuss some matter. She was upset. I feel I should go to her.'

'Of course, my dear. I would not have you shirk your family duty.' The clipped edge remained in his voice. It should have alerted her to his stifled anger, but she was too frantic to make her escape to heed its warning.

She smiled abstractedly and pulled away from her husband, needing all her self-control not to break into a run. Outside the pavilion, the light was failing fast. With a furtive glance over her shoulder, Georganna veered away from the path to the house and sped across the lawns to the Chinese folly.

Inside it was all but devoid of light. The last rays of the setting sun fell upon the stone bench opposite the door. The place was empty. Disappointment clawed at her throat with a long, searing ache. Could he not have waited such a short while? A heartfelt groan was wrenched from her.

Her heart was lacerated by despair. She had risked so much to be here. Her face burned with humiliation and she put shaking hands to her cheeks and leaned against the cool stonework of the building, battling against her threatening tears.

Then, from out of the deepest shadows of a recess, a light flared and she smelt the smoke from a cheroot.

'I thought I had been forsaken,' his deep voice proclaimed.

'Why did you not say you were here?' Her voice throbbed with relief.

He stepped out of the darkness, his handsome face enigmatic. 'Your humble servant awaits his lady's pleasure.'

She ran to him, throwing her arms around his neck and kissing him in frantic passion. He sounded so cold, angry even. 'I could not get away. Thomas kept me by his side. I had to lie in the end. And I am such a poor liar, but I was so desperate.'

106

'You are here now.' He pulled her down on to the bench and his hand tugged impatiently at her skirts. 'Too much time has been wasted.'

The first of the fireworks lit the sky. In his anger he was rough with her and spoke no words of tenderness. When he pulled away and adjusted his clothing, his voice was terse. 'I promised to make a fourth at cards with Lady Clarissa. She will be displeased if I am late.'

'But the fireworks have not finished.'

His face was a satyr's mask as cascading rockets illuminated the folly. Georganna could not stop her pain at his callous manner and blurted out, 'You knew we were to meet. Can you not stay longer?'

'You were the one who said we must be careful.' He seemed already to have distanced himself from her. 'One of us must be seen at the display. Or would you have our secret discovered? I would enjoy testing your husband's skill in a duel.'

'That must never happen!'

He stooped to drop a perfunctory kiss on her brow before striding from the folly. 'Wait at least ten minutes before you leave.'

Georganna sat up slowly and brushed away the tears on her cold cheeks. Tonight he had been uncaring of her emotions in his unseemly haste, leaving her feeling ill used and ashamed. This side of him had frightened her, and she realised how little she knew of him. For this stranger she had risked her marriage and her future, and she was deeply ashamed.

Misery engulfed her as she straightened her crumpled gown. She could not believe the change in her lover.

The fireworks ended in a climax of explosions and magical fountains of coloured stars. Their splendour left Georganna unmoved. Her step was leaden as she made her way back to the house, joining the last of the guests filing inside. In the pale moonlight, bats darted overhead, and she scratched absently at her arm and neck and found her flesh covered with gnat bites. Light spilled from the windows of the great house on to the lawns, and the sound of music and laughter greeted her entrance. She stepped through a door into the room filled with card tables. The players were intent upon finding their partners or making up the numbers for the first game. As she moved on through to the corridor she paused by an anteroom, where her attention was caught by Tamasine's excited voice.

'Adam, St John, Thomas, at last we are all together. Will you not greet our dear cousin Tristan Loveday?'

There was a frozen silence from her husband and cousins. Georganna moved forward on legs that seemed to be wading through mire. She was shocked at the naked fury on Adam's face.

'Tristan, what trickery did you use to gain my sister's acquaintance?' Rigid with anger, he bowed stiffly to Tamasine. She was wide-eyed with shock, her hand raised to her face to veil her expression. Adam clipped out, 'You have made a grave error of judgement inviting this scoundrel into your home. I refuse to acknowledge him as kin. If you are wise, you will ask him to leave at once.'

'So speaks a true grandson of George Loveday,' replied Tristan with equal venom, though his voice was hardly above a whisper reaching only to the family. 'Unforgiving to the end and still believing your twin's lies.'

'I know what I saw that night. You brought shame to us all,' Adam flared.

'In the heat of the moment – we all had much to answer for that night. Do you think that I have not regretted what happened? I was a youth caught up in such turbulent violence I did not know what I was doing. Did any of us? I am not that same person today. Did that night not change you, cousin?'

Still bristling with fury, Adam swivelled on his heel and marched from the room. Throughout, St John had allowed his twin to speak, a look of horror on his face.

Chapter Twelve

'What possessed Adam to take so violently against Tristan?' Tamasine regarded Thomas and St John with horror.

Thomas shrugged and looked equally perplexed. He only vaguely remembered Tristan living at Trevowan. He thought he had run off to sea and their grandfather had renounced him as an ingrate and refused to have anything further to do with the youth. The year Tristan had left was one when his mother had been unwell and they had not visited her old home in Cornwall.

St John shifted uneasily and glared at Tristan with contempt. 'How dare you trick our sister in this fashion? What lies did you use this time to slither your way back into our family?'

Unperturbed, Tristan held his cousin's condemning glare and adjusted the ruffles at his wrist. 'Your sister has a kinder heart than my Trevowan kin.'

'She does not know how you betrayed us. I will not remain in the same room as you.' St John also marched away.

'I'll go after him,' Thomas suggested to appease Tamasine. 'He had better have a good reason for his rudeness.' He paused to regard Tristan. 'Unless you would care to explain.'

Tristan shrugged. 'With respect, I make a point of never explaining. Besides, your family only listen to what they want to hear.'

Thomas headed after St John and caught up with him just outside the door. He fired several questions at the younger man, and St John's face was strained as he snapped out replies before marching in the direction of the gaming tables. Briefly Thomas stared back at

Tamasine and lifted his hands, showing her that he was none the wiser.

Georganna had been horrified at the exchange and backed away to conceal herself behind a potted palm in the corridor as Adam strode past. She had remained frozen when Thomas confronted St John a few feet away from her hiding place. Now she held her breath when her husband turned and saw her watching him.

Thomas continued to glower at his wife. Her world had fragmented in pieces around her and she closed her eyes against the anguish that tore through her. Was her guilt obvious? Did Thomas suspect that Tristan was her lover? Her conscience condemned her to the worst her husband could throw at her. She braced herself for his further scorn, but when she opened her eyes Thomas had disappeared. Tristan had not moved, neither had he acknowledged Georganna. She did not know whether to be pleased or disheartened.

Tamasine regarded Tristan with a mixture of alarm and concern. 'What did you do that was so terrible?' she demanded.

Not a flicker of emotion showed on his pale face. 'We were children. You know how Adam and St John are rivals over everything. An incident between us got out of hand.'

Though his tone was dismissive, Tamasine detected a more rigid set to his shoulders, showing an inner tension. It made her challenge him. 'I had not thought Adam would bear a grudge over some trifle.'

'Then mayhap you do not know him as well as you think.' Tristan bowed curtly. 'I had thought they were men enough to forget the indiscretions of our youth. Clearly it is not so. I will not spoil your celebrations by this discord. I shall leave in the morning.'

'No. You are our guest.' Tamasine was appalled at the anger she had witnessed and at the affront she had given Tristan by her comment. She had planned this reunion to be a grand surprise and she was mortified that it had gone so terribly wrong. She had never seen Adam so furious and she did not believe that he would act so violently without just cause. Yet Tristan had always been the most amenable and perfect of gentlemen when they met. Though in truth their meetings had numbered no more than six before he had arrived at Beaucombe. Nevertheless, she was confused and embarrassed. At least her brothers had kept their voices low despite their anger, and no other guests had appeared to notice the friction between them.

Also aware how malignantly gossip could spread, she glanced anxiously outside to the hall. To her relief it was deserted. Conscious that she had failed miserably in her duties as a hostess, she said, 'Your pardon, Tristan, I must go after Adam.'

'I warned you a surprise meeting might not be to my cousins' liking.' Tristan seemed to be taking a perverse pleasure in her embarrassment. 'I remind them of something they would rather forget. Guilt has hardened their hearts towards me.'

'Whatever did they do?' She was desperate to understand the animosity. Was it a childhood misdemeanour, or something more sinister? She was inclined to believe that if Adam was involved it must be the former.

The smile Tristan turned upon her was tolerant, as though he were a priest granting his cousins dispensation from their sins. 'That is not for me to say. They were young and impressionable and their grandfather took against me. I was fourteen and old enough to make my own way in the world. I did tell you I ran away to be free of the old man's tyranny.'

'I thought you exaggerated.' Tamasine frowned. She knew little about her grandfather, George Loveday, other than that he had expanded the shipyard from a small affair building fishing luggers to constructing ships capable of weathering rougher seas and sailing across the English Channel. Adam had once mentioned that he had the devil's own temper when crossed.

'I can only apologise to you for my brothers' behaviour, Tristan,' she appeased. 'I will not have my guests insulted – especially when they are family. I would not have their ill manners drive you from my home.'

He took her hand and raised it to his lips. 'You have a kind and forgiving heart. It is best that I leave. But I am indebted to you for your friendship and hospitality. I hope this incident will not destroy that.'

For the first time she saw the brittle calculation in his stare and she wondered if she had not been overhasty in extending her friendship to him. 'You must do what you think best.'

'I will depart before anyone rises on the morrow. My presence will cause contention and I would not spoil this celebration.'

She extracted her hand from his and went in search of Adam. It would be too public to confront St John at the gaming tables.

Tristan narrowed his eyes as he regarded her departure. He should never have allowed Tamasine to talk him into this reunion. He should have known his hot-headed cousins had not forgiven him – would, in fact, never forgive him for his betrayal of their family. His blood burned at this further indignity. His damned cousins always thought themselves so superior to him. He knew different. They were not so innocent. One of them had a guilty secret he would not want made public. Yet he, Tristan, was the one who had suffered. Had he not lost everything and been thrown back into the gutter from where George Loveday had rescued him?

But as yet all was not lost. He intended that the Lovedays would pay for the humiliation he had suffered.

Tamasine found Adam alone, staring bleakly out of a landing window across the lawns. His hands were on his hips and every muscle in his body was tight with tension. Through the panes of glass the moon could be seen high in the sky above his head, its reflection silvered in the rippling water of the lake. The sound of muffled laughter and the strains of a string quartet carried incongruously to them. She stood back from her brother; made uncertain by the cold fury she could feel emanating from him in waves.

'Why will you have nothing to do with Tristan? I thought he was your long-lost cousin.'

'Not lost for long enough,' he replied with venom. He did not turn to look at her and a muscle throbbed along his jaw as he combated his rage. 'I thought he was dead.'

'Then do you not rejoice that he is alive?' She was shocked at this unforgiving side to Adam's nature. She knew he could be ruthless in dealing with enemies, but family loyalty had always been important to him.

'Only so that now I can have the satisfaction of calling the blackguard out and running him through his treacherous heart.'

She shivered as an icy finger ran down her spine. 'But he speaks only praise of you and your family,' she protested. She was mortified that her brother was filled with such hatred and could not understand it.

Adam twisted round and leaned back against the window. His knuckles were white as he gripped the sill. He glared at her, the pale light from the candle sconces set in the wall flickering over the chiselled lines of his face, which was now set in a macabre mask. 'And by so doing he tricked his way into your circle of friends. For the sake of your reputation I hope he has not fleeced them, or used some other means to part them from their money.' His full lips drew back in a snarl. 'Betrayal is his speciality.'

Outside, an owl hooted sinisterly. Even though the hairs at the back of her neck prickled at this disclosure, Tamasine refused to believe she had been so wrong about Tristan's character. Had not Max also met and liked him? Georganna had met him more than once on her afternoon visits to the Deverells' London home. She had never shown any doubts as to his integrity and seemed to enjoy his company.

'It is many years since you knew him,' she placated. 'He could have changed, Adam.'

He briefly closed his eyes, and when he opened them they were dark with compassion for her. 'A knave of his ilk does not change. He is a ne'er-do-well of the worst order. Max must ask him to leave, or he will bring discredit to what should be a joyous occasion.'

Her cheeks stung with the heat of her distress that Adam found her so lacking in perception. 'Then you must tell me what he has done that is so disreputable that he must be barred from my home. Max found nothing amiss in his character.'

Adam clamped his jaw shut, refusing to elaborate further, and a fraught silence stretched between them. Finally Tamasine snapped, 'We all make mistakes. Tristan said he had not had contact with any of our family for twenty-five years. He must have been very young at the time.'

'He was fourteen and old enough to betray us in the basest manner after my grandfather had given him a home and an education. He was no better than a guttersnipe when Grandfather learned he was living off the streets. He was then ten, with no home or money and clothed in rags.' He rubbed the back of his neck. 'This is not the time to drag up painful memories. You have guests to entertain.'

She stood her ground, feeling utterly wretched. 'Tristan has shown me nothing but kindness. He hinted that he had done many foolish things in his youth and it was now his deepest wish to make amends to those he had wronged.'

'He is a knave, and a scoundrel who has no concept of honour. Do not trust him.'

She flinched at the harshness of his accusation and was stung to remind him, 'Some may have said that of your cousin Japhet. He was a charming rogue. Many dubbed him a fortune-hunter when he wed an heiress. Did he not spend a year in Newgate without cause? He was transported to New South Wales for his infamy even though he was later pardoned. He is still there now seeking his fortune.'

Adam's features contorted with anger. 'False evidence was laid against Japhet, as you are well aware. He is a saint compared to that shyster Tristan.'

'Then you must tell me what he has done.' Tamasine folded her arms across her chest and tapped her foot. Her own uncertain temper was dangerously close to erupting: how could her brother think she was so naive as to be duped by a fraudster?

Their eyes locked in challenge, and to her surprise Adam dropped his gaze first. 'It was a long time ago. Believe me when I tell you that he is corrupt and evil. He will not change. Get him to leave, or I fear for the consequences. I am not prepared to say more.'

As he walked away she ran after him. 'That is not enough. I will not turn him from my home, though he has suggested he will leave to prevent unnecessary conflict. But do I not deserve to know what it was he did that was so terrible?'

'Grandfather swore us to secrecy. I cannot break that vow.'

Tristan paced the moonlit garden, still fuming at the injustice of his cousin's accusations. So much for the Lovedays and how they prided themselves on family loyalty, he thought sourly. Though his own branch of the family was not so illustrious as Adam's, was he not also the great-grandson of Arthur St John Loveday, the founder of the Trevowan Loveday dynasty?

Adam's grandfather was George Loveday, who according to the family Bible was the only child of Arthur and his wife Anne. There was no mention of his second son, Walter, who had been so like his irascible father the two had been at loggerheads throughout his childhood. Walter was three years younger than George and both had tempers and a reckless nature. Like Adam and St John they constantly fought and argued. No amount of punishment dealt to them by Arthur could bring a truce between the brothers, who had come to loathe each other with a vengeance. The rivalry between Adam and St John was nothing compared to the hatred George and Walter felt for each other.

The wilder side of the Loveday blood governed their actions. Walter wanted a life of adventure and his hero was his swashbuckling grandfather who had sailed with Drake. Not that Walter craved a life at sea; he had heard too many stories of how hard that existence could be. For him there would be other ways to win fame and glory.

While George channelled his energy into an interest in ships, a passion he shared with his father, Walter resented being expected to help in the shipyard without pay or reward. When he turned twelve Arthur demanded that he either enter the navy or serve the family in the yard. When Walter refused, his father threatened to disinherit him. In response Walter ran away, taking a few pieces of his mother's jewellery. To further spite his family, he rejected the family tradition of a life at sea and enlisted in the army as a drummer boy. There he was drawn to the criminals who had been tricked into taking the King's shilling. He was an apt pupil, and they taught him how to pick pockets and not be detected, and how to open any lock. The hardship of army life soon lost its appeal, and at fifteen he deserted and turned to crime.

The family did not hear of him again until he was dying from a knife wound received in a street fight. His life had been filled with adventure but no glory, and the only fame he had earned was as the leader of a gang of thieves who had terrorised the streets of Bristol. On his deathbed, he was smitten with a pang of conscience and wrote to his father asking him to care for his young wife, Kitty, and daughter Alice. He confessed that Kitty, the daughter of a haberdasher, was unaware of his criminal life. Her widowed father had died the previous year, leaving her his shop, which Walter had sold, squandering the money on a year of extravagant living. She would be destitute on his death.

The letter was ignored or never delivered. Tristan believed that Arthur Loveday had deliberately ignored it, cutting Walter and his family from his life.

His memories of his own childhood were bitter. Kitty had reared Alice in poverty and squalor and drunk herself into an early grave by the time her daughter was fourteen. She had died cursing Arthur Loveday and made her daughter vow to return to Trevowan and claim her birthright as the granddaughter of a wealthy shipbuilder. Alice had never honoured her vow. A handsome trickster and cutpurse who had led her into a life of crime had seduced her but never married her. His sharp wits had provided them with a lucrative income for three years as they worked together swindling the gullible out of their life savings, until the law finally caught up with them. Alice had escaped over a rooftop to a garret in the next street, but her lover had been shot and plunged to his death. Five months later Alice had given birth to Tristan. Terrified of being caught by the law, she had stayed in hiding in the squalor of the gin-sodden back streets of the city. In her more sober moments she would regale her son with the stories her own mother had told her of their cousins in Cornwall.

'I did not honour my vow to my mother,' she lamented to Tristan.

She would sit in the only chair they possessed in front of a pitiful fire in the single room they rented in a dank basement that always stank of boiled turnips. Her hair was matted and straggled down her back and her clothes were filthy rags. Tristan sat barefoot on the floor, his bony arms and knees protruding from the threadbare cloth of his breeches and shirt. Alice coughed incessantly, frequently bringing up blood.

'I was a city girl and scared of the thought of living in the country, where our nearest neighbour could be a mile away and there was nothing of interest to do,' she reminisced. 'Ma reckoned my grandfather were rich, drove a fine carriage and had a score of servants. They were proper gentry. And that was our birthright. Don't you make the same mistake, Tristan. You're a bright lad. I'm not long for this world. I've written to the old man's son at Trevowan – your great-uncle George. You're his nephew. You deserve what is yours by right.'

'You ain't gonna die, Ma.' Tristan swallowed his fear, and held out a pie that he had stolen from the tray of a pie man. 'This will make you strong. What do I want to live with that old bastard for?'

'I don't want to hear such disrespect from your mouth. You talk properly like you've been taught and you will go far in the world.' His mother's rebuke ended in another bout of coughing, and she fell back gaunt and exhausted on the mildewed pillow. During the last month her face had broken out in open sores and her rotting teeth had all fallen out. She looked like a hag from Hades, but for all that Tristan loved her.

'If they are so fine, they'll not want a guttersnipe reminding them of their family shame. You always said that Walter Loveday was a rogue. And I can look after myself. Haven't I fed you? Even stole money for your gin, though I hate it when you're drunk.'

'You've been a good boy.' Her skeletal, chilblain-reddened hands stroked his matted hair, which had been unevenly shorn off to his shoulders with a knife. 'But I don't want to die thinking this is the only legacy you know. You may be in the gutter, my son, but you can look up at the sky and dream you are amongst the stars.'

Alice had died two weeks later, and with no money for a coffin she had been condemned to a pauper's grave, her body thrown into a lime pit with a dozen others. Tristan had stood in the pouring rain, which disguised the tears that washed his cheeks, and made a vow that one day the Lovedays would pay for abandoning his mother. The resentment that had once fired the blood of Walter Loveday ignited in his grandson's veins. How had the grandsons of George Loveday fared whilst their cousin lived in poverty? Tristan doubted they had been so hungry that they cried from the pain, or so cold in the winter that their bare feet were swollen and inflamed, making every step torture.

Had they ever lain awake at night when they were four years old shaking with fear as a drunk broke into their room and raped their mother? With his young heart beating wildly, Tristan had flung himself at the attacker, striking at him with a poker, only to have the weapon snatched from his tiny hand and turned on himself. With a

117

final kick at both his victims, the attacker had stolen the few pence his mother had earned sewing mobcaps until her fingers bled. Alice had crawled to Tristan and hugged him close, her sobs shaking his skinny body with such violence that his teeth rattled. The next day she came home with a bottle of gin, or her little bit of comfort, as she called it. She was rarely sober again.

The day of the funeral, the landlord threw Tristan out on the street and new tenants moved into the squalid room. For a month he lived on the streets, scared and trusting no one. He stole what food he could, and when his ragged clothes fell apart, he covered his grimy body with a patched coat stolen from a dead beggar that was so big it dragged on the ground behind him. Somehow he scavenged an existence on the streets, curling up at night in any rat-infested hole that would give him a measure of shelter. A week of torrential rain and no food brought him to the brink of death.

That was when George Loveday's agents found him. George's gentle wife, who believed that no decent man could allow his brother's grandchild to rot in the gutter, had prompted his great-uncle to search for his kinfolk.

George Loveday had undoubtedly saved Tristan's life, but it was no fairy-tale happy ending.

Chapter Thirteen

Adam found the confined space of the ornate bedchamber stifling and restrictive. He needed fresh air to clear his thoughts. The shock of meeting his cousin face to face had shaken him. Images that he had thought long suppressed ricocheted through his mind with a sickening clarity, and his hand trembled as he ploughed his fingers through his hair. He had thought Tristan out of his life for good, and with him the secret and the shame he had buried in a place in his memory too deep to be resurrected. How wrong he had been. One glimpse of his cousin's cynical face and the feelings of revulsion had come rushing back. Even now, after a quarter of a century, he was loath to face them.

At that moment he could have throttled Tamasine for her meddling. Yet how could anyone as sweet and innocent as his sister even begin to suspect that her new-found family had such a dark and sinister secret, or Tristan such malevolence?

Anger poured like molten lava through his veins. His first instinct was to denounce his cousin. But how could he do that without implicating himself and St John? His next reaction was to call the knave to account and salvage the family reputation in a duel. A younger Adam would not have hesitated, but now wisdom prevailed. A duel might release his own rage at his cousin's misdoings, but it would also rouse gossip and speculation, and old memories that were best forgotten would be resurrected.

His breath felt sucked from his lungs, and he clawed at his stock to loosen its suffocating folds. From the terrace below his window, the distant music and the sound of laughter mocked his need to protect his family. The years of respectability and righteous living slid away and the raw panic and terror he had felt as a child threatened to swamp him. He had to get away – find space to breathe and think clearly.

Wrenching open the door, he marched through the house, taking the servants' stairs two at a time. A middle-aged maid called after him.

'Can I help you, sir? The stairs you need are . . .'

Her voice was lost in the pace of his rapid descent. This was the only way he could break free and not encounter any inquisitive guests. His shoes pounded on the flagstones of the narrow corridor, past the major-domo's small office and the boot boy's cubbyhole. With an unerring sense of direction, he continued along another corridor, passing the ironing room where valets and lady's maids gossiped as they pressed the finery to be worn by their masters and mistresses the next day. As he neared the great kitchen there was the clatter of cooking pans and dishes being washed in the large stone sinks and the giggling of the scullery maids. He hurried on and almost collided with a footman strolling out of a deep cupboard adjusting his breeches. Behind him came the muffled gasp of the maid he had been making love to as she pulled down her skirts. Unaware of their consternation, Adam turned down another corridor and finally saw the door to the servants' entrance at the side of the house.

Outside, the moon was almost full and bright enough to light his passage as he continued at this furious pace past the stables, the coach house, the row of visitors' parked coaches, and on through the walled vegetable and fruit gardens to the open fields.

Here the music and revelry could barely be heard and no guest would venture. He was breathing heavily when his pace finally slowed and he found himself by the kitchen fishpond stocked with trout. Tormented by his dark memories, he continued his walk. Grazing rabbits scattered before his progress and the ground began to slope steeply up a hill towards a dense wood. Only when he found his path blocked by a fallow deer stag did he realise that he had circled the estate towards the deer park.

Dimly he noted the rustlings of the deer herd as they moved through the undergrowth. Sitting down a fallen tree trunk, he stared towards the great house. In the distance the windows, illuminated by the light of hundreds of candles, blazed like a chain of office across its façade. Gradually the rapid thumping of Adam's heart stilled, but the solitude and silence brought him no peace. The sense of horror he had felt as a youth of ten when Tristan had betrayed their family honour cut as sharply now as it did then.

Tristan at fourteen was an angry, troubled young man scarred by the deprivations of his childhood. But that was no excuse for the events of that fateful night. He had been treated as an equal to his younger cousins by Adam's grandfather. George Loveday had been appalled at the life led by his brother's family. His sense of loyalty had led him to want Tristan to carry the name of Loveday with pride, and to be given the chance to take his rightful place in the world that had been denied his grandfather and mother. Although George Loveday might have been a stickler for honour, he was also cantankerous and irascible and a hard taskmaster. Taking on the guardianship of Tristan had been one of his few unselfish acts. It was also why his grandson's betrayal was impossible for the old man to forgive.

Adam, St John and Tristan had been beaten for their exploits that night. They had decided on a night-time adventure and taken a bottle of the twins' father's brandy to the cave in Trevowan Cove. What had begun as a boyhood prank had all changed when they were caught in a violent storm. St John had passed out drunk and Adam was unsteady and his wits disorientated. Tristan, who had been drinking gin for many years during his life in the slums, had been hardly affected by the alcohol, and taunted Adam for his weak head. It had made Adam more reckless to prove that he could hold his drink as well as his cousin. That had been his downfall.

Yet there were no excuses that could condone Tristan's actions that night. Adam, with misplaced loyalty, had lied to his grandfather to spare his cousin from the repercussions that would lead to his disgrace. They were lies that haunted him to this day.

George Loveday knew the measure of hardened men and he saw through to the rotten soul of his great-nephew. Even so, family pride sustained him. To prevent the Loveday name being sullied, he declared that as soon as it was light the next day Tristan would be dispatched to Plymouth and sent to sea as a midshipman. In defiance Tristan not only ran away but also stole several small pieces of silver and four of his great-aunt's rings.

For days George Loveday threatened to summon the authorities to find his great-nephew, and the devil with the consequences for the youth. But it was an empty threat. Even he feared the gossip that could ruin the family if the truth of that night was known, and Tristan's involvement in it.

'We are well rid of the scoundrel and from this day he is dead to us,' he had declared. 'Neither his name nor the incident will be mentioned again unless you wish to join him in his exile from the family.'

The shame Adam had felt all those years ago returned with humiliating clarity. The events leading up to Tristan's disgrace had been savage and unacceptable, the stuff of nightmares. It had been a night when circumstances unravelled out of control and emotions ran high, a night of unnatural and unearthly events. A night of valour that had turned to unspeakable horror. It had been the worst storm that Adam had ever experienced. His memory conjured the cannonade of thunder and the flash of incessant lightning. It was the night that had changed him irrevocably and shown him the path of his future and the code he would live by. It had taught him never to take life or the blessings it bestowed for granted.

He sank his head into his hands and struggled to find the path of reason. George Loveday had ranted that Tristan had reverted to type and that bad blood would always out in the end. Yet did not that same blood run through all the Lovedays' veins?

The words Tristan had flung at him rang through his mind, harsh and accusing: 'Did that night not change you, cousin?'

It had changed him, drastically. Was it possible that it could have changed Tristan too? Had he reformed? Somehow Adam doubted it. And he had an uncomfortable feeling that now that Tristan had made his presence known, it did not bode well for the future.

For two hours Adam wrestled with his thoughts before returning to the house. Some of the guests had already retired for the night. St John was still at the gaming tables, his face flushed with drink. He did not appear intoxicated and he raised his glass to Adam when he saw his brother watching him from the far side of the room. Adam was relieved to see that there was a healthy pile of coins lined up in front of him. St John was obviously winning. He felt a momentary stab of anger that his twin clearly had not allowed his encounter with Tristan to spoil his evening or, from the looks of it, trouble his conscience.

He saw Thomas and Lucien in one of the larger withdrawing rooms engaged in conversation with a group of men. Adam did not wish to interrupt them. As far as he recalled, Thomas knew nothing of the incident that had resulted in Tristan's disgrace. What alarmed Adam was that Tristan would be aware that Tamasine had not been connected to their family when he had lived with them. He was concerned at how much Tamasine had told him of her parentage. Tristan would not hesitate to use it against her if it proved to his advantage. Blackmail would come as easily as breathing to him.

Adam did not sleep that night and was still angry in the morning. He sought an early meeting with Max before his time was occupied with his other guests.

'How is Tamasine this morning?' Adam asked.

'Naturally distressed.'

There was censure in Max's manner, which Adam had expected. Max was an exemplary man, bold and dashing, or he would never have won Tamasine's heart, but there was a greater restraint about his nature than any of the Lovedays possessed. Would he understand how the deep-rooted wildness of their blood could never be governed by convention? Even Adam had been forced to battle with his nature on occasion, and not step over the line and flout propriety and the law when his blood was fired by the lure of adventure, passion or injustice.

Max continued in a quiet voice that had an edge of tension, 'I am surprised you reacted so strongly, my friend. I met your cousin three times before he was invited here and he seemed a genuine enough fellow. A little brash perhaps, but Tamasine was charmed by him.'

'He can be charming when it suits him, but I assure you he cannot be trusted.'

'So why was your sister not warned against him? Indeed, she remained ignorant of his existence.'

'Nothing had been heard of him for twenty or more years. It was assumed at the time of his disgrace that he had run away to sea, fled abroad or been killed. He mixed in dangerous company and had spent his formative years as a guttersnipe on the streets of Bristol. Our grandfathers were brothers. His had turned to a life of crime and died in a knife fight. Tristan was reared as a trickster and cutpurse. His mother took to drink. It was not something of which our family was proud.'

'Many families have insalubrious ancestors they would rather forget. But that would make Tamasine all the more prepared to bring Tristan back into society. She will see it as the birthright that he was denied.'

'That is why she must understand that he cannot be trusted.'

'How can I persuade her of that unless you tell me what he did that was so terrible?'

It was the question Adam most dreaded. How could he accuse Tristan without also implicating himself? 'My grandfather made us swear an oath of secrecy on the matter. I cannot tell you. You have to trust me on this.' He realised with greater sadness that his promise to George Loveday had made this the only secret he had kept from his wife.

'That will not satisfy your sister.' Max did not look pleased at his evasion. 'But I will not press you.'

'I will deal with Tristan as is fitting.' Adam hoped to make amends to his brother-in-law. 'I intend to speak with him at once.'

'He has already left,' Max informed him. 'He went at first light.'

'Then I must go after him. If he does not agree not to force himself upon our family or acquaintances, I will call him to account for his perfidy. Is he returning to London?'

'He did not say, and Tamasine was too upset to question him.'

Adam's relief that at least Tristan had left rather than create a scene was short-lived. It meant he had to hunt down his cousin. And that would take time he could ill afford. Yet he had no choice. Now that Tristan had resurfaced, Adam could not allow him to destroy the reputation of his family and all they had worked for.

'I am sorry this came to pass, Max. I hope Tamasine will not allow it to stop her coming to Boscabel later in the year as planned.'

'She cares for you too much to allow a disagreement to come

between you. But she is upset by your actions. The surprise she had planned had meant a great deal to her. She thought she was repaying you for all you had done for her by healing this rift between you, St John and Tristan.'

Adam's guilt that Tamasine had been hurt intensified. 'I will ask her pardon before I leave.'

It was not an easy interview. Tamasine was still angry with him and they parted after a heated exchange. Lady Clarissa interrupted them before Adam could make his sister understand that he had no choice but to pursue Tristan. Her mother-in-law breezed into the room and without an apology for breaking into their conversation began to list a number of matters concerning the welfare of their guests that needed Tamasine's urgent attention.

While Tamasine attempted to reassure her ladyship that everything would be done to ensure their guests' comfort, Adam left and sought out St John, who even this early in the morning had found another four men to play cards.

'You will excuse my brother, gentlemen. There is an urgent family matter I must discuss with him.'

'It can wait until later.' St John scowled.

'It must be dealt with now,' Adam replied in tones that would not be argued with.

St John threw down his cards with ill-concealed displeasure and followed Adam into a quiet anteroom. He glowered at his twin. 'I dislike being summoned like some common lackey.'

'Have you no concern that Tristan has dared to show his face and tricked Tamasine into receiving him? He left at first light but he cannot be trusted. He needs to be warned in no uncertain terms that we will not tolerate him mixing with our family.'

'If he's run off like a cur with his tail between his legs, we will not see him again.' St John remained surly. 'We made our feelings for him plain enough last night. I do not intend to curtail my pleasure here.'

'He needs teaching a lesson,' Adam fumed. 'I am going after him this morning.'

'Then you teach him,' St John snarled and walked to the door to wrench it open. 'He'll have run to ground. And one of us should remain to escort the women back to Cornwall.'

Adam was shocked at his brother's lack of concern. Was St John so lost in his obsession with gaming as to forget all family loyalty? Then to hell with him! Adam would deal with Tristan on his own.

Swallowing his anger against his twin, he now had to explain to his wife that he would be abandoning her. He found Senara in a quiet place in the garden whilst most of the guests were breakfasting in the dining hall.

'You will look into your heart and do what must be done,' she said without hesitation after he had explained his plans.

He took her into his arms and held her close. 'And you must think my actions out of character, yet you do not question me. I will confront Tristan alone. It is time these ghosts were laid to rest.'

She leaned her head against his chest. 'I love and trust you, Adam. You will tell when the time is right for you. But I pray you take care. For you to deal with this with such urgency means you will risk much in bringing your cousin to account.'

He let out a tortured breath against her hair. 'You are my rock, my love. Thank you for your understanding. If I do not return by the time the others are to leave, journey with them to Boscabel.'

It was three weeks before Adam saw his family again. In that time there was no sign of Tristan returning to his old haunts in London. Yet Adam knew his cousin did not intend for the matter to end as it had. Tristan was playing for time and wanted to ensure any future reunion was upon his own terms.

Chapter Fourteen

After the upset at Beaucombe, Senara was relieved to return to her home to enjoy some peace in the soothing routine of the estate. The journey home, sharing the coach with St John and Felicity, had been anything but restful. The couple had bickered continually, with Felicity constantly nagging St John about his gaming and deserting her. She refused to let the matter rest concerning the mystery surrounding Adam's early departure and the connection of Tristan to the family.

'He is a ne'er-do-well,' St John had repeated, each time angrier than the last. 'That is all you need to know.'

When they were not quarrelling, the couple were sulking. Senara had always disliked dissension and she was also concerned for Felicity's welfare. St John's wife was pale, her eyes hollow from lack of sleep. The vicious lurching of the coach as it plunged into the deep ruts that were a hazard throughout the journey made her complain of nausea. But it was the tight lines of pain about her mouth that worried Senara most. By the time Felicity alighted at Trevowan she could barely walk, and Senara advised her to take to her bed for a couple of days for a complete rest.

The coachman was to drive Senara to Boscabel before returning to Trevowan. The sun was low in the sky and dark rain clouds were coming in from the sea. She could already smell the dampness in the air. Before they parted, she addressed St John. 'Give my good wishes to Amelia and Elspeth. I will visit them tomorrow. If I delay now, I will not get home before dark and the children will be asleep.'

He nodded, but at the tension in his face she added, 'Do not be too hard on Felicity, St John. Her pregnancy is a difficult one. Make sure she rests and does not get upset. It would be a tragedy if she miscarried.'

'Is that possible?' He was shaken at her words.

'I state it as a precaution.'

His jaw jutted at a stubborn angle. 'Why did she risk the journey? She should have stayed at home.'

'Sometimes a woman will risk everything for love. She loves you and is trying to be the wife to make you happy.'

He did not immediately reply, and when he spoke his voice was thick with disappointment. 'Then she will give me a son.'

She suppressed her anger at his words. If St John loved his wife he would be concerned for her safety. He placed more importance on her giving him a son. That so much resentment had beset the marriage in so few years did not bode well for the couple.

The familiar walls of Boscabel were a welcome sight. In the last rays of sunlight the stonework was cast in a mellow ochre light. Senara ran through the house, eager to hold her children and breathe in the sweet smell of their skin and hear their excited chatter. She was also anxious to learn if Bryn had recovered his memory, or if there had been information about his identity from the reports in the news-sheets.

Nathan had grown another inch taller in his last term at Sherborne and was now more self-conscious, bowing formally to her. She abandoned etiquette and hugged him close, declaring, 'I have missed you.' He blushed and squeezed her tight.

The younger children danced around her, all clamouring for her attention at once. When they quietened she sat on one of the beds in the twins' room with Rhianne and Sara on her lap. Joel was too excited to sit still and bounced on his own bed as she told them of the entertainments she had seen and the news of their cousins. Nathan sat on the floor at her feet, and as she had insisted that Bryn remain with the others after she had greeted him, he sat quietly on the window seat.

'Did you get held up by a highwayman on the journey?' Joel demanded with gleaming eyes.

'Did you want us to be held at gunpoint and robbed?' Senara regarded him seriously.

'That would have been really exciting. Dancing and music are boring,' he replied with apparent unconcern at the dangers they would have faced. He jumped from his own bed on to Rhianne's and lay on the covers hugging his knees to his chest. 'And Uncle Thomas's play did not sound much fun if it was about silly old politicians trying to gain favour with our fat Prince George. He should have written about pirates plundering the Spanish Main and finding lost treasure.'

'All you think about are your silly pirates.' Rhianne dug her twin in the ribs. 'I want to know about Aunt Hannah and cousins Florence and Abigail. They are more fun than Charlotte, who is always telling tales on us, and Rowena thinks she is too grown up to spend time with us now.'

'You have to remember that Charlotte had her mother's sole attention before Felicity married your Uncle St John. She may feel excluded from your games,' Senara replied. 'Aunt Hannah says your cousins miss you all. They are looking forward to coming back to the farm later in the year.'

Senara smiled at her youngest child. Sara was snuggled against her chest, contentedly sucking her thumb, her eyes wide with amazement at all that had been said. Senara hugged her. 'You are very quiet, my dear. What have you been doing while I have been away?'

'I made friends with a fawn whose mother was shot by a poacher. Aunt Bridie showed Rhianne and me how to feed her like they do with lambs that have been abandoned by their mother. Her name is Shadow as she follows me everywhere. She is locked in the barn at night with the goats.'

'You must introduce Shadow to me in the morning,' Senara said. 'And when she gets older we must teach her how to forage for herself.'

'She will not have to go back to the wild, will she, Mama? She is my special friend.' Sara looked close to tears.

'When she can take care of herself she must make that choice herself. Would you like it if you were kept from your family, never to see them again?'

Her words made her glance anxiously at Bryn, who had stayed on the window seat apart from the family reunion. Senara had not intended to ignore him, but her children had been demanding of her attention until now.

'And how are you, Bryn? You look well. Have you and Nathan become friends? Joel can be possessive of his older brother.'

'Joel has been very good. We are all friends,' Bryn answered loyally.

'Have you recalled anything of your past?' Senara asked.

He shook his head. From the way he was chewing his lower lip, she was worried that he thought she would be annoyed.

'You know you have become part of our family,' she was quick to reassure him. 'We want you to be happy, but like the fawn we would not want you feeling that you should be part of another life.'

His expression brightened. 'I think I am happier here than I have ever been in my life, Mrs Loveday. But I do not expect you to continue to support me. I want to help on the estate farm all I can.'

'It is good of you to offer, but it is not necessary, Bryn.' She was nevertheless touched by his sincerity. 'And you have your education to consider. My husband would not hear of you neglecting your studies. Your tutor is impressed with your progress.'

'I would not wish you to think that I am ungrateful.'

She disengaged herself from her own children and crossed the room to affectionately ruffle his hair.

Bryn felt a glow of pleasure. He desperately wanted to be a part of this family. His past remained firmly locked away and a mystery. The terrifying nightmares he still suffered were of a dark, forbidding place, voices screaming abuse and a sense that his life was in danger.

His only regret about his lack of memory was that he could not recall who had been in the coach with him. Whoever it was, he was certain that they had risked everything to save his life.

When later Senara had tucked her children into bed and kissed them good night, her mood remained unsettled. She had hoped Adam would be at Boscabel on her return but he had sent no word. The celebrations at Beaucombe had been clouded by Tristan's arrival. Even his departure had not lightened the mood. Georganna and Thomas were strained in each other's company and she believed that on the last day they had quarrelled. Thomas had suddenly announced that he and Lucien would return to London for the present, but that he would travel to Cornwall later in the summer.

Georganna and Aunt Margaret were to spend a few days at Highcroft with Hannah and Sam before travelling to Trevowan.

With the children ordered to their beds, Senara retired to a withdrawing chamber: a small, intimate room with comfortable horsehair-filled leather chairs and a view across the rose garden to the paddock. After spending two days in the coach she was tempted to walk through the moonlit garden. Before she could collect her cloak, Carrie Jensen bustled into the room carrying a tray of cooked meats and bread and a small glass of cider for her meal. The maid looked ready to burst with suppressed news.

'So what has been happening while we have been away, Carrie?' Senara said with a laugh. She treated all of the servants in an informal manner, and Carrie most of all. Carrie had worked for her since the early days of her marriage and was the daughter of Pru and Toby who ran the Ship Kiddley at Trevowan Hard.

'Daisy Tonken from Trewenna and Mary Cresswell from the yard have had their babies, both boys. Ben Mayfield from Polmasryn wed Trudy Wibbley and they do say she be three months gone with child. Old Ma Martin from Penruan died and were buried three days past. Ollie Trenance, a gentleman from Bodmin, have called three times in a month upon Hester Lanyon. That be Hester Moyle that was, since she weren't rightly wed to Lanyon on account of him being wed already. They do say that Hester bain't averse to his calling.'

'Hester deserves some happiness after all that has happened to her.'

Carrie was not so forgiving. 'She brought most of it on herself with her uppity ways and carrying on with Harry Sawle after she thought herself wed. I never did like her. But that bain't the half of what's been happening. You'll never guess what were found under a pile of stones in the wood at back of the long meadow that Cap'n Loveday had left fallow until now.'

'If it had been a pot of pirate treasure I am sure Joel would not have been able to keep it to himself.' Senara bit into some cold chicken, enjoying teasing her servant. It was obvious that Carrie had left the juiciest news until last.

'It bain't no jesting matter, Mrs Loveday. Nothing were said to the children. It could have given them nightmares. Truth be, I don't

131

rightly know how to tell you. It were a body that were found. Eli discovered it and he said it turned his stomach sour.'

A piece of chicken stuck in Senara's throat and she felt herself gag. Quickly she drank some cider but the succulent fowl was like pebbles sticking in her throat. She coughed and spluttered and Carrie looked even more alarmed.

'Oh, what a fool I be, telling you such news when you be eating.'

Senara managed to force some more cider down her throat and recovering her composure said, 'Was it a recent death? This is shocking news. Tell me all you know.'

The maid's eyes were round as trenchers. 'Horrible, Rudge said it were. The flesh had long rotted away and half the bones had been taken by foxes and carrion.'

For the first time in her life Senara felt herself close to swooning. She dragged in a sharp breath. 'Were the authorities informed?'

'Eli sent word to Sir Henry Traherne as the nearest Justice of the Peace. Sir Henry ordered Rudge to search through the man's pockets and from what he found he thought it be that lieutenant who'd gone missing. But there bain't too much of the body to identify.' Carrie gasped. 'Oh heavens, Mrs Loveday. You've fainted.'

She hurried to the side of her mistress, who had slumped forward in the chair. She pushed Senara's head between her knees and patted her wrists to try to revive her.

'I am well enough, Carrie.' Recovering her wits, Senara found the strength to reassure her maid. 'The journey and now this shock, and I have eaten little all day.'

'I should never have told you such dreadful news.' Carrie was distraught. 'Parson Loveday were to tell you. He'd have been more careful what he said, knowing you'd be upset. I weren't thinking straight. We've all been upset since the discovery. The parson wouldn't have shocked you half to death.'

After a night of little sleep, Senara was glad the next day was a Saturday and Bridie would not be teaching at the yard. It was early in the morning when she visited her sister and mother at Polmasryn parsonage. She entered through the kitchen door and found her mother seated by the Cornish range with a bowl of peas she was shelling between her knees. The tall yew trees in the churchyard cast a shadow over the back of the house, and if a fire was not always burning, the rooms soon became damp. The rocking chair was Leah's favourite place, the heat from the range providing a welcome relief to the pain in her swollen joints. Her wrinkled face creased with delight at seeing her elder daughter.

'Welcome home. Did you enjoy your junketing? Was it all as grand as you feared?'

Senara nodded. 'Tamasine's home was twice the size of Fetherington Hall, and every minute was filled with ensuring that everyone was royally entertained. Tamasine was a splendid hostess.'

'I be sure you were a credit to your husband. I look forward to hearing all that passed. Bridie be in the church. She picked some wildflowers this morning for the service tomorrow.' There was a rumble of deeper voices from the direction of Peter's study, and Leah explained, 'Peter be with his churchwarden.'

There was a crash outside, and moments later Dora, the servant, appeared, her round face bright with embarrassment. Behind her trailed young Michael, holding a bright red ball in one hand and clinging to the back of Dora's dress with the other. His long skirts were splattered with muddy water and his fair baby curls twisted into natural ringlets about his shoulders. Apart from his slender frailty, he was the image of the cherubs Senara had seen in paintings in the grand houses of the Lovedays' acquaintances.

'He be soaked, Dora.' Leah tutted with annoyance. 'Have your wits gone begging? The child could catch his death. Change him at once.'

'His ball went in the pail that was half filled after two days of rain,' Dora wailed in her distress. 'He managed to tip it up when he tried to retrieve it. He was so fast I could not stop him.' She picked up the infant, pulled a set of his garments from where they had been airing on a rail over the range and carried him upstairs to change.

'Bridie will cosset him all day when she learns he took a dousing.' Leah shook her head. 'She fusses too much to my mind.'

'I am sure Michael will come to no harm. It is a warm day outside,' Senara reassured. 'And it is good that he is getting into scrapes. It shows he is getting stronger.'

'That's as may be, but the foolish girl knows better than to let him get wet. He takes a chill so easily.'

133

Senara frowned as she heard Michael coughing in the room above. 'This house is so damp, it cannot help.'

'The parsonage be dryer and far better than many of the places we lived when you and Bridie were that age. The roof of our gypsy caravan was always leaking as I remember, and so did the roof of the cottage in the clearing until Adam had it repaired for us. An old sail was all that kept us dry when we first returned to my parents' home after they had died.' Leah sniffed, and her stare was accusing. 'Happen you've forgotten your roots, living as you now do in such fine houses, daughter. Bridie were a sickly child. She survived far worse than a bit of dampness.'

Senara put her basket on the table. It contained a freshly killed hare trapped by Billy Brown, and two pigeons. There was also a selection of spices recently delivered to the kiddley, and a cone of sugar. Bridie grew her own vegetables, and kept chickens and a sow and her litter, but a parson's stipend stretched to few luxuries and Senara never visited her mother and sister empty-handed.

'I could never forget my heritage and my blood,' she said briskly. 'I am not ashamed of the years I lived with my father's family on their travels.'

Leah nodded, apparently satisfied. 'I grow crotchety in my old age. Pay no heed to me. Bridie and you fuss too much over Michael. She overcame the rigours imposed on her by her twisted back, and look at her now. She be strong and healthy and takes any adversity in her stride. She be a supportive parson's wife, and the villagers love her because she understands what it be like to have been poor and face prejudice.'

'Ma, you have no need to tell me how wonderful is our Bridie. There is no one more proud of her than I am.'

'What have I done to receive such praise?' Bridie giggled as she put her basket that still contained a bunch of bluebells on the table. She did not wait for a reply as she kissed her sister's cheek. 'How lovely that you are back, Senara. Have the rest of the family returned to Trevowan? You must tell what news there is from Hannah and when she will be at the farm. And of course Tamasine. Was the baby adorable? Well, all babies are adorable. So does Olivia resemble Tamasine or Max?'

The questions continued to tumble forth as Bridie busied herself filling a pottery vase from the jug of water that had been drawn from the garden well and arranging the bluebells in it. Their sweet scent mixed with the fragrance of the herbs drying in bunches on the low beams and the smells of a rabbit roasting over a spit on the fire and freshly baked bread.

Senara answered, curbing her impatience that she had so many questions of her own crowding her mind.

Bridie had brewed a pot of tea, and they had drunk it before her questions dried up. Yet not once had she mentioned the body found on Adam's land. Did she not know about it? That seemed unlikely to Senara. Gossip would be rife about such an occurrence.

'We sold every piece of lace made by the local women at market last week,' she related proudly.

'That were a wonderful thing you did, Bridie,' Leah interrupted her daughter's babbling. 'Getting that loan from Sir Henry Traherne for bobbins, thread and a spinning wheel and persuading Martha Keppel to teach the women to make lace. The sales made a big difference to their lives this winter. No one went hungry.'

'We are all proud of you, Bridie,' Senara said. 'Did you hear of—'

Bridie cut in before she could get further, 'Yesterday Gert Wibbley had a fight in the street with her sister-in-law. She accused Cathy of playing fast and loose with a pedlar who came through the village. She chased after her with a pair of scissors, threatening to cut off her hair for bringing shame to her family. Cathy gave Gert a black eye and they were rolling about in the dirt in the most undignified fashion until one of their girls screamed so loud Peter heard her. He separated the two women and received a split lip for his pains. He put both of them in the stocks for half a day and they did nothing but yell abuse at each other.'

Senara forced a grin. Gert Wibbley was a troublemaker and a gossip, but Senara was now certain that Bridie was gabbling out of nervousness, delaying the moment that her sister would ask her own questions. She held up her hands to halt the stream of conversation, and Bridie cast an anxious glance at her mother.

Leah shrugged and bent over the fire to turn the rabbit on the spit. Fat splattered into the flames and some sparks spat out from the wood on to her black skirt, which she quickly brushed off before they could singe the cloth. 'She's obviously heard about the body, Bridie. You can't spare her by not letting her speak.'

Bridie sat on a stool opposite Senara at the table but could not look her sister in the eye. 'Since you do not question Ma's comment, you must have heard, then?'

'That a body was found on our land? Yes. Is it true?'

Bridie paled and nodded.

'Did Sir Henry identify the corpse as Lieutenant Beaumont?'

Again her sister nodded and kept her gaze fixed upon the bunch of carrots lying on the table. They had been pulled out of the earth that morning and needed washing. She brushed the soil from them with her fingers before she risked a glance at Senara. Then she said in a low voice that their mother would be unable to hear, 'I know what you are thinking. Were you the last person to see him alive? Or were you responsible for his death? That is nonsense, Senara. You were not on your land when you encountered him.'

'He could have died shortly after I met him. I told you what I did. What if I was the cause of his death and he crawled away to die?'

'You were angry. You acted in self-defence. What you say makes no sense. Why would he head towards Boscabel? It is more likely that he was killed and deliberately left there.'

'What are you two saying? Speak up,' Leah demanded.

'It's nothing, Ma.' Senara did not want her mother worrying.

'It bain't nothing and don't think I be a fool,' the old woman retorted. 'That man were no friend to you or your husband. Adam believed he were responsible for his father's death. But he wouldn't kill him, if that be what you afear.'

Leah could not be further from the truth. Senara had no doubt that Adam was innocent of Beaumont's murder. But was she?

At that moment Dora clumped down the stairs carrying Michael, and Peter could be heard ushering his churchwarden to the front door. He called out that he would ride to Trewenna to discuss an urgent matter of church business with his father. The door clanged shut behind him before anyone could tell him Senara had called.

'I'll fetch him back,' Bridie apologised. 'He is much preoccupied over raising funds to repair the church roof. He can tell you more about the body and Sir Henry's conclusions about this matter.'

Senara shot her sister a warning look, nodding towards Dora. She wanted no gossip or speculation on the subject. Bridie turned to the servant, reaching out to take her son. 'Dora, the windows in the parlour and the parson's study need cleaning. I could not see out of them when the sun was shining yesterday. Do the study first before the master returns.'

They waited until the woman had collected the cloth and a bowl of water and left them before Bridie rose from her stool and placed Michael on Leah's lap. His grandmother gave him a pod to break open and he squealed with delight, extracting a pea and putting it in his mouth. 'Ma, you'll keep an eye on Michael for me, won't you? I need Senara to take a look at one of the piglets. I noticed this morning that it was not feeding. It's not the runt of the litter and I fear the mother may have lain on it and harmed it in some way.'

The sisters walked towards the pigsty, which was next to the stable that housed the two horses and the dogcart that Bridie drove.

'There is nothing wrong with the piglet,' Bridie confessed. 'I guessed you did not want to talk in front of Ma. You are worried about this body being found.'

The sow had heard their approach and reared up on her hind legs to rest her front trotters on the wooden door of the sty. She sniffed the air to detect the tidbits they might have brought to feed her. Senara scratched the pink head and found a piece of chopped carrot in her pocket that she carried with her in case she was called upon to tend a sick animal. The sow grunted with pleasure until Bridie shooed it away from the door. Her sister leaned on the wood, staring at the nine piglets.

'You know what I did?'

'You saved the life of a child and a woman from being raped by that monster. I do not blame you for the anger you launched at him when you last saw him. But you did not kill him.'

'How do we know that for sure?' Senara's eyes were dark with fear. 'I have to know how he died. I will go to Sir Henry.'

Bridie held her arm. 'Do not make more of it than you have to. Talk to Peter.'

'How can I? He more than anyone would be appalled at my actions.' Her voice shook from the force of her emotion. 'He is driven by his piety. He is quick to condemn me that I do not attend church as often as he believes I should. And he is suspicious of my knowledge of herbs. He will not allow you to use what I taught you to tend the sick of his parish.'

She felt the trail of tears running down her cheeks and impatiently brushed them away. 'If he ever found out about my encounter with Beaumont he would forbid you from seeing me, fearing I would corrupt you. He could even testify against me, and you know what that would mean.'

'You are allowing your fears to run wild.' Bridie was shocked at the state of her sister. Senara was always the calm one, the one in control. 'Peter and you are family. He would never do anything to harm you.'

'But what if his prejudice is governed by his religious fervour? He would see it as his duty.'

Chapter Fifteen

Senara returned to Boscabel hoping that she had convinced Bridie not to mention the encounter with Beaumont to her husband. Even so, she remained unsettled. She had no one to whom she could confide her fears. This was one matter she hoped would never reach her husband's ears. She was so ashamed of her actions. Adam had always understood her reverence for the ancient ways. Had they not been married at the winter solstice following the old rites at the stone circle at Avebury? That had been the most memorable day of her life. Believing Adam was to wed another and knowing herself to be carrying his child, she had fled Cornwall. She had loved him too much to share him with another. He had spent months searching for her, defying his family when he declared he would have no wife other than Senara. He had found her on the morning of the solstice; that night she had given birth to Nathan and the following morning they were married by gypsy lore. On their return to Trevowan they had married by the law of Adam's church so that there would be no claims upon the legality of their marriage.

Yet Senara had never entirely abandoned her old religion and had found a way to merge the old with the new that had worked in perfect harmony — until she had come upon Beaumont acting so despicably. She felt she had betrayed her husband's trust and her own integrity by summoning the old gods in an act of retribution.

She held her hands to her cheeks, her heart racing with shame. She had broken the one law that she honoured above all others: harm none. To find some measure of calm from her anxiety she visited the waterfall on the estate, accompanied by Scamp. As she walked, she picked wildflowers, until she came to the concealed grotto by the waterfall. Here she placed the spray of poppies, cornflowers and daisies on a large flat stone. Scamp ran off, searching for birds hiding in the reeds further along the stream. This was Senara's special place, where she sought solace when she was troubled.

She sat very still on a boulder and closed her eyes to listen to the water tumbling over the rocks and the birdsong high in the branches. Her senses were filled by the scent of wild honeysuckle and the moist smell of the earth. The sound of the water was soothing and she allowed its melody to flow through her until her whole being reverberated with a slow, deep pulse. It was the rhythm of nature itself and she felt her spirits lighten and soar. After the noise and clamour of people at Beaucombe, the peace of her sanctuary was as hallowed as any church.

She was reluctant to break the spell that had woven around her, but aware that the air had grown cooler, she opened her eyes. On the opposite bank of the stream a pair of bright, intelligent eyes stared back at her and her heart leapt with joy to witness the rare sight of a female otter and her two cubs climbing over the bank. The mother slid into the water, and for some moments the cubs chased each other and rolled over in mock fights. Then they too plunged into the stream and swam off towards where their mother was waiting for them. Senara realised she had been holding her breath and let it out in a contented sigh.

Her attention was now taken by a kingfisher landing on a nearby branch with a tiny fish in its beak. In a flash it was gone and she saw a glimpse of bright blue as it disappeared into a hole on a sandy part of the bank where it was nesting. Moments later it reappeared and flew on to another branch to hunt for more fish. From out of the nest appeared three heads. The chicks were almost ready to fledge and would leave the nest in the next day or so.

The sightings of the otters and the kingfishers were a good omen. A sign of thriving and contented families. Not only had the wildlife given Senara a great deal of pleasure, the omen gave her the strength to overcome her fears.

Senara's sense of well-being did not last for long. When she returned home, Carrie informed her that Parson Loveday was in the parlour.

140

Senara shook out the folds of her gown and brushed away a few pieces of grass that clung to the muslin. She paused only to sleek a hand over her hair before squaring her shoulders to face whatever censure Peter would throw at her.

When she stepped into the parlour she was surprised to see him playing chess with Bryn. At a hand's width less than two yards high, Peter was the shortest of the Loveday men, but was still considered taller than average height. But then there was nothing average about her husband's family in Senara's opinion. His figure was wiry rather than muscular like Adam's and without any spare flesh. As usual he was dressed in his cleric's black and Geneva bands, and his dark hair, cut short to his ears, had a natural curl, which gave him a boyish air that softened his often sombre expression when dealing with his parishioners. The cut lip he had sustained from Gert Wibbley was testament of his diligence to his pastoral duties.

'Good morning, Peter. What brings you to Boscabel? I trust you have not been kept waiting too long.'

He stood up and inclined his head in acknowledgement of her greeting. 'Your young charge has been keeping me company. He was on the way to beating me at this game.' He smiled at the boy. 'Run along, Bryn, I must speak with Mrs Loveday. You have a sharp mind. Thank you for the game. And take care that you read your Bible daily and say your prayers every night.' The admonishment was delivered in a light tone and carried none of Peter's usual harsh judgement.

His relaxed manner was not what she had expected, though a frown hovering upon his brow alerted her that he was displeased. He waited for her to be seated by the hearth before saying, 'I have a suspicion that Bryn may have been brought up a Papist. Though when questioned he recalled little of any religious teachings. That I find strange, as the Lord's Prayer and the Papist rites are learned by rote and the responses become all but automatic.'

'Not all families follow a strict religious doctrine.' She hoped her voice sounded neutral. She had no wish to provoke his anger with her own views. 'Such teachings may have been neglected in one so young, and I believe those of the Catholic faith are still viewed with suspicion and worship in secret.'

'That is so. Though several of our great nobles are Catholics.

141

Since they believe that theirs is the true Christian faith and Protestants will burn in everlasting hell, any Catholic family would be diligent in ensuring that their children followed their teachings.' His expression darkened. 'I find Bryn's lack of religious understanding disgraceful. It must be remedied. I would not have his soul imperilled.'

'Though I suspect you would have him follow the Church of England's teachings,' she challenged.

'It is the faith of our country. King George is the head of our church, not the Pope.'

Senara had no wish for a lecture on religion but was goaded to answer sharply, 'Bryn receives the same instruction as my children, which is overseen by your own father. And his memory has still not returned concerning his family. We know he was beaten. If he was subjected to religious tyranny, he could also have blocked that from his mind.' She braced herself for a lengthy lecture.

'You are a compassionate and wise woman, sister.' He startled her by this statement. Then a grin transformed his dour expression to one of intense pleasure. He went on, 'But this is not a day for debate on religious matters. Today is a joyous one. I have come straight from Trewenna. And I praise the Lord that my brother and his family have returned to us safe from their exile.'

Shock turned to a delicious thrill of excitement. 'Japhet is in England? And Gwen and the children? When? Where is he?'

'At the rectory. His first call naturally was upon Papa and Mama. He had arrived an hour before my visit this morning.'

'Oh, Adam will be so vexed he is not here to welcome him.' Her relief that Peter remained ignorant of her talk with Bridie was so great that she found it impossible to contain her joy. 'That is wonderful news. But we only heard a couple of months ago that he intended to sell his homestead and business interests. The voyage alone from Sydney usually takes nine months.' Forgetting her usual restraint in Peter's company, she flung her arms around him and gave him a hearty hug.

'Once his mind was made up, they were impatient to leave.' It was a sign of his elation that he showed no embarrassment at her lack of decorum. He could not stop smiling. 'Japhet never lets the grass grow under his feet, or in this case let the waves settle. They had a fast passage. The ship docked in London two weeks ago, but Japhet wanted to surprise us all. And he has arrived in style. Dressed in the latest fashion and driving his own curricle.' A thread of censure had entered his voice. 'Though I would have thought he would seek to draw less attention to his return. There will be many who will remember his fall from grace.'

'It is a bold move that you would expect from Japhet. He would want to prove to those who proclaimed him a rogue and a fortune-hunter that Gwen had not erred in marrying him.'

'It will take more than a show of wealth to prove that,' Peter pronounced with a parson's primness. 'His honour and integrity have been questioned. Some will assume that it is his wife's money that has provided these trappings of new prosperity. Botany Bay is a penal colony. Its purpose is for punishment, not to make its inhabitants rich.'

'It is also a new colony that is attracting many settlers from our shores.' Peter's high-handed manner made Senara bristle with indignation. 'You sound as though you still condemn him for his old life. If you cannot accept that marriage has changed him, how can you expect others not to judge him?'

Peter blushed and did not meet her angry stare. All his life he had resented the popularity of his older brother. He had used his piety like a cloak to shield his frustration and protect him against the demons of his own wild blood that he sought to exorcise. He exhaled sharply, and when his gaze again locked with hers, she could see that he had conquered the insecurities of his past.

'I suspect Japhet has been to hell and back,' he continued more humbly. 'You will see a difference in him. It is not the brutality of the penal system that has tamed his ungodly pursuits, but the love of an exceptional woman. However, there is a more cynical edge to his charm, which is as blatant as ever, and I have never seen a man more in control of his own destiny. I respect him for all he has endured and how he has triumphed when many would have crumbled under such adversity.'

This time there was respect in his voice for all his brother had suffered. Senara wished he would lower the shield he kept so close around his emotions more often. It would make him more compassionate and insightful in his role as a clergyman.

'Will they be staying with Joshua and Cecily?' she asked. 'Their property is on a yearly lease to a tenant farmer which does not end until after the harvest. The rectory will be cramped with the children, though Cecily will adore having them around her. However, I know Adam would be delighted if they stayed here.'

'I doubt Mama would appreciate the gesture. She could not hold back her tears of joy, and her grandchildren were locked firmly in her arms throughout my visit. She would have them safely back in her nest for a time at least.'

'As would any mother,' Senara laughed.

Peter lifted a dark brow and his mood again was condemning. 'Mayhap not the Lady Anne. Japhet and Gwendolyn have gone to Traherne Hall. Both are apprehensive as to how her mother and sister will receive them. Though I have no doubt that Sir Henry will heartily welcome the return of his old friend.'

'Lady Anne Druce still refuses to have Japhet's name mentioned in her presence, even though he and Gwen have been wed for eight years and have two children. Gwen has always adored Japhet and he has been steadfast to her.' Senara was passionate in her defence of the couple. 'He did not return to England when his pardon was granted because he wanted to prove to the world that he had reformed. He also wanted to create a fortune for his children with his own hands. Her ladyship would have a cold heart indeed if she shut them out of her life. Though I suspect it will not be an easy reunion.'

'Then we will pray for them.' Peter riveted his stare to hers, challenging her to defy him. He knelt on the floor and placed his hands together. 'Come, sister, you will join me in this.'

The preacher within him had never given up completely on converting Senara. Until now she had defied his insistence on prayers for every important occasion. Today it felt right. Although her mind had been distracted by this joyous news of Japhet's return, her conscience was still troubled over the discovery of the body. She had much to pray for.

Joining Peter on her knees, she bent her head as he intoned a prayer for his brother and his family. She remained with her hands clasped devoutly together as the prayer led into another for the redemption of lost souls, and finally she joined in when he began the Lord's Prayer.

She felt calmer as she rose to her feet. Peter smiled his approval and bowed to her, intending to leave.

'I have heard other news since my return which is not so welcome,' she confessed, halting his departure. 'Is it true a body has been found on our land?'

'A tragic event. Fortunately he was identified and placed in a coffin and conveyed to his home parish.'

'Was it Lieutenant Francis Beaumont?' She found herself holding her breath as she awaited his reply.

'Unquestionably. Though it is a mystery what the knave was doing on Adam's land.'

Her hand clasped the pendant she wore at her throat and her voice cracked as she asked, 'How did he die?'

His eyes flashed with scorn. 'Does it not concern you that he was on your land? That on another occasion when he trespassed in such a manner that knave shot Uncle Edward? Deliberately shot, I must add, on the absurd assumption that he was resisting arrest for allowing contraband to be hidden here. Beaumont hated Adam with a vengeance. They had been enemies for years.'

'Do people believe that Adam killed him?' She gripped the back of a chair for support. 'He was not the officer's only enemy.'

'Of course Adam did not kill him!' Peter was clearly horrified. 'And he certainly would not have left a body where it was bound to be discovered. As you rightly say, Beaumont had many enemies. Not least was Harry Sawle. The body had lain there for many months. Sir Henry was of a mind that the smuggler must have killed him before his own arrest and hanging for the crimes of abduction, smuggling and other murders. The corpse was likely left on Adam's land at the time when Sawle was doing everything in his power to destroy our family. What better revenge could Sawle have upon us than if Adam was suspected of Beaumont's murder and arrested?'

Senara's legs no longer seemed to have the strength to support her and she sank heavily on to a chair. Her heart was pounding so fast she could barely snatch her breath. She had done such a terrible thing. She was as guilty as Sawle for wanting Beaumont dead.

At seeing the effect of his words upon her, Peter was immediately contrite. 'Your pardon, Senara. I am an imbecile to speak to you in such a manner. You must be deeply shocked.'

She drew several long breaths to steady her nerves. It also gave her time to collect her wits. Even so, her voice quivered and she hoped he would think it was dread for her husband. 'So Sir Henry believes Harry Sawle murdered Beaumont?'

'Without a doubt.'

'How did he die? Was it possible to tell?'

'Any bullet or knife wounds would long have been destroyed. The body was just a skeleton. But since the back of the skull was smashed, Sir Henry determined that a blow to the head was the cause of death.'

Senara was not convinced. Had the injury been caused by man or some other force? There was no resolution to her own fearful secret. It would be impossible to prove at this stage that Sawle was the murderer.

At her silence Peter put a hand on her shoulder. He was awkward in his movements, unused to expressing compassion by touch. 'The authorities were satisfied with the verdict. Two villagers from Trewenna said they saw both Sawle and Beaumont in the area on the same day. The murder has the smuggler's handiwork stamped all over it. Even Beaumont's widow did not question their findings. She has since wed another and her dead husband's body was barely settled in its grave.' His hand withdrew self-consciously and he cleared his voice before concluding, 'It was well known that the excise man had kept away from these parts, fearing Sawle would kill him. It was Sawle's cargo hidden without permission on Loveday land that was the reason Edward was shot. The contraband was confiscated and that would have cost Sawle a great deal of money. More than he could afford to lose. Something important must have dragged Beaumont from his lair to return here. Sawle was more than capable of baiting a trap for his enemy.'

He stepped back, and when Senara still did not trust herself to speak, said more kindly, 'You must put this incident from your mind. Sawle paid for his murdering ways on the scaffold. He must be laughing in hell that he could still cause us suffering by this deed long after his death.'

Chapter Sixteen

'This will be a disaster, I know it.' Gwendolyn blinked rapidly to halt the tears that threatened to fill her eyes. Her restless fingers pleated the folds of her sprigged muslin gown, the large sapphire ring that Japhet had bought her in London, to mark their triumphant return to England, catching the sunlight as they rode in the open-topped carriage. There was a raucous cawing from the rookery that sounded like a sentence of doom to her taut nerves. The redbrick Queen Anne house loomed threateningly close as the perfectly matched greys trotted along the drive to Traherne Hall. She bit her lip, and unable to contain her anguish said, 'We should at least have sent Mama word that we were in England. That we would visit this week.'

'I would not want the Lady Anne or Lady Traherne inconvenienced by arranging a welcome feast on my account,' Japhet could not resist mocking. He took his wife's slender fingers in his large tanned hand and squeezed them. Then he glanced up at the score of nests in the tall trees as the birds continued their incessant screeching, and grinned. 'Hark, they herald our arrival like a fanfare of trumpets greeting the return of a queen.'

'They sound more like a funeral dirge to me.' Gwendolyn looked down at her fingers, browned from the months she had spent in the sun in New South Wales and the long voyage home. Even a parasol or sitting in the shade had not prevented her skin from turning as brown as a peasant's in the heat. 'Mama will declare we have returned looking like vagabonds who spend their life traipsing the highways. She always declared that a lady of good breeding had the complexion of the palest English rose. She despaired of my copper hair and freckles, and I am covered with the wretched things that no amount of powder will hide.'

'I think you are beautiful and I would have you no other way.' He raised her hand to his lips. 'Your mother never saw your virtues, your strength of character or your loyalty. I owe my freedom to you, Gwen. More importantly, I owe you my happiness. No other woman has won my heart as you have, or could keep my undying devotion.'

She knew that at this moment his words were sincere. He adored women, and the fact that he had been faithful to her throughout their time in Australia was something she would always treasure. Back in England, she suspected that the fashionable beauties would one day be too great a temptation for him to resist.

She wanted to tease him in return, but she was so nervous at this reunion that her wit failed. She had never judged him. From her youth he had captured her heart with his careless charm and rakehell life. His former paramours had been great beauties and it had seemed no woman could resist him. She had never dreamed he would look upon her as more than a childhood friend and neighbour. He had always teased her and her infatuation had grown to an abiding love where no other man could match him. She knew his weaknesses, and though they would bring her pain, she would always forgive him.

The slow, lazy smile that showed his even white teeth and crinkled the corners of his hazel eyes still had the power to set her heart scudding. In London he had shorn to a fashionable crop the long black locks that she had adored running her fingers through. He had also shaved off his goatee beard. She missed it, as it had given him a commanding and prepossessing appearance. Clean-shaven, he looked younger. He had travelled the world and triumphed over the cruellest of adversity, but remained devastatingly handsome. Now he was dressed in the latest fashion, his broad shoulders restricted by the impeccable cut of his jacket and short waistcoat, his head held high by the intricately wound cravat around his neck. He would not look out of place amongst the Prince of Wales's set at court.

Seeing her worried frown, he grinned irrepressibly. 'The Lady Anne cannot fault your style. Your grace and beauty have a radiance unparalleled, and your sister will be choking on her envy at your wardrobe in the very latest mode. She will be a veritable dowd by comparison.'

'I care not a fig for fashion,' Gwendolyn groaned.

'But Lady Traherne does.'

Gwen was not convinced. 'We should have followed convention and sent Mama word to expect us. This is her "at home" afternoon. All her friends will be present.'

'All the better. The Lady Anne will be too proud in front of her friends to cause gossip by having me forcibly removed from her home, as she has threatened in the past.' He was unrepentant and his relaxed manner showed that he was enjoying this moment.

'You are incorrigible. Mama will be furious. What if she refuses to acknowledge us? It will be so mortifying to have her friends witness my shame. They will likely be our neighbours when we take up residence at Tor Farm.'

'You worry unnecessarily. Sir Henry would never allow you to be banished from the home he provided for you. And he has no reservations about our marriage. He has remained a loyal friend.'

'He will not stop Mama and Roslyn venting their venom. Mama will never forgive me for marrying you against her wishes.' Her hands clenched in outrage and frustration. Her mother would never acknowledge the good in Japhet or how happy her life was with him. She would have seen her married to any man of noble lineage and not cared that they had wedded her for her fortune. Gwen would have been miserable and would have come to despise her husband. None of that would have mattered to Lady Anne. She had not sought her daughter's happiness, only her submission to her will. Until Japhet had shown an interest in her, Gwendolyn had always been timid and quick to obey her mother, at whatever cost to her own pride and feelings. Japhet had shown her that she had a powerful personality of her own and a rare courage that would not bow to convention. And that was what her mother would never forgive.

'Will you stop doubting yourself?' Japhet read her mind. 'Have not your mother and sister been reconciled with the rest of the Loveday family? And more importantly, to the Lady Anne, do we not arrive in style?'

'Mama will not be impressed by our fine clothes. You know how she frowns upon trade. She will know that the wealth you acquired in New South Wales came from acting as agent for Adam and his investors in the new colony, and also from the sawmill and the property you built.'

The faintest sign of irritation creased the angular planes of Japhet's face. 'Then she will do well to remember that Sir Henry was one of those investors. They gambled that household goods, farm tools and livestock would sell at a vast profit to the new settlers in the penal settlement. Those profits saved him from financial constraints after the tin mines on his land failed.' He nodded towards the two large Italian marble statues of Roman warriors that now guarded the steps leading to the entrance of the house. 'Roslyn has been spending her husband's profit from such trade with her usual ostentatious taste.'

Gwendolyn was unimpressed by the statues, which must have taken a goodly portion of Sir Henry's profit from his first voyage.

At the time of Roslyn's marriage, Traherne Hall had not been so grand. Gwendolyn's sister had spent the greater part of her dowry refurnishing and renovating the house in the very latest mode. Yet in an age of restrained elegance, her taste became more ostentatious as the years progressed. Gwendolyn wondered if it did not make up for the lack of love within Roslyn's marriage and covered her injured pride at Sir Henry's roving eye. Roslyn, always a shrew, was jealous that Gwendolyn had married the man she passionately loved. That Japhet had reformed his libertine ways after their marriage and had remained faithful to his wife, Roslyn's envy could never forgive. And Gwendolyn knew that at one time before her sister's betrothal she had set her own cap at Japhet and he had paid no interest to her.

As the curricle drew to a halt at the foot of the entrance steps, Gwen fell silent. Japhet raised a dark brow, his expression sombre. 'I have been thinking to change the name of our estate. I thought the Loveday Stud. We will be breeding horses.'

A gush of laughter burst from Gwen, diverted from her worries at the meeting ahead. 'Mama will claim you named it after yourself and you have no shame.'

He grinned. 'But it has brought a smile back to your lovely face.'

'Oh, you are beyond redemption.' She playfully slapped his arm. She was still laughing when she alighted from the carriage.

Sir Henry's head groom came forward to take the horses of so seemingly important a guest. He bowed briefly to the occupants, but his gaze was engrossed in appraising the matched greys and he did not at first recognise the passengers.

'What do you think of them? Quite something, are they not?' Japhet said with a laugh.

The older man's head shot up. 'Good Lord, Mr Japhet! And Miss Gwendolyn! Begging your pardon, I mean Mrs Loveday.' His shock was all too clear at their unexpected return.

Japhet took no offence. 'You will not fault those thoroughbreds. I doubt even the Prince of Wales himself has their equal.'

'You always had an eye for horseflesh, sir. They be beauties. I'll take the very best of care of them, don't you fear, sir.'

Gwendolyn said under her breath, 'It will take more than the finest matched pair in England to soften Mama's condemnation.'

Japhet lifted his two sons, Japhet Edward and Druce, from the vehicle and regarded them sternly. 'Take extra care to be on your best behaviour. Our arrival will be a shock to your grandmama and aunt. And they do not approve of boys who do not know their place.'

Gwendolyn rubbed her finger across Druce's cheek to remove a smudge of dirt and straightened the lace collar of Japhet Edward's jacket. Both boys were in cut-away coats and breeches made for them in London, but Japhet Edward fidgeted with his jacket, which was riding too high on his waist. Gwendolyn swore he had grown since it was made for him.

'Remember everything I have taught you about good manners,' she warned. 'And do not forget to address your grandmama and aunt as your ladyship, or my lady.'

They nodded solemnly and Gwendolyn's heart swelled with pride. As they prepared to enter the house, she silently prayed that the boys would remember not to run, or talk too loudly. They had been so boisterous running free at the homestead in New South Wales and still had an excess of energy from so many months cooped up on the ship to England.

Japhet said in an undertone to the groom, 'If Sir Henry is at home, it might be as well to inform him that we are here. He usually makes himself scarce when his wife receives her friends.'

'I shall send a boy to inform him of your visit, Mr Loveday.'

'Usually Sir Henry likes to take his *Gentleman's Magazine* to read quietly in his study at this time of day and will not be away from the house.' Japhet expressed his fervent hope to Gwendolyn. Despite his show of calm, he was nervous. The Lady Anne had made her dislike for him plain on several occasions.

They walked through the grand vestibule, greeted by further statues in Roman armour. Japhet whistled softly, and observed, 'From whom is Roslyn defending her home? An invasion by Henry's mistresses?'

Gwendolyn nudged him in the ribs at his irreverent humour. 'More likely it is from recalcitrant relatives who would defy their ladyships' sense of decency.'

'Very true. Perhaps we should have discarded our finery and dressed in sackcloth and ashes to ask their humble forgiveness. There could be fireworks from the grand saloon when we appear.'

Gwendolyn was glad of her husband's arm to lean upon; her legs were becoming increasingly unsteady. Her nervousness increased as a maid, Mary, who had served her family for a dozen years squealed with delight upon recognising her and bent her knee in a curtsey low enough to honour a princess.

'Welcome home, Miss Gwendolyn. And Mr Loveday.' Her eyes gleamed with tears as she straightened and turned to hurry up the stairs to announce them.

'Please do not announce me to her ladyship, Mary. I would rather surprise her. I presume at this time of day that Lady Anne and Lady Traherne are in the grand saloon.'

'Yes, Miss Gwendolyn.' Mary's joy turned to uncertainty and she wrung her hands together in a moment of doubt. 'They are taking afternoon tea with visitors.'

'Who are her guests?' Gwendolyn asked.

'The Dowager Lady Fetherington, Lady Fetherington and the Honourable Mrs Bracewaite.'

'Not too daunting a trio,' she whispered to Japhet. Then confidently to Mary, 'I will tell her ladyship that I insisted we arrive unannounced. You will not be blamed for failing in your duty.'

★

The day was hot and the windows of the grand saloon of Traherne Hall were opened to catch the light breeze. Sunlight sparkled off the large crystal and gilded chandelier in the centre of the ceiling. At the unexpected appearance of the family, who halted inside the door, the drone of conversation in the room ceased as though cut through with a sabre. In the recesses of the marble fireplace carved with fat cherubs, the tall Venetian mirrors reflected the tableau of five women's faces frozen in shock, their teacups raised halfway to their lips.

Japhet bowed to them. 'Your obedient servant, ladies.'

Gwendolyn curtseyed and tugged on her sons' hands to remind them to bow.

'Well I never! Japhet Loveday.' The Dowager Lady Fetherington was the first to speak. A stalwart woman of venerable years, she had always liked Japhet and had been particularly pleased when she learned that on his marriage he had purchased the estate that bordered her own land. Her late husband had kept a prime pack of hunting dogs and had encouraged Japhet in his decision to breed racehorses. 'You look to have fared very well from your travels, Mr Loveday.'

Japhet bowed to her. 'I was sorry to learn of the death of your husband, my lady. No hunt will be the same without him.'

She nodded graciously.

Alice Bracewaite, who had married Sir Henry and St John's friend the Honourable Basil Bracewaite after Japhet's transportation, closed her gaping mouth with a snap and whispered to Marcia Fetherington seated beside her, 'Is that not the one sent to Botany Bay for highway robbery?'

Gwendolyn saw her mother and sister stiffen at the words and braced herself for their retort. She held her breath, praying that they would not actually summon the servants to have them escorted from their presence. It was a mortifying possibility. Neither the Lady Anne nor Roslyn had spared her blushes in the past when they had castigated her for some foolishness or disobedience. They saw her marriage not only as defiance, but as the ultimate betrayal of their family.

Japhet parried the remark, which had no power to embarrass

him. His concern was for his wife, who he knew was desperate for this meeting to go well. 'So fate did brand me, my innocence cast to the winds, dear lady.' His stare was sharp and unrepentant, causing the young woman to blush. He added with a twinkle in his hazel eyes, and the slow smile that had the power to set most women's pulses racing, 'But with respect, I would remind all present that the scales of justice were turned by the steadfast devotion of my beloved wife, and I received a royal pardon.'

The young Lady Fetherington fluttered her eyelashes, unashamedly intrigued and captivated. 'How extremely romantic.'

'Bringing shame and disgrace to our family is far from romantic.' Roslyn's shrewish tongue had not mellowed in their exile. There was no welcome in her chilling glare.

Japhet turned his attention upon Lady Anne Druce. She was glaring at them, clearly furious that they had forced themselves upon her without warning. Hatred blazed in her eyes before she masked it from her friends. Japhet seized the opportunity to make their reconciliation. His mother-in-law might revile him in private, but her pride would not allow her to be the butt of gossip amongst her friends. For his wife's sake he was prepared to show humility and deference. His bow to her was of the deepest reverence. 'I paid the price for the reckless ways of my youth. I humbly ask your pardon for any pain or distress my conduct may have caused this family. Any recrimination you may wish to utter can be no worse than the condemnation I have heaped upon myself for the shame I have brought upon my wife. Gwendolyn is the most noble-minded and honourable of women; my love for her is inestimable. Without her I would be nothing – not for her wealth do I say this, but in honesty as to my character and happiness. My wife has shown me the true meaning of honour, loyalty, integrity and courage. She is my redeemer and my salvation.'

Marcia Fetherington gave a little gasp and looked quite overcome with emotion.

'Prettily spoken, but you always did have a silver tongue,' Roslyn spat.

The Lady Anne put down her teacup, and placed a restraining hand on her elder daughter's wrist. She studied the couple, appearing to weigh her words carefully.

Alice Bracewaite broke into the uncomfortable silence, stammering with embarrassment at her earlier indiscretion. 'How very dashing and noble of you, Mr Loveday.'

Lady Anne sucked in her breath, but her answering tirade was halted when Gwendolyn stepped forward holding the hands of her sons.

'Will you not greet your grandsons, Mama? Flesh of your flesh as well as Papa's. He would never have turned against me for being steadfast to the man I chose above all others to be the one to whom I bequeathed my heart.'

They stood in the light of the window, the sunlight playing over their figures. The folds of Gwendolyn's gown quivered at the intensity of emotion that passed through her in waves. The boys regarded their grandmother with puzzlement that she had not scooped them into her arms with tears of joy as Grandmother Loveday had done.

Lady Anne stared at the younger of the two, her eyes widening with recognition and pain.

Gwendolyn pronounced, 'Mama, is not Druce the image of Papa?'

'How clever of you to name him Druce,' the Dowager Lady Fetherington said with a wry smile. 'No one could ever doubt the young man's heritage. You have two charming sons, Gwendolyn. My dear departed Fetherington always believed in your innocence, Japhet. Will you breed horses as you planned and live at Tor Farm?'

'It was always our intent. How could I fail Hannah after the care she has taken of my mares?'

'Elspeth speaks much of their pedigree,' said the older woman. 'She has a good eye for horseflesh.'

Her ladyship's approval was enough to allow Lady Anne to save face. 'I am quite overcome at your arrival, daughter. You know how I dislike surprises. I suppose you have become used to more barbaric ways in recent years.'

'To be present at the birth of a nation was an experience I would not have missed for the world,' Gwendolyn returned.

A hearty bellow resounded behind them as Sir Henry strode into the room. 'You have seen sights I could not even begin to imagine. I look forward to hearing of your travels.' He kissed Gwendolyn unceremoniously on the cheek and took Japhet's hand and pumped it enthusiastically. 'Welcome home. You'll be staying here, of course.'

'Mama expects us to stay at the rectory,' Japhet explained. 'And Adam in his last letter spoke of us staying at Boscabel when we returned.'

'Nonsense, there is more room here. I am sure Lady Anne and Roslyn would not have it any other way.'

Lady Anne looked as though she had swallowed a plum stone and Roslyn as though she had trodden barefoot in pigswill. Lady Anne recovered first. 'Sir Henry is most generous. I have been parted from my daughter for too long.'

The Dowager Lady Fetherington rose. 'Delightful as it is to welcome you back to England, you will wish to be alone with your family. Percy will be expecting you to visit before too long, Japhet.'

The other women also took their leave. Roslyn remained tight-lipped and condemning in her silence.

'This surprise has rendered my wife speechless. A rare occurrence,' Sir Henry jested tartly. 'There is no question but that you must live here for the time being. It has been some time since Traherne Hall played host to our neighbours on any grand scale. A welcoming feast would be most appropriate to celebrate your return.'

'And what if our neighbours shun us?' Roslyn was aghast. 'Not everyone is as forgiving as you, Henry. Pardoned or not, Japhet *was* convicted of a serous felony. One that is the scourge of our highways, making the roads dangerous to travel.'

'Then we will find out who our true friends are, will we not?' Henry stressed with such force that Gwendolyn felt Druce flinch as she stood with her hands on his shoulders. 'And we will show our solidarity as a family.'

'Do I have no say in my own home?' Roslyn retaliated.

'This is not a subject to be discussed in front of the children, sister.' Gwendolyn faced her with a resilience she would never have shown in the past. 'And I thank Sir Henry for his generous offer, but we will stay at Boscabel where we will not face constant judgement. The Lovedays know the meaning of family loyalty.'

'What does Japhet think?' Sir Henry turned to his friend.

'More than anything I would like to see my wife reconciled with her family, but I will not be the cause of dissension in your home, my friend.'

'There will be no dissension.' Sir Henry was adamant. 'You are my business partner as well as my brother-in-law. I will stand by you, and to hell with the neighbours if they choose to act otherwise. And we must think of your sons. My boys are just home from school and will enjoy getting to know their only cousins. Also the three girls are upstairs. I shall send for them.'

'They can meet later,' Japhet replied. 'This was intended as a brief visit, so that you did not hear of our return from a third party. Sir Henry, I appreciate your offer for us to stay here and accept providing that their ladyships have no objection.'

When neither woman commented, he bowed to them, saying, 'You are most gracious. We will come at the end of the week. I think Mama would be heartbroken if we did not spend a few nights at the rectory.' He held their stares, his voice contrite. 'For myself I do not expect or ask for your approval, but I hope that in future you will realise I have only the happiness of my wife and children at heart.'

'Roslyn!' Sir Henry prompted.

Her thin lips twisted into a bitter smile. 'It is our Christian duty to forgive you, if you truly repent of your sins. I hope Sir Henry will not regret his generosity.'

'And one day, sister, I hope you will eat those words,' Gwendolyn replied, showing where her first loyalty would always lie.

'Then the matter is settled.' Sir Henry rubbed his hands in approval.

Gwendolyn smiled at him with genuine affection. 'Thank you, Sir Henry.'

'You will not regret your kindness, my friend,' Japhet added, and bowed again to the ladies. 'I am your humble and obedient servant.'

'Let us hope so,' said Lady Anne. 'The past is behind us. If I judge you at all, it will be upon your conduct in the future.'

Chapter Seventeen

In his search for Tristan, Adam went first to London and the address given to him by Max. He had decided against staying with Thomas, as it would have meant revealing the real reasons for his distrust of their cousin. His own guilty conscience made him loath to disclose more than was absolutely necessary.

Tristan's lodgings were next door to a respectable chophouse in Holborn. The landlord, a burly man with vast side-whiskers, became instantly antagonistic at the mention of his tenant's name. He barred the doorway to the lodging house, his arms folded across his barrel chest, whilst he regarded Adam shrewdly, assessing his character.

'What did you say your name was?' he demanded.

'I did not. I just want to know where I can find Tristan Loveday.'

'Then I've got nothing to tell you.'

Adam considered for a moment before stating, 'We were at school together in Cornwall. I met a cousin of his and promised to look him up.'

'Then you've made a long journey for nothing. He's not been here for some weeks and I don't know when to expect him back.'

'But he still resides here?' Adam queried.

'He's paid his rent until the next quarter-day.'

He made to close the door in Adam's face, but Adam put out a hand to stop him, asking, 'Perhaps I could speak to some of your other lodgers? They may know where I can find him.'

The landlord squinted sourly and prepared to close the door again when two foppish gentlemen in their middle twenties appeared in the hall.

'I heard you mention Tris. Friend of his, are you?' said the shorter of the two, who had heavily ringed fingers.

'We were at school together,' Adam repeated. 'Have you any idea where else I may find him, if he is still in London?'

'The usual clubs, old boy.' His companion sprinkled some snuff on the back of his hand and sniffed it. 'White's. Brown's. Drury Lane and the Haymarket are favoured theatres. The cockpit is another haunt. The Royal Exchange another.'

'Doubt he'll be in London for a week or so,' the first man added. 'He was off to visit relatives in the country. Dorset, I believe he said. A big country house. I regret I cannot be of more help.'

'Thank you for your time, gentlemen.'

'You could always call on the actress, Polly Parsons. He is a regular caller upon her.' The shorter man winked knowingly. Then he slapped his hand to his brow and groaned. 'I've forgotten my purse. Left it in my room.' He hurried back inside, followed by the lumbering landlord.

As Adam turned to walk down the steps to the street, the second man held out his card. 'If you find Loveday, I'd appreciate you letting me know where he is.'

'Does he owe you money?'

'I could not as a gentleman possibly say.'

Adam drew his own conclusions and expected more of the kind as he made further enquiries about his cousin at the establishments the two men had suggested. To his surprise he discovered a different side of Tristan's nature. He seemed well liked, and several people asked warmly after him, some extending invitations for him to join them at their estates or in Bath during the Season. That Tristan could be both charming and ruthless confirmed Adam in his belief that his cousin was a confidence trickster.

Following a night at the cockpit, only one man corroborated Adam's suspicions of his cousin's true character. The gentleman was in his cups and indiscreet. 'Tristan Loveday has the devil's own luck at cards and I would not want to be a man late in paying a lost wager.'

'Why is that?' Adam had a feeling he would not like what he heard.

The intoxicated gentleman put a finger to his nose. 'Just a word

159

of caution, dear boy. There's been an unpleasant accident or two when a debt is not settled promptly.'

His grandfather's words from the past, when Tristan had run away from the consequences of his misdeeds, rang clear in Adam's mind: 'You can take the boy out of the gutter but you can't take the gutter out of the boy.' Clearly Tristan had reverted to type.

He had wasted enough time trying to find his cousin. He was needed at Boscabel for the harvest and the handover of the *Good Fortune*. If Tristan did not want to be found, there were too many places where he could hide. Adam hoped that the violence of his and St John's condemnation had warned their cousin away from having any further dealings with his family, especially Tamasine, who was made vulnerable by her own need to be accepted by her relatives.

Even so, when Adam returned to Cornwall he remained uneasy. Had he not been so engrossed with his own worries he would have observed that Senara looked pale and edgy, and that when he called at Trevowan there was a strained atmosphere, even though the family was ecstatic at Japhet's return. St John had stayed only one night in his home after the arrival of Aunt Margaret and Georganna, declaring that he had business in Bodmin. Felicity had taken his departure badly and, complaining that she was exhausted by all the upsets, had taken to her bed. Amelia, Elspeth and Margaret clucked and fussed like hens around each other whilst Georganna spent hours walking along the cliffs and beaches.

Adam was annoyed that Tristan was the cause of his not being at his home when Japhet and Gwendolyn had arrived. When he called at the rectory the next morning there was only a maid to greet him.

'Mr Japhet Loveday is not at home,' she informed him. 'Mrs Cecily Loveday be with Mrs Gwendolyn Loveday and they have taken the boys to visit their cousins at Traherne Hall. The reverend be in the vestry.'

The usual musty smell of the old church was sweetened by swathes of honeysuckle draped around the pulpit and windowsills. At the sound of Adam's step on the flagstones, Joshua rose from where he had been kneeling at the altar. His movement was stiff, the cold having seeped into his joints, but there was a proud tilt to his head that had not been present for many moons. He grinned broadly at his nephew.

'Every day since Japhet's arrest I have prayed for him,' Joshua said. 'Now I give thanks for his safe return to us all. I'm afraid you've missed them.'

'The maid said Gwendolyn and Aunt Cecily were visiting the Hall. I hope that means Lady Anne is reconciled with her daughter.'

'I would not quite go that far, but they are building bridges. The children help. Druce is the image of his grandfather. For that the Lady Anne can forgive Gwendolyn much.'

'And Japhet? The maid did not say that he had accompanied them.'

Joshua gave a wry laugh. 'He knows when to keep his head low. Gwendolyn's mother and sister are being chillingly polite. He is at the farm putting the horses through their paces. He is delighted that Hannah has cared for them so well, and the quality of the foals has exceeded his expectations.'

'Then I shall visit him there.'

Joshua nodded. 'Japhet was disappointed you were not here when he returned. But then it has been overwhelming for them both. They were kept apprised of most family events through our letters, but he did not know that Hannah had remarried. I sent word to her and a reply came yesterday that she will arrive for a short visit next week. She is overjoyed at the news of her brother's return. Unfortunately, Sam and Charlie will not be able to accompany her. The terms of the late Lord Eastley's will are unnatural and virtually make the boy a prisoner on the estate.'

They walked out into the church porch. A blackbird perched on a gravestone as it proclaimed its territory. Joshua paused in his stride, his expression now serious.

'Senara told me that your cousin Tristan was at Beaucombe and that Tamasine was much taken with him. She also said that your meeting with him did not go well.'

'How could it when he betrayed our family in so dastardly a manner?'

'It was a long time ago, Adam. He could have changed. He was but a lad and he had had a difficult childhood. Perhaps he thought he only stole what was rightfully his father's.'

'He did more than steal.' Adam felt his rage building. 'He showed himself unworthy to bear our name. And what trickery did he use to gain Tamasine's trust? He could so easily have destroyed her reputation.'

'It is not like you to judge so harshly.' Joshua studied him with a frown. 'When Tristan was at Trevowan he was young and scarred from his earlier experiences. My father was strict and showed the boy little attention. Perhaps Tristan felt he was never fully accepted by the family.'

'He had not a shred of common decency. That was why he did not fit in.' Adam clenched his fist to control his anger. Then, unable to bear his uncle's scrutiny, he turned away, wiping a hand across the back of his neck.

'What did he do that was more terrible than stealing from your grandfather?' Joshua demanded. 'You and St John were with him that night of the storm.'

Adam backed away as though his uncle had struck him. 'He is no kin of mine. I will not have him destroying my sister's happiness.'

He left without further explanation and rode his horse at a furious pace to Hannah's farm. The wind whipping through his hair, and the power of the gelding's muscles beneath his thighs channelled some of the frustration that had been with him since his reunion with Tristan. He prayed that his cousin's disappearance meant he would stay away from his family for good. Yet a nagging sense of unease, which refused to be quashed, warned him that life was never that simple. Tristan had always felt that the Lovedays owed him something for the poverty his mother had suffered. A few stolen trinkets would not appease that obsession. Especially after the judgement George Loveday had passed on him.

Obsession was a family trait that could be either good or evil. Four generations ago it had driven Arthur St John Loveday to put aside his buccaneering ways and ally himself to one of the oldest wealthy families in Cornwall by marrying the heir to Trevowan, Anne Penhaligan. He had started the shipyard as a means to continue his passion for the sea. His son George had furthered the family fortune by using his skill as a shipwright, learned by spending every moment he could steal in the yard, to raise the reputation and esteem of the business. Edward Loveday had had an even greater vision to expand the yard and build larger ships that would be the best in their class. The yard had also been Adam's obsession. His years in the navy had given him an understanding of the large sailing ships that crossed the oceans. Each ship he designed had proved itself in speed and manoeuvrability, and had it not been for the war with France, which made merchant adventurers and investors nervous of losing ships and cargo to the enemy, the yard would have been one of the most illustrious in the south of England. Adam's pride would not allow him to fail after all his forefathers had achieved.

It was a more sinister need that held St John in its grip. Insidious and addictive, it would lure him towards perdition with tantalising moments of good fortune when it seemed the world and all its riches was within his grasp. The turn of a card or the throw of a dice was a compulsion that had become as necessary to him as breathing. It was excitement he craved and which had been denied in his home life. Although he refused to see gaming as anything other than a pleasant pastime, its grip was tenacious as a hawk's talons fastened upon its prey, and just as lethal. For a month the gaming tables had been good to him and he felt invincible, and it made him dangerously reckless.

He was playing hazard tonight at a gaming house in Bodmin. Percy Fetherington and Basil Bracewaite had both dropped out of the game an hour ago and gone home to their beds.

'Your luck has changed,' his lordship had advised St John before he left. 'There is always another evening.'

'But the night is still young,' St John protested, his body tingling with the thrill of the game. His friends had grown more staid since their marriages and St John found their maturity boring. He sought the company of younger bloods to keep him entertained and became oblivious of the passage of time. The ring of gamblers around the table cheered and hooted at each roll of the dice. Up until an hour ago his luck had not failed and a thousand guineas had been piled in front of him. His every throw had been cheered and he had been flushed with the power of his success. Now he was down to his last few guineas. St John was sweating, his mouth sucked dry of moisture, a quiver of excitement deep in his gut. The dice felt warm and alive in his hand. He could almost hear them telling him they would fall in his favour.

'Talk to those bones and throw those sixes,' one of the gamblers demanded. 'You've done it before. You'll do it again.'

'Or hand them to another if you have lost your nerve,' someone else jeered. He was a stranger to St John, with a thick Spanish accent and something of the look of a brigand about his swarthy face, despite his fine clothes. St John did not trust foreigners, and he felt the need to show this one that an Englishman was superior to any Johnny foreigner. The dark eyes across the room glittered, malicious in their taunting. 'Have you lost your touch? Show us, proud Englishman, your faith. I wager you a hundred guineas that your skill earlier was pure chance.'

St John could not meet the wager with the money in front of him, but this was a matter of pride. The dice were pulsing in his hand.

'Come on, Loveday, show us your mettle,' a young fop urged. 'Here's a hundred guineas says you can do it.'

The thud of St John's heart increased in tempo, sending the blood rushing to his ears. So much was at stake; he could not lose. Not now. Lady Luck would not abandon him. The dice were old friends, warm and coercing in his palm. He could not turn his back on them. He had never felt so good or so alive. To win now would prove that he could outshine even the most hardened gamesters. It would prove to those who had ridiculed him in the past for his wastrel ways that they were wrong.

'Looks like you're out of funds, my friend,' sneered the foreign voice across the table.

The air was thick with a blue haze of tobacco that partially obscured the ring of spectators that had gathered around their table as word spread of the size of the pot to be won. A central oil lamp burned above their heads, the whale oil adding to the smell of closely packed sweating male bodies and the cheap perfume of their accompanying whores. It added to St John's feeling of light-headedness, his sense of conquest. Yet his elation was tinged with fear. He had no further money to match the last wager. Then, with a sense of triumph, he remembered.

'I have a stake,' he declared exultantly, pushing his hand down into the pocket of his waistcoat. His fingers closed over the warm metal of a ring and he drew it forth. A ruby the size of a man's knuckle threw out sparks of red fire in the light of the lamp. It was a showy piece and little to St John's liking. It was the last of his cache from the coach accident. He had brought it to Bodmin to sell to fund his gambling, but so far he had not needed the extra money. There was a loud gasp from the spectators as he tossed it amongst the coins. 'That more than covers your last wager.'

The foreigner picked up the ring and examined it briefly. His eyes narrowed as he tossed it back on to the table. 'A pretty enough bauble.'

St John shook the dice in his hand and released them. They rolled to a halt, displaying two sixes. A cheer filled the room as he collected his winnings.

St John continued to play, but within another three throws he had lost everything, including the ring, to the foreign man, as well as an IOU for another hundred guineas wagered on the last throw. Only two other gamblers remained at the table when he decided to call it a night and set off in a drunken haze back to his inn. He had only the vaguest idea how much he had lost or how many IOUs he had written, but it could not be far short of a thousand guineas. The brandy he had drunk remained sour in his belly, echoing his mood, and he had the beginnings of a headache, which he suspected would turn into an unholy hangover. Nothing was going right for him this night.

As though the gods had heard and continued to mock him, he became aware of two men blocking the street ahead of him. Before he could evade them they closed in and a pistol barrel was pressed against the side of his head.

A rough voice cackled in his ear, 'I'd not put up a fight. Not if you want to live. Nor lie. Now tell me where you got that ring you just gambled so carelessly away.'

St John froze, terrified that they meant to kill him. Then the words penetrated his fear. The information they wanted was more important to them than his life. Clearly they had recognised the ring, but was it the boy they were hunting, or the lost treasure? And what would they do if they believed he had stolen the casket of money and jewellery that night? They would not be thanking him, that much was certain. The least they would do was to denounce him as a thief, and he could be hanged or transported as Japhet had been. First he would be thrown in gaol, and his past experience of that filled him with dread. He suspected though that their motives were more sinister. His life would mean nothing to them. They must never know the truth.

His mind fastened upon and discarded half a dozen excuses in as many seconds, until his instinct for survival kicked in and he affected a drunken slur. 'Garish little trinket, that ring. Did not much care for it myself. Won it at hazard whilst in Dorset ten days ago. Niece of mine was christened and half the lesser nobility in those parts were present plus some who had come down from London.'

'What part of Dorset?' his attacker demanded, spraying him with spittle and the stench of rotting teeth.

'About twenty miles from Dorchester.'

'The place bain't of consequence,' snarled the inquisitor's accomplice. 'Whom did you win it from?'

'I cannot rightly recall. We had been gaming most of the night like tonight. There were a dozen of us. But I think it was a chap from Bristol. Yes, that was the one. The son of a merchant.' He frowned and hiccoughed. 'Not quite top drawer, if you get my meaning. Lost all but the shirt on his back if I recall.'

'His name, damn you!'

St John felt his guts turning to liquid and willed himself to continue his ruse. 'I really cannot recall it.'

'I would try very hard if you want to live.' The pistol barrel was drawn in a line from his temple to his mouth and clanked against his teeth as it was forced inside.

St John's eyes bulged with fear. 'Carstairs or Carfax, I think. Rum sort of cove,' he mumbled against the metal, and then he gagged and vomit gushed from his throat.

With a curse his attacker jerked back and St John toppled to the ground.

'He bain't no use,' growled the accomplice, who was swathed in a greatcoat and muffler. 'They said they'd likely head for a port. We've been looking in the wrong place.'

Before St John could register that he had been reprieved, pain exploded at the back of his head as the pistol was smashed against his skull, and he passed into oblivion.

166

Chapter Eighteen

Senara needed to banish Beaumont's death from her thoughts and immersed herself in her work. In the spring she had begun to lay out a herb garden behind the stables at Boscabel. The plants grown there would save her hours of searching the woodland, fields and moor for the healing leaves, seeds and roots she needed to help the sick. She had gathered seeds or uprooted specimens of all the local varieties, and whilst at Beaucombe had found some other new species to expand her collection. These she had dug up and transplanted into a wooden box to bring home with her. Fortunately they had survived the journey, and she placed them under a glass frame to propagate more seeds to be planted later in the year. None of the servants were allowed to tend her herb garden, and it brought her great satisfaction to feel the soil beneath her hands, which gave her a connectedness to nature and the earth. Yet today, when she needed to still the turmoil in her mind, the garden brought her no peace.

Instead, the need to visit the waterfall became all-powerful, and eventually she put aside her work and returned to the kitchen. There she placed some fruit, grain and a stoppered pitcher of mead into a wicker basket. She added to these three perfect white lilies, and paused at the chicken coop before walking to the river with a determined tread.

At her special place she laid out the flowers, fruit and grain on the granite slab by the water, then, chanting a brief invocation, she raised the pitcher above her head before pouring the mead on to the ground. These gifts she offered to the ancient goddess of the earth and to the nature spirits who were her acolytes. She sat back and closed her eyes in silent prayer, asking for forgiveness and a way to make amends for contravening the sacred law forbidding the wishing of harm upon another. Her grandmother had always warned her never to call upon the old gods in the heat of rage, or for vengeance. Intense emotion increased the potency of their power, and when they had done your bidding a sacrifice must be paid in blood. That cost could be greater than you were prepared to make.

No matter that Sir Henry and Peter were convinced that Sawle had murdered the excise officer and hidden the body on Loveday land to cause further trouble for the family. Senara could not shake off her guilt that she had also been party to his death. Had she not uttered the most powerful of ancient curses – called upon the old gods to strike him down? The snake was a potent symbol of the old ways and ancient wisdom. It was considered divine as it lived within the earth and the healing elements of nature. It had the power of life and death. Had the vipers been summoned from the underworld by her invocation, or had Beaumont stumbled upon their nest by accident? Even if the ancient ones had not killed Beaumont on her command, she believed they had in some way weakened him, enabling Sawle to bring an end to his life.

She now had to appease the old gods and pray that her sacrifice would satisfy their blood lust. She prayed also that Harry Sawle's death would be another atonement and that further bloodshed would be spared. That Beaumont and Sawle had been dead for so long boded well. Even so, she would make the necessary offering. Drawing her dagger from the belt at her waist, she stared at the chicken on the grass in front of the stone. The bird, held by its legs, had been frozen into stillness. Now, as though sensing its end was near, it lifted its head and squawked. The sound was cut short by the dagger plunging into its breast, and blood from its severed artery pumped over Senara's hands and the ground.

The ritual left her unnerved. It was many years, long before she had met Adam, since she had performed such a rite. When she stared at the blood seeping into the earth she was ashamed of her actions. These ways were no longer her ways. She had paid her homage and her dues, but she knew that she would never again revert to the religion of her childhood. It was part of her old life, and when she had married Adam, that life should have been put firmly behind her.

However, a personal sacrifice was also needed to ensure that the blood curse she had called upon Beaumont brought no further harm to her family. Again she raised her arms to the sky and throwing back her head proclaimed, 'This day I renounce the old ways and will honour the faith of my husband's family and attend their services every Sunday. My knowledge as a wise woman will be used only to ease the suffering of those who are ill, and to that end I dedicate my skill to save lives. This is my solemn oath. So mote it be.'

She then removed her shoes and stockings and walked barefoot to Trewenna. Joshua was sitting on a bench by the village pond enjoying a quiet moment smoking his clay pipe. He was horrified to see her carrying her shoes and the bloodied state of her feet.

'I have walked here barefoot as an act of penance,' she said before he could question her. 'Will you baptise me?'

Joshua Loveday was not a man easily shocked, but this request from his nephew's wife momentarily made his jaw drop. 'You have never been baptised! What of Bridie? She is wed to a clergyman! If she has not been baptised he could be unfrocked for marrying a heathen. And they were wed in church, as were you and Adam.' He clutched the cross resting on his chest and for a moment she thought he would raise it to ward off evil. Instead he shook his head sadly. 'Adam has condoned you risking your soul and living outside the protection of the Church.'

'I am to blame, not my husband. He thought I had put the old ways behind me. I should have come to you before this.' She clasped her hands together, her eyes beseeching him to believe her. 'And do not concern yourself with my half-sister. Bridie's upbringing was very different from mine. Because she was born so frail, Mama insisted she was immediately baptised.'

Joshua could not hide his shock, and in supplication Senara lifted his cross and touched it to her lips. 'I repent of my sins. I will do whatever penance you see fit to show I am truly repentant and have renounced the old ways. Will you baptise me? And can it be done now without anyone but the two of us being present? I would not have gossip spread that Adam has been married to a heathen all these years.'

'It is most irregular,' he began, but at seeing the anguish in her eyes he nodded assent. 'Come into the church now, my child. Our Lord will rejoice in this day. But what has brought about your change of faith?'

She bowed her head, knowing that to reveal her secret and accept his condemnation was part of her penance. They knelt together at the altar and Senara confessed her sins.

'These are grave and ungodly revelations indeed, my child. Ones for which you could be prosecuted under the witchcraft laws.'

'But I am no witch,' she emphasised with passion.

'Do you swear you did not serve the devil in your ignorance or craze for vengeance?'

'In the past I called only upon the Mother Goddess to bless my work when healing. I am no devil-worshipper, nor ever have been. Herne, the horned one, is a god of nature, not a devil. And did not the ancient Greeks depict their male gods with horns to show their divinity? Because a deity is pagan, it does not make it evil.'

'Our Lord came to show us that the old religions were misguided and to teach us a more benevolent way.'

Senara bit her lip and bowed her head. She still had respect for the old teachings, but with her decision made, she would not break with her new chosen faith.

The interrogation continued for some time until Joshua was satisfied that Senara had truly recanted. Then he opened the phial of holy water that he had brought from the vestry earlier and blessed her as he poured the water over her head. Finally he raised her to her feet. 'This will remain between us. Trust in the Lord and you will be redeemed of your sins. I am sure that Beaumont died at the hand of Sawle. All life is in God's hands, and whether the vipers' attack weakened the officer or not, they are all God's creatures. Our Lord works in mysterious ways that man cannot always understand.'

Senara was not the only Loveday to have undergone an epiphany. When St John regained consciousness in the yard of the inn, his clothing and hair were drenched from a downpour. The chill of the rain soaking his flesh had recovered his wits, and he found his teeth chattering and his body shaking. As he struggled to his feet, every bone and muscle felt that stampeding horses had trampled them. For a moment he needed to cling to the rough brickwork of the inn and shake his head to clear the last of the fuzziness from his brain. It was not the cold that had set his body reacting so violently; it was fear of the discovery of his deceit and theft on the night he had found Bryn and the coach. Instantly he was chillingly sober. The demons that possessed his blood had again taken hold this night. He was appalled that he had risked his livelihood and reputation on the turn of a card.

His family had forgiven him many misdemeanours in the past, but they would never condone that he had put Trevowan at risk. Though even that paled into insignificance beside his callous actions on the night of the accident. That no one had come forward to claim Bryn as kin had given him a false sense of security. The ring and the bracelet he had taken from the dead woman were not the only valuables he had appropriated that night. The small chest he had tripped over had been filled with gold coins and more jewels. It had taken all his strength to carry it away from the broken coach and hide it under a pile of boulders. It had remained undiscovered by the thieves who came later and stripped the vehicle of all its valuables.

At the time he had excused his own conduct by blaming his inebriated state for being too drunk to reason clearly, and he had seen the money as a godsend after losing so much gaming. When Adam's servants had returned from the scene of the accident and declared that everything had been stolen, he had kept silent about the hoard. He was ashamed of his actions and too cowardly to admit what he had done in case his family saw through his excuses. In the following weeks there had been moments when his conscience had troubled him, but his increasing dependency on drink soon clouded his integrity. His growing discontent over his marriage, and the shackles of responsibility of living with a house full of women, were further burdens he resented. Gambling and drink brought a temporary ease to his dissatisfaction. Always weak in the face of temptation, he had been blinded to the hold gambling had taken upon him. Even now he refused to acknowledge that it had become as relentless as a fever, and just as lethal.

The rain and the beating had sobered him to a devastating awareness of how low he had sunk. His stolen cache had been lost in his excess of gambling. Even when he had won a large pot he had not known when to stop. Winning made him feel invincible: a man of prowess and distinction. He had lost count of the times he had staggered from a gaming table with his purse empty and sought oblivion in more brandy. Before he had even gone to Beaucombe he had lost all the money in the chest. He had left his sister's home having signed IOUs amounting to several hundred pounds. And he had no idea how he could honour them when the holders presented them in the near future.

How could he have been so foolish as to gamble so heavily? And since then, in desperation to recoup his losses, he had fallen deeper into debt. He had raised money from several loans from money-lenders. None of them was for more than a few hundred pounds and each he was convinced could be paid back from his next winnings. Last night he had lost the last of the loan money and the ring, which he was convinced would restore his fortune. How cruelly fate had mocked him. He was no longer certain how many debts had been raised against Trevowan. Though he doubted that even a bumper harvest would settle all of them. The only chance he had to recoup his fortune was to win a pot like the one that had been on the table last night.

He still had the bracelet. But what if that was recognised, as the ring had been? Again he shuddered. The fear of the theft being discovered returned to haunt him. He had given Bryn little thought in the last weeks, or that he could have robbed the boy of the only means he would have to make his way in the world. Had his attackers been employed by the boy's family? But they seemed more interested in the lost valuables than the youth. Even now St John's thoughts centred upon his own dilemma. It had always been in the back of his mind that he would win enough to replace all that he had stolen, and that he would make a magnanimous gesture and restore it all to the boy if his family never claimed him. If they did find the boy, then the smugglers would be blamed for the money going missing and his name would be in the clear.

All that now stood between him and ruin was the diamond bracelet he had slipped into his pocket that night. He had no choice but to sell it and pray that his luck would change and one large winnings would restore both his and Bryn's fortunes.

He had the bracelet hidden in the lining of his travelling bag. He had not left it at Trevowan, since he did not trust Felicity not to snoop through his possessions. In his opinion his wife was developing a clingingly possessive and sly nature, bent upon depriving him of the carefree exploits and entertainments available to a gentleman.

St John staggered back to his room at the inn, and by noon the next day he had sold the bracelet for a quarter of its value to a back-street fence he knew from his smuggling partnership with Harry Sawle. The fever was again building in his blood that this money would be his salvation.

He was not pleased to discover that his gaming companions of the previous evening had left town and he would be denied the opportunity of recovering his losses. Nevertheless, he had no inclination to return to his home and a household of demanding women. Then, whilst drinking in the taproom of the inn, he over-heard two men recounting that one of the county's most notorious black sheep, the rogue Japhet Loveday, had returned from exile. St John was so delighted at the information, he bounded up the stairs to pack his belongings, forgetting to call the men to account for slandering the good name of his cousin. With Japhet back in England, life would take a more exciting turn.

When he returned to the lodging house in London, Tristan summoned his landlord. The bulky figure scratched at his side-whiskers as he stood inside the door of his chambers. The interior was spartan, with no personal possessions on show that would have revealed the nature of the occupier. A cloak hung on a peg behind the door and a cracked shaving mirror was on the wall above the washing pitcher and bowl. The wooden shutters across the window were partly closed, casting deep shadows into the room. To a more observant eye it had an air of impermanence about it.

'Like you expected, a man came looking for you,' the landlord declared with the sly grin of a man who had been paid well for his trouble. 'Though he did not seem the sort who'd be easily duped. But like you said, he didn't want to hear well of you.'

Tristan stood with his arm resting along the mantelshelf above the fireplace. It was an indolent pose but there was a tense set to his shoulders. The coal-black eyes showed no expression, but his tone was sharpened by anger at what he perceived was a further injustice.

'Didn't seem to have a very high opinion of you!' the landlord expanded. 'Your friend Bagshawe here played his part as well, intimating that you owed him money.'

'You can tell Bagshawe I'll cancel his debt for his show of loyalty,' said Tristan.

The landlord chuckled. 'Like you insisted, I had a watch put on the Cornishman when he left. He was asking over town about your habits. Your gentleman friends told a different story. They declared you a champion fellow, though one suspected you had a ruthless side.'

Tristan grunted, and the seam of his lips compressed into a bitter line. 'That would not have disturbed my cousin.'

The older man eyed him suspiciously. 'Happen you know what you're doing. Rum do that you did not care your kin thought you a scoundrel.'

Tristan shrugged. 'My affairs need not concern you.' There was a dangerous edge to the warning that made the landlord take a half-step back. 'A man who cares about public opinion, or indeed anyone's opinion about himself, will always limit his potential to achieve his aims.'

Tristan dismissed the landlord and sat for a long while deep in thought. During the afternoon he summoned other men whom he had paid to spy on his family. He had not expected his cousins to welcome him with open arms. That suited his purpose. Their fierce pride and code of loyalty were predictable. They thought they knew him, but they judged him on the misfit he had been as a child. He had been as good as dead to them for twenty-five years. They knew nothing of the man he had become, whilst he had kept himself informed of all their exploits in recent years. While he knew their strengths and weaknesses, they had only a prejudged conception of him. That was his ace card. On the day George Loveday had cast him from his home, after allowing him to glimpse the privileged life he might have led had his grandfather not been similarly exiled, Tristan had vowed that the Lovedays would acknowledge him not only as their equal but as their superior.

For most of his lifetime he had been waiting for this moment. So far everything was going to plan. He did not intend to fail.

Chapter Nineteen

Japhet refused any celebration to mark his return that involved their friends and neighbours. Sir Henry had wanted to hold a ball, and the prospect had horrified him. They had been living at Traherne Hall for a week, and twice Japhet had been snubbed in public by former acquaintances amongst the gentry. The censure did not trouble him. It was no less than he expected. In time he would prove his worth and those people would eat humble pie and accept him. His worry was that Gwen and the children would suffer. Japhet Edward had already had a fight in Trewenna when some of the local boys had called him a 'convict brat'. Though not yet seven, he had fought bravely. He had faced taunts from the hardened children of convicts in the colony, and fought regularly in New South Wales, frequently emerging the victor. Whilst Japhet had been proud of his son's courage, Gwendolyn had been appalled that he had brawled like a common street urchin.

'You cannot blame the boy for fighting to defend his name,' Japhet had counselled.

'When Mama learns of this I shall never hear the last of it.'

'She should be proud her grandson stood up to bigger boys and did not run away. There is no shame in him fighting, only shame had he been craven.'

'But he is so little to have to fight such battles.' Gwendolyn had been unable to hide her distress.

Japhet was immediately contrite. 'I cannot change the past. Japhet Edward has nothing to be ashamed of. The local boys will respect him for taking them on. As they will come to admire him as a gentleman of courage as well as position.'

Gwendolyn had not looked convinced, but she did not chastise her son for fighting. Japhet was now in the gunroom at Traherne Hall with Sir Henry. Their images were reflected in the glass fronts of the mahogany gun cabinets. Two of the walls were covered with swords dating back to when Sir Henry's great-grandfather had raised his own troop to fight for the King during the Civil War. Several steel lobster-pot helmets and breastplates were also mounted on the walls.

Japhet's friend was proud of his new shotgun, made by the finest gunsmith of the day, Joseph Manton. One of the purchases Japhet himself had made during his stop in London before travelling to Cornwall had been a pair of Manton's duelling pistols. Earlier the men had set up targets and spent an hour testing the guns, and were now cleaning them.

'Can I not persuade you that I should host a welcoming party and invite our neighbours?' Sir Henry again broached the subject.

Japhet gave an emphatic shake of his head. 'I appreciate the gesture, my friend, but I intend to live quietly and concentrate on horse-breeding as I had planned after Gwen and I married. Delighted as I am to be home, let any celebration be only for the family.'

'But a ball will show everyone our solidarity. You were innocent of the crime you were arrested and tried for. You received a King's pardon.'

'But I was first found guilty. That is what many will remember. I want to put the past behind me and not cause Gwen any further suffering. If any one of our old friends or neighbours slights us, it will be Gwendolyn who will be hurt, not I. And I would first build my bridges with my mother-in-law and your wife.'

'The matter is resolved between them.' Sir Henry paused in polishing the gun butt.

Japhet looked down the barrel of the pistol he had cleaned and laid it on the table before answering. 'Because you ordered it so. It is not the same. If I cannot convince them that I married Gwendolyn purely for love, how can I expect the rest of polite society to view my marriage?'

'You have the approval of Lord Fetherington, his mother, Squire Penwithick and myself.'

Japhet returned the duelling pistols to their box and snapped the lid shut. 'You mean well, but this is something I have to prove to others. Whether it takes a month, a year or a lifetime, I will not rise in the world through my wife's purse strings.'

'You always were stubborn where your own destiny was concerned.'

'And it is not just Gwen. The boys are old enough to be troubled by gossip. I will not have their future damaged because of the recklessness of my youth.'

Sir Henry nodded, and there was genuine respect in his voice when he replied. 'And you will succeed. I am proud to call you brother.'

Japhet shifted uncomfortably with embarrassment. 'You have been a loyal friend. And I have much to repay my family for, not least Hannah. Because of her hard work and sacrifice I have some fine horses to start the stud farm. She had problems of her own and I failed her by not being here for her in her time of need. I am looking forward to seeing her again and thanking her for all she has done for me.'

'You may allay your fears on that score,' Sir Henry reassured. 'Your sister surprised us all by her resilience when her husband died. Not only did she take on the farm and the care of the mares you had picked for your stud farm, but she also stood up to Harry Sawle when he used your land to store his contraband. She was a veritable Amazon in her wrath and defiance. But all the Loveday women have proved feisty.'

Japhet threw back his head and laughed. 'They have indeed, but the men would be bored in a month with a mealy-mouthed mouse, no matter how beautiful and efficient in running our household.' He cocked his head to one side and looked thoughtful. 'Though I am not so sure about St John's new bride. I only met her once. She did not seem his usual type – rather insipid compared to the red-blooded Meriel. His first wife certainly kept him in line. Felicity seemed more vapid.'

'Meriel was a shrew and a gold-digger. Nothing but wealth and more wealth would satisfy her. Her greed got St John mixed up with her brother's smuggling band and she cuckolded him when she saw her chance for a better life, or so she thought.' Sir Henry frowned. 'Felicity is a strong-minded woman. I think the problem in that marriage lies with St John. He can be selfish and unfeeling. Felicity had a calming effect on your cousin in the first year of their marriage. But St John has reverted to his old ways of gaming and the pursuit of pleasure, and she is quick to remind him of his failings. He is often away from Trevowan.'

'I hope St John can hold his drink better than the days I remember. It made him reckless in his gambling and he lost more often than he won.'

'If rumour is true, nothing has changed,' Sir Henry said sadly.

'Then he is a fool.' Jake spoke with a flash of heat. 'He does not deserve Trevowan. I am surprised Uncle Edward did not make Adam his heir. St John was always a wastrel. Has he learned nothing about responsibility?'

'He resents that he was deprived of the shipyard, which was the financial support of the family.'

'St John is no shipwright. He would have brought it to ruin in a year. In Adam's hands it has prospered. Trevowan is a large estate. Surely the home farm can support the family?'

'It did to a great extent when Edward was alive. He supervised its running himself. St John relies too heavily on Nance. There have been bad harvests.'

'You cannot govern the weather. Therefore I am surprised that he was not one of the investors in Adam's venture to supply the colony in New South Wales. St John had Uncle William's legacy he could have invested, did he not? You reaped the rewards of such foresight.'

'It helped having you as our agent, I am sure.' Sir Henry finished reassembling the shotgun before adding, 'It was the old rivalry and jealousy of his twin's success that stopped St John investing. He knows how to spend money but has little head for making it.'

'That does not bode well for the future of Trevowan,' Japhet said heavily.

'Adam would never allow his brother to destroy all his father worked for. Even though the heir usually gets everything, other members of the family become dependents or have to seek the means to make their own way in the world. It cannot have been easy for you, growing up knowing your cousins had so much whilst you were beholden to Edward Loveday's generosity for your education.'

Japhet shrugged. 'It was harder for me to accept the constraints of being the son of a vicar. I knew I could never live up to society's expectations of such a role. Father was content with his calling because he had lived a dashing life before he married and settled down. Peter was an exemplary son. I was compelled to rebel against all things pious and respectable. I paid the price, but along the way I was truly blessed with the love of a remarkable woman. Gwendolyn saved me from the hell I had created.'

'You are proof that man can triumph over any adversity. Is it true you have returned to England an exceedingly wealthy man?'

'I am comfortable enough.' Japhet grinned evasively. 'I have no need for my wife's dowry to establish one of the best stud farms in England.'

Sir Henry sat back in his chair and eyed the box of duelling pistols. 'They are superb weapons, perfectly balanced. But I trust you bought them for sport, not for their true purpose.'

Japhet, who had been relaxed and at his ease, lifted his gaze to regard his friend. 'They were bought with one intent only.' His voice was coated with frost. 'The man who was the cause of my transportation will one day answer for his treachery.'

Sir Henry sighed. 'Can you not let it go? You have Gwen, the boys, the stud farm and the beginnings of a fine string of brood mares. Would you throw all that away? Does not Gwen deserve a time of peace and prosperity – of true happiness?'

'She deserves all that and more.' Japhet continued to hold Sir Henry's stare, although his resolve did not falter. 'It is why I am prepared to wait until the stud farm is established.'

As he spoke, Japhet's genial manner changed. His features hardened and Sir Henry glimpsed the merciless side of his nature. It had been honed with a brutal code of honour, without which Japhet would never have survived the deprivations and hardships of a year in Newgate, transportation in the squalid depths of a prison ship, and five years as a settler conquering the elements and horrors of life in a penal colony. Not only had he survived, but he had prospered beyond all his dreams. A remarkable feat. How he had achieved such wealth he had so far been reluctant to reveal. Somehow Sir Henry doubted it was all honestly come by.

He rose and put the shotgun back on its mount in the cabinet, then closed the glass doors and locked them. From the bunch of keys in his hand he selected another and unlocked a chest. Solemnly he lifted a slender oblong shape wrapped in velvet and placed it on the table before Japhet. 'To protect yourself from old adversaries you will have need of this.'

As soon as Japhet's hands closed over the velvet he felt his heart leap with excitement. Reverently he rolled back the cloth and his swarthy features split into a grin. His hand tightened over the sword and scabbard and he sighed with pleasure as he withdrew the blade. He flashed a white-toothed smile at his companion. 'I cannot tell you how much I would have given in the last years to have this in my hands. It is an old and trusted friend.'

'All your possessions were put in the attic here after you were arrested. But I kept this close at hand. I knew you would return for it. I am not sure that your wife will approve.'

Japhet stood up and tested the weight of the sword and its balance in his hand. 'A pity the days have gone when a man never ventured forth without his sword at his hip. Has Adam kept up his practice now he has become a respectable shipbuilder?'

'He and Peter practise on occasion.'

'Peter?' Japhet raised a querying brow. 'He despises swordplay and all its evils.'

Sir Henry laughed. 'You have a lot to learn about your little brother. He has greatly changed and you may even find him your match with a pistol and sword. Though he is not above sermonising on the use of weapons in violence against our fellow man, unless, as we are today, at war with another country.'

'I had noted the change in Peter.' Japhet looked amused. 'He has a greater confidence and self-possession than I remember. And if I was not mistaken an unspoken challenge in his eyes when we were reunited. During our first evening alone, Papa proudly told me how Peter fought his own battles with the smugglers and won. Yet he always remained true to his calling. I admire him for that. I was always too impetuous and hungry for adventure. And I certainly have had my fill of that in recent years.'

'And your impetuousness?' Sir Henry teased.

'Ah, let us hope it has been tempered.' Briefly Japhet's eyes clouded and Sir Henry could only guess at the adversity and perils that had carved the deeper lines about his friend's handsome face.

When Japhet replaced the sword in the scabbard he said, 'I have learned a greater measure of patience. The recklessness of my younger days has been put aside in favour of the maturity of the reformed, if not the wise. I've had seven years since my arrest to plan my revenge upon the man who produced false evidence against me. When the time is ripe he will not escape my justice.'

Chapter Twenty

It had rained all morning whilst Senara had been at Trevowan Hard tending the patients who had need of her remedies. With only four people calling on her services, she had occupied her time making a syrup of comfrey root boiled in wine, which she then sealed in small bottles. It was a remedy that cured many ills: it helped disperse the spitting of blood or passing of bloodied urine, speeded the healing of bruises and open wounds and cleared rheum from the head and lungs. It also settled the fluxes of the stomach and blood. Her herb room contained shelves full of neat rows of elixirs, balms, ointments and tinctures prepared and ready to distribute to her patients.

Fortunately today there had been no serious complaints for her to tend to. There had been a baby with croup, a young screaming boy who had been stung by several wasps when he had thrown a stone at a swarm in a tree, an apprentice carpenter who had been larking about and had sliced a deep gash in his forearm that needed to be stitched, and a grandfather brought in on a cart by his daughter from Trewenna with unhealed ulcers on his legs. Senara had shown the daughter how to cleanse the sores and change the dressings as soon as they began to smell, and had given her a large pot of unguent for the wounds.

When Senara emerged from the herb room she glanced at the sky. The black clouds were low on the horizon and edged with amber where the sun was slanting through, and in places the sky was patched with pouches of blue. After the heavy rain the sun was warming the timbers of the ships under construction, and steam rose from the wood to drift across the decks.

Careful to avoid any puddles, she walked to the stables. Noticing Adam on the *Good Fortune* supervising the placement of the cannon, she waved to him when he looked in her direction. Every inch of the ship would be inspected and its fitments and workings examined before it set out for its sea trials in a week or so. Adam paused in his work and returned her wave. He would not be returning to Boscabel until the evening.

As Senara rode towards the crossroads at the top of the coomb that led down to the shipyard, her thoughts were on the tasks she intended to accomplish that day. She still worried about their young guest. Apart from his continued loss of memory, Bryn showed no other lasting effects from the coach accident. But it was now two months and it troubled her that no one had replied to the notices in the news-sheets about the boy. Surely loving parents would be frantic with worry about him. His identity remained an unsettling mystery. At least Bryn was happy in his new environment and did not seem to be fretting at his lack of a family. Perhaps he had been miserable in his past, which was why his mind continued to block the memories. He had a pleasing manner and she had become very fond of him and knew that she would miss him greatly when he had to leave them.

She was so deep in thought, she started violently at hearing her name called as she approached the crossroads. Seeing Georganna sitting on a fallen tree trunk under the shelter of an oak tree, she frowned. The older woman had clearly been caught in the earlier rain. Her shawl and dress were wet and her hair was sleek against her skull, droplets of water still clinging to its tendrils. She was not dressed for riding and neither was there sign of a horse. It was a long way for her to have walked.

'What are you doing all the way out here, Georganna?'

'I walked from Trevowan. All Margaret, Amelia and Felicity can speak of is babies and children. And Elspeth thinks only of the horses. It can be wearisome at times.' She grimaced. 'Besides, I hoped I would see you.'

'What is so urgent? You are soaked. You'll catch a chill.' Senara regarded the agitated fluttering of the older woman's hands, yet when she looked into her eyes, what she saw seemed at odds with Georganna's distress. She had a tingling premonition, but instead of the delight she expected Thomas's wife to be feeling, there was sadness in every line of her body. It caused Senara to ask sombrely, 'Are you sure I can help you?'

'You know, don't you?' Georganna bit back a sob. 'You have guessed my terrible secret.'

Disconcerted by the outburst, Senara dismounted and looped the reins of her mare around the branch of a tree. She sat beside Georganna and took her hand. It was icy and trembling. 'Why do you not tell me everything? I thought you would pleased, if my instinct has not failed me over your condition.'

'I have no one to turn to but you.' There was desperation in Georganna's voice. 'I have been so wicked and foolish and now I am to be punished.' The words tumbled forth like a dam bursting. She spoke so fast that Senara had to strain to understand her words. 'I am so frightened. No one must know of my shame. Especially Thomas. No one will understand.' By now she was almost incoherent in her distress and burst into tears.

Senara squeezed her hands. 'Breathe deeply and calm yourself. You can tell me whatever you wish and it will be in confidence. But is this such a dreadful thing? You are with child, are you not? Thomas will be delighted.'

It took several moments before Georganna had calmed her emotions enough to speak; even then her voice was a faint whisper. 'The child is not my husband's. There, I have said it. You will think me despicable.'

'It is not for me to judge.' Senara controlled her shock. Georganna had always been rather prim and emotionally self-contained. She wanted to put her at ease, for it was obvious the older woman was desperate to confide in someone. 'You are a loyal and devoted wife to Thomas. But your marriage cannot always have been easy.'

'It is not Thomas's fault,' Georganna defended with unexpected heat. She twisted her wedding ring on her long, artistic finger. 'How can I have this child? Thomas will never forgive me for dishonouring his name.'

Senara could feel the pain and misery rolling in waves from the distraught woman. In these situations it was always the woman who carried the greatest burden and paid the highest price in terms of consequences. Of all of Adam's male cousins, Thomas was the one she felt least drawn to. His intellect and cutting wit often left her cold, and there was an aloofness to his manner that was used as a shield to stop people getting too close. Yet he had never been less than charming and solicitous towards her, and in the early days of her marriage that had meant a great deal to Senara. Even so, he was too quick to take affront and she was not impressed by his reputation as a crack shot and swordsman. His fierce pride and rash temper had led him to injuring several men in duels. However, amongst his good traits, he could not be faulted in his loyalty to his family. His generosity in loaning them the bank's money at low interest had saved Edward, Adam and St John from financial ruin on many occasions. But Thomas also had a ruthless and selfish streak and Senara knew that Georganna had often been neglected when he pursued his own interests.

She chose her words carefully, not wishing to alienate or upset Georganna further. 'Thomas should have considered the slur upon his reputation when he did not share your marriage bed. You have been marvellous in your support of his friendship with Lucien Greene. It is a dangerous path he takes and he risks disgrace and arrest. He may be delighted that you are with child. By acknowledging it, he could save his own reputation.'

'Thomas will give me no peace until he learns the name of the father, and then he will call him out. One of them will be hurt, if not killed. I could not bear that.'

'Who is the father?'

'I will take my own life rather than say.' Georganna drew back from Senara, and although her words were theatrical, her voice and expression showed her determination to carry out her threat. 'This is my punishment. Only you can help me, Senara. I know you have the skill. Give me something to rid myself of my shame.'

Senara swallowed against a knot of pain in her chest. This was a moral dilemma that always upset her. 'I have not the right to take a life. A child is a special gift. Thomas will understand. He could not expect you to be celibate all your married life.'

'Thomas would have turned a blind eye to a discreet affair, but not to this. You must give me a potion to take my shame away.' She gripped Senara's hands so hard that her nails broke the skin and blood ran through her fingers.

Senara did not feel the pain in her hands, so great was her agony at Georganna's suffering. It took all her willpower to remain firm. There had been occasions when a mother with too many mouths already to feed and too little income had persuaded her to help, but it had never sat easily with her conscience. After her vow to Joshua it would be impossible to agree to Georganna's plea.

'I cannot do as you ask,' she finally answered.

'But you are my only hope,' Georganna begged.

Senara held her cousin's stare for a long moment before replying. 'Do not ask this of me.'

'Then it would be better if I killed myself.' Georganna wrenched her hands away and stood up to pace in an erratic circle.

Worried at the older woman's growing hysteria, Senara needed to make her see reason. 'It is a mortal sin to take your own life. And you would carry the double sin of another death. You cannot mean to do that.'

'But I will die anyway,' Georganna wailed.

'That is nonsense,' Senara countered. 'Thomas will never admit to the world that it is impossible that he is the father. Margaret has prayed for a grandchild for years. She will dote on the child and insist you have the best midwives and doctors to tend you—'

Georganna cut into her speech. 'Not only did I betray my vows to Thomas, but the reason our marriage worked and we have found happiness together is that I never wanted children. Not after my mother died in childbirth. I was terrified I would die the same way.'

Senara attempted to reassure her. 'Your mother's death was unfortunate. Although there are hazards in giving birth, most women come through it safely. There is no reason why you should not do the same.'

Georganna shook her head, her voice cracking. 'You must help me. I cannot go through with this. I will die in childbirth like my mother.' She sobbed inconsolably, and Senara gathered her in her arms.

'Ssh, you must not think that way. I will not take the life of a child, Georganna, especially as you have the means to give it a good life. And you will be as much at risk if you try to rid yourself of it. If you really cannot face Thomas, then there are places you can go to hide away and await the birth. Your baby will be looked after and you can return to London with no one the wiser. At least the child will be spared.'

'Tamasine was miserable at being sent away as an illegitimate child. What life is that?' Georganna broke away from Senara and wrapped her arms around her own body, rocking back and forth in her wretchedness.

'And look at all Tamasine has recently achieved. She is a wonderful, vibrant woman and very happy in her life.'

'Her story is exceptional and she was fortunate to have Edward as a father.' Georganna sniffed back her tears and wiped her cheeks with the skirt of her gown. 'He would not see his daughter suffer the indignity of one who is base born. Her mother was a great lady and yet she had no power to help her illegitimate child.'

'Does the father know of your condition?'

Georganna shook her head. 'There is no future for us.'

For a moment Senara was tempted to do as Georganna asked, but as soon as the thought formed, she knew she could not break her vow. The potions were not always successful and could cause terrible complications for the mother, even death.

'If Thomas will not accept the child, then you must tell the father. Edward regretted not being part of Tamasine's childhood. He would never have abandoned her. No honourable man would.'

'Tamasine's mother had no choice but to keep her birth a secret. Her husband shut her away afterwards.'

'I cannot see Thomas being so unfeeling.' She put her arms around Georganna and allowed her to cry on her shoulder. When she was calmer, Senara said, 'I want you to consider what I have said. You have a large share in Mercer and Lascalles Bank that you inherited from your father. It was that share that saved Mercer's Bank and was the reason why you and Thomas married. You can provide a good future for the child. It need not want for education, dowry or the means to establish a career.'

Georganna palmed away her tears and drew a shuddering breath. 'I am more scared of the birth than of my husband's wrath,' she confessed. 'My mother screamed in agony for days before death released her from her torture. I am not brave.'

'It will not be the same for you.'

'Can you promise that?' Georganna said sharply.

Senara sighed and blinked aside her own tears. 'No one can make such a promise. But you are unnecessarily fearful. Your mother was unfortunate. But she loved you and she loved your father. You were her lasting gift to him. Life was her loving gift to you. Instead of the gift of life, would you have fear be the legacy of her death?'

Georganna stared at her feet, her breathing loud and ragged. She took several gulps of air. 'I do not want to go away to strangers. Will you tend me? Let me stay here until my time comes.'

'In that case Thomas must be told,' Senara insisted and stroked the wet hair away from the distraught woman's face.

Georganna nodded reluctantly. 'My marriage will never be the same. He will not forgive me.'

'Thomas has much to answer for himself in his neglect as a husband. He should ask for your forgiveness. He cannot shirk his responsibility that his actions are as much to blame as yours. But I think you worry in vain. Thomas will be a good father. If he loves you, he will love your child.'

Georganna summoned a weak smile. 'Happy endings only happen in plays and novels.'

Senara lost patience and, gripping Georganna's arms, gave her a firm shake. 'No more talk like that. From unusual circumstances you and Thomas have created a good marriage. You have been happy together and you will be again.'

Chapter Twenty-one

St John had planned to visit Japhet at Traherne Hall on his own. As soon as the women of his family learned he was going, however, all of them except Elspeth insisted on joining him, and Jasper Fraddon was summoned to prepare the coach and horses.

'It is a bright sunny day and I will ride ahead of you and meet you at the hall,' declared St John.

Felicity pouted with displeasure. 'Is it too much trouble to ride with us? We have not had your company this fortnight.'

'Would you prefer we are all crammed into the coach and suffered the heat and discomfort?' he returned.

'I shall ride with Papa,' Rowena declared, smiling smugly at Felicity. She was often in competition with her stepmother to claim her father's attention.

'You will be staying here to keep Charlotte company,' Felicity snapped.

'Papa, that is so unfair,' Rowena wailed. 'I often used to ride with you to visit the Traherne girls. They have been my friends for years and are my age. Charlotte can play with Rafe. They are so childish in their games.'

'You may visit the Traherne girls another time.' St John groaned with impatience. 'My intention was to welcome Japhet home, not be escort to a gaggle of women partaking of afternoon tea.'

'We have no wish to inconvenience you, husband.' Felicity paled at his rudeness. She felt humiliated before his family but was determined not to allow her pain to show in front of their guests. 'Since Lady Anne has been so accommodating towards Japhet and

190

seems prepared to put the unpleasantness she caused over his wedding behind her, it is diplomatic that we visit and show our unity, is it not?'

He replied in an offhand manner. 'I thought you were too indisposed to travel and needed to rest as much as possible.'

'I am much stronger now. Margaret wishes to see as much of Japhet as possible while she is in Cornwall.'

'And I thought you had been taught better manners.' Aunt Margaret rounded on her nephew, her lips white with anger. 'When did you become so churlish, St John?'

He rubbed his fingers across his brow, but there was little contrition in his voice. 'Your pardon, ladies. I have a lot on my mind with estate matters. I intended my visit to be brief. You will wish to converse at a more leisurely pace.'

'If you had not spent so long in Bodmin away from your duties, you would not be pressed for time now,' Felicity retaliated. 'We will do very well without you as an escort, husband. I would not keep you from your duties here, which have been neglected of late.'

He scowled in her direction. 'I shall inform Lady Traherne and Lady Anne Druce to expect you within the hour.' He bowed curtly and strode from the room.

'He was ever headstrong but I have never seen him so disagreeable,' Aunt Margaret said, patting Felicity's hand with concern.

'He is like that when he has been gambling and losing. He thinks I do not see through his moods.' She tried bravely to hide her despair. 'He has been gambling heavily for months. Where does the money come from? He refuses to discuss it. Uncle Joshua has tried to reason with him to curb his wastrel ways, but St John will not listen. He regards any criticism as interference. And he is too quick to take offence that the family feel Adam would have managed the estate more efficiently.'

'St John may be reckless but he would never risk Trevowan or the security of you and the children,' Margaret assured her.

'That is what I believed until recently,' Felicity groaned. 'May God spare us from his obsession.'

St John was delighted to find Japhet and Sir Henry in one of the outer fields on the approach to Traherne Hall. Both men wore thick gloves that covered their arms to their elbows and had falcons on their wrists. On the far side of the field the gamekeeper was flushing rabbits from their burrows with ferrets. When one darted across the grass, Japhet removed the hood from his bird and raised his arm to set it in flight. There was a thrumming of air as its great wings rose and fell in a graceful arc lifting it skywards. There it soared briefly, its wings outspread and the leather jesses on its legs dangling. With a tinkling of the bells around its legs, which could be heard from a considerable distance if the bird refused to return after its flight, it then swooped with merciless speed towards its prey. The rabbit weaved across the ground in an erratic attempt to escape the hunter, but the falcon was relentless, and with unerring certainty its talons fastened over the fleeing animal. There was a squeal from its prey and then its body went limp.

Japhet whistled and the falcon beat its wings to fly back to his outstretched arm whilst the gamekeeper collected the dead rabbit and secured it with string around his waist, where several others already dangled.

'Such power, such majesty, such lethal accuracy,' Japhet observed as the hawk bit into its reward of meat held between his fingers. 'A noble bird for a noble sport. I feel quite humbled to feel that power and majesty obeying my commands.' He deftly hooded the falcon, which sat tall and proud on his arm.

St John dismounted, calling out, 'Welcome home, cousin. Was there such sport to be had in the new land?'

'Good day to you, St John. I have seen sights you could not begin to conceive.' He grinned roguishly. 'But it is good to be home.'

Sir Henry hailed St John and signalled to the falconer and his helper to come forward and take the birds and return them to their mews.

'They are two fine birds, Sir Henry,' St John said appreciatively. 'I have not flown a hawk for some years. It is no longer such a popular sport.'

'I had a fancy to take it up again,' the baronet replied. 'I had the mews repaired and hired a falconer to train the birds. I shall breed them next year.'

'And Henry has generously given me this bird that I may use

whenever I choose, until I can build mews of my own. Have you not thought of taking up hawking again, St John?' Japhet enquired of his cousin. 'Adam seemed much taken with the idea.'

'He has the yard to support his grand claims,' St John snapped. 'I have too many other responsibilities.' Then aware that he had again appeared churlish, he added more convivially, 'For all your hardships and travels you look well, cousin.'

Japhet nodded and a self-mocking smile stretched across his lips. 'My travels and experiences served me well enough. And I am more of a man because of them.'

'Then the horrors they speak of,' St John taunted, 'of murdering man-eating natives, beatings, starvation, unendurable heat and deprivation, are not true?'

'The natives were not cannibals.' Japhet did not elaborate further.

'So your luck stayed with you, and you not only survived but prospered?'

Japhet regarded him solemnly. 'My luck came to me, having risked her life to carry my pardon to those inhospitable shores. Because of Gwendolyn's sacrifice I came home the richer of another son.'

'A man has untold riches when he is blessed with sons.' St John could not keep the bitterness from his voice.

Japhet frowned. 'Much as I delight in your company, you never did accept your blessings with good grace, did you, cousin? You have two daughters and another child on the way, and a new, beautiful, loyal and faithful wife.'

Anger and resentment flashed through the younger man's eyes. 'You chose an exceptional wife. Who would have thought that Gwen, so meek and timid as a young woman, would brave so much? And, of course, her vast dowry did not come amiss in rescuing you from your fall from grace.'

Shrewd hazel eyes assessed the twin who had inherited so much and yet did not find contentment. Japhet had seen such lines of dissipation and discontent in too many men's faces during his years as a rakehell not to know the demons that haunted St John. If any man but one of his own family had so accused him, he would have challenged them to answer to his sword. He bit back his flash of anger. The years of transportation had taught him how to control his hot temper. 'This time I will not call you to account for such words. But I did not marry Gwen for her fortune.'

Tension, barely checked, emanated from Japhet, whilst St John was sullen and antagonistic in his jealousy. Sir Henry stepped between them with a conciliatory smile. 'Is this any way to welcome Japhet home? You are squabbling as though he had never left.'

Japhet saw the lunacy in their antagonism and good-naturedly slapped St John on the shoulder and gave a throaty laugh. He refused to take offence and was again relaxed and at his ease. 'Is that not then a true welcome – that nothing has changed? I've missed our rivalry.'

St John regretted his bullish manner. He had always looked up to Japhet as the older cousin, and envied him his carefree lifestyle and devil-may-care manner. Whatever riches his cousin had brought back from the new colony, he had paid a high price for them in hardship and loss of reputation. 'To see you having prospered and in good health and spirits makes me proud to own you as kin. I know it cannot have been easy for you.'

'Strangely, once Gwen joined me I would not have missed those experiences. For all the hardship it was a beautiful land habited by wildlife the like of which you could not imagine, and like nothing else known to man. It is a land which will prosper once more settlers voyage to its shores, and they will reap the rewards of the new continent.'

'You almost sound as though you regret leaving.' St John regarded him in puzzlement.

'Regret is a waste of time. There are unlimited adventures for those willing to engage in them, but my home is here. I am glad to be back.'

The Loveday carriage could be seen as it turned into the drive leading to Traherne House. 'My womenfolk are about to call upon you,' St John commented.

'Gwen is not expected back for another hour. She has taken the boys to visit Mama, who insisted on Peter retrieving our wooden soldiers from the attic for them to play with. I was about to ride to Hannah's farm and work with the horses. Elspeth and Mark Sawle have trained them well but they have yet to be tested in races. I need to employ a groom to tend them.'

'Sawle will not like that. He prefers working with the horses than on the land,' St John goaded. 'Your old friend Nick Trescoe advised him how to train them. But Sawle is Hannah's overseer.'

'Sawle is a good man, but his first work must be on my sister's behalf,' Japhet returned. 'I will not be the cause of any further disruption to the farm's productivity. It is Davey's future, and Hannah has done so much for me, I can never repay her.' His expression cleared as he changed the subject. 'Is Nick still in Cornwall? He purchased a couple of my foals, did he not? I would be interested to learn how they fared if he raced them.'

'I believe they have won a race or two,' Sir Henry replied.

'That is good to hear.' Japhet turned his attention back to his cousin. 'Since you are here, I will ride to the farm later.'

Sir Henry interrupted. 'I will leave you to catch up on your news. I must speak with my gamekeeper before I greet my guests. I shall see you both back at the house.' He fell into pace beside his gamekeeper and falconer as they returned to the mews.

St John, leading his mare, walked at a slower pace beside Japhet. 'We could ride together. There is much news to catch up on which will be of little interest to the womenfolk.'

'I must pay my respects to my kin. I would not have them think I slighted them.' Japhet reminded his cousin of what was expected of them. 'Mama always wrote glowingly of Felicity in her letters. I look forward to becoming better acquainted with your dear wife. She is a genteel and refined woman. A credit to you, St John. Unlike the fast baggage you hitched yourself to the first time you were wed. Meriel had beauty to tempt any man and spirit to match, but she had no heart and a black soul. Take pride in your new wife. She will only bring credit to your name.'

'Fate dealt with Meriel appropriately,' St John snarled. 'I suppose such gossip reached you.'

Japhet nodded, not surprised at the bitterness in his cousin's voice. 'One should not speak ill of the dead, but you are well rid of that scheming minx. All the more reason to honour the wife you have now chosen.'

At St John's darkening looks he added, 'You did chose her, did you not? There was no shotgun at your head that you can blame this time.'

'Just a pile of debts I thought marriage to an heiress could solve.' St John grimaced. 'The deed was done before I learned she had but a moderate income.'

'Trevowan is no small prize and is large enough to support your family in comfort. Can you not be content with that?' When St John remained sullen, Japhet lost patience. 'You made your choices. Learn to live with them and make the best of your situation. You have much to be thankful for. Do not throw it all away.'

This time it was a different pain that flickered behind St John's eyes. 'The estate is like a succubus; its demands are never-ending.'

'With privileges comes responsibility. Are you not proud of your heritage?'

'Of course I am, but . . .' St John caught himself up short.

Japhet sighed but did not press him. He had seen the bleakness and fear in a man's eyes too often in the gaming circles he had once made his own. 'Gambling is not the answer. I say this not out of judgement but experience and understanding. It was almost my downfall.'

'I do not wager beyond my means.'

His denial was too strident. Japhet knew his cousin was not being honest with himself. Until he admitted his problem he would forever be in the power of his addiction. Since this was their first meeting in many years, Japhet did not want it to end in a quarrel. Yet he would do his cousin no service by staying silent. 'I am glad to hear it. Only a fool would risk his home and heritage on the vagaries of Lady Luck and the turn of a card or throw of a dice.'

St John's scowl told him he had guessed right. His cousin was gambling beyond his means. But this was not the time to pursue the matter and he tactfully changed the subject. 'One of the greatest burdens I carry was not being here when Edward and the family faced so many problems with Harry Sawle. Your father was a great and good man. I would have given much to have been here to see Harry Sawle dancing at the end of a rope after all the evil he committed in these parts. And Beaumont is also dead. Another scoundrel who did not deserve to die in his bed.'

He grinned to lighten the mood between them. 'It appears that I have returned in time to enjoy a period of peace amongst our family. And there is currently a cessation in hostilities with France. We at least are now free of enemies.'

St John kept his gaze fixed on the ground ahead as they walked. 'There are still those amongst our own who would make mischief. They must be dealt with.'

Japhet frowned but could not resist teasing, 'It's not Peter who is still condemning us all to hellfire for our sins, I trust? I thought his piety had mellowed.'

'It is not Peter.' St John stopped abruptly in his tracks, causing his horse to throw up its head and prance. It took a moment to calm his mount before he declared, 'A devil would worm his way back into our favour. Our ne'er-do-well cousin who threw our trust and generosity back in our faces. Namely Tristan Loveday.'

'Tris!' Japhet did not hide his surprise. 'I had all but forgotten him. How is the gutter brat Grandfather took under his wing?'

'On his way to hell if there is any justice,' St John flared. 'He is bent upon mischief which will do us no good at all. And he dares to proclaim he is our kin.'

'We cannot deny his blood.' Japhet shrugged. 'But what has he done apart from survive? He was always a wild card. Yet is that so surprising considering the poverty he endured as a child?'

'Have you forgotten that he repaid us by treachery? How can you defend him?' St John bristled with outrage.

Japhet was unrepentant. They walked more slowly as they approached Traherne Hall and would soon be overheard. 'He taught me a trick or two that served in my favour.' Then, seeing his cousin's look of disdain, he amended with a challenging edge, 'Perhaps as the son of a parson I also felt the injustice of watching others with so much take their good fortune and grand lifestyle for granted and squander it away without compunction.'

He was startled that childhood resentments still smarted when he thought he had long ago laid them to rest. He shook his head impatiently. 'Even though Hannah, Peter and I never had the advantages that came so easily to you and Adam, your father saw we were never hungry or in want of education or clothing. We were still brought up to be gentry. Tristan had all that taken away from him when he was becoming used to a more prosperous way of life. Until Grandfather became his guardian, the only laws he understood were those of how to survive in a feral and squalid environment. And to be truthful, he was ever regarded as an outcast by the family.'

'You would defend what he did?'

'I was not with you the night of the storm, and his fall from favour was never allowed to be discussed. You and Adam never spoke of it. And within a week you were back at school.' Japhet frowned as the memories of the young Tristan returned. He had been like a stray dog: at first wary of any kindness, then gradually learning to trust and eager to please. Yet despite his lowly past, there had remained a steely core within the youth and a fierce competitive edge to prove he was the equal of his cousins. 'To tell you the truth, I liked Tris. We were of an age and I know he desperately wanted to be part of the family. Even though he had been beaten for whatever scrape he had been involved in, I was shocked that he ran away. He once confided in me that he was terrified of facing poverty again, and of having to live on the streets. More than anything he wanted to be respectable. He would fight tooth and claw to retain that.'

'He ran away rather than face the consequence of his actions.' St John scowled.

'A beating alone would not have made him flee. He was used to such treatment from the older urchins who worked in gangs. What did he do that was so terrible?' Japhet queried. 'There was more to it than just the theft, was there not?'

St John's jaw set in a rigid line. 'If there was, it is a mystery to me. We had taken a bottle of brandy to the cave at the foot of Trevowan cliffs and I passed out drunk. Tristan and Adam went off together when they saw a ship sailing too close to the rocks further along the coast. It was obvious the ship would founder. Adam will not speak of the incident. We were all given a hiding the next day. Grandfather was strict. Adam and I took our punishment like gentlemen. We did not steal and turn to treachery.'

Japhet would wager his last guinea that St John was lying, or at the least not telling the whole truth. 'It was a brave and foolhardy venture. The seas were rough. They could have been killed trying to rescue survivors from the wreck. If I recall aright, there were none. Is it any wonder Grandpapa was so furious with them?'

St John did not answer for several moments and then his tone was dismissive. 'It was too long ago. I had a hangover the next day and remember little of the incident.'

'But if you were all beaten, why did Tristan run away?' Japhet remained sceptical. 'He had so much to lose. The only home he had known and a chance to make something of himself. He would take any number of beatings to ensure he had an education and could make his own path in the world, away from his old life and crime. And why will Adam not speak of that night?'

'Ask him!' They had reached the front of the house where the Loveday carriage stood empty. St John threw the reins of his horse to Fraddon and strode off, leaving Japhet unsettled by his evasion.

Chapter Twenty-two

Throughout the following days, Japhet put his plans for his new life in order. When he and Gwen visited Tor Farm, he was pleased at how well it had been maintained. The tenant's lease ended on Lady Day. Half the harvest of grain was already cut and the haymaking would be finished in a fortnight. Japhet was impatient to move into the home he had bought to start his married life and had never lived in. He repaid the tenant half a year's rent, the cost of the livestock he had purchased, and agreed a generous settlement for the grain and hay yet to be cut. The farmer, who had no family, agreed to move out at the end of August. Another stable block would be needed to house the mares reared on Hannah's farm, and work on it would start as soon as Japhet was able to engage a team of men.

The barn and also the roof of the house had been retiled whilst he had been in Newgate, but there remained further renovations to be done on the residence. The granite building had been erected over a hundred years ago and was of a good solid structure. The main part of the house was three storeys high, with two storeys added to the side thirty years ago. There were six family bedrooms, with two further bedrooms in the attic for the house servants, two parlours, a dining room, music room, small library, kitchen and pantry. Three tied cottages and rooms above the stables provided accommodation for grooms and groundsmen. These were currently empty and in need of renovation. With fifty acres of fields and meadows, it was a good-size estate for a stud farm.

Compared to the log cabin Japhet had built for his family outside

Parramatta in New South Wales, the farmhouse was a palace. He put his arm around his wife's waist as they inspected it, and expressed his plans. 'We could extend it in a year or two, or even knock it down and build a more modern home.'

'I love this place with its warren of rooms,' Gwendolyn enthused. 'Add another wing if it is necessary but do not knock it down. I do not wish for a house gilded and decorated with elaborate plaster-work as Roslyn has done at Traherne Hall. I want a cosy family home like Boscabel and Trevowan.'

'But you are worthy of a grand mansion.' He pulled her close and kissed her hair. 'I want only the best for you.'

'You are my life, not stones and mortar. And you are all I ever wanted. This is perfect.' Having heard the fervour in her husband's voice, she sought to calm the fierce ambition that could so easily consume him. 'Roslyn has a grand mansion but she is not happy. Her husband does not love her and she is obsessed with making the house a showpiece, as though to disprove Henry's infidelity. All I want is a family home for us. You and I have nothing to prove to each other and I care not what the world thinks.'

'But I do, not for my own, but for your sake.' His eyes sparked with passion. 'It is lack of respect of all that is wonderful about you if people believe I wed you for your money.'

She smiled with confidence and contentment. 'Then those people are blinded by jealousy when they see how happy we are together. Let the quality of the racehorses you breed be your testimony to the success of our marriage. And admit that you would never be happy in a gilded mansion that is a testament to wealth, and not a home. The Loveday name will be renowned throughout England for its fine thoroughbred racehorses. Concentrate your energies on that goal, my love.'

He chuckled, his body relaxing. 'You know me better than I know myself.'

With his own world finally falling into place, Japhet remained concerned about the tension within his family. He had too many secrets in his own past, which he had kept hidden from the family, not to know when others were evasive of the truth.

When he next visited his parents, Peter had also called. Gwendolyn was determined to become better acquainted with her sister-in-law and she had taken an interest in the lace-making industry that Bridie had created for the local women. This afternoon she had joined the circle of women who met in the parsonage at Polruggan.

The crop of apples from the orchard had been harvested and the three men were working at the cider press, stripped to their shirtsleeves. The smell of the crushed apples brought a lump of nostalgia to Japhet's throat. They had performed this task together for so many years that it was a potent childhood memory.

'There is nothing like the good wholesome taste of your cider, Papa,' he observed. 'We made our own beer in the colony and rum was almost a currency amongst the settlers, but even the French wines and brandy can't match this on a hot summer's day. Cornish cider, sunshine and the time to idle away an hour or two are sweet memories. Adam and St John would say the same.'

'Such idleness no doubt led not only to sore heads but many an indiscretion,' Peter commented.

'It was harmless fun,' Japhet returned. 'You happily joined us until the day you were sick to your gut. That turned you to preachifying its evil.'

'Taken in excess, it is still the devil's brew,' Peter began, but was silenced by Joshua holding up his hands.

'You've had your fair share of my cider in recent years, Peter, as I have myself. A man deserves some pleasure in this hard life.'

'Drink has turned many a decent man into no better than a beast. It has ruined lives.' Peter was not prepared to be so indulgent. 'It will be the ruin of St John if he does not curb it. He'd not have so many gambling debts if he drank less. It makes him less cautious.'

'Peter has a point,' Joshua interceded. 'It was a boyhood drinking prank that led to Tristan's disgrace, if I recall correctly. Strange that he should rear his head again after so long. Adam and St John were furious he had tricked his way into Tamasine's confidence.'

'Perhaps he was delighted to find a member of our family who did not judge him,' Japhet offered. 'They are cousins. Both were outcasts in their youth, though I doubt either has spoken of those incidents. Yet somehow their experiences could have formed a bond between them as great as the ties of blood.'

'It is because of her childhood that Tamasine is susceptible to his persuasion,' Peter said, energetically twisting the screw of the cider press. A gush of apple juice ran into the wooden pail.

'And what do you know of Tristan?' Japhet flared. 'You were six when he ran away.'

'I was seven. And I never liked him. He was the one who started calling me Pious Peter, and he never wanted me to be part of your games.'

'Probably because you were always telling tales on us,' Japhet mocked.

Peter glared at him. 'He had bad blood and it will always out in the end.'

Joshua held up his hand. 'Enough. Five Loveday youths will inevitably squabble. As the youngest, Peter, you were bound to feel excluded. I found Tristan eager to please and polite, despite his rough edges. However, he did have a temper and egged the older boys on to some dangerous and wildcap scrapes. He could be a disruptive influence.'

'None of us were that innocent the year he left,' Japhet confessed. 'Well, Peter probably was. But it was only boys' pranks, the mischief we created. Nothing too terrible.'

Japhet realised he would learn nothing further from his father or brother. With so many matters to occupy him, he should have been able to forget their scapegrace cousin, but his thoughts kept returning to Tristan.

A few days later, when Japhet learned that Adam was home, he visited the shipyard for the first time since his return. He was surprised at how it had expanded and that the shipwrights' cottages now formed a small hamlet. A large merchant ship looked almost completed as it bobbed in the water by the jetty. Its masts, rigging and sails were all in place, but carpenters could be heard at work below decks. The ship's name, *Good Fortune*, was painted on its side; surely a good omen for the yard after all the misfortune Adam and his father had suffered in recent years.

Several curious glances were lifted in Japhet's direction: some by men who looked away in confusion, while others' eyes narrowed in speculation or suspicion. Japhet was becoming used to such curiosity, and held any man's gaze with defiance and also challenge.

Toby Jensen was rolling an empty beer keg to stack behind the kiddley and paused in his task to regard Japhet. Immediately he grinned and straightened. Toby had lived in Trewenna before he wed Pru and had worked in Sir Henry's tin mine before it closed.

'If it bain't Mr Japhet Loveday,' he said with genuine pleasure. He was several years older than Japhet and now sported thick side-whiskers and a paunch that showed how well he suited life as landlord of the kiddley. 'I heard you were back. Botany Bay not grand enough for you after Cornwall? Bain't many returned from those shores, but you be a sight for sore eyes, so you be. Cornwall be a dull place without you to liven it. I'll stand you a quart of our finest ale, once you finish your business with Cap'n Loveday.'

'I'll take you up on that quart, Jensen. And how is your lovely wife?'

There was a throaty chuckle from Pru as she joined her husband. 'I thought I recognised your voice. Still the flatterer and charmer of old. It be grand to see you looking so well, sir.'

A group of four women had gathered outside the store with their heads bent together as they stared at Japhet in fascination. He bowed in their direction, ever the gallant. 'The ladies of Trevowan Hard are as beautiful as I remember. Good day to you, ladies.'

He turned away, ignoring the younger women's giggles, and dismounted to tie Sheba to the hitching post. He had been delighted at being reunited with his Arab mare, although she was now past her prime as a racehorse. He had won many races on her in the past, and that success had fostered his dream to breed thoroughbreds. She had produced two foals in the years he had been away and the two-year-old colt showed the potential to be faster than his mother.

Adam hailed his cousin, having been notified of his arrival. 'I regret not being here when you returned.' He slapped his cousin on the back and swallowed against a lump of emotion. 'Nothing has seemed the same without you. You must have some amazing experiences to relate. Some you would probably wish to forget.'

'There was the good with the bad.'

Adam nodded in understanding. 'You look well and prosperous.'

Japhet gazed around the yard. 'I have much to thank your father for. The time I spent here as a youth acquiring some carpentry skills was invaluable. By the time I left the colony I had several convicts and a dozen ticket-of-leave men working for me in the sawmill. I trained them as carpenters as best I could, which was adequate enough for them to build shops and homes in Parramatta for the new settlers arriving regularly from England. There was a mine of money to be made in property, with Parramatta and Sydney expanding rapidly. With more convicts having served their time but with no money for a passage home, they were eager to spend any wages in taverns, which I also invested in.'

Adam guessed that Japhet was ruthless enough to make money from the seamier side of tavern life, supplying not only drink but also women and gaming.

'Time enough for me to tell you of my adventures on other occasions. Now show me the improvements you have made here.'

Adam spent an hour showing Japhet the changes and giving him a tour of the merchant ship before they entered the office to sit at their ease.

Japhet was fulsome in his praise. 'The captains during their time in Sydney Cove praised the speed of *Good Fortune*'s sister ship, *Pride of the Sea*. She took three weeks off the usual sailing time to New South Wales.' He prowled the room with long-legged strides, too restless to sit for long. 'It was a shrewd investment to send goods to the colony and it gave me the chance to establish a trading store that was the turning point in my fortunes.'

'I did not do so badly from the venture,' Adam said. 'Without you as our agent it could have been a very different outcome. I gather the militia were feathering their own nests from any cargo that arrived. I doubt they stood complacently back and allowed you to take their monopoly away from them.'

'Once Gwen arrived in the colony, her name and presence carried a great deal of weight with the governor. Winning over the militia would have been impossible without his support. They ruled by brutality and treated the settlers little better than the convicts when they first arrived.' He flung himself down in a vacant chair, but his long, lithe figure remained taut as though at any moment he would spring into action. 'Without Gwen making such a sacrifice by undergoing the voyage to bring my pardon, I would not have stayed after it arrived. She has been the mainstay behind my success in the life we made for ourselves.'

'She is a remarkable woman,' Adam agreed. 'How have her mother and sister treated her since your return?'

Japhet sat back in his chair, his mood flippant. 'The boys have melted Lady Anne's heart and Sir Henry will take no nonsense from Roslyn. He likes a quiet life. We are gradually building bridges. I intend to move to our estate at the end of the month. That will ease the tension.'

'I wish you well with your new venture. You must be pleased with the foals Hannah kept for you.'

'I never expected her to work so hard. I have much to thank her for.'

'She would not have had it any other way. Working with the mares and foals kept you close to her, especially after Oswald died.'

'She seems to have found a good man in Sam Deighton. Though she has promised to visit Rabson Farm in time for the end of the harvest in a few days, it is a pity it will be some time before I meet her husband,' Japhet said. 'And he is not the only member new to our family during my absence. I never got to know Tamasine properly, meeting her only briefly at my wedding before my arrest. It would not have been appropriate for us to meet during the time I was in Newgate and she was in London. She sounds quite a character, from her adventures and her eventual marriage to Deverell. Both Gwen and Hannah filled their letters with news of her exploits.'

'She is a true Loveday, very like Hannah. Loyal, dependable, fun-loving and adventurous, with a strong sense of duty. You will find her delightful.' Adam's laugh ended in a frown as he recalled the recent events surrounding his sister at Beaucombe.

'From your expression, do I take it that even now she is married she remains wilful and headstrong as well as fascinating?'

'She has a heart of gold, but she is vulnerable because of her childhood.'

'St John mentioned that Tristan had become part of her circle of friends. He was furious and refused to talk about our cousin.' The tight clamp of Adam's jaw showed that he was similarly disinclined. Japhet wanted to get to the bottom of the mystery. 'You also look displeased. Tristan had problems when he lived with you, but was he such a bad sort?'

Adam dipped his head and ran his fingers through his hair. 'He is not to be trusted and will cause trouble for her.'

'St John would not speak of the night of his disgrace. What was it he did that was so terrible?'

'He stole from us, after all Grandpapa had done to give him a better chance in life. Is that not enough?' Adam did not look up, his elbows resting on his knees and his hands dropped between his legs as he stared at a spider crawling across the flagstones on the floor.

Japhet cocked his head to one side. 'I know evasion when I hear it. What really happened that night? Tris wanted desperately to fit in. I never understood what could have been so bad that he had no choice but to run away.'

Adam sat straight in his chair, his expression strained. 'It was a long time ago, Japhet.'

'And Tris is as much my cousin as yours. I liked him. We have all done things we regret, none more so than I. I would need a very good reason to treat him like a social leper. What happened to the Loveday belief in family loyalty?'

Adam's mouth remained clamped shut as he held Japhet's challenging glare. Eventually he let out a harsh breath. He rose and crossed to a brandy decanter and poured two large measures into glasses, handing one to his cousin and drinking half of his own before he spoke. 'I think the time has come when I need no longer feel bound by my oath to Grandpapa. With our temperaments I expect we all have regrets, or a secret so painful that no matter how hard we try to bury it, it will haunt us until our death.'

He remained standing, his body tense as he tossed back the last of his brandy.

'Not you, Adam.' Japhet was incredulous. 'You are the most honest, upright man I know.'

'You may feel differently when I tell you what happened that night. How Tristan tricked us all and revealed his true colours. He could have brought us to ruin in the most dastardly manner, our name reviled, decent society shunning us.'

Japhet crossed his legs and sipped his own drink. 'Nothing you can say could shock me. I have seen too much.'

'This may very well change your opinion of me,' Adam shot back before pacing the room for some time, his cousin watching him in silence. He had wrestled with his conscience so many times in recent weeks, his old fears and feelings of disgust stripping away at his self-esteem. He had carried the burden of his guilt for so long, it would be a relief to confess.

Chapter Twenty-three

'It all started as a boyhood prank . . .' As Adam began to speak, the years rolled back and he relived that night with vivid intensity. Tristan was fourteen and the twins ten years old.

The three of them had taken a bottle of brandy from the cellar to the cave on Trevowan beach. It was evening and a storm had been predicted all day. Lightning was already streaking the sky when they reached the cave. The thunder was earsplitting and when the rain started it was like a dam bursting its side. Within minutes the wind was lashing at the sea, churning it to a frothing monster as it flung itself on the shore. It was the worst storm Adam could remember, and being on the beach at the mercy of such menacing elements made the escapade both frightening and exhilarating.

The boys sat on boulders in the mouth of the cave. St John uncorked the brandy and gulped down a large mouthful. He coughed and pulled a face before passing it to Tristan. There was always tension and rivalry between the three of them. Adam often found Tristan sullen and antagonistic and too ready to take offence at some imagined insult. He also disliked his constant bragging, turning every conversation into a challenge to outdo his cousins. That night the storm seemed to charge them all with a reckless energy.

'What scars have you got from doing something dangerous?' Tristan demanded, lounging back on the rock and scrutinising the twins through narrowed eyes.

St John greedily snatched back the brandy and gulped at the liquid. His eyes watered and he could not suppress a shudder.

Tristan taunted, 'Bet that's the first time you've drunk spirits, milksop. I had my first gin at six. I used to have a cup every night.'

'We've had watered wine on feast days,' St John blustered.

'Watered wine is for old women, parsons and babies,' jeered Tristan.

Adam took the bottle from his twin and drank a mouthful. It burned his tongue and blazed a fiery trail down his gullet, making him gasp. As it settled in his stomach, its warmth chased the cold from his flesh.

St John rolled down his knee hose over his calves, proudly declaring, 'I got this scar when I fell through the roof of the old barn and landed in the hayloft.'

'That's nothing,' Tristan snorted. 'It wasn't dangerous, just plain stupid to fall when climbing. I regularly ran across rooftops if I had the watch after me for filching something.'

'He got a beating for disobeying Papa. We were forbidden to go on the roof,' Adam defended his brother.

'Still kid's stuff.' Tristan grabbed the brandy from Adam. 'What about you?'

Adam shrugged and rolled up his sleeve to reveal a jagged scar on his upper arm. 'Does this count? I got it fighting Harry and Clem Sawle when they were giving Dan Holman a ducking in the sea. They were always picking on poor Dan. He could not help being a halfwit. Dan is from a family of estate workers. A Loveday has to defend their own. Sawle went for me with a meat hook.'

'I suppose that was fairly brave, but it don't match this,' Tristan bragged. He lifted his shirt to show a puckered red triangular scar on his shoulder. 'I got this from a flat iron. I was fighting a man who was beating my ma 'cos we couldn't pay the rent. He would have killed me if I hadn't kicked him in the balls. While he was rolling on the floor in agony, Ma hit him over the head with a poker. Knocked him out cold, she did. We dragged him out in the street, then we had to wrap all we had in an old cloth and run for our lives, lest he came to his senses and set the watch on us.'

'That was dangerous,' Adam said, appalled at the picture of violence and squalor his cousin had painted. 'That wound must have hurt very badly.'

'You get used to pain when your only reward for a night's

thieving is a kick in the ribs from your gang leader who thinks you're keeping stuff back from him.' Tris puffed out his chest. 'You bain't done much compared to me. What was the most dangerous thing you two ever did? I don't suppose it will be any more impressive than the last answer.' He took another swig of brandy and passed the bottle to St John.

The flashes of lightning showed the anger in the older twin's face at being ridiculed. 'My most dangerous adventure,' St John boasted, 'was to sneak out of the house one night when Clem Sawle said his pa was landing a cargo. I stayed up on the cliffs all night. If the smugglers had caught me they would have buried me up to my neck in sand so I'd drown at the next high tide.'

'Bet you stayed hidden behind a rock, shivering with fear,' Tristan sneered. 'Where's the danger in that? I suppose you had Adam to hold your hand.'

'No. Adam was toadying up to Grandpa at the time. He had sailed with him to deliver a fishing lugger to Looe,' St John protested indignantly. 'And I don't need him to defend me in a fight.' He threw a punch at Tristan, which the older boy nimbly ducked with a sarcastic laugh. It goaded St John further and he snapped, 'It was brave, too. You don't mess with the smugglers.'

'I don't suppose they're any worse than the criminal gangs in the cities. They'd slit your throat for working on their patch,' Tristan bragged. 'So, Adam, what do you think of your twin's exploits? Are you the braver one, or is he?'

Adam drew his legs up and rested his chin on his knees. After his second swig of brandy, he was beginning to feel light-headed. 'I don't suppose you will consider this dangerous, but I did once save a toddler from being crushed by a runaway cart in Penruan. A farmer was delivering two piglets to a house halfway up the coomb and one of them got free. It ran off squealing round the horse's hooves. It was a skittish mare and the noise the pig was making frightened her, and she bolted down the hill towards the quay. The fishwives were gutting the fish and some of them had their children playing nearby. Dozens of gulls were screeching as they scavenged the entrails, their cries drowning out the carter's shouts and the sound of the approaching horse and cart. Annie Moyle had come out of her father's chandler's shop to play. She was always dressed better than the other children and they resented it. One of the girls pushed her over into a pile of entrails, ruining her dress. She was sobbing and screaming in temper. No one paid her any heed, and when she saw the horse bearing down on her she froze in terror. I was the nearest and threw myself at Annie, scooping her into my arms and rolling us both away from its hooves just as it sped past.'

'It's a wonder they don't call you St Adam.' His cousin remained unimpressed. 'I could pick a pocket or a lock better than anyone in our gang,' he bragged. 'Twice I was caught as a sneak thief stealing silver inside a big house and only escaped by stabbing a footman in the leg on the first occasion, and by jumping from a first-floor window the second time. You two don't know what danger is. You've been cosseted all your lives. I risked the hangman's noose every day when I stole food so Ma and I would not starve.'

Tristan had grown steadily more angry and continued to down the brandy, which seemed to have no intoxicating effect on him. The angrier he became, the more scorn he heaped on the twins, becoming increasingly scathing in his resentment of the comfort and luxury of their childhood. It was the only time he had spoken of the squalor and hardship he had endured, and while his tales had shocked Adam, St John mocked him for exaggerating. To boost his own bravado, St John had drunk more of the brandy than Adam and his speech was slurred and his movements uncoordinated. Another insult from Tristan, lost to Adam by a boom of thunder, had St John and his cousin at each other's throats, rolling about the floor as they fought. Tristan, the older and heavier, smashed his fist into St John's nose and eye, and the light from the lantern they had brought with them showed the younger boy's face was streaked with dark trails of blood.

'Damned guttersnipe,' St John raged as his fists failed to find their target.

'Stop it!' Adam jumped on Tristan, hauling him away from his twin. 'Is that how you win your fights, by picking on someone smaller than you? Where's the courage in that?'

Several blows landed on Adam's chest, knocking him down.

'I hate you both,' Tristan spat. A flash of lightning showed his face twisted with fury. He was kicking out, his temper out of control as St John squirmed to get out of his way.

'You think you're better than me,' Tristan screamed. 'I hate you and your hoity-toity family. I hate George Loveday. He turned his back on my ma when she needed help. She'd be alive now if he had shown just a scrap of mercy. I don't need him and I don't need any of you.'

Adam rubbed his chest, which was bruised from the blows, and struggled to regain his breath. 'It was not Grandpapa's fault you lived as you did. His brother ran away and cut off all connections with us. Blame him.'

'Go to hell. All of you can go to hell!' Tristan stumbled to the mouth of the cave.

St John was crouched on the floor of the cave vomiting. 'I'm dying,' he groaned. 'That bastard has done for me.'

'You're drunk.' Adam lost patience with his twin as St John flopped on to the floor. He was worried that Tristan in his drunken anger would do something stupid and he followed him outside. He had been appalled at what Tristan had revealed about the deprivation and horrors of his upbringing.

To his relief Tristan had not gone far. His dark shape was staring out to sea. Thunder resounded like cannon fire and when lightning lit up the shore like daylight, Adam saw the ship that held Tristan's attention. It was too close to the shore, and though it had missed the rocks of Trevowan Cove, if it did not immediately change its course, it would certainly founder on the next headland.

Adam's experienced gaze had seen that the tattered sails would make the vessel slow in responding. He doubted anything could save her, but he could not stand back and do nothing. Picking up the lantern he shouted, 'The ship will smash on the next rocks. We've got to try to warn them.'

'A shipwreck! There could be rich pickings,' Tristan shrieked as he sped along the beach to the cliff steps.

'No!' Adam protested as he ran after him. 'We have to see if we can save any lives.'

The icy rain had drenched him, helping to chase away the fogginess to his wits induced by the brandy. His lungs seared with pain from the pace of his run as he swung the lantern, hoping that it would warn the sailors of the closeness of the rocks. The wind was at gale force and at times he had to stoop double or risk being blown over the cliff to his death. The ship had already disappeared around the headland, and minutes later, as Adam stood at its edge, his worst fears were realised. She was already on the rocks on the far side of the cove, and between the crashes of thunder he could hear the sharp crack of timbers splintering. More alarmingly, he heard the screams and cries of terrified crew and passengers. He could just make out a jumble of bodies clinging to the rails and shredded rigging.

Then, as he watched, the ship's prow rose up like a rearing horse as the vessel was thrown forward by the surge of the tide. At the same moment the fore mast sheared off and toppled sideways into the water. The ship was tilted at a dangerous angle, the waves crashing against its sides. The sea around it was a bubbling cauldron of foam and debris and it was impossible to see if any bodies were in the water.

The cliffs above the rocks where the ship had gone aground were sheer and there was no way down them from the top without ropes and pulleys. The tide was at its highest and it would have been impossible to reach the ship from the shore as the rocks were too far out and a dinghy or fishing boat would also risk being smashed on the granite needles beneath the water's surface.

Adam gazed helplessly around him. The sailors and passengers would drown if help did not reach them. But what could be done? By the time he ran back to Trevowan to raise the alarm it would be too late. Even as he regarded the disaster, a huge wave slammed over the deck, dragging several bodies into the sea. Already the beach was dotted with cargo and smashed timbers, and he prayed that some of the bodies would still be alive when they were washed up on to the beach.

He scrambled down the slippery cliff face, which was treacherous on this side of the cove, although it sloped at a climbable gradient to the beach, his fingers grabbing at clumps of sea thrift to keep his balance. He was aware of Tristan already on the beach below him running towards the shoreline. At the same time he became conscious of a group of distant lights and of other figures looming out of the shadows of the cliffs in the middle of the cove. It made his already chilled heart turn to icy fear. Those distant lights and so many men meant only one thing. The scourge of the Cornish coast. Wreckers.

To claim the vessel as salvage there must be no survivors. Any passenger or sailor who made it alive to the shore would be clubbed to death so that there would be no witnesses to the heinous events of the night. Adam knew his own life would be in danger if he was caught, but he could not leave helpless victims to be murdered without trying to save some of them. He noticed a score or more men on the sand dragging anything of value higher up the beach, and hoped that in the confusion he would be undetected.

When his feet hit the firmness of the sand, he sped towards the churning waves. The sound of the thunder was growing fainter and the lightning bolts were further apart. The storm was moving out to sea and heading to the coast of France. The wind also, having done its worst, was losing most of its force and Adam no longer had to bend double. Between the illuminating beams of lightning the scene was cast into a Stygian darkness except for the tiny pools of light from the wreckers' lanterns. A few bodies writhed in the foaming waves, their cries for help pitiful, and their arms flailing in desperation to fight off the fiendish creatures intent upon killing them. Other hellish demons ignored their cries as they dragged casks and boxes to the shore. The wreckers were too engrossed in their evil rampage to notice Adam as he kicked off his shoes and plunged into the waves up to his thighs.

The first body he encountered was floating on its stomach, and as he turned it over, the gaping mouth and sightless, staring eyes of the only dead person he had ever touched brought a rush of nausea to his throat. He spat it out and steeled himself to face more such gruesome sights if there was ever to be a chance of him saving someone. Five, six, seven more bodies were similarly discovered drowned, until the cries from the ship no longer carried above the gushing of the waves. They were replaced by the shouts and arguments taking place on the shore as the wreckers fought over the rich spoils.

The scene was a nightmare. Adam's teeth chattered from the cold and his strength was ebbing from his battle to stay upright in the fierce undercurrent. No one appeared to have survived the wreck. If he stayed in the water much longer he would be too weak to wade ashore, and every minute he remained on the beach he ran the risk of being recognised and even attacked by the wreckers to conceal their own identity. Fortunately, until then the men had been too engrossed in their greed to notice him, but for how much longer could he escape detection? He had swum in waist-high water almost to the centre of the cove where the wreckers were working. He dared not venture ashore; his size would give him away as a youth, and he had seen only men working on the beach. His only chance would be to swim to the edge of the cove and retrace his steps up the sloping cliff face.

Then his attention was caught by a slighter figure on the edge of the shadows on the beach. It was Tristan, and he was fighting with a figure on the ground. Adam gasped with shock, for it looked as though his cousin had attacked a survivor. At that moment a wave crashed over Adam's head and he lost his footing, powerless to save himself as the current dragged his body under and his mouth and nostrils filled with water. His body cartwheeled along the bottom of the sea bed, scraping over rocks, his legs fighting for leverage to kick upwards to the surface. The current was too strong for him to stop it sucking him backwards into deeper water. His father had taught him how to swim when he was five, and every summer he had spent hours in the sea, becoming a strong swimmer. His grandfather had also told him never to fight a current but allow his body to float with it.

Now his survival instinct took control, and when his head broke through the waves he managed a gulp of air. He had been carried away from the wreckers and the ship towards the opposite cliff, and he struck out with his arms, knowing the incoming tide would take him towards the headland. Here the danger lay in being dashed against the rocks. A fork of lightning allowed him to get his bearings, and as his knees grazed against granite boulders, he managed to get a handhold in a cleft in the rock. The waves continued to buffet him and his life depended on not losing his grip. A swell in another wave enabled him to both find a foothold and haul himself higher, and as the sea receded he prayed his strength would not give out as he heaved himself above the waves. He clung there for several moments recovering his breath. He dared not wait too long, for with each breath his skin grew colder. Inch by inch he forced his battered and almost exhausted body forwards. His feet slithered on the seaweed-coated rocks, and his knees and hands bled from the razor-sharp granite.

Weakened from his climb, he collapsed on the ground and must have passed out. His next memory was of Tristan and St John trying to haul him to his feet. He vaguely remembered staggering home, and the humiliating interview with his grandfather.

'You were lucky to survive!' Japhet broke into Adam's narrative and with an effort he pulled his thoughts back to the present.

'I was in bed with a raging fever for a week. By then Tristan had gone and Grandpapa refused to have his name or the wreck mentioned.'

'When did St John reach the beach? Hadn't you left him unconscious?'

'He said he had roused himself enough to follow us. He saw more than I did and said Tristan was stealing jewellery from the body of a woman who had been washed up on the beach. There was a gold cross in his pocket. Tristan swore he was innocent, but Grandfather said the cross was damning evidence. He and St John were beaten that night and I got a hiding once I had recovered from my fever.'

'Then why did St John not tell me that, instead of insisting I hear the story from you?' Japhet frowned.

'That is typical of St John.' Adam was too disturbed by the vividness of the memories to pay much heed to his twin's evasion. 'I am deeply ashamed of what happened that night. It was as though by being on the beach we were party to the evil of the wreckers. There were no survivors, and by morning the ship had broken up. Once word got out, villagers from all around swarmed to the shore to find what pickings they could from the cargo. No arrests were made. By running away, Tristan as good as admitted his guilt. It was not a proud day for the Lovedays.'

217

Chapter Twenty-four

Since the attack upon him at Bodmin, St John could not shake the feeling that he was being followed when he was away from Trevowan, and he made fewer visits to Truro and Bodmin. It was worse when it was dark, as everywhere had concealing shadows where an assailant could lie in wait. The current fashion of tight-fitting breeches, slim cut-away coats and short waistcoats made it impossible to secrete a weapon about his person. Even the close-fitting top boots were too tight to hide a dagger along his calf, and it was not done to wear a sword. September was proving too mild a month to don a greatcoat, where at least he could have hidden a small pearl-headed pistol. Much to his twin's amusement and ridicule, St John had taken to carrying a walking cane, much favoured by the fops of the day. Effeminate as the cane might appear, it did conceal a thin sword blade within, but it was inconvenient to carry.

When Basil Bracewaite called at Trevowan intent upon a night of cards, St John welcomed the diversion. They decided on a gaming house in Fowey and took rooms at a nearby inn. For most of the evening the cards favoured St John, and when they turned against him, the fire to recoup his earlier winnings consumed him. He was deaf to his friend's advice to cut his losses, and was not even aware when Basil declared he was leaving. He had just won his first hand in an hour and was convinced that his luck had changed. Two hours later he finally conceded that fortune had again deserted him. He staggered to his feet having signed several IOUs, which could only be settled by means of raising another loan.

Outside, the port was eerily quiet. St John peered at his hunter watch in the glow of the lantern hanging over the door of the gaming house. Four a.m. The quietest hour, before the port began to stir at dawn. The moon was almost full and he could see no figures lurking or sleeping in doorways, and the inn was only a dozen paces away. The cobbled streets were sequinned with a thousand moonlit stars after a shower of rain. The downpour had freshened the air and washed the debris from the runnels into the gutters and down into the quay. The masts of a score of sailing ships forested the skyline above the quay. The only sound was the ringing of a solitary bell marking the change of watch on a vessel moored in the river channel. The sharpness of the fresh air after the heat and smoky atmosphere of the gaming house increased St John's light-headedness from a night of heavy drinking.

When he entered the inn, only a single light burned in the taproom and a sleepy potboy was slumped over a table. A fat ginger tomcat lay stretched before the dying embers of the fire, a dead mouse on the flagstones by his front paws. He opened one eye as St John passed him on the way to the stairs. All the rooms were occupied. Behind one door he passed, someone was urinating noisily into the night pot. Several men could be heard snoring, and further along the corridor there was the rhythmic thudding of a bedpost against the wall and the grunts of a couple fornicating.

St John had paid extra for the privilege of not sharing a room, and as he stumbled inside he yawned, more than ready for his bed. He never reached his destination. A cover was thrown over his head, and before he could shout a protest, a thud to the side of his head knocked him unconscious.

When he next came to his senses, his first impression was of a band of steel tight about his brow. His throat was parched and his tongue thick from a night of excess. That was no different from any other hangover. What was strange was the weird dipping and rising motion of the bed. He groaned and opened his eyes to meet with total darkness. It was not until he tried to move his cramped arms and legs that he realised he was tied and blindfolded. Panic ground through him. There was also a gag stuffed into his mouth and he was unable to make a sound. He thrashed wildly for several minutes, the ropes rasping the flesh on his wrists and ankles. There was no slackening to their bite and he finally lay still, his mind frantically trying to make sense of his surroundings. It was not the alcohol that was causing the weird motion. The slap of water against timbers told him that he was a prisoner aboard a ship.

The women at Trevowan were seated at the dining table. The chair at the head of the table remained vacant. Elspeth stared at it and gave an exaggerated sigh. 'That scapegrace nephew of mine ever neglects his duties. How long has he been absent this time? Four nights. Even Bracewaite was abandoned by him. He called this afternoon and was shocked that St John had not returned. The estate will not run itself.'

'It is Felicity I feel sorry for,' Margaret replied. 'She has taken to her room claiming that this pregnancy exhausts her, but it is her husband's neglect that ails her.'

'At the very least St John should inform her of his whereabouts,' Amelia said. 'We do not know where he is. His cavalier manner is disgraceful. One would almost think he did not care about his inheritance.'

'Adam should have been the heir to the entire Loveday estate.' Elspeth sniffed her disapproval. 'It was by chance that St John was drawn first from the womb when they were delivered by Caesarean. Edward would have been within his rights to decide which of them was the more dedicated and appropriate heir. He should have put aside tradition. St John is driven by his selfish hunger for pleasure. He is a wastrel and will never change.'

'I pray that Felicity gives him the son he craves.' Amelia fidgeted with her napkin. 'He resents working when he believes the estate will pass to Rafe. A son could give him a greater sense of purpose – of ancestry and continuity.'

'If he does not change his ways I wonder if there will be an estate left to pass on,' Elspeth snapped. 'As his youngest son, Edward could provide little security for Rafe apart from a small annuity. He will have to make his own way in the world.'

'He will not go without,' Amelia corrected. 'Richard, as the son of my first husband, naturally inherits all of Mr Allbright's property. When I married Edward I still had most of the inheritance from my parents and Edward insisted that this would be placed in trust for Rafe.'

'Younger sons never have it easy,' Margaret observed. 'Rafe may yet take after my brothers Hubert and William and join the navy. Richard chose such a life and he is now a lieutenant.'

'It is not without its hazards and dangers, especially whilst we are at war.' Amelia could not suppress a shudder. 'I do not think I could bear to have both my sons fighting for our country. It is four months since I have received a letter from Richard. He could be in the midst of a sea battle right at this moment, or a French privateer could have sunk his ship.'

'Supposedly there is a lull in the fighting,' Elspeth reminded her. 'The navy is a noble profession. You must take comfort in his courage and that he is prepared to give his life for his country.'

'Lull or not, I still worry. Many of the ports are the cesspits of humanity. I am but a weak and selfish woman.' Amelia flashed her sister-in-law a fierce glare. 'Your words are no comfort to a mother.'

'Rafe could take the cloth like Uncle Joshua and cousin Peter.' Georganna, who had been pushing her food around her plate and eating little, joined in the conversation, contributing a stab of irony. 'Though they are the only two Lovedays to engage in a more sober way of life.'

Margaret tutted in annoyance. 'How can you deny the sobriety of your own husband? Thomas is a banker. His bank is one of the most prestigious—'

'Mama, you know very well he is only happy when he is writing his plays,' Georganna flung back with unwarranted heat.

'Perhaps if he had a son he would be more settled . . .' Margaret began.

To everyone's astonishment, Georganna rose from her chair and ran from the room.

'That was not very tactful.' Amelia raised her eyebrows. 'You should go to her, Margaret.'

The older woman pressed her hand to her head. 'Georganna has been acting strangely of late. And why has Thomas made excuses not to join us here? I would have thought he would be delighted at Japhet's return.'

'All of the family seem troubled since their return from

Tamasine's,' Elspeth snorted. 'That tyke Tristan has unsettled everyone.' The atmosphere in the dining room was taut with tension. 'His presence must have been a shock. He was a waif and a child who was one of life's unfortunates.'

'Was he not an ingrate who threw Papa's kindness in giving him a home back in his face in the grossest manner?' Margaret snapped. 'Once a guttersnipe, always a guttersnipe.'

'Perhaps too much was expected of him,' Elspeth said with unaccustomed generosity. 'Though he tried hard to be accepted he was ridiculed for his rough manner and speech. There was always rivalry between him and the twins. St John made it no secret he did not like him. Papa barely tolerated him. Edward was hardly ever here, spending all the hours God sent at the yard. Margaret was married and living in London and I was more interested in my horses. He was very much a boy in need of a mother's love and a father's guidance.'

Margaret stared at her sister in astonishment. 'You defend him after he stole from us?'

'I often wondered if I should not have done more to make him feel welcome. But I am not naturally maternal. Providing the house ran smoothly and the boys were fed and clothed, I never paid them much attention. The twins never suffered from it. But Tristan had lost his mother just before he came here. He must have mourned her terribly.' The usual stern line of her mouth quivered and she hid her emotion by blowing her nose in a lace handkerchief. 'The lad was always on his guard. Emotionally, he would let no one close. But he loved the horses and took to the saddle like a duck to water. He was a good rider, never sawing on the bit or pushing his mount too hard, or for too long, as many a madcap would do. He spent hours in the stables grooming and tending the horses. He was not all bad.'

'Because he showed an interest in horses!' Margaret scoffed. 'Elspeth, my dear, you have a strange concept of what it takes to make your way in the world.'

'All I am saying is that it showed he was not without some good points.' Elspeth banged her hand on the table. She hated to admit any failing within herself, and to be ridiculed for it was unendurable. 'I do not know what he did that night that was so terrible, but before he ran away I found him sobbing in the stables. I do not believe it was from the beating, or anger. The lad sounded as though he was heartbroken. When I tried to console him – although probably not very compassionately – he backed away, his fur ruffled and spitting like a feral cat. "They'll never believe me. I'll never be good enough. I'm not wanted here. They can keep their grudging charity. I don't need it. I don't need anyone."

'I told him to pull himself together and not be so weak. I should have been more understanding. He was gone the next morning.' She dabbed her napkin to her eye. 'I feared that if he had died I was partly responsible. At least he survived and seems to have made a success of his life.'

'It does not change his attitude,' Margaret pronounced. 'He deliberately set out to trick his way back into the family. I have great regard for Adam's judgement. If Adam does not trust him, I am inclined to believe his opinion. He was a witness to all that happened that night.'

The following day Hannah arrived at Rabson Farm with her four children. The dairymaids and servants were excited at her arrival and fussed over the children. After the grandeur of Highcroft, the rambling timber-framed farmhouse seemed cramped in comparison. But to Hannah, who had spent ten years happily married to Oswald Rabson before his untimely death of a wasting sickness, it would always have its own special charm.

When the young ones ran off to explore and greet old animal friends, Hannah spent two hours talking with her overseer Mark Sawle and was delighted to see the rows of workers in the fields and that the haymaking was already underway. She was also pleased that Mark had found another half-dozen shops and kiddleys to take the extra milk produced by the increased number of cows they had reared. She also inspected the buttery, which was run under the supervision of Mark's wife Jeannie, who made the cheese and butter sold at local shops and markets. Everything was spotless and in perfect order, and rows of maturing cheeses lined the storeroom. Each smell and sight at the farm filled her with nostalgia, but as the new baby moved within her, she had no regrets at the changes in her lifestyle since her marriage. She adored her second husband and

223

could never believe that she had found such a fulfilling love for a second time in her life.

During Oswald's illness she had run the farm with the help of her present husband Sam, but she had been the one with the experience and had made all the decisions. Now she was determined that the farm, which was her eldest son's inheritance, would continue to prosper until he was old enough to take charge. But Davey was still only fourteen and it would be some years before he made his life here.

Outside, the livestock were all well fed and healthy and her only moments of sadness were to see the empty stalls and paddock where Japhet's mares and foals had been housed. The horses had been part of the farm for the last seven years. Her sadness was fleeting, for their absence brought the greater joy that her brother had installed them at Tor Farm.

Impatient to be reunited with Japhet, she would discuss the rest of the farm details with Mark later and summoned her children to join her on a visit to Tor Farm.

As her carriage entered the drive, she saw Japhet exercising a colt on a leading rein. She ordered the driver to halt, and waving excitedly she forgot all decorum as she leapt to the ground and ran across the fields. Her heart pounded with happiness and tears of joy blurred her vision as she watched Japhet tether the colt to a post and stride purposefully towards her. Laughing, she ran into his arms and held him close as he hugged her against his chest. For several long moments she clung to him, her throat too locked with happiness to speak. The touch of his warm lips against her hair and his deep answering laughter steadied her composure and she breathed a heartfelt sigh as she lifted her head to gaze up at him. Somehow she managed to find her voice. 'I have missed you so much, dear brother.'

With a grin he wiped the tears from her cheeks. 'I missed you too. And I am unworthy of your tears.'

She brushed the remnants of them away. 'I never meant our reunion to be like this. How foolish of me to cry when I am so very happy.'

He held her at arm's length. 'Let me look at you. You are as beautiful as I remember, and I owe you a great debt for all the sacrifices you made to keep my dream of breeding horses alive. The mares and foals are all I hoped for and more. And you also found tenants for Tor Farm who tended it well. Yet you had so many problems of your own. I regret not being here for you when Oswald died. He was a man I much respected and admired.'

'Your letters were a comfort.' She could not drag her gaze from his handsome face, seeing the lines etched by his experiences. 'You have returned to us safe and well, and also with two wonderful sons. We have so much news to catch up on, but for now, hug me again so I know this is not a dream and that you are really home.'

After the Sunday service at Trewenna, as it was such a bright sunny day the family were standing in groups in the churchyard and Tristan's name again rose in the conversation. Adam's revelations about the night of the storm were now known to them all, but Japhet remained sceptical of their cousin's blackguard reputation.

'I'm still inclined to give him the benefit of the doubt,' he declared. 'Adam by his own admission did not see much of Tris's actions that night. He could have been fighting a wrecker, not attacking a survivor.'

'They found a gold cross and a ring in his pocket,' Hannah said. This was the last day of her short visit, which had allowed her to be at the farm during the harvest as well as be reunited with Japhet. They were returning to Dorset tomorrow. The sun was hot on her face and she twirled her parasol in her agitation.

'Thieving had been a large part of Tristan's life since a young child. The temptation to take something from a dead body could have been too great for him. That is a far cry from knocking a survivor unconscious,' Japhet pointed out.

'You always defend the underdog, Japhet,' she replied.

'Because I know how dangerous speculation can be to a man's reputation.'

'That is all very well, but Tristan often made me feel uncomfortable. He was always showing off and trying to prove he was better than the twins.'

'And what youth doesn't act that way?' Japhet said with a harsh laugh. 'It was his way of proving his courage and trying to fit in.'

'I do not think any of us even came close to knowing the real Tristan,' Hannah said with more sympathy. 'I doubt he has many happy memories from his time with us. Perhaps he saw Tamasine as a kindred family spirit, that was all, and he had no sinister intentions to use her power and influence to fleece her friends. Did Adam even give him a chance to explain himself? Or did his own feelings of shame about that night cloud his judgement? Tristan was a reminder of something he very much wanted to forget.'

'Since the twins made their feelings so clear to our long-lost cousin, I doubt we will see anything of him again. Not in this part of the country at least,' Japhet declared.

Aware that Senara was standing quietly and not joining in the conversation, whilst the men continued to speak of Tristan, Hannah said softly to Adam's wife, 'Was news of Adam's involvement with wreckers on the beach a shock to you or did you already know of it?'

'Adam was sworn to secrecy by his grandfather. He did not tell me of the incident and I would not have expected him to in those circumstances. He is too honourable. And I am not shocked, for Adam tried only to save people that night. It was his cousin's treachery in joining the wreckers that so greatly shamed him, and the fact that he could not stop him.'

To change the subject that had again brought tension to her brief stay with her family, Hannah said, 'Speaking of cousins, St John still appears to be avoiding his responsibilities. Aunt Margaret is upset she has seen so little of him. How long has it been since he was at Trevowan? Ten days? That is excessive for him, and no one knows where he is.'

St John had lost track of how long he had been a prisoner. At one time, from the noise on deck and the motion of the ship, he could tell they had set sail. His arms and legs remained bound and he had been given no food and only fetid water once a day. He had repeatedly been beaten when he did not give his interrogators the answers they wanted. Weak and slipping in and out of delirium, he was certain he was going to die, his body thrown overboard to wash up half eaten by fishes on some unknown beach.

His legs and arms were locked in agonising cramps as he lay

226

stinking in his own filth, and he was racked with thirst and hunger. Finally his greed and his obsession with secrecy and gaming had brought him to this miserable end. No one knew where he was. There could be no rescue, and whether he confessed the truth to his captors or not, he was convinced they would kill him anyway. The hours alone in the darkness had given his conscience free rein and all his failings had been recalled to mock him. He had been so wrapped up in his pursuit of pleasure that he had lost sight of the priorities that could have brought him lasting happiness. He had seen Trevowan as a millstone around his neck instead of an accolade to all his ancestors' achievements. He resented his marriage because Felicity had not brought him the easy wealth he craved. Yet in the early days she had been intelligent and witty company, adoring and undemanding. She had been everything he had wanted in a wife except immensely rich, and he had allowed that to ruin everything. Amelia and Elspeth's drain on his resources had also irked him. How quickly he had forgotten that Elspeth had brought him and Adam up and been the only mother they had ever known. She had sacrificed her youth and possibly her chance of a good marriage, for despite her quick temper she had been a striking and vivacious woman in her younger days. He had also conveniently forgotten that Amelia had used her personal income to save Trevowan from ruin on more than one occasion. It made him ashamed. He had seen his ownership of Trevowan more as a triumph over his twin than the life of privilege it was capable of giving him. Was it too late now to make amends? Would he be allowed to return to his home and show the appreciation to his family that they deserved?

There was a draught of air across his body as the door to his cell was opened.

'Quite the hero, ain't you, Mr Loveday?' The cruel voice that had led all the interrogations taunted him anew. 'You saved the life of a boy from a coach accident. But what happened to the valuables on that coach?'

'I told you, I know nothing. The boy was badly injured and my only concern was to save his life.'

'Very noble!' his antagonist mocked. 'But who'd leave a fortune in jewels and gold coins scattered about the countryside? What did you do with the valuables?' A vicious kick to his already bruised ribs sent pain crashing through his body. 'Maybe that will remind you. If not, you'll tell us in time.'

'I was on my own. It was dark. The boy was in pain. I gave no thought to possessions. There was a woman dead inside the coach, and also the driver.' He focused over the gruelling pain to keep to his original story. He had failed his family in so many ways, but he could not fail them in this. They would only be safe if he pleaded ignorance. 'I could do nothing for the woman or the driver, but I could help the boy. If you know of the crash, do you know who the boy is?' He attempted to turn the questioning back on them. Perhaps this way he would convince them he was innocent and they would let him go. 'The lad has lost his memory. My family have been trying to discover his identity to reunite him with his family.'

'The news of the crash is commonplace. The boy does not interest us. What happened to the valuables?'

'I do not know. I told you, when our servants reached the scene they found that the coach had been stripped of everything.'

'I don't believe you.' A fist slammed into his face and another into his gut. 'Stop lying. There was a cash box and of course the ring you claim you won at hazard, and other jewellery, expensive clothes and furs, family silver.'

'How do you know so much if you do not know who the family were?' St John gasped through his pain.

'It's for us to ask the questions.'

Several more punches left him hovering on the edge of consciousness. He battled to speak, suspecting this could be his last chance to save himself. The words were slow to come but were listened to without interruption. 'They must have been taken by smugglers. There were signs of pack ponies along the track. They must have thought it was their lucky night. It is amongst their number that you must ask.'

'Yet you have squandered hundreds of pounds on your gambling losses in recent months.'

'Trevowan is a wealthy estate.'

'Not according to rumour. Bad harvests, poor management.' A kick to his head had him falling into nothingness until a dousing of cold water was thrown over his body.

'I am a rich man,' he blustered. 'I have no need to steal.'

When a sadistic burst of laughter echoed behind him, St John drew upon the last reserves of his courage and strength. 'To know so much you must know the family. Who is the boy? Surely they would pay you a reward for finding him?'

There was a faint smell of expensive cologne in the room and St John sensed another's presence. A heavily accented, cultured voice said, 'Enough of this savagery. If he took the money, he has lost it at cards. He does not have it now. Not according to the number of IOUs he has recently written. The man is a wastrel. He is of no use to us.'

The words faded. St John was too weak to fight the battle of keeping his wits. All he wanted in that moment was to escape the pain and he allowed the darkness to close in around him.

'He has passed out again,' the foreign voice declared. 'Get rid of him. At least we know for certain the boy recalls nothing or prefers to remain anonymous, or he would have spoken of his past by now. But who would believe him anyway?'

Chapter Twenty-five

Georganna was feeling isolated from the Loveday family. She had sworn Senara to secrecy about her pregnancy until she told Thomas. Senara had agreed, provided that she promised to do nothing foolish in return. She had always dressed eccentrically and now wore a knee-length loose Roman-style tunic over her high-waisted gown. Nothing of her condition showed. She had no sickness, and unlike Felicity she suffered no debilitating tiredness. Only her appetite had been affected, her worry making all food unpalatable, which was why she had remained so slim. Senara had examined her and agreed that she was about four months into her pregnancy. In a few weeks' time it would be impossible to hide her condition. She had expected that Thomas would have joined the family in Cornwall by now, especially as Japhet had returned. Yet he had made his excuses to both herself and his mother in letters that had arrived three days ago. A bank was interested in merging with Mercer and Lascalles and the negotiations were at too critical a stage for Thomas to leave London.

Each day Georganna was finding it harder to live with her guilt. It was unthinkable to confess to Thomas of her condition by letter, and she had woken up this morning considering taking the post chaise to the capital. Whatever the consequences and Thomas's reaction, at least she would know the worst. If he refused to acknowledge the child and wanted nothing more to do with her, she would make a fresh life for herself. Although the prospect of bringing up a child alone was another fear she had to face. To create such a new life for herself would first mean that she had to survive the birth, and despite all Senara's reassurances, she still lived with the terror that she would die as her mother had done. She knew she was being irrational, but she could not shake from her mind the thought of her mother's screams and the ordeal she had suffered. It did not help that she had no one but Senara to confide in. Even the fact that neither Felicity nor Hannah had voiced any such concerns for themselves, and they were expecting their third and fifth children, could allay her dread. Felicity was convinced that this time she was carrying a boy, and a son would change St John's attitude to her and stop his gambling and safeguard the future of Trevowan. Hannah, as with everything else, took her pregnancy in her stride.

Georganna welcomed the solitude she found during her long walks. This morning, after they had taken their breakfast together, Felicity had gone upstairs to lie down, Elspeth had left on her morning ride and Margaret and Amelia were in the orangery. As Georganna approached, she could hear the two older women cooing and fussing over Thea. In her present mood she knew her control over her emotions would snap if she joined them. The weather remained fair, and without stopping to collect her Indian shawl she left the house and headed for Trevowan Cove.

For a long while she stood at the top of the cliff, surveying the horizon. She ignored the breeze that dragged the pins from her hair so that tendrils writhed around her face. There was a gentle swell to the sea as the waves rolled up the beach. The sound of them lapping against the shore was comforting, like the whispers of an old friend. Dotted on the skyline she could see the pale sails of Penruan's fishing fleet, and a Falmouth packet was heading towards its port. Two local sloops that had probably loaded a cargo of slates or tin from Par beach were heading along the coast. A barque transporting china clay from the recently built harbour at Charlestown was also visible. She was beginning to recognise the different types of vessels that sailed on these waters, and Adam had explained where many of them loaded and unloaded their cargoes.

Two cormorants were on the water by the headland, and for a moment she thought one of the tenants' children was swimming in the bay until she realised it was the head and sleek body of a grey seal. For a moment her inner tension eased. Here was a peace and tranquillity that she could never experience in London.

Attracted by the antics of the seal, she climbed down the cliff steps to the beach and sat on the sand. She drew her knees up to her chin and her expression was taut as her gaze drifted sightlessly out to sea. The seal had dived and disappeared from the cove. Her mind churned again in its ceaseless turmoil. Guilt. Shame. Fear. But mostly loss. The loss of her ideals. The loss of innocence. The loss of feeling so completely a woman. The loss of the thrill from a lover's tryst. The loss of passion itself. She did not delude herself that Tristan had loved her with the same wild intensity that had made her forget all pride and honour in the heady sweetness of their affair.

A shuddering sigh escaped her and she angrily dashed a wayward tear from her cheek. She had not come here to feel sorry for herself but to seek a solution. She had no idea where her lover was, and after the reception he had received from her family at Beaucombe, she doubted she would see him again. Perhaps that would be for the best. They had no future together. How could they when she was married?

Her thoughts were abruptly cut short by the shadow of a man's figure that loomed across the sand in front of her. Aware that she was alone and out of sight and calling distance to summon help from the house, she gasped and spun round, her heart hammering with fright. Her fear dissipated like spindrift in the sun, but her pulse continued to race.

'You! I never hoped . . . Never expected . . . Oh, my love.' She rose to throw herself into his open arms.

'Did you think I would abandon you?' His mouth was hot against her neck and ear.

'Tristan, I did not know what to think.' She moved back in his embrace to stare into his face. The passion she saw there fired her blood, but she could not help a furtive glance up to the cliff. 'This is madness. Anyone could see us.'

'Then come into the cave. We will be safe there. I have been watching the house for some days and noticed that most mornings you walk here. I would risk everything for you, my darling.' He took her hand and they entered the narrow opening of the cave.

Once within its darkness, Georganna held back. She was disconcerted that he had spied on her when she was unaware of his presence, and neither did she feel comfortable here. Her initial joy at being reunited with her lover ebbed, replaced by the dread of discovery. When he drew her closer and started to kiss her with urgent passion, she leaned back and placed her fingers on his lips.

'We must talk, Tristan. But not here. There are too many ghosts of unhappy lovers.'

'What fancy is this? Some ill-fated tryst of Adam's or St John's?' He laughed. 'There were no stories of ghosts when we were boys.'

'It is where Captain William Loveday shot his wife and her lover. This is where they met. Uncle William then took the bodies out to sea and drowned himself. It was not so many years ago.'

'I had old William down as a confirmed bachelor. I could understand him fighting a duel with his wife's lover, but killing her and then himself is not what I would expect at all.'

'Lisette tricked him into marriage. She wanted the respectability William's name could give, whilst his absence at sea allowed her to take any lover she chose. And there were many.' The story had always chilled her. It had all the pathos of a Greek tragedy and within its sinister echoes she could almost hear the lovers' laughter mocking her own dilemma. Her voice shook as she forced herself to continue. 'Her lover was also her brother, Etienne Riviere. The bodies of the two of them were never found. We think Uncle William drowned himself to make it look like an accident at sea and save the family from scandal. His body was washed ashore some time later.'

'The Lovedays and their pride and honour!' Tristan scoffed, but feeling her draw further back from him he added, 'I have taken a house in Charlestown. Come to me there.'

She shook her head. 'This cannot go on, my love. It has to end. I have wronged Thomas. Am I any better than Lisette?'

'I am not your brother.' His rigid stance warned her that he was offended.

'But there is no love lost between you and your cousins. Etienne hated Adam. He was jealous of the affection Lisette once had for him.'

'Is that how you see me? I do not hate Adam. I have no quarrel with *him*.' Tristan dropped his hands to his sides, anger sparking in his eyes. 'Do you think that I am less honourable than Thomas or St John?'

'No!' Georganna cried out in protest. 'You do not understand.' She broke off, unable to control her anguish. 'You have spoken of the Loveday pride and honour. How can we avoid enmity? I am to have a child. Your child!' She hugged her arms tight about her chest.

His face was frozen into an expressionless mask. Was it shock? Or was it horror? She cursed her foolishness in so stupidly blurting out her news. She had handled this so badly; of course he was shocked. 'Stupidly I thought this would never happen to us. It is all such a mess. I do not know if Thomas will forgive me, or accept the child. But I do know that he will not rest until his honour is satisfied. One of you could die. How can I be responsible for that? He must never know that you are the father. I shall take that secret to the grave.'

'And deny me the right to acknowledge my child?' His outrage flayed her. 'I would not abandon you to suffer the anger of your husband, who has been no husband to you at all.'

'You must never say that.' A new fear consumed her. 'I will never allow Thomas to be so maligned. It would destroy his reputation. It could put him in prison.'

'Then he will accept the child. If he continues to see his catamite, why should we not also continue as lovers?'

'You make it sound so sordid. So degrading.' She put her hands to her ears. 'I will not bring shame to my family. Our affair must end now. I will bear the consequences of my actions. I want our love to remain pure.'

His laughter was cruel and mocking. 'Pure is not the word for an illicit affair, my dear. Have these last months meant nothing to you? Or would you just cast me aside as the rest of your family have done?'

He had not moved, and through his sarcasm she detected the pain of rejection inflicted on him by the Lovedays. She shook her head. 'I love you, Tristan. But I love Thomas as my friend and husband. My loyalty must be to him.'

'It does not have to be that way.' His voice was brittle and the set of his body rigid and uncompromising. A chasm opened between them. 'We can go away from Cornwall and London and start a new life where no one knows us.'

'The scandal would wreck the reputation of the family. Recent gossip almost ruined them. Society will tolerate only so much before they will be considered outcasts. I owe Thomas too much to destroy the Lovedays.'

Tristan remained stiff and unbending, so devoid of emotion that an insidious thought wormed into her consciousness. Had that been her lover's aim from the outset? She was under no illusions that her looks had enslaved him. She was too plain. Had he used her to get back at the family he believed had wronged him? In their latter meetings he had made no secret of his anger at how George Loveday had tossed him back into the gutter. Even though he had become a wealthy man, he had been secretive about the manner in which he had come by his fortune. He had described himself as a speculator with an eye for a profitable deal. She suspected that many of them would have been underhand. That made him more dangerous than she had realised. How could she have been so blinded by passion? The weight of her foolishness threatened to crush her. She had glimpsed something of the ruthlessness of Tristan's nature at Beaucombe. What if he was as evil as Adam had hinted? A man like that would want revenge upon the family who he believed had wronged himself and also his mother.

She proceeded more cautiously. 'Our love is wrong. But it is always something I will cherish, and I will have our child, which will hold you for ever in my heart. Yet duty binds me to my husband. When I married Thomas I knew we would never be lovers. I did not care. He rescued me from a life of boredom and repression. Before our marriage I dreamed of being part of the theatrical world as my father had been. I wanted to mix with our great playwrights and poets. It is an important part of my life.'

'And I am unimportant?' Again the lethal edge harshened his tone.

'You have shown me what it is to be a woman. I will never forget you.'

'It cannot end like this. At least come to Charlestown while Thomas remains in London.'

Again she shook her head. 'I cannot. I will sacrifice our love for the sake of the child.'

'And if your husband abandons you, casts you out from the life you say is so important, what will you do?' The contempt was now thick in his voice.

'I will make the best of it.' Her chin jutted with determination. 'But Thomas will not cast me out. We will continue to show a public face to our marriage.'

'If he challenged me to a duel, there is no certainty that he would be the victor. If he died we could marry.'

'And our child would be brought up living with the shadow of murder over its head, whether the death be yours or Thomas's. I would not condemn it to such a life. It is better this way.'

'Bah! Your excuses are feeble.' Contempt sparked in his eyes. 'Be honest, you are no different from my cousins. You think I am not good enough. Then damn you and all your kind.' With a violence that swirled around him like a cloak, he turned on his heel and strode out of the cave.

Georganna was shocked by the fury that had erupted. She could not let him go with such bad feeling between them and ran after him. He was already halfway up the cliff heading towards Penruan where he must have left his horse.

'Do not leave it like this,' she shouted. 'I beg you. We must talk further.'

He ignored her and climbed the cliff with a speed and expertise that was beyond her. She sank down into the sand and covered her face with her hands. The enormity of her sin and the repercussions it could have for her family filled her with dread. For a moment she was cast into the blackest despair and the sea beckoned temptingly. Why not end her life as Captain William Loveday had done? Her death would keep the secret of her pregnancy and she doubted anyone would then listen to any tales Tristan might spread about her marriage.

She rose shakily to her feet, staring at the kingfisher-blue waves. How easy it would be to walk until the water covered her head. She could not swim. Then she felt the faintest fluttering like butterfly wings in her stomach. The child had quickened. Senara had told her it would feel like that. The movement changed everything. It was not just her life she would end by drowning. She could not murder her child. A warm glow of love spread through her entire being. It was so unexpected she felt humbled. She had believed herself without maternal yearnings or desires.

Her head titled back with defiance. It was time to face whatever fate threw at her.

Several slaps to St John's cheeks dredged his wits back to consciousness. He coughed, spitting out the foul taste of salt water. His eyes seemed plastered shut, pincers of light trying to burn through his lids. His throat was on fire with thirst and his body felt as though it was coated in ice. Another stinging pain flared along his jaw, breaking through his stupor. When his eyes opened, shafts of agony shot through his skull at the intensity of the sunshine. He groaned and rolled on to his side. As his wits slowly cleared, he found himself sprawled on a beach, his feet still in the sea.

'He be alive,' said a husky female voice.

St John struggled to sit up, only to discover that he had no strength, and slumped back on to the sand. The woman was kneeling on the beach, bending over him. Her face was in shadow and she wore a red kerchief tied over her long straggling hair, whilst her patched clothes gave off a musty, mildewed smell.

'Where am I?' St John groaned and managed to heave himself on to his knees. His shirt was in ribbons around his arms and his moleskin breeches were covered in brown bloodstains and ripped in places. His feet were bare.

'Mount's Bay, along from Porthleven. There bain't no sign of a wreck. Did ye fall overboard? Ye be lucky to survive a night in the sea. Ye've taken some hammering on the rocks.'

He noted that he had been washed ashore behind some low rocks. His wits were clearing and he remembered the beating he had been given on board a ship. Porthleven was a great distance west of Fowey. It was near to Penzance, at the very end of Cornwall. His captors must have thrown him overboard expecting him to drown. He staggered to his feet, and when he swayed weakly the woman grabbed his arm.

'Hold on to me, my lover. You bain't strong enough to walk far. But we should make it to my shack. I'll tend your wounds. I be Izzy. Who be ye?'

'I'm . . .' He paused. With his clothes little better than rags, he looked more like a peasant than a gentleman. He was ashamed of the events that had led him to this beach. At least he could spare his family further shame by not revealing his identity. He doubted he would be recognised this far west and away from the main towns. 'I'm John. Johnny Trelawny.' He picked his grandmother's unmarried name.

Izzy chuckled and he encountered the most startling blue eyes he had ever seen. She also appeared to have most of her teeth in far better condition than some women of her age and class. He also saw that beneath her grubby complexion she was plump and if cleaned up could be considered passingly attractive.

'You lean on me, Johnny, my lover. Izzy will take care of ye. I bain't got much. But once ye be rested and fed, ye'll be feeling more yer old self again.'

Chapter Twenty-six

Japhet was delighted with his stock of thoroughbred racehorses and the degree to which they had been trained. Mark Sawle was a natural with horses, and Japhet had much to thank Hannah for, as she had unselfishly kept his dream alive. He also owed a great deal to his old friend Nick Trescoe, who had coached Sawle how best to train the horses. Nick would be a good source of information for what was happening on the current race circuit and the opposition his horses would face.

A week after his family were settled in their own home, he rode to the Trescoe estate. Both the groom who had come to take Sheba's reins and the footman who answered the door to him were strangers. Once he would have known the names of all the servants here. It was a sign of how long he had been away. He presented his card and was told to be seated in the hall. Nick had been his friend since childhood and Japhet had never had to wait attendance upon the Trescoe family, and it gave him an unsettling feeling. Although he made excuses that the footman did not know him, he would have expected that the name Loveday would have been enough to have him ushered immediately into the presence of the family.

He removed his high domed hat and paced the hall, hearing distant movements from the family and servants. Trescoe Manor was as large as Traherne Hall, built in local stone in the shape of a square during the reign of William and Mary. The hall was long and panelled in oak, with several rooms leading from it. The footman had disappeared into the yellow saloon, where the family usually gathered at this time of day. At the sound of the door opening Japhet turned, expecting Nick, his father or one of his friend's sisters to have waved aside formality and come to greet him. When the footman carefully closed the door of the yellow saloon behind him before advancing, Japhet felt his stomach knot with unease.

The footman held out Japhet's card and bowed stiffly. 'Lady Trescoe and her daughters regret that they are not at home, sir. Neither will they be at home to either you or your wife should you call upon them again.'

Japhet saw the contemptuous smirk behind the servant's eyes. The damned man had the audacity to look at him as though he was dirt beneath his shoe. Japhet felt his temper start to rise and unconsciously his fist bunched. Briefly his eyes flashed dangerously and the footman paled and took an involuntary step back. It took all Japhet's willpower to quell his anger. He knew that not everyone in polite society would accept him with open arms, but he felt betrayed by the Trescoes. He had assumed that such close friends would realise that his pardon meant he had been innocent of the robbery that had sent him to prison and transportation.

'My good wishes to the Trescoe family,' he clipped out, recovering his composure. He breathed slowly and evenly to combat his humiliation as he walked sedately to where the groom continued to hold Sheba. After he had swung up into the saddle, he flipped a silver coin to the lad, whose jaw dropped in astonishment at his generosity. It was more than the youth earned in a month. It was an ostentatious gesture and unworthy of Japhet, but giving the groom a simple pleasure that he could now easily afford soothed his ruffled composure.

His glance swept the windows at the front of the house. There was movement behind one of them as someone stepped back from regarding him. Doubtless it was one of Nick's two unmarried sisters, both of whom had been friends of Gwendolyn. That made it a double betrayal. He clicked his tongue, setting Sheba at a demure trot until he was out of sight of the house, then he touched his heels to the mare's sides and gave her her head. It was two hours before his temper had cooled and he returned to his home.

Yet he should have known that he could keep nothing from Gwendolyn. The moment she saw him, her expression was anxious. She was with a sewing woman in their bedchamber, a bolt of blue and gold brocade spread across the bed as the servant measured the carved posts for new hangings and a canopy. She ordered the woman to continue with her measurements and linked her arm through her husband's, drawing him outside. 'What has happened? Did the Trescoes not receive you? I had hoped for better from them.'

'It must be distressing for you, my love.' His face was dark with anger. 'They can cut me from their lives if they will, but not you. Eugenie and Beatrice Trescoe were your friends. You deserve better from them.'

'They will be governed by the dictates of their mother. Was Nick there? I cannot believe he would shun you, especially as he bought your foals.'

'I was informed that we would not be received. I assume that Nick was not present. His father never approved of me. Nick and I led each other astray in our wilder days. Though Lady Trescoe would naturally lay the blame at my door and her husband is equally judgemental.'

Gwendolyn could feel the tension pulsing through his body. 'I do not care what they think. We have nothing to be ashamed of. We have made our home here and if they do not care to receive us, then it is their loss.'

He folded her in his arms. 'My bold fighter. I will prove to all those who would so basely judge me that they are wrong. With you at my side, how can I fail?'

'We rose above far more dangerous adversaries in New South Wales and we shall do the same here. Give us a year or two and Lady Trescoe will be begging to be received at one of our banquets or soirées, for the cream of society will be present. Anyone who is anyone will want to be the owner of a Loveday thoroughbred. They cannot buy one of our line and not admit that the finest of horses was bred by the finest of men.'

Japhet made an elegant bow, twirling his hand in an extravagant flourish, his accompanying laugh teasing. 'God bless you, ma'am. But you're a rum one all right.'

She smiled, relieved that he could jest when she knew that the snub from the Trescoe family must have wounded him deeply. 'We have survived far worse than this cruel censure, my love. Adversity has only made us stronger. We knew it would not be easy returning to Cornwall where your name and reputation were so well known. We have nothing to be ashamed of. I hold my head up with pride. There is much to occupy me here transforming the old farmhouse into a comfortable home. I have no regrets and neither should you.'

St John awoke to the smell of fish cooking. For several moments he lay dazed, unable to remember where he was. He stared around a dwelling lit by the orange glow of a fire. The single room was deserted and he swung his legs to the floor, trying to remember how he had got here. He was on a truckle bed with some kind of seaweed-stuffed mattress. He gazed uncomprehendingly at the bare mud floor, the three-legged stool, and the iron cooking pot steaming over the flames in the centre of the room. There was a fish speared on a stick propped near the fire to cook. A roughly made cupboard looked as though it had been thrown together with driftwood, and hanging on a wooden peg on one wall was a nondescript item of clothing. There was no window, but daylight was visible between many of the wall timbers. A rickety door hung crookedly on a broken hinge. Some kegs and small crates were piled in a corner together with a long coil of rope, dirty sacks, and an assortment of the kind of artefacts that would normally be thrown on a scrap heap. What the devil was he doing in this hovel?

He made to stand and swayed alarmingly. His whole body throbbed with pain. He kept his head bent to avoid banging it on the ramshackle wooden roof. There were cracks between the timbers that showed it was partially covered in oilskin. Other gaps showed the fading light from the sky.

'So you be awake then, my lover.' A throaty female voice startled him. A woman entered dragging a broken branch of a tree. 'Found this on the shore. It will keep the fire going for some while.'

She tossed the wood in a corner and straightened to put her hands on her hips. Her tattered skirt did not reach her ankles and she wore one lady's ankle boot and one man's shoe stuffed with rags that stuck out around her ankle. She was also dressed in a man's shirt with only one sleeve, a black-laced bodice and over this a man's stained and torn brown leather jerkin.

'What the devil am I doing here?' snarled St John.

242

'That bain't much of a greeting being as how I saved your life,' she snorted. 'Don't ye remember, I found ye on the beach two days gone. You'd been shipwrecked I reckon, or fallen overboard. The sea washed you up. You be lucky to be alive, Johnny Trelawny.'

She sniffed and wiped her nose on her bare arm, studying him shrewdly. 'If that be who ye be. Said ye be a fisherman afore ye passed out. Ye talk like no fisherman I know. More like a gentleman.'

'I've been here two days?' He was incredulous. 'What day is it?'

'Same day it be when I woke up.' She cackled at her inane joke. 'Bain't heard no church bells so it bain't be a Sunday.'

Who was this imbecile? St John shook his head to focus his wits. There was enough light coming through the door for him to see the bright blue of her eyes, and they somehow looked familiar. So did the wild hair that resembled tangled kelp. 'Where is this place?'

'Along from Porthleven. I make my living from what comes from the sea. Ye be the first merman that ever got washed up.' She grinned at her cloddish humour.

'I need a boat to take me to Fowey,' he declared.

'Oh, ye be gentry all right, ordering folk like they be servants.' Again she cackled. 'You look more like a beggar. And seeing you've forgotten my name as well as your manners, I be Izzy.'

St John stared down at himself. His shirt and breeches were ripped and stained and there was some kind of binding around his ribs. He touched it tentatively.

'Ye were battered by the rocks,' she informed him as she squatted by the fire and hooked out the fish. 'Reckon afore ye go anywheres ye'll be wanting some food.'

St John realised that his stomach was growling with hunger. He eyed the fish suspiciously. It certainly smelt good. 'Is there anything to drink?'

'Some rainwater in a butt. It runs off the roof. You had the last from a wine keg that washed ashore on the spring tide. I thought it might strengthen and warm ye.' She pulled a knife from her waistband and cut the fish in half, then put one piece on a battered tin plate and held it towards St John. 'Better sit yourself down and eat. 'Sides, it will be dark in an hour. Best ye stay till the morrow. Passage to Fowey will cost ye money and ye bain't got no money or valuables as far as I can see to pay for it.'

He was loath to return to the bed, which was covered in an evil-smelling blanket, though since he had spent the past two days lying under it, he supposed it could do him no further harm. The fish was hot and he blew on his fingers as he scooped its flakes into his mouth. It tasted surprisingly good.

Izzy picked up a pottery ewer from the floor by the fire, tipped some water into a cracked horn beaker and passed it to him. He ate in silence. Porthleven was a long way from Trevowan, probably a day's ride. And the woman was right. He had no money to pay for his passage. A glance at his fingers revealed that his father's gold ring was missing. He remembered that his captors on the boat had stolen the ring and his hunter watch, which had also belonged to his father. His misery increased. Even in his most desperate hours gaming, they had been too precious to put at risk. Now they were gone, and for what? The price of his own selfish stupidity, he supposed. God, how low had he sunk in his depravity? He closed his eyes and hung his head as the memory of his ordeal on the ship flooded his mind.

'You've had a rough time of it,' Izzy said with a kindness he knew he did not deserve. 'Stay here tonight and you'll find things look better in the morning. Ye be alive. Happen the good Lord saved ye for a reason.'

Those words hit him harder than any reprimand or censure. Why had his useless life been saved? He had failed his family yet again. He had no idea how great were his debts. Alcohol and gambling fever had clouded his judgement and recollection. But he had a sinking feeling they were vast. At the very least he would have to sell a sizeable amount of Trevowan land or lose the entire estate.

'It would have been better for everyone if I had died,' he groaned, overcome by self-pity.

'And I thought the landed gentry be obsessed with their heritage.' The woman snarled her scorn. 'Or do ye be a younger son with no prospects?'

St John gave a derisive snort. 'What would you know of the burdens of responsibility? They say wealth is a privilege; sometimes it is a curse.'

Izzy sat back on her heels and chewed thoughtfully at her fish. 'It be true I bain't got much in the way of possessions. Just what the sea gives me. Even this place could blow down in a bad storm. I bain't never been wed and me pa, a miner, threw me out when I got big with me first child. Me ma were dead and I had no other family. The babby died, so did two others I birthed. Seemed nothing I did were right. I wandered the roads scavenging off the land, used by men, not much proud of the life I'd been dealt. Not seeing any way to improve my lot or end my suffering.'

St John held his aching head, her witless ranting destroying his patience. 'I'm not interested in your life story, woman.'

'Then I met an old soldier on the road,' she said, ignoring his protest. 'He'd been blinded in battle and had lost a leg and lived by begging. He'd seen the worst life could do for anyone but he had this wonderful joy in everything. He played a brass whistle so beautifully a soul could soar or weep with joy or longing. He had faith in people, that no matter how dire things might be, there be joy in some part of your day if folk bain't be too blinded by self-pity to see it.'

St John scowled. Now it seemed he was stuck with a madwoman for the night.

Izzy gave a mirthless laugh. 'Happen I like to hear the sound of my own voice. It be rare I have company apart from the gulls to hear my ravings.' She sighed, a stillness settling upon her squatting figure. 'That old soldier would make me stop and listen to a birdsong, or smell a sweet flower. He'd say that while such simple things could bring a person joy, how could they consider the world an evil place, or that God had forgotten them. He reckoned you could change the world by a simple act of kindness. His gift was his music. He was never happier than when he could make others happy and forget their troubles. He changed my life.'

'And what happened to this latter-day saint?' St John sneered.

'I hope he be still bringing joy to others. Our ways parted after a few days but he showed me there were a different way to view how you live. He also told me to trust that if you need something badly enough it will be provided.'

St John stared at the woman as though she was simple. 'Then why are you still living little better than a vagabond?'

She smiled. 'What we want and what we truly need bain't always the same thing. Since I met that soldier I bain't never been hungry,

I bain't never been without a roof over my head. And what be best of all, I've got my freedom. Izzy don't call no one master.'

The note of satisfaction in her voice astonished him. She lived hand to mouth in the worst squalor he had ever encountered. Yet he realised that she had shared her precious food with him and given him the last of the wine that must have been the only luxury in her sparse existence.

As though to prove his reasoning she laughed. It lit her face with a radiant serenity. 'And now I've got you. A gift from the sea. What the sea gives must be respected. That binds us, my lover. The sea gave me your companionship for a time but it gave you your life and brought you here so I could help you. We be bound all right.'

She fixed him with an unearthly stare that sent a shiver through his flesh. What had her crazy mind devised now? He had to get away, but when he tried to stand, his legs remained weak and his body was gripped by pain.

'I am married and live far from here. We are not bound,' he sharply informed her.

'I don't doubt you be a fine upstanding man. But the sea brought you to me, we can't escape that. Your loved ones would not want you dead, my lover. You called out many names in your sleep. Treasure what you have.' Her expression was one of pity as she stood up and took his empty plate. 'You who have so much know the value of nothing.' She went out to wash the plate in the sea.

St John staggered to the opening and clutched at the doorpost for support. The woman was singing an eerie jumble of words of no song he had ever heard. Mad Izzy unsettled him. He had to regain his strength and get away from the squalid hovel as soon as possible. Everything about it disgusted his sensibilities. And how dare the woman, who knew nothing about him, presume to lecture him? How dare she say he knew the value of nothing or presume that because he had been washed up on this beach they were in some way bound together? He had never heard such nonsense.

He saw her by the shoreline with her skirts now pulled between her legs and tucked into her waistband. She was picking over a tangle of fishing net and humming a tuneless song. She was obviously quite mad. He would not stay here a moment longer.

Suddenly Izzy let out a yell and started dancing round, further convincing St John the woman was a lunatic. She held her hand aloft and ran pell-mell towards him, shouting and laughing.

'Look 'ee here, my lover!' She held her hand upwards to show him a man's leather shoe. Didn't I say trust and what you need will be provided?'

'It's a shoe, woman. A single shoe, not even a pair. What am I supposed to do? Hop back to Fowey?' he snapped in exasperation.

'Dummy! It what be on the shoe that be important.' She chortled and turned the footwear round to display a tarnished buckle. 'Bain't that silver? Bain't never had such riches as this afore. Reckon this be worth a walk Helston way. There be a kiddley on the road where a man will buy this. It'll give you money to get yourself passage to Fowey and I'll get myself a new shawl for the winter.' She continued to dance an improvised jig in her excitement.

His irritation turned to astonishment. 'I could not take such a generous gift from you. The sale of that buckle would feed you for months and buy you more than a shawl. It would buy you some real comforts.'

'I've done without so-called comforts for years and you need to get home. I can't see a fine gentleman like yourself trekking so far. You'd not last a night on the road without food.'

St John knew she was right. He had never been without money. 'There will be someone on the road who will give me a lift.'

'Happen, or happen not. You bain't shaved in days and your clothes bain't much better than rags. Most people don't take kindly to beggars.'

St John self-consciously rubbed his hand across his jaw and was startled by how thickly his beard had grown. He must have been held captive on the ship for several days.

Izzy eyed him with unmistakable challenge. 'We be bound by this buckle and the money it brings.'

The fact that she intended to share her bounty with him was strangely humbling, but the other implications were unnerving.

Chapter Twenty-seven

Censure upon St John mounted within the family when he remained away from Trevowan. He had been gone for two weeks and the harvested corn remained unsold in the barn. This was not the first time that St John had put Trevowan's harvest at risk by his absence. The last time had nearly brought the estate to ruin, and this year much depended on the money from the crop if harsh cutbacks in expenditure were not to be imposed.

Whilst he searched for passage on a ship that would take him to Fowey, St John was aware that the family would regard this absence as another of his failings. His humility that Izzy had sacrificed so much when she had given him half of the few shillings they had received for the sale of the buckle had dissipated within a day of his search for a ship. He had spent half of that money replacing the rags he was wearing with a cheap shirt and uncomfortable boots and had paid a barber for a shave. A fisherman at Porthleven had agreed to take him only as far St Mawes. A night in an inn and a simple meal had left him just enough money to get a passage as far as Mevagissey. No amount of inducement that he would pay handsomely once he landed at Trevowan could persuade the fisherman to take him further. Apart from the sea, the only entrance to Mevagissey was through a coomb, the harbour sheltered by the steep walls of the hills on either side. The village, with its cob houses and narrow streets spilling down to the harbour, did not welcome strangers no matter how well spoken. Like many isolated villagers, the people were wary of outsiders who could be in the pay of the preventive office.

From his own days as a smuggler St John knew that landing sites in this part of St Austell Bay were worked by men from the harbour village. But he had arrived when the fishing fleet was out at sea, unlikely to return until the following day.

To avoid delaying his return to Trevowan further, he had been forced to walk. Before he had even climbed the steep track to the cliffs above the harbour, his ill-fitting boots had rubbed several blisters and the skin had burst and was bleeding. He winced with every step and it was not long before his earlier gratitude towards Izzy for saving his life was replaced by anger. Within another agonising mile this had turned to outrage at all the indignity he had suffered. He had conveniently forgotten that it was his own greed at stealing the possessions from Bryn's coach that had been the cause of all that had befallen him.

He trudged on for some miles, wrapped in his misery. Several horsemen had cantered past without looking at him. A coach lumbered by with two clergymen inside and did not even falter in its pace when he called for assistance. So much for their pompous teachings of Christian charity, he fumed. Yet he himself had never stopped his carriage or paid any attention to a stranger walking the highways when he had been comfortably cantering along the lanes.

The vehicle had covered him in a coating of dust that made him look even more dishevelled than before. One farm cart with five male labourers squashed in its back amongst some crates of cabbages and carrots did pull over when he hailed it.

'You looking for field work?' the farmer demanded in a surly voice.

'No, but I'd be grateful for a ride as far as you are going.'

'I need labourers.' He clicked his tongue and flicked the reins for his horse to move on, ignoring St John's shout that any distance would assist him.

The midday sun was hot on his back, and apart from a few figures walking in the distance the track was deserted as it stretched across rolling hills towards St Austell. Parched with thirst, he climbed a stile into a field whose boundary was a row of willow trees and a trickling stream. He knelt and cupped the water in his hands to drink, more exhausted and wretched than he had ever felt in his life. Crouched on all fours, he panted like a dog as he gathered his reserves of strength and pushed himself upright. If he kept walking he could reach the comfort of his home an hour or two after dark, but he was so weary it looked as though he would spend the night under a hedgerow with his stomach growling with hunger.

Despondently he climbed back over the stile, then sat on its top rung and dropped his head into his hands. What he would not give for the arrival of a coach containing a friendly face. So much for Mad Izzy's theory that what you needed always turned up. He was annoyed that she had pushed into his mind. He had taken her money and given her the slip, having no intention of honouring any notion of a bond. He had his own troubles. Fate had not only knocked him down but it had kicked him. He stared bleakly at the road ahead. He was not that far from Trevowan. Surely someone he knew would pass by. He did not care that they would mock him for the state of his dress, or that he had obviously fallen so low on his luck. He'd tell them he had been attacked and robbed, which was not far from the truth. Had not Father's watch and ring been taken by his assailants?

He clenched his jaw against the pain in his feet as he forced himself onwards. He had walked another mile when a rumble from behind him warned of the approach of a cart or coach. He ran a hand through his unkempt hair. A phaeton was approaching at a smart pace. Such a vehicle had to belong to a gentleman of his acquaintance, though he did not recognise it. Its highly glossed yellow paintwork glistened in the sun. As it drew closer he held up his hand for the phaeton to halt. At first it did not slow and he had to flatten himself against the hedgerow to avoid being run down.

Swallowing the dregs of his pride he shouted, 'Stop! I am St John Loveday of Trevowan. I've been attacked and robbed.'

When the phaeton drew to a halt several yards in front of him, the sun was in his eyes so he could not see the identity of the driver. He ran forward, relieved that his ordeal was at an end. 'Your servant, sir. It is good of you to stop. I was robbed and beaten. I thought I was doomed to spend the night in the hedgerow. I am so grateful—'

A harsh laugh cut off his speech. 'Gratitude is not something I ever expected from you, St John Loveday.'

He froze and moved position to regard the driver, who was the sole occupant of the fashionable carriage, but he was certain he could not have mistaken that voice.

Tristan Loveday grinned malevolently. 'A night under the hedge might be the making of you. Teach you some compassion for those less privileged than yourself.'

When St John backed away to the sound of his cousin's mocking laughter, Tristan added, 'You look like you have received your just deserts for all your deception. You do not relish a night being a prey to the elements. It never bothered you that that is what you condemned me to.'

There would be no lift for him and now he had to endure this humiliation. 'Drive on in your fancy phaeton,' he snarled. 'I would rather walk than take any favour from you.' He broke into a brisk march, biting the inside of his mouth to stop himself limping in front of his enemy. The pain from his bleeding feet was excruciating. He also mentally cursed that the lane was narrow and there was no sign of any gaps in the stone walls leading to a farm so that he could escape this hateful encounter.

'How the mighty have fallen!' Tristan scoffed. 'How does it feel to be on the receiving end of adversity? You look little better than a beggar. It does not take much to strip the trappings of wealth and position from a man and leave him to the vagaries of fate.'

St John trudged on, ignoring the jibes, as the horses walked slowly alongside him.

'Do you want a ride? I'm sure you are not too proud now to accept help from someone you so profoundly wronged.'

'Go to hell!'

'Do you think I have not been there?' Anger replaced the mockery. 'But I don't suppose that in your cosseted youth you ever gave a thought to what I might have suffered. Or even cared.'

'You got what was coming to you,' St John raged. 'You abused my grandfather's trust. You stole from us. You reverted to type, guttersnipe.'

'If anyone reverted to type, it was you. And how easily you twist the truth. Or is it that over the years you have convinced yourself that your lies *are* the truth? I suppose that is the only way you can live with yourself.'

St John refused to rise to his baiting, his gaze doggedly fixed on the lane ahead. As the elder youth, Tristan had constantly mocked him for his weaknesses. Until Tristan arrived at Trevowan, St John had, despite their rivalry, held a certain power over Adam. He could goad his twin beyond reason with his taunting that he was the heir and Adam would always be the poor relation. Adam would fight him to win supremacy but Tristan, with his low cunning that had enabled him to survive on the streets, had used mockery and tricks to reveal to the family St John's failings. No insult St John threw at him could touch his thick hide; no underhand trick succeeded and it was always turned back upon himself. His rivalry with his twin had paled at the hatred he felt towards the interloper in their lives.

'You are a liar, a cheat, a useless wastrel, selfish and arrogant because you thought as the heir to Trevowan you were above reproach.' Tristan continued to flay him with his scorn. 'How many times did your sly accusations earn me a beating? I never stole anything from your grandfather. If valuables were taken, it happened after I left. Neither was I the one who shamed the family that night of the storm. You made sure you got your story told first. Adam could never have seen clearly what happened on the beach that night. You convinced him I was the guilty one.' Tristan leaned over the high footboard, his eyes glittering with contempt. 'But we know who was the thief and the one who attacked a helpless victim, don't we, cousin? I was fighting with you to stop you killing him in your greed.'

'You ran away and that professed your guilt,' St John jeered. 'You did not have the mettle to face the consequences. And I would not have killed that man, whatever you think. Taking his purse was enough. There were wealthy passengers on that ship and all but that man were dead before we reached them.'

'I was blamed for your greed. Like Adam I wanted to save those souls. That would have made me a hero in George and Edward Loveday's eyes. Their respect and acceptance was all I wanted. I'd had enough of thieving on the streets. That life sickened me.' Tristan forced himself to swallow and control his anger. Righteous indignation had not helped at Beaucombe and it would not do so now. In a calmer voice he continued to pour out his scorn. 'You planted that gold cross in my coat. I knew that I had been condemned of the one thing your father and grandfather could never forgive. It did not matter that I was innocent. But who would believe me, the guttersnipe, as you were always quick to ridicule me? I knew that being accepted as a Loveday was the best thing that could happen to me. I would never have jeopardised it. But you were jealous that your grandfather saw the same spark in me that he had possessed as a boy. Ruthless and ambitious, but not scared of hard work. And you were ever a disappointment to him. Though he liked Adam well enough, for from an early age your twin had shown a flair for working in the yard and he was a natural leader.'

Tristan laughed, unimpressed by the hatred in his cousin's eyes. He went on without mercy. 'George Loveday wanted your father to make Adam his heir, but your father was too honourable a man to put the elder son aside. Was your twin's fiery temper his downfall? When I heard that he had been sent away to the navy I guessed you were somehow behind it. Did your petty jealousy provoke one fight too many? Your father had no patience with your rivalry. Adam's banishment would have delighted you. There was no one to show you up for the incompetent wastrel you were. Yet Adam's time in the navy served him well. It taught him all he needed to know about ships and the management of men. It made him a hero. And you were denied your full inheritance because he was so obviously the more worthy heir to the yard. I wager that rankled and still does.'

Tristan was enjoying this unexpected meeting with St John so much at the disadvantage. 'And as for myself leaving Trevowan, unable to return because of your lies! That was the making of me. I had been given an education and learned how to be a gentleman in my time there. I had learned that heritage is important as a means of getting on in the world, and most importantly I had learned that I would never return to the gutter or my former life. Indeed, I have much to thank you for, St John. You gave me a reason to succeed and one day return and prove to the world how craven and deceitful you are.'

That brought St John to a halt and he could not resist gloating. 'Then you made a mistake in coming back here where you are known as an ingrate and a thief. No one will ever believe you. I am master of Trevowan. A man of standing in this community.'

'Money opens many doors.' Tristan pulled on the reins so that

253

the horses also stopped. From his superior position on the phaeton he looked down at the scowling figure below him. He saw through the arrogance as bluster; any gentleman worth his salt would have challenged him to a duel for the accusations he had flung at him. But St John was too craven; he was no more than a passable swordsman, and a pistol made the odds even. 'Lack of money when it is lost through idleness and incompetence is as lethal as the plague for slamming doors and losing friends. How many friends will be loyal to you once they learn the truth of your recent losses and exploits?'

St John glowered at him. 'You will always be the guttersnipe and I will always be master of Trevowan.'

'But only for as long as you can settle your gambling debts. You've already sold some land. How much more are you prepared to risk?'

He clicked his tongue and the horses moved forward. He tipped his hat to his cousin. 'I look forward to our next meeting. Soon everyone will learn the truth. You cannot escape it. We will learn then who is the master and who the guttersnipe.'

St John was shaken by the encounter. His hatred for his upstart cousin had not lessened in the intervening years. It had grown and he felt no guilt for his lies. He was angry that Tristan had come back into their lives richer and more powerful then he himself would ever be. If anyone accepted Tristan's story about the night of the storm, St John would be ostracised by his friends and neighbours. Arrogance shored up his flagging confidence. He had succeeded once in destroying Tristan's reputation. Whatever anyone said, mud stuck; his lowly past would always count against him. Whereas St John prided himself that he had power and influence to crush the upstart.

Throughout the rest of his journey St John schemed to vanquish his cousin. Eventually he arrived at Trevowan, having been given a ride on a tinker's cart. The last two miles had been covered in silence, the surly tinker clearly not given to conversation above an occasional grunt to any comment St John attempted. He had been perched uncomfortably between a knife-grinding stone and a pile of ironware.

'Let me off here,' he demanded as they drew level with the drive of Trevowan.

When the tinker saw the grandeur of the house, he lost some of his surliness. It had been dark for two hours and the lights in the upper windows showed that the women had recently retired for the night. At least St John would not have to face their criticism at his unkempt appearance. There was bound to be an inquisition in the morning. His mood darkened. He would take no further censure. It was time the womenfolk who enjoyed his hospitality learned to respect him as master of Trevowan. If they did not like the way he lived his life, they could take up residence elsewhere.

The tinker's voice jolted St John from his reflections. 'This where you live? I could do with a bed for the night. What's the master like? Do you reckon there be a place for me in the stables?'

'I doubt it,' St John snapped. The last thing he needed was for the tinker to be gossiping to the servants about the state of the man whom he had brought here. 'The master does not take kindly to vagrants on the estate.'

'I bain't looking for charity. I'll sharpen knives or mend pots to pay my way.'

'There is an inn at Penruan. There will be more work for you there.' St John jumped down from the back of the cart. His knees almost buckled at the pain shooting through his feet where the blood had dried and the movement pulled at the skin around his blisters. He limped slowly along the drive and let himself into the house through the servants' entrance.

Jenna, the children's maid, who had been sitting in the kitchen mending a tear in a pair of Rafe's breeches, gave a small scream of alarm at St John's unexpected appearance. He put his fingers to his lips to silence her.

'Thank God someone is still up. I need hot water for washing, food and a flagon of brandy. Take care you do not wake the mistress. I do not want the ladies upset by my appearance. I was set upon and robbed. Mind you keep that to yourself until I have spoken to my wife and aunts.'

Jenna handed him a candle to light his way to his chamber and he hobbled up the stairs. He had been carefully rehearsing excuses for his long absence during the ride. He had no intention of telling

255

his family of the money he had lost gaming, or that he had been kidnapped and questioned about the coach accident.

His hand was on the doorknob of his chamber when he noticed a movement and saw Felicity watching him from the door of her room adjacent to his.

'So you have come skulking back to your lair. Sneaking in like a thief in the night.' Her fair hair was loose about her shoulders and her night robe showed her stomach swollen by her pregnancy. There was no warmth in her greeting. She put a hand to her nose and shuddered with disgust. 'You reek of the midden where you have been cavorting with gamesters and no doubt whores. And look at the state of you. Did you indeed lose the shirt off your back this time? You shame us all.'

After all the humiliation he had endured, he had no patience left for her prissy hauteur. He could imagine how his womenfolk had gossiped and maligned him during his absence. It was time they remembered who housed and fed them and provided them with every luxury.

'For your information, madam, I was attacked and robbed,' he informed her coldly. 'Get back to your bed. We will talk in the morning. But I will listen to no lectures and I hope a good night's sleep will put you in a more congenial frame of mind. And you can tell your coven of crones that if they wish to continue to enjoy my hospitality, they will remember that I am master of Trevowan. How I conduct my business is none of their affair.'

Chapter Twenty-eight

The next morning St John had weightier concerns than facing a gaggle of women who needed to be reminded of their place. He left Trevowan before any of them had emerged from their bed-chambers.

Although the price of corn was high, a hurried consultation with Isaac Nance, his bailiff, warned him that the crops would not yield the money he needed to meet his debts. It did not help that he had no real idea how many IOUs he had written in the last three months, or their amount. It would be another lean year and more land would have to be sold to meet the interest on the latest bank loan. To avoid the family knowing his business, he had borrowed money from a bank in Bodmin rather than from Thomas. He still had an outstanding loan from his cousin, but at least the interest on that was reasonable. Momentarily panic punctured his composure. The list of his debts seemed endless and fewer than a third of them were entered in the estate ledgers. He had become lax in keeping records, trusting that a good win at cards would keep all his creditors at bay.

Still shaken by his encounter with Tristan, he rode to Boscabel to speak with Adam before he left for the yard. Adam was in the stable yard talking to Billy Brown. St John dismounted and threw the reins of Edward Loveday's old horse, Rex, to Brown. The animal was past its prime and its head drooped from the hard ride.

'Are you trying to kill Rex?' Adam demanded angrily, running a hand over the horse's muzzle. 'He is too old for a long gallop. Why are you not using your hunter? And where the devil have you been? Have you no sense of duty?'

'My horse was stolen. I was attacked and robbed. And how I lead my life is none of your damned concern. *I* am master of Trevowan, not you.' He was cross with himself for so quickly losing his temper and retaliating in so childish a fashion. 'We need to talk in private.' He walked away and waited for Adam to follow him.

'We will go to my study. No one will interrupt us there.'

The tension remained between them as they entered the house and enquired after their respective families. St John snapped, 'I arrived at Trevowan late last night and one shrewish encounter from my wife was enough. I suppose the others are well and enjoying my hospitality whilst complaining bitterly how I fill my father's shoes so inadequately.'

'We are all concerned at the rumours that your gaming has been excessive and that you have lost more often than won.'

'I do not risk more than I can afford,' St John lied, instantly on the defensive. 'I would never place the estate at risk.' When the study door closed behind him, he realised he needed to deflect his twin's anger. 'There was more than robbery behind the attack in Fowey. I think it was you they were after, not me. They were very interested in the coach accident and the boy. The attack upon me was not just a robbery. I was knocked out and taken captive on board a ship. I have no idea how long I was their prisoner but it was several days.'

'Why do you think they were after me?' Adam queried.

'Because the boy lives with you. Perhaps they thought if you had him you would also be in possession of any valuables from the coach. I told them how they had been taken by smugglers.' St John twisted the truth enough to make Adam feel he was responsible for the ordeal he had suffered. He then spoke of his interrogation and how he had been thrown overboard, presumably expected to drown. 'I always thought the boy would be trouble. You should have packed him off to an orphanage when he was well enough,' St John concluded.

Adam was used to St John spinning some tall story as an excuse for his negligence of duty. This was different. There were yellowing bruises and freshly healed cuts on his face, and one eye remained swollen and bloodshot. His brother was haggard with strain and there was a haunted look in his eyes. He suspected that St John was still keeping something from him, but there was no mistaking that he was badly shaken from his abduction and that those terrible events had not been fabrication.

'I do not understand why these men were more interested in the valuables on the coach than in the passengers,' Adam queried.

'They didn't care if the boy was alive or dead. I was in too much pain at the time and cannot swear to it, but they did seem relieved he had no memory of who he was. Whether they will be content with that . . .' He shrugged. 'By keeping Bryn here you could be endangering your family.'

'I have promised the boy a home until his memory returns. I will not break my word,' Adam stated. 'Do you have no idea at all who these men were, or who they worked for?'

St John shook his head. 'Only the boy has the answer to that. If only he could remember. Do you not find there is something sinister about the way no one has come forward?'

'He could be an orphan, or illegitimate. Many such children's identities are kept secret from the world. There could have been important papers amongst the possessions that were stolen that could have given us a clue to his family. But nothing has come to light and I doubt it will after so many months. If it was smugglers who plundered the coach, they would see no value in such papers and would have destroyed them.'

Adam paused, considering the gravity of St John's story. 'Something is not right about that attack. Yet we may never learn the truth. You were lucky to survive. And for that we are all grateful. Your ordeal must have been frightening.'

St John rose. 'I wanted to warn you about the boy and the danger he could present.'

'I appreciate that. But Senara is fond of Bryn. She will not hear of him being put in an orphanage. I will apply to be made legally his guardian until his family are discovered.'

'Can you trust him? Our family was betrayed last time we took in a waif and he had our own blood. Did you know Tristan was back in Cornwall? I saw him on the road to St Austell.'

'Then he had better stay away from us.'

'I've problems enough without that cur adding to them,' St John said.

Adam nodded. 'This year the harvest has not been as good as expected and I think Trevowan has been hit harder than other estates. I am sorry about that.'

'However hard we work we cannot rule the weather.' St John's eyes sparked in challenge. 'You at least have the yard to support you. You have more orders now and the merchantman is finished.'

'The yard is also a huge drain on finances. The orders are for repairs, not new ships.' The old antagonism flared and the atmosphere was again charged between them. But aware of how much St John had recently endured and that he had taken the time to warn him of Tristan's presence in the area, Adam changed the subject. 'Has Tristan been to Trevowan while you were away? He's not been here.'

'Not according to Fraddon or Nance. But I don't trust him. He's here for a reason and I doubt it will be to our benefit.'

Adam suspected his twin was right.

The brothers returned to the stables, while outside the window of the study Bryn sat with his head in his hands. He had not meant to eavesdrop, but when he heard his name mentioned he had been concerned as to his future. Adam Loveday remained true to his word. He did intend to become his guardian. His relief was immense. Of late he had been having terrifying dreams, and although his memory had not completely returned, the dreams showed him a dark, locked cellar where he had sometimes spent days at a time shivering with fear at every sound. If the darkness was horrifying, it was as nothing to when the door opened and the tread of a man's steps descended the stairs. He never knew if he would be physically beaten or shouted at that he was worthless and useless. There had been days when he had longed to die to escape the misery. He drew his knees to his chin and brushed away the tears spangling his cheeks. He did not want to relive those wretched times even in his dreams. He pushed them aside, determined to forget them. He was happy here – happier than he had ever been, though once there had been warmth and love even further back in his past. But that had also become a dream where the truth eluded him.

As the twins rode together, Adam was aware of the surliness and wariness in his brother's manner. 'I still do not understand what has brought Tristan back. You would think this was the last place he would want to be. There is nothing for him here but disgrace.'

'He tricked his way into Tamasine's life but he will not trick us again. We know him for the cur he is.'

Adam was thoughtful for a time. 'We could not have got those incidents that night wrong, could we? Japhet was astonished that Tristan ran away. He said he was desperate to fit in with our family.'

'Bad blood will always out in the end,' St John snorted. His eyes narrowed as he regarded his twin. 'Japhet would side with the underdog. He is not so innocent despite his pardon. He lived very close to the wrong side of the law for years before his marriage.'

Adam rode along the lane in silence as he considered the differing opinions about Tristan. His twin's face was red as his anger blasted forth. 'You were there. You saw what happened. Tristan attacked an innocent victim: that is what you told Grandpapa.'

'But it was difficult to see clearly. There may have been other youths with the wreckers. What if I was wrong?'

'At the time you were certain of what you saw. The storm proved what a tyke Tristan was. It showed us his true colours. We were well rid of him.'

'Did it never occur to you to wonder why he would risk so much?' Adam persisted. 'It puzzled me. I thought he was happy here. He'd know Grandpapa would not tolerate the way he attacked that man on the beach. It was inhuman. Japhet would not believe it of him and he knew him better than us.'

'He tricked us all.' St John turned away to glower at a carrion crow pecking at a dead weasel in the hedgerow. 'He was like a madman that night.'

'But you were not on the beach until later. You'd passed out with the drink.' Adam shot him an assessing glance.

St John tightened his lips and kept his narrowed stare averted. 'You told me what happened.'

'Were you on the beach earlier?' Adam accused. 'Did you see him attacking that man? He swore he had been trying to save his life. I was caught in the current and too far from the shore to see exactly what happened.'

'I was on the cliff. I helped save your life, if you remember,' St John snapped. 'Most of what happened after we went to the cave was blurred by how much I had drunk. And it was nearly a quarter of a century ago. If Tristan was not guilty, why did he run away?' He urged Rex to a faster pace.

Adam clicked his tongue for Solomon to follow but he kept slightly behind his brother, gauging the stiff set of his shoulders and his tense figure. What was St John keeping from him? Now that he had recovered from the shock of seeing Tristan at Beaucombe, he did wonder if they had not over-reacted. Over the years St John had often lied to escape judgement from his family.

'How was Tristan's manner to you when you saw him, St John?'

Unwilling to go into the circumstances of the meeting, he shrugged. 'Mocking and belligerent. He hates us: that was obvious at Beaucombe. He is twisted with jealousy that he was the poor relation. He will do anything to lie and cheat his way into people's regard at the expense of our reputation.' He turned his accusing glare upon his brother. 'And why are you defending him, Adam? Is my word not as good as Japhet's?'

They had reached the crossroads where Adam would leave him to continue to the yard. St John kicked Rex into a canter, raising his hand as a gesture of farewell. Adam stared after his departing figure. St John had been edgy and Adam doubted that he had been honest about either his encounter with their cousin or the attack that had led to his capture. If his brother was hiding something, Adam hoped it was not so serious that it would have repercussions for those at Trevowan.

Chapter Twenty-nine

Thomas finally arrived from London. He had sent word about the time he would arrive in Launceston, and Jasper Fraddon had been sent with the coach to collect him from the post chaise. Ever since his missive had arrived, Georganna had been restless as a bee, unable to settle to any task for longer than a few minutes before moving on to something new. Two days of rain had made it impossible for her to escape for her usual walks.

'This is the longest you and Thomas have ever been apart,' Margaret commiserated when the women were seated in the orangery, expecting Thomas to arrive within the hour. Margaret, Amelia and Felicity were embroidering a layette for Hannah's baby. 'You must be excited that he will be with us soon.'

Instead of the words being reassuring, they had filled her with panic. It had been difficult to listen to the others twittering on about babies and reliving their memories of their own children when they were first born. She felt that her infidelity and shame were branded across her brow. Everything she ate gave her acute heartburn, and since that first faint fluttering the baby's movements were now stronger and more insistent. It was as though the child demanded to be acknowledged. Unable to stand her guilt, she mumbled an excuse and hurried from the room.

'Georganna has been acting most oddly.' Amelia frowned at the younger woman's departure. 'Yet the sea air at Trevowan has been good for her. She was so peaky at Beaucombe and now she is positively blossoming and has even put on a little weight.'

Margaret exchanged a meaningful glance with her sister-in-law.

'Do you think she could be with child? It has been my most fervent prayer. She and Thomas have been married for so long. I feared I would never hold a grandchild in my arms.'

Amelia raised a questioning brow. 'If I were a gambling woman I would be inclined to place a wager upon it, but surely she would have said?'

'Georganna may be a bluestocking and have more knowledge crammed in her head than is good for any woman,' Margaret responded, a glow of pleasure now lighting her cheeks, 'but she can be naive about more worldly matters. She has not to my knowledge seen a doctor. Also, such joyous tidings are not something she would care to put in a letter. The father should be the first to know.'

The two women smiled. Amelia reached forward to squeeze her friend's hand. 'We shall know for sure in a day or so. After so many travails and the poor harvest, our family needs some uplifting news.'

Margaret sighed and closed her eyes, her hands clasped as though in prayer. 'I do hope we are right. A family is what Thomas needs. He spends far too long away from home in the company of Lucien Greene.'

When the coach arrived, Georganna sought the company of the other women to welcome her husband. She was dreading facing him alone. Thomas greeted the women effusively, but Georganna detected a coolness in his manner when he bowed over her hand. He was still angry with her. That did not bode well for what she must tell him. But her time at Trevowan had given her the opportunity to review all her options. She was no less guilty than Thomas in dishonouring their marriage vows. As a married woman she had no rights even upon her own property, but her pregnancy had given her purpose and strength. The child was the innocent party and she was determined that it would not suffer or be cast aside.

She spent a tortuous two hours while Thomas wanted to hear how Japhet had fared since his arrival. He was clearly eager to be reacquainted with the cousin closest to him in age, and was impatient that Japhet was away from his home at a race meeting.

'He is eager to establish the quality of the horses Hannah reared.' Georganna felt this was safe ground to break the ice between them. 'He will be back the day after tomorrow. How are negotiations progressing on the bank merger, or will they buy us out?'

'The lawyers seem to do everything they can to complicate matters.' Thomas did not hide the boredom in his voice. 'It is a slow and frustrating procedure.'

'I wish you would reconsider.' Margaret showed her distress. 'The bank is your heritage.'

'My heart has never been in banking, Mama,' Thomas tartly reminded his mother, and Georganna was glad that she was not the only one to face his censure. She breathed more easily as he continued. 'I have given twenty years of my life to it. Am I not now entitled to pursue my passion in the theatre? Our future is secured and we can all live extremely comfortably from the proceeds of the sale.'

Margaret cast Georganna a look of longing and hope. 'Can you not reason with him? What if circumstances within our family were to alter?'

'In what way?' Thomas demanded in a tone that was both irritable and uninterested. 'I will not change my mind.'

'But Georganna is still young. She could—'

A gasp from Georganna halted her pleading. The younger woman could feel the colour draining from her face, leaving her cheeks chilled and stiff. She guessed Margaret was on the brink of declaring that they might yet have a child. From the conversations she had overheard between Margaret and Amelia, her mother-in-law believed that with a child Thomas would want the family business to continue. Her voice was sharp as she addressed them. 'Thomas must do as he believes is right. Nothing that might happen in the future should change how he feels.'

Margaret waved aside her protest. She was a formidable woman who believed in family tradition and loyalty. Her first allegiance remained with her late husband and the bank that had been his life. 'You have your head in the clouds because your father was a playwright. But it was his brother who provided for your security and fortune by continuing to run Lascalles Bank when your father turned his back on his duty and became a sleeping partner.'

Thomas stood up and bowed stiffly to his mother. 'You have made your opinions obvious in the past, Mama. It is not a subject for family discussion. I came here to escape the pressure of my working life.' He turned to the other women. 'I will take a stroll in the grounds before it is time to change for dinner. It has been too

265

long since I took the sea air. The dust from the coach is still in my nostrils.'

'I will accompany you, husband.' Georganna joined him and linked her arm through his. She was disheartened when she felt him stiffen at this unusual show of affection.

'Yes, I am sure you two have much to discuss.' Margaret smiled knowingly at Georganna. 'The sea air has been of great benefit to your dear wife. She walks every day. I have never seen her so blooming in health.'

The couple did not speak until they had left the house. Georganna grew more nervous with each step. As they passed the Neptune fountain, the spray from its falling water drifting on the breeze blowing off the sea to settle in droplets on their hair and shoulders, she spoke to break the tension between them. 'Has the sale been so troublesome?'

'They are haggling like fisherwomen over the price. I cannot let all our families have achieved go for a song. If they want the prestige and clientele that Mercer and Lascalles will give them, they will pay for it. It is a matter of principle.'

The couple were almost of a height, and Georganna easily matched her long stride to her husband's pace. 'And have you decided where you will build your new theatre? That is still your dream, is it not?'

He did not answer immediately. They had reached the steps leading to the beach and were forced to walk in single file. Thomas proceeded down to the shoreline and his words carried back to her as she ran a few steps to catch up. 'I have seen two sites between the Haymarket and Piccadilly where land is available and the buildings on it can be demolished. But to build and establish a theatre will take most of my share of the sale of the bank after Mama has been provided for. It will mean many changes to our lifestyle.'

'Nothing remains the same for ever. I cannot go on living as we do.' She sighed and before her courage failed blurted out, 'Oh Thomas, I have ruined everything that was good in our lives. But you must realise that we cannot go on as we are. Our marriage is a mockery. You spend more time with Lucien than myself now. Once you start work on the theatre we shall hardly see each other. I have little in common with Margaret and her friends. I think it would be better for us both if we led separate lives. Perhaps it is time for me to live quietly in the country.'

'Where the devil has this notion come from?'

'I am with child,' she stated baldly, all her carefully rehearsed words vaporising in her anguish.

A gust of wind pressed her muslin dress to the contours of her figure. Her rounded stomach was obvious and Thomas stared at it with a sneer of disgust. 'And who do I congratulate upon being the father? I have suspected for some weeks that you had a lover, but not who it was.'

She shook her head. 'The father is not important.'

'Not important!' he raged. 'The identity of the man who has dishonoured my wife and my name is immensely important.'

Her head shot up at his accusation. 'If anyone has dishonoured me then you should stand first in line. I have never been your true wife. You could divorce me. You have the grounds. Our marriage has never been consummated. But then there would be gossip and speculation, even more than there is now. Our marriage was expedient to us both at the time.'

'I seem to remember that it was your idea. I told you I would never visit our marriage bed.'

'You are not to blame. I am. But I would remind you that my share of Lascalles Bank saved Mercer's from ruin. And I escaped an unhappy existence with my uncle's family. But now everything is different.'

The darkening red of his countenance and the throbbing of a vein on his broad brow showed the depth of his anger. Though it was pure ice that dripped from his tongue. 'You made your views on childbearing plain when you proposed to me. I never wanted to marry and you never wanted children. You were terrified of conceiving.'

'Yes, I was. I still am. But I also have had to face the ridicule of being thought barren.' She stood her ground, refusing to back down under his fury. His reaction was understandable and no less than she had expected. 'Please, Thomas, do not turn this upon me. You have never wanted me that way. I had your affection and respect, and until recently I thought that was enough. I never thought I would have carnal feelings . . .'

267

'So the frigid virgin has turned into a whore.'

She slapped his face and her wrist was caught by the rigid vice of his fingers. She did not flinch at the bruising intensity of his hold and her stare locked with his as she repaid his scorn. 'That comment is cruel and unworthy of you. I have never once slated you for your preferences. Have I not accepted Lucien as a friend and given respectability to your relationship?' She flexed her fingers, and he dropped her hand and stepped back from her.

'I have the right to know the name of the man who would foist his bastard upon my family. The knave deserves to be called out. In honour I have no choice.'

'He is not important. The affair is over. I will not see him again.'

'Honour must be satisfied.'

His back was straight as a ramrod, arrogance refining the thickening contours of his face. This unyielding and unforgiving figure was a stranger to her. It goaded her own anger at the injustice of his censure after all the years she had turned a blind eye to his liaison.

'I never thought you a hypocrite, Thomas. How can you not be aware that there is much gossip in the City about you and Lucien? Whenever the three of us appear in public there is a flurry of whispers and titters. I am surprised it has not rebounded upon the bank. Or that Margaret has not heard it. She adores you, Thomas. The scandal would kill her. That is why I have kept alive the sham of our marriage. And why I have allowed your friends in the theatre world, many of them men of your persuasion, to snigger at me behind my back.'

'Anyone who slanders my reputation or yours will answer to my sword. As will this knave who debased you.' The wind lifted the fair curls from his brow and she noticed how his hair had thinned and was turning grey. The harsher light of the sun over the sea had deepened the lines scored into his handsome face. Behind his anger and hauteur was also pain.

Her voice softened. 'He did not debase me. I loved him. But it was a foolish, impossible love.' She wrapped her arms close about her chest. 'I am deeply sorry for the wrong I did to you. I do not regret my affair, for it showed me what love can be like for a woman. I want this child and I want to finally allay my fears about my mother's death.'

He stared for a long moment out to sea before replying. 'I was wrong to marry you. You were too young to know what a sacrifice you were making. But I cannot allow you to live with this lover.'

'That was not my intent. It is over between us. Wherever we go scandal will follow us. I do not want that for my child. I thought if I lived quietly in the country there would still be some hope that scandal could be averted. By accepting my child, you would slay much of the gossip about you and Lucien. No one will know it is not yours.'

'Your lover will know the truth. I assume he has been informed.'

'He will not speak.'

'How little you know of men,' he scoffed. 'He will gloat. I demand his name. You owe me that at least.'

'It will do no good. Hate me if you will. And if you will not accept this child, I will set myself up in my own establishment and rear it alone.'

'And you think that will not cause gossip?' His laughter was harsh and cruel, twisting in her heart like a knife. 'It could stop the sale of the bank and destroy Mama. Good God, woman, you have made a Greek tragedy of our lives. Had I written this as a plot it would have made me the greatest playwright of the day.'

Despite his irony, he remained outraged. A duel would destroy them all. She had to say something that would salvage his pride and give hope for the future. 'Whatever happens, gossip is inevitable. Thomas, had we been brother and sister and not man and wife, we would have adored and respected each other. Do not let your pride destroy what was once right for us and made us happy for many years. Can you not at least accept my child as you would that of a sister?'

'Tell me the name of your lover and I will consider it.'

'You are my husband. In law you are its father. I will never reveal his name. We can live together or apart. That is for you to decide.'

He picked up a stone and hurled it into the water, watching it skip across the waves before sinking.

'Leave me, madam. I have much to consider.'

Chapter Thirty

Georganna could not face the curiosity of the family alone. She hoped to gain her chamber and await the decision of her husband. When she approached the house she saw Margaret standing by a window watching the path to the cliff. She was about to veer away to take refuge in the orchard but Margaret waved frantically to her and there was no escaping a meeting. She knew her mother-in-law would follow her if she ignored the summons. Margaret did not like mysteries concerning members of her family and she would be aware that relations between her son and Georganna had been strained at Beaucombe.

As she entered the house, she slowed her pace and breathed deeply and slowly to achieve a semblance of calm. Margaret was waiting for her in the hall, her face alight with expectancy.

'Where did Thomas go? Have you told him? Is he not delighted?'

'Told him what?' Georganna drew on her knowledge of acting to keep her face impassive. 'I am sorry, Mama. I have no idea what you are referring to.'

'But surely . . . your news . . . you look so well . . . putting on weight . . . We guessed . . .' At the blankness of her daughter-in-law's stare, she finally faltered. The excited anticipation faded from her countenance, her eyes shadowing with puzzlement. 'Are you not . . . ? I mean . . . We all thought . . . Oh, my dear, I must be blunt. Are you not then with child?'

Georganna's composure snapped. She did not want to discuss her condition until she knew how Thomas would react after he had considered their situation. 'Why is everyone obsessed with my fecundity? If I had such news, would I not share it without you having to speculate and pry? Do you not think that after so many years of marriage I am not humiliated by the sly looks and pitying conjecture that I am barren?' Unable to bear more, she rushed past the older woman and fled up the stairs to her chamber.

'My dear, I did not mean to pry or offend you,' Margaret called up to her. She took several steps to follow, then halted and chewed her lip. Through her own disappointment she realised how cruel her anticipation must have been to her daughter-in-law. She would apologise later, but perhaps for now it would be better if she left Georganna to recover her composure. She returned to the orangery and shook her head wearily at Amelia's smiling stare. 'It seems we were wrong. And now Georganna is upset and has taken to her room. Thomas has not returned from his walk.'

'You said things had been strained between them for some months, and especially at Beaucombe.' Amelia was appalled at how insensitive they had been. With Hannah and Felicity with child their talk had revolved around babies throughout Georganna's visit. No wonder the poor woman had taken so many walks. They had virtually driven her away with thoughtlessness. 'Thomas would not have helped by staying so long in London. Perhaps we should just give them the space to resolve their differences.'

'I should go to her.' Margaret again chewed her lip, allowing her uncertainty to show. 'I thought their marriage was happy, but in recent months Georganna has been tense and uncommunicative. She spends hours on her own. Something is clearly troubling her.'

'Probably the least said, the soonest mended,' Amelia advised.

When Margaret heard Thomas return an hour later, she went to intercept him before he could go to his wife's chamber. 'I think I may have upset Georganna. We have been thoughtless. Ever since she arrived, our talk has been of babies. We even wondered, as she was looking so hearty and had put on weight, whether she was herself expecting. Of course she would not have mentioned it to us until she told you.'

'What did you say to her?'

The coldness in her son's voice alarmed her. She twisted her hands, now certain that there was a rift in the marriage. 'I am a foolish, thoughtless old woman. I wanted to know if I would be a grandmother. It appears I was wrong. But you must not blame her for her barrenness. Not all couples are so blessed. It is God's will and Georganna has been a loving and supportive wife.'

'I will go to her.' Thomas took the stairs two at a time. His temper had cooled during his walk. There was not only her condition to come to terms with; much of what Georganna had said had been a shock to him. Their marriage could never have been easy for her. Yet she had never complained, and he had thought she was content with their life. In their early years together they had been friends, sharing many interests. Latterly he had neglected her and taken her complaisance for granted. He had never considered himself to be a hypocrite. His anger that she had conceived a child was due to wounded pride, not jealousy. Yet how could he with honour allow a man to cuckold him without calling the knave to account? That she had stubbornly refused to name her lover had added to his anger and sense of injustice.

He knocked on their chamber door before entering. Georganna was reclining on a day bed, a book unopened on her lap. Her features were drawn with misery, tears bright on her cheeks, and the rounded shape of her stomach was clearly evident beneath the high waist and soft folds of her sprigged muslin gown.

When she swung her legs to the floor to rise he said, 'Do not get up.'

The softer roundness of her face made her look younger than her thirty years. He had forgotten that there was ten years between their ages and that she had been a naive and unworldly young woman when they married. The theatre world was not known for it sobriety or its chastity. Yet until this year she had remained a devoted and faithful wife. A wife whose dowry had released his family bank from debt. She had saved the reputation of his father, who had killed himself rather than face the shame of his bad investments, which could have brought ruin to many wealthy families, including Thomas's Uncle Edward.

No other woman would have been so understanding of his neglect.

She ruffled her gown to hide her figure. 'I have been such a fool, Thomas.'

He raised a hand to silence her. 'I was accosted by Mama as I came in. She fears she has upset you. What she said also made me realise the pressure she must have put on you in her expectations for a grandchild.'

'It is only natural.'

'But unfair in the circumstances. I am sorry you had to face censure that you did not deserve. My family can never repay the debt or the sacrifice you made by our marriage. You should not be penalised for my failings.' His apology was unexpected. To Thomas, family pride was everything.

'I made no sacrifice. I never wanted a child. I have nightmares about what could happen to me now. But I loved you. No, more than that: I adored you, Thomas. I believe that in your own way you loved me as much as you could ever love a woman. I should have remained content with that. I was the one who failed you. I ruined everything.' She covered her face with her hands. 'I am so ashamed. But I cannot give up my child. Neither will I ever reveal the name of my lover. I could not have the blood of the baby's father, or yours, on my hands.'

He dropped to his knee beside her and gently took her fingers from her face. 'Is the affair over?'

She nodded. 'And you are not to believe that he abandoned me to my fate. He promised to support me but I had already served you too ill.'

'Would you be happy with him?' His voice was strained and he was surprised at how difficult it was to ask the question.

'How could I be happy in a relationship built upon betrayal? I thought I loved him but it was an infatuation. Despite what I said earlier, I love the life you have given me. We have always been good friends and had so much in common. My life would be empty without those shared interests. I do not expect you to forgive me, Thomas. But if you could understand and find it in your heart . . .'

He put his finger to her lips. 'Do not plead.'

He stood up and paced away from her. The rigid set of his shoulders showed that his anger had returned. He spun round to deliver his verdict, each word a barbed arrow piercing her heart.

'There is much to consider. Honour should be avenged. You are upset. I will not force you to give the knave's name at this time. But clearly we cannot allow the situation to drift. You cannot conceal your condition for much longer. Gossip will be inevitable. It could endanger the sale of the bank. I would avoid that.'

'You will not cast me out? You will accept the child?'

'Do I have a choice?' His eyes flashed with suppressed fury. 'When we return to London, you will move in with Mama. She will be delighted to fuss over you. You will want for nothing. After the sale of the bank, the building of the theatre will take all my time. I shall inform Mama accordingly and move to lodgings closer to the work.'

'But I did not intend to return to London. Senara is the only one I trust to attend my travail.'

'You will have the best doctors. There will be gossip if you stay here.'

'There will be more gossip if we are both in London and it is obvious that we are living apart. Margaret will be so delighted by the coming baby she will talk of it incessantly. That will convince any gossipmongers that the child is yours. She will explain my eccentricity at wishing to have the reassurance of Senara at the birth.'

'Have you then spoken to Senara of this?'

She nodded and twisted her fingers in her lap, unable to hold his gaze. 'She guessed my condition. I had to confide in someone that I had sinned. I even asked her if she could rid me of my shame. She refused, and she has not told Adam of my condition.'

'The family must be informed. Your pardon, but I have no appetite for hearty congratulations. I came to welcome Japhet home. I will stay but a few days. We will announce the impending arrival of the child the evening before we leave. But I insist you accompany me to London. We will show a united face to the world. Only that will quell gossip. I promise you, the Queen's physician himself will attend your lying-in.'

It was more than Georganna had hoped for. As to her fears about her confinement without Senara, whom she trusted, that would be her punishment for the shame she had brought to her husband.

Throughout the remainder of their stay at Trevowan, Thomas

was an accomplished enough actor to play the role of adoring husband. Only when they were alone did the strain return to their relationship.

Georganna had no need to act. She was grateful to Thomas for not shaming her in public. It made her realise why she had cared so deeply for him. He had always been honest with her and had given her the life she had wanted by their marriage. She hoped that the truce between them would lead to a return to the closeness and companionship they had once shared. And she would also have the child to love. That was if she was spared the birth. Her nights were broken by dreams of her mother in labour, and when she woke crying and sweating, Thomas was the one to calm her fears. It deepened her sense of shame of the wrong she had done to him, and made her more determined to make a success of their life together.

As promised, the evening before they were to leave for London, he announced the news of her pregnancy. From his performance, no one suspected that he was still seething that Georganna had refused to reveal the name of her lover.

An ecstatic Margaret accompanied them back to London. As their carriage pulled away, Georganna wondered if she would ever see Cornwall or this part of her family again.

The completion of a ship was always a time for celebration at the shipyard. The *Good Fortune* had successfully executed her sea trials, and a crew had been engaged to sail her to her home port of Dartmouth. A few days after Thomas and Georganna's departure, the final payment would be made and she would sail from the yard. During the last month there had been additions insisted on by the owner that had delayed the process.

The handover was always a special event, and the larger shipyards often invited local dignitaries to show the importance of the yard. Adam decided such a celebration was appropriate. Squire Penwithick, Sir Henry Traherne and several parish councillors of Fowey, Trewenna, Penruan, Lostwithiel and St Austell were to attend. The yard had been decorated with coloured bunting and on the flagpole proudly flew the Cornish flag, a white cross on a black background. A fiddler and a singer and a troupe of dancers had been engaged to entertain the guests, and wine and cakes were available in the kiddley for after the ceremony, with ale and pasties for the workers. Later a bonfire would be lit, and the fiddler would play for the country dances that would continue for the workers long after the family and guests had departed.

Adam was disappointed that Thomas had left Cornwall before the celebration, but his cousin had been adamant that he had pressing engagements in London, with the sale of the bank and purchasing the site to build his theatre.

With everything in readiness at the yard and most of their guests arrived, Adam anxiously noted the absence of Mr Heathcote, the lawyer working on behalf of the mysterious client who had commissioned the merchantman. It still irked him that the customer's identity had not been revealed. No matter how many times he told himself that he was making too much of it, he remained unsettled by the secrecy. Yet every instalment had been paid as soon as it was due, and the commission of such a large vessel was good for the prestige of the yard. Two new customers had asked for tenders to be sent to them, but as yet no new orders had been placed.

The family arrived early. Benches had been arranged along the jetty for the women to be comfortably seated. The air was festive with laughter, the workers' families colourful in their Sunday best. Also decorated with bunting trailing from her prow to her stern, *Good Fortune* bobbed majestically in the water as the tide rose. Besides their neighbours, half a dozen dignitaries were mingling with the guests. A string quartet played in the background as they waited for Heathcote to arrive by coach.

St John, Adam and Japhet mingled easily with the guests, who were loud in their praise of the size and lines of the merchantman. As the time for the ceremony drew near, there was still no sign of Heathcote, and Adam kept glancing anxiously at the entrance to the yard, his gut tightening with apprehension. He checked his hunter and tried to relax. Heathcote had hinted that the *Good Fortune* could be the first of others commissioned by his client, if the ship lived up to his expectations. Orders remained slow. There were three ships booked in for repair from storm damage, and another in the dry dock that had been holed below the waterline by a French privateer. Fortunately it had managed to limp to port for temporary repairs before continuing to the west coast of England. That work would keep the shipwrights busy for most of the winter.

The reputation of a shipyard spread by word of mouth. A satisfied customer could bring in several new orders from other merchants impressed by a ship's performance. Much could depend on this day. Many of the guests had been given a tour of the ship earlier by Adam.

A wine importer from St Austell who chartered ships to transport his cargo engaged Adam in conversation, hinting that he might be interested in such a vessel but was hesitant because of the war with France.

'I have been dealing with German vineyards using ports at Rotterdam and The Hague. It is not so risky as the Mediterranean. The import of Canary and Madeira is still much in demand. I see *Good Fortune* is well equipped with cannon to protect her.'

'A ship carrying valuable cargo is always at risk. It is good policy to protect her,' Adam replied. 'And we can but hope that there will soon be a lasting peace with France. Did not the beginning of this year see a major step with the reforms brought about by Prime Minister Pitt to pacify the Irish?' Adam glanced up again in case there was any sign of Heathcote. 'After the riots in that country the Act of Union was passed last year joining Ireland to Great Britain and creating the United Kingdom of Great Britain and Ireland. Pitt is also working for Catholic emancipation.'

'I cannot see the Irish so easily subdued. They want independent rule. And how does including them in this new grand view of a United Kingdom help trade? The Irish have no navy. Britain was great as it was in my view.'

Adam was about to answer when a shout from the river drew everyone's attention. A schooner was approaching the jetty and Adam saw Heathcote's immense figure on deck. He made his excuses to the merchant. 'I am always available if you wish to view the plans of any of our ships. Your pardon, sir, I must greet these guests.'

The schooner was mooring alongside the merchant ship, with a half-dozen men on deck. The willows on the far bank stirred in a freshening breeze and four mallard flew squawking skywards.

Adam's gaze was on the fashionably dressed man beside Heathcote. He was wearing a caped greatcoat and a broad-brimmed beaver hat that concealed his features. The man kept his head bowed as he stepped ashore, but Adam's sharp ears detected a gasp from amongst the women of his family. Heathcote's bulk blocked his view of his companion until the lawyer stepped aside in front of Adam.

'Mr Loveday, may I present the owner of *Good Fortune*, Mr Tristan Loveday.'

There was an angry shout from St John, and from the corner of his eye Adam saw Japhet put a restraining hand on his cousin's arm.

Adam felt his blood heat with anger. '*You* commissioned this ship?'

'I thought it might surprise you.' Tristan grinned and regarded the crowd on the jetty. 'I did not expect so grand a welcoming.'

'Curse you!' Adam growled in a hoarse whisper.

'We don't want anything to do with your money.' St John broke away from Japhet and glowered at the newcomer. 'Tell him, Adam.'

Tristan broadened his grin. 'I think your brother will find that he is bound by our contract. And you have no say in the affairs of the yard. You never had the aptitude, which is why Uncle Edward bequeathed it to Adam.'

Adam battled to overcome his own anger. In front of so many important people, prospective customers amongst them, he could not make a scene. Already St John had caused such a stir that their guests were putting their heads together, whispering among themselves. Most of them would be aware that Tristan had once lived with them at Trevowan and that he had run away with something of a cloud over his departure.

He glared at Tristan. 'Come into my office and we will discuss this in private.' He turned to his other guests. 'Enjoy the entertainment. There are a few papers to sign, then all will be completed.'

St John scowled at his brother. 'You may be prepared to sell your soul to the devil, but I am not.' He strode to his wife and daughters. 'We are leaving.'

Felicity looked alarmed, then hung her head, confused and ashamed of her husband's outburst in front of so many of their friends. Rowena was red-faced with rebellion, but even she was shocked at the intensity of her father's fury and for once did not try to exert her wiles to get her own way. St John glared at Peter and Japhet. 'Where is your loyalty to Grandfather George?'

Japhet shrugged. 'This was never my fight.'

'Perhaps it is time to do as our Lord advises and turn the other cheek and look into your heart for forgiveness.' Peter was prim in his piety, mindful of the curious stares directed at his family. 'A business contract cannot be broken, even one as underhand as this.'

'If he thinks that by making us indebted to him he can worm his way back, he is mistaken,' St John spluttered in his rage. Then he marched from the jetty, leaving an embarrassed Felicity to trail behind him. The harsh voices had upset Charlotte and she was clinging to her mother's hand and sobbing.

'Who is that man?' Rowena demanded, causing even more speculation to stir amongst the guests. 'Why is Papa so angry with him?'

Adam nodded to Japhet and Joshua, indicating that they should accompany them to the office. Peter followed, refusing to be left out. Tristan had not allowed his smile to falter. He walked as though he was out for a leisurely stroll and appeared oblivious of the sensation he had caused. When the office door closed behind them, he did a slow perambulation around the room. 'Apart from the new models and paintings on the walls of the ships you are now building, it has not changed since your grandfather's day.'

'What is it you want from us, Tris?' Japhet asked.

Tristan turned to his oldest cousin. 'Even from you there is no "it's good to see how well you have prospered". Clearly they did a good job of blackening my character.' He shrugged. 'It was all a long time ago. What point to continue with old grievances? The one who knows the truth is the one who has stormed off in a temper. Perhaps it is fear and guilt that has sent him into hiding from a confrontation.'

'Of what are you accusing St John?' Joshua demanded.

Tristan spread his hands. 'If you have not seen through his lies and deceit, then I am not the one to reveal his craven character. Japhet, you asked what I wanted from you all. First I wanted a merchant ship that was the best money could buy. Where else would

I go for that except the Loveday yard? Secondly, I hoped at least for a chance to explain – to be accepted enough to be given the benefit of the doubt. It is time to lay some ghosts. Or is the prejudice against hearing my side of the story too deep?'

He turned to Adam. 'Your attitude at Beaucombe showed I was still regarded as the interloper. The outcast. Despite inner rivalries the Lovedays pride themselves on family loyalty, on standing united against their foes. Where was that loyalty to me?'

'You ran away, Tristan,' Adam threw at him. 'A sure sign of guilt.'

'You had already closed ranks against me. I was not the one who shamed our name. He is still festering amongst you. You were blinded by family pride. It is time for you to live with the consequences.'

He drew an envelope from his pocket and tossed it on to the desk. 'There is your final payment for the ship. You built her well. Just remember that it was my money that saved your precious yard from ruin, Adam. That demands some loyalty, but all I ask is that you keep an unbiased mind. I intend to expand my merchant fleet. Whether they are built here or in another yard is a matter for discussion. I have taken a house in Charlestown. We shall be neighbours. Do not seek to blacken my reputation with old rumours, or your family may find they are the ones who have the most to lose when the truth is known. Good day, gentlemen.'

Japhet moved to stand in front of the door and stop him leaving. 'You cannot go without explaining fully.'

'You are all outraged at finding yourselves beholden to me. Now is not the time. When your minds are cooler and you have thought about what I have said, you know where I am. The time of reckoning and the revealing of secrets will soon lay bare the truth. Now my crew is at hand and the tide awaits me.'

'You cannot come here and make those accusations then just leave.' Peter bristled. He was so incensed he grabbed Tristan's shoulder and spun him round.

A knife was in the older man's hand before anyone saw him draw it. 'Stand back, Peter. I did not come here to fight and I am sure Adam does not want a brawl on his hands with so many dignitaries in the yard.'

'My intent was not to fight but to listen.' Peter stared at the knife.

'You have shown your colours yet again. You cannot be one of us. Your background betrays you.'

Japhet took his brother's arm and drew him aside. 'I think we all need time to cool off.'

Tristan looked from Joshua to Adam. 'You can keep your prejudices against me or not. But this is not the last you shall hear of me.'

With that he opened the door and gestured to Mr Heathcote, who joined him together with the crew who would sail the ship from the yard. Adam started forward, unwilling to let the matter end there.

'Let him go, Adam,' Joshua said. 'He is right. Now is not the time. For saving the yard from ruin, you owe him that much loyalty.'

'But to be beholden to him of all people!' Adam's fists were bunched, ready to go out and fight. 'Why did he do it? Not just to feel superior over us; it must be more than that. He wants something. I do not trust him.'

'Whatever he wants will be revealed in time,' Japhet said. 'Now it would be wise to join your guests. You have built a great ship and that alone is cause for celebration.'

Chapter Thirty-one

There were few visitors to Tor Farm throughout September apart from family. Japhet was too busy with the renovations to the house and stables for it to overly concern him. He was happy to live quietly until the gossip surrounding his return died down and spend the time establishing his stud farm. Gwendolyn had encouraged his plans, and as she was used to the isolation of their farm in New South Wales, she was equally happy to live in seclusion.

Japhet knew that for a year or so, wherever he went his past would be a cause of speculation, and people would be watching and waiting for him to return to his reprobate life. As far as he was concerned they would have a long and fruitless wait.

By not attempting to thrust themselves back into society, and apparently leading an exemplary and industrious life, they pricked their neighbours' curiosity. When rumours spread that no expense was being spared in renovating and refurbishing the house, Gwendolyn's mother and sister were in great demand from the matrons who refused to receive Japhet, and were interrogated as to the style and quality of the redecoration of the house. Whenever they sniggered that Gwendolyn's fortune would soon be dissipated by such reckless spending, Lady Anne indignantly sought to silence them.

'Every penny of Gwendolyn's inheritance has been put in trust for the children,' she declared. 'Any money that was used in the first years of their marriage has been repaid. My son-in-law has an income now that far outmatches that of his wife.'

Unfortunately, Lady Anne's comments served to add to the speculation as to how Japhet had made his money. Few believed it could have been by legal means. In their ignorance of the recent expansion of the penal colony in New South Wales with eager settlers, the gossips concluded that a continent of convicts only nurtured criminal activities. Such comments ensured the couple were rarely out of local conversation. When news filtered through that the furniture arriving at Tor Farm was direct from Mr Chippendale's workshop and the carpets were of the finest Persian quality, the women were regretting their haste in excluding the couple from their circle. They were intrigued to discover how extravagantly Tor Farm had been changed.

Aware that many now considered him to be an outcast, Japhet had more empathy with Tristan than the other members of his family. He had been appalled at St John's attitude towards his cousin at the shipyard. If the revelations they had made about the wreckers were true, and Tristan had attacked one of the survivors and robbed him, then he had shamed their family and acted beyond any form of decency. Japhet certainly would not condone such brutal behaviour, but somehow such conduct did not fit with the young Tristan he had known, who was desperate to be accepted by his new-found family.

Japhet abhorred hypocrisy. If he wanted his neighbours to accept that his own innocence had been proved by his pardon, then he needed to hear Tristan's side of what had happened that night before he judged him. However, his plans to seek out his cousin were waylaid when he learned that Tristan had again left the district.

Japhet had been in his new home for two months when he disappeared for a fortnight. Despite Gwendolyn's insistence that he was tending to business matters, greying heads nodded sagely and tongues developed a vicious tendency to condemn him for returning to his old life of womanising and gaming.

In the first week of November he returned to Tor Farm riding a five-year-old black Arab stallion, Emir Hassan. The colt had been trained by one of the best in the business, Frank Neale, who had won five Derbys for his owners since 1782. One of them had been HRH the Prince of Wales's horse, Sir Thomas, in 1788. The owner of Emir Hassan had died and his widow had auctioned him at Tattersalls. Japhet had outbid fierce competition from the stables of Lord Grosvenor, one of the foremost owners, who had already won the Derby three times. Emir Hassan had come a respectable third in the Derby himself and won a total of fourteen races in all. Japhet would continue to race him, but had great hopes that in the future he would sire a future Derby winner. Then the name of the Loveday stud would be assured. As this news spread, the landed gentry to a man were intrigued as to Japhet's intentions for the new stud.

When Japhet's old associates on the racing circuit learned that Emir Hassan would service exclusively the mares of Tor Farm, wagers were placed on who would be the first to offer a price exorbitant enough to make the reformed rogue change his mind.

Japhet and Gwendolyn heard the gossip and laughed at the pomposity of their old acquaintances. They in turn had their own wagers on which of them would be the first to eat humble pie and open their doors to receive them.

While Japhet and Gwendolyn contentedly laid the foundations to achieve their dreams, others within the family were also more satisfied with their lives. With the French and British coffers drained from a ten-year war, rumours of a treaty to be negotiated had seen an improvement of trade with the Continent in recent months. Fewer men-of-war in the waters, both British and French, also increased the free-trading. It had prompted an order for a brigantine from a shipping line in Bristol and a cutter for an agent in Guernsey who supplied contraband to smugglers on the Sussex and Kent coast. That meant that Adam had been able to refuse to build another ship for Tristan, stating that those orders would keep the yard in work for another eighteen months.

There had been a terse letter from Tristan sent through Heathcote's office, declaring that as Adam had shown no honour towards him as a past customer who had saved the yard from ruin, or family loyalty, Tristan felt he had no family or loyalty obligations towards his cousins. It was a puzzling statement and sounded like a veiled threat. But that was Tristan's way when crossed, and Adam did not take it seriously. Yet when Japhet expressed an interest in visiting the newly built harbour at Charlestown where Tristan had taken a house, Adam joined him. He had an order to place with the rope-maker for a lugger being overhauled in the dry dock at the yard.

The day of the visit was sunny, with a crisp autumn breeze that sent the clouds scudding like small sailboats across the sky.

'This is very different from when I left Cornwall,' Japhet said with a low whistle as he rode down the main street to the port. It was now the widest street in Cornwall to accommodate the china-clay-filled wagons arriving from the pits through St Austell to Charlestown. 'There were only a few fishermen's cottages then. It was an unremarkable place with beaches on either side.'

He studied the port filled with horse-drawn carts also carrying copper and tin, and the scores of men now employed here. The crook of the harbour arm swept out to sea, and within its shelter were moored the long, narrow pilchard boats. An inner basin had been constructed which was large enough for several tall-masted ships, and as the tide went out a dock gate could be closed across this to retain the water. At its north end was a long ramp that held three slipways used for shipbuilding, and around these were workshops, a timber yard and a smithy. Charles Rashleigh had built the harbour and basin and the small port had been given his name. A row of cottages ran along the side of the quay, and warehouses and coopers' sheds vied for space with rope- and net-makers, lime-burners and brickmakers. The main purpose of the port had been for the use of the china-clay industry, and a steady file of men pushed wagons filled with Cornwall's white gold to be loaded on to the waiting ships.

A fine mist of white dust from the clay drifted over the harbour, frosting the rooftops, ships and ground. Whilst Adam tended to his business, Japhet explored the expanding port, and his curiosity took him to the two-storey house that Tristan had rented. The place looked deserted, and his discreet enquiries informed him that his cousin had left the port last month and was not expected to return. No one seemed to know much about the gentleman, but as gossip about any newcomer was rife, Japhet learned that Tristan had taken a house in Truro for the winter. So their cousin had not left Cornwall. Neither was there mention of him from their neighbours who had visited the county town. For reasons of his own Tristan was living quietly. For a man who could afford to invest in a merchant ship, little was known of his business interests.

Tristan was too wily to do anything without reason. To be accepted amongst the elite of Cornish society would take more than money. Japhet's brief meeting with his cousin at the yard had shown him a man who like himself had been to the depths of hell, and had not only survived, but triumphed. Tristan was not a man to swerve from the ambition that drove him. If he had an axe to grind against the Lovedays, they would not escape its sharp edge. He would be an opponent like no other they had faced before. He would fear only failure, and if Japhet assessed his cousin correctly, failure to Tristan was not an option. He would be relentless, ruthless and merciless in achieving his goal.

Although it had clearly served his own ends, Tristan had nevertheless offered an olive branch by giving a much-needed order for a ship to be built in the yard. The twins' refusal to accept him back into the family was a serious error on their part. Tristan would see it as one more betrayal. Japhet admitted that if circumstances had placed him in Tristan's position, he would never have accepted being made an outcast from the very people who should support him.

With the Loveday blood running hotly through Tristan's veins, coupled with the dog-eat-dog survival code of the underworld he had inhabited as a child, the twins needed to be on their guard. If Tristan's aim was to be accepted by the community, he would make sure that whatever means he took to strike against his cousins, he would have right on his side.

Whenever Japhet tried to reason with Adam and St John, the stubbornness of their pride rose against him. St John stormed out and Adam shook his head. 'A leopard cannot change its spots. What ill could I cause if I let him back into our family?'

Japhet wondered if the greater ill did not come from excluding their cousin. It was better to keep your enemies close and give them enough rope to hang themselves, rather than have them lying in ambush waiting to plunge a knife into your back. That had been how he had triumphed over his enemies in New South Wales. He hoped the twins' obstinacy would not be their downfall.

For many people the winter brought dissent. Anger was growing against the King and Parliament, and there were reports of food riots. The price of wheat and other food reached even higher levels, bringing more suffering to the poor.

Throughout the country tension was rife, and relations also

remained strained between Adam and St John. The poor harvest had forced St John to tighten his purse strings and avoid his gaming haunts, a fact that was reflected in his irascible mood.

Japhet was weary of the conflict that was again raging through his family. Adam had at least accepted the fait accompli of Tristan tricking him into building a ship for him. St John was behaving like a boar with a sore tusk and was the main cause of the tension within the family. This was certainly not turning out to be the joyful homecoming Japhet had yearned for.

It did not help that he was being snubbed by as many of his old acquaintances and neighbours as those who were happy at his return. That was a separate problem and he would deal with it in his own way and time. First he must establish his credibility as a racehorse breeder, and to this end he focused all his time. He trusted no one to ride Emir Hassan but himself, and though he had some knowledge of horse-racing, he was aware that he had no expertise in training that would give his stallion the best chance of winning the Derby. The best trainers were in the pay of the elite of society, and he doubted any of them would give up working for a lord to take employment with an unknown stables whose owner had a criminal record.

It was a problem he put aside for now. Firstly, Tor Farm had to be transformed into an efficient stables and training yard with proper gallops for the horses to train upon. His main reason for purchasing the farm before his marriage had been the long, flat meadow that would be ideal ground for the gallops.

Two weeks after Emir Hassan arrived in the stables, Japhet received a visit from his oldest friend. He was putting the stallion through his paces in the meadow along the drive to the house when he saw a horse and rider approaching. The mount had similar markings to one of his mares, and he recognised the slim, fair-haired figure of Nick Trescoe, who had purchased two of his fillies. After being snubbed by Nick's family, Japhet felt his spine stiffen in resentment at the memory of the treatment he had received. Yet Nick had proved his worth as a friend by helping Hannah and Mark Sawle train Japhet's fillies and colts on Hannah's farm.

Japhet dismounted, tethered Emir to a hitching post and smiled a greeting to his friend. He clicked his heels and bowed to him. 'According to Hannah, I have much to thank you for.'

Nick dismounted. 'I regret not being here when you returned. I was furious to learn that Mama refused to see you and Gwendolyn. I hope I am still received by you.'

'You are not responsible for your mother's censure. And she is not the only one to view me with suspicion and disfavour. You are most welcome. Did you come to see this fine beauty?' He indicated the stallion.

'I have to say I was curious.' Nick laughed. 'But where is the beauty you married? I came to pay my respects. Gwendolyn is an exceptional woman for following you so loyally to the far ends of the earth. I am ashamed that my family will not receive her.'

Japhet shrugged, but his body remained tense. He told himself that acceptance would take a while and would be won from one person at a time. He slid the stallion's reins from the post and nodded to Nick to follow him to the stables. 'Gwen will be delighted to see you. First I must see to Emir.' They entered the stables and led the stallion to his stall. As Japhet loosened the girths and removed the saddle he said, 'Before we join my wife and she quizzes you on how many hearts you have broken and what adventures you have been engaged in since last we met, tell me how the mares you bought from Hannah have fared on the racing circuit. I heard they had won a race or two.'

'In the last two seasons they have competed fewer than a dozen times: they won three races, and had two seconds and a third between them. They are fine horses, and I have been delighted with their success.'

'That is heartening news.' Japhet beckoned to a groom to rub the stallion down and turned his full attention on his friend.

Nick was grinning. 'I have to say that for your sins you look disgustingly pleased with life.' His easy-going manner refused to take any offence at the stiffness of Japhet's demeanour. 'Many said you would skulk in the southern hemisphere to the end of your days, too ashamed to return. I knew you would make your fortune and thumb your nose at society.'

As he spoke, Nick could not take his gaze from the stallion. The Arab's ebony head was held proudly as he posed as regal as any potentate.

'Who will train him?' Nick asked.

'I have not decided. I have not the skill for a horse of his standing. I bought him primarily as a stud and prefer him not to leave my stables unless he is racing.'

'He has a few more years in him, and every race he wins adds to both his and your status in the racing world. To achieve that, you need an insight into how the top trainers work today.'

Japhet frowned. His money had enabled him to outbid the other interested buyers, but the racing fraternity was tightly knit and wary of any whose reputation was not impeccable. 'And how am I to get them away from the most acclaimed owners in the sport?'

'You go for a newcomer. Someone who knows the ropes but has yet to prove his mettle. I know just the one. Tim Coates. He's not a trainer but has worked in a couple of the top yards as a stable lad. He was dismissed under something of a cloud after selling information about runners. He's a bit of a wild card, but you'd be the man to keep him in line. He loves the sport but has only been able to get work as a groom this year.'

'Usually I would be the first one to give a man a second chance, but with my reputation still tainted . . .' Japhet did not need to finish his statement. Nick knew only too well that the credentials of a racing yard must be impeccable for them to be accepted at the highest levels.

'Coates has a knack of getting the best from a horse,' Nick replied. 'You have fillies and colts that need such a trainer. A racing stables and stud takes years to become established.' He ran his hand appreciatively along the dark glossy neck of the stallion. 'A reputation is built by the number of races won. I know where Coates is working and we can go together to meet him if you wish.'

This was Nick's way of making amends for the treatment Japhet had received from his family. It would have been churlish to refuse such a generous offer. It was also unlikely that any of the top trainers would wish to be associated with an untested stable yard. Nick had thrown him a valuable lifeline and he would take it. An opportunity such as this might not come his way again. It would be a major turning point in establishing the future of the stable yard.

Chapter Thirty-two

'I have a son!' St John shouted as he entered Boscabel like a whirlwind. 'Where is everyone? At last I have a son.' It was the beginning of December, and the morning mist had formed droplets on his cropped hair.

Adam and Senara had been seated at breakfast and both rose at his cry. When the older twin filled the doorway, his hair dishevelled from the pace of his ride and his face beaming with pleasure, Adam was the first to congratulate him.

'Joyous news indeed, brother. How is Felicity? We had no idea that she had gone into labour.'

'The boy was born very quickly. Her first pain was at three this morning and, thinking it would be several hours, she would not hear of me calling Senara or another midwife or doctor to attend her until morning. My son was born five hours later, hale and hearty. Dr Yeo attended Felicity before I left and proclaimed her well, and there were no complications following the birth.'

'Have you decided on a name?' Senara asked.

'George Arthur, after Grandfather and Great-grandfather.'

'And after our sovereign and the fabled King Arthur. Noble names indeed,' Adam agreed. He went to the sideboard and collected a flagon of claret and three glasses. 'We must toast the health and prosperity of the child.'

From his brother's flushed countenance, it was obvious that St John had started celebrating the birth long before he came here. But who could blame him? When he left an hour later, after several more glasses, he was swaying tipsily and intending to visit Joshua and Peter.

When Adam and Senara called at Trevowan later that afternoon, they noted the dramatic change in the atmosphere. There was an air of brightness everywhere, like the sun bathing the countryside after a storm. The women were excited and light-hearted, and the children were playing with their hoops, running unrestrained across the gardens with the family dogs chasing them. Even the servants had a greater jauntiness in their step and a smile quivering on their lips.

Felicity was propped up on her pillows, looking more contented than for many months. George Arthur nestled in her arms and she could not stop smiling down at the infant. 'He is just so perfect, is he not, Senara?'

'And, from the speed of his birth, impatient to experience life,' Adam chuckled. 'Japhet and Gwen have just arrived. I will leave you ladies to your talk of babies.'

'Did my husband not return with you?' Felicity frowned. 'He has waited so long for a son, I thought he would want to be at home to welcome the well-wishers.'

'Do not judge him too harshly on this occasion,' Adam said gently. 'He is so proud he cannot wait to tell all his friends.' He bowed and left, hoping that now St John had his heir, he would take his responsibilities more seriously and restrain his excessive pursuit of pleasure.

St John returned as his guests were leaving. Their horses had been brought from the stables and the cousins were saying their goodbyes when St John was seen swaying in the saddle as his horse walked up the drive. They waited for him to dismount, which he did almost pitching himself face down on to the flagstones. He was only saved by Adam catching him under the arms. His breath was sour from a day's heavy drinking and his legs were in danger of giving way as he clung to his saddle for support.

He grinned inanely and waved a finger in Adam's direction. 'I have partaken of a drink or several to toast my son. No one would begrudge me that.'

'He is a fine boy, St John,' Adam said, keeping a firm grip about his twin. 'I think you should sleep off your celebrating before the women see you in this condition.'

'I will not be judged by those cackling hens,' he hiccoughed. 'I have a son at last. Every man needs a son to be proud of and to continue the family name; girls suck a man dry with their expectations of a dowry. I weary of being surrounded by women.'

'But you will respect their gentility by not offending them by being drunk in their presence.' Japhet took his other arm. 'We will get you to your chamber by the servants' stairs.' He frowned over St John's sagging figure to his wife. 'This will take us some minutes. I suggest you await us in the orangery, Gwen.'

Senara had seen Rowena watching her father from the doorway. She had clearly been awaiting his return with anticipation, and now her lovely face crumpled in distress at witnessing his condition and his cruel words. She ran off towards the orchard. 'I think Rowena has need of us,' Senara told her husband. 'She has been her father's favourite for so long and never saw Charlotte or Thea as a threat to St John's affections. Everything will change for her now that George Arthur is born.'

The following week Japhet took Gwendolyn to Truro to buy Christmas gifts for the family. Whilst Gwen enthusiastically visited the shops with her maid, hunting for toys for the children, Japhet purchased a sapphire pendant and matching earrings for his wife and was on his way back to their room in the inn when he saw Tristan entering a coffee house. This was his chance to speak to his cousin, and he followed him. By good fortune Tristan sat alone in a wooden booth at the back of the shop, which would afford them some privacy.

Japhet approached the table. Tristan had picked up one of the news-sheets available for the customers to read, and when he glanced up from it, his surprise was obvious as he recognised his cousin.

'Do I intrude?' Japhet asked. 'Are you meeting someone?'

'I have an hour to pass before I have an appointment across town.' Tristan's voice was guarded. 'You are welcome to join me if you do not regard me as a social leper.'

Japhet sat down and ordered a pot of coffee from the approaching serving wench. The coffee house was only half full and there was no one sitting close enough to overhear their conversation. 'I have been intending to meet with you for some time, but I believe you left Cornwall shortly after taking possession of your ship. Your dealings with my cousin were a surprise.'

'I needed a ship.' Tristan shrugged and regarded him with hooded eyes. 'Are you of the same opinion as the twins? Have you come to warn me away?'

'I am intrigued as to why you have returned,' Japhet said honestly. 'Your disappearance was a mystery to me for years. The reasons, other than that you had shamed the family, were silenced by Grandpapa. And Adam and St John refused to speak of the matter. I thought you would have done everything in your power to stay here. I thought you wanted to be accepted.'

'It was made obvious to me that such a thing would never happen.' Tristan's expression was closed and all emotion stripped from the indolent response. 'Nothing has changed from your side of the family. Even Adam has shown where his loyalty lies.'

'What did happen that night?'

The eyes regarding him narrowed. 'I will make no excuses to you for my conduct. But I was not guilty of what I was accused of. That is all I will say on the matter.'

A dozen questions stalled on Japhet's tongue. He bowed his head in acceptance. He had not really expected Tristan to confide in him on their first meeting. 'It gladdens me that you have prospered. The years have treated you well.'

'Like you, I turned circumstances to my advantage. We are similar in many ways. I doubt you would wish to reveal all of your enterprises in the new colony.'

Japhet gave a soft laugh. 'Very true. Also, my life was far from exemplary before my marriage. Yet whilst I visited several of our larger cities, including London, I never heard anything of you in all those years.'

'I spent some time abroad. France. The Channel Isles. Venice – now that was a city for a hot-blooded male. Boston. But once my fortune was acquired, Cornwall remained a potent lure. It must have been the same for you. With so many settlers sailing to Sydney Cove, a man of your talents could soon acquire riches beyond your dreams. Yet you returned to our native shores. Was that to prove how much you had been misjudged?'

293

Impressed by the places Tristan had visited, Japhet wondered if the greatest truth had been in his final question.

'I owed much to my wife. Whatever the opportunities for advancement in New South Wales, Gwendolyn deserved the genteel civilisation England offered. Did you ever marry?'

'Twice. But again I am a widower.'

'Any children.'

'I was not so blessed.'

'Do you intend to settle in Cornwall?'

Tristan spread his hands, and the piercing black of his eyes challenged Japhet's hazel stare. 'I am a man of chance and opportunity. Who knows what the future will hold?'

'Do you wish to be reconciled with our family?' Japhet was curious to know.

There was a long pause before Tristan announced cuttingly, 'The future relationship between my Loveday cousins and myself is in their hands. I learned long ago that loyalty starts with being true to oneself.'

He refused to be drawn further on the subject and was only interested in hearing of Japhet's exploits in the last two decades. When Japhet left his cousin, he was not much the wiser of his past or his intentions.

In the weeks following the birth of George Arthur, St John was a changed man. He was rarely from home and curbed his drinking. He spent hours in his study concentrating on the running of the estate and planning ways of improving the beef herd and making it more profitable. It was a shock for him to discover the extent of the loans he had raised on the estate, and that he had sold a quarter of the land during the last year to meet his gambling debts. Even the house itself was now encumbered by a hefty mortgage. How could he have allowed his drinking to so cloud his judgement? Trevowan was teetering on the edge of ruin if he could not raise more money to invest in stock to improve the beef herd. The land he had so recklessly sold had been prime fields for planting.

He threw down the quill he had been using to write down columns of figures and sat back in his chair. His hesitation was only token before opening a bottle of brandy and pouring himself a large measure. In front of him were unpaid bills from milliners, corset-makers, hosiers, shoemakers, tobacconists, tailors, seamstresses, tailors, candle-makers and farriers amongst sundry others. None of which he had the means to pay. He cursed Felicity for her extravagance. Many of these articles had been for Rowena, who was fast growing into a young lady, and if Rowena had new shoes or a gown, Felicity also purchased the same for Charlotte, doubling the expenditure. He ignored his own tailors' bills, which were twice the size of anything spent on his wife and daughters.

His despondent stare skimmed the book-lined walls and paused briefly upon the head-and-shoulders portrait of George Loveday. The old man glared accusingly back at him. St John raised his glass in salute to the painting. 'A hair of the dog, Grandpapa. The Lord knows I've reasons aplenty to drown my sorrows.'

The ormolu clock on the fireplace showed a quarter before ten. The wintry sun was low in the sky and dazzlingly bright through the window. He rubbed his hand across his eyes. A headache was starting from the pressure of his responsibilities that had been too long neglected.

It had only now dawned on him that so many months after the sale of the land, the new owner had ploughed none of the fields. At first he had been relieved that they had been left fallow, for strange workers would have raised the family's suspicions that something was amiss, but the fact that those fields had not been put to profitable use made him uneasy. He had no idea who had purchased the land.

Also nagging at the back of his mind were the IOUs he had written. They were now due for payment and he was unaware of the extent of his gambling debts. He had nothing left of significant value to sell. All but a few paltry trinkets of Felicity's jewellery had been pawned, and once she had risen from her lying-in after the birth, his wife would be demanding why they were not in her jewellery casket. He could stall her for a few weeks, saying that he had noticed that the clasp of her diamond necklace had broken and he had left it with a jeweller to repair.

He downed another brandy, savouring its welcoming fire in his gut, before he dropped his head into his hands. How could he have let his debts mount so heavily? It was ill luck that just when he needed it most, he could no longer call on Thomas for a low-interest loan. A letter from his cousin had arrived before the birth of George saying that he had sold the bank and that the present loan St John had with them would now be subject to a higher rate of interest. Thomas had suggested that in future he might be better served by dealing with a local banking house. What no one knew was that the most prestigious ones had already turned him down because of the outstanding loans already taken out on the property.

He could not even ask his cousin for a personal loan, as all Thomas's private money would now be tied up in the vast expense of building his new theatre. For a moment despair gouged like talons in St John's breast. His hand shook as he poured and drank another fortifying brandy. He must not panic. All was far from lost, he told himself stalwartly. For the sake of his son's future, there must be some way he could save the estate from debt. He pulled the sheet of figures he had been working on towards him, but the brandy had dulled his wits, and the debts now appeared insurmountable. The drink also turned his thoughts morose. He would not be in this mess if his father had not given his birthright to his twin. The yard had always supported the estate when the harvests had failed. His resentment flared. It was not his fault Trevowan now faced this crisis. His father should never have separated it from the source of its main income.

The estate ledgers lay accusingly on the desk. The interest on the loans he had raised mounted with every week. He had only a vague idea of how much was owed altogether and no stomach at this moment to learn the extent. He would deal with that another day. He shoved the ledgers back in the desk drawer and slammed it shut. A frequent occurrence in the last year.

To escape his guilt he craved diversion. Outside he could hear Rowena and Charlotte quarrelling, the shrillness of their voices stabbing through his skull. Elspeth's voice was also raised in the house as she chided Rafe for running pell-mell like a guttersnipe through the corridors. When there was a scream from Charlotte and an outburst of tears, all patience deserted him. He poured himself another large brandy, seeking solace in a drunken haze. If he could not find a way to repay his debts, the banks and moneylenders would foreclose on their loans. That did not bear thinking about.

He could be declared bankrupt and Trevowan sold to pay his debts. There had to be another way. He could not allow his son to lose his inheritance.

The brandy bottle was half empty when a sharp tap on the door roused him from his melancholic torpor. Jenna entered and bobbed a curtsey. She was carrying a letter on a silver salver.

'This came by messenger from Bodmin, sir. He said he were to wait for your reply.'

St John scowled at seeing the seal of Lancombe and Fairweather, a lawyer's office in the town. He doubted the letter contained news to his advantage. It requested a meeting with him at his first convenience to avoid a writ being entered against him by a creditor, and advised that he give this matter his immediate attention, as delay could prove detrimental if he wished to safeguard his family name and reputation.

St John screwed the letter into a tight ball and threw it into the fire. An icy sweat broke out on his skin and the wings of panic battered inside his chest. His creditors were baying at his heels. If he did not comply, he would face imprisonment. He could only hope that the bank would now look favourably at his request for a loan against next year's harvest.

'Inform the messenger that I shall attend at eleven tomorrow forenoon,' he forced out through the tight ball of fear lodged in his throat. 'Pack for two or three nights, Jenna. I will leave for Bodmin as soon as my horse is saddled. Urgent business awaits me. Do not tell the mistress until I have left.'

With good speed he could make Bodmin by nightfall. There must be some way he could save his family from disgrace.

St John's mood had not improved by the time he reached the old stannary town just as the innkeepers were lighting the lanterns over their doorways. He had never cared much for his own company, and having partaken of an evening meal, he was drawn by boredom to one of the gaming houses. With only ten guineas in his pocket, he had no expectations of much entertainment from the cards. He sauntered around the tables watching the play in progress. He recognised many of the gentlemen from his visits in the past, and the first threads of hunger to participate stirred. With each win of the steadily increasing wagers upon the tables, his need became a craving.

'Not like you not to be playing, Mr Loveday,' a sybaritic voice challenged.

He turned to regard a short, stocky man, the shiny elbows and lapels of his coat proclaiming him of dubious repute. 'I saw you win two hundred guineas here not two months past.'

'I am in town on business,' St John replied, his blood circling with a fiery glow as he recalled the game in question.

'Two hundred guineas won on the turn of a card. There is nothing like that elation, is there, Mr Loveday?' the man persisted. 'You had a skill and a cool head I much admired. Will you be playing tonight?'

'I arrived too late to call upon my bank. I have not the funds until tomorrow.'

'Ah, a pity, sir! I heard tell that in the back room there would be a game for high stakes later. It would have been a wonder to watch a man with your skill at play.'

The flattery fanned St John's pride. His mouth was dry and he ran his tongue over his lips in anticipation of such a game.

'Would you do me the honour of accepting a drink from a humble admirer?' The man bowed to him. 'Jonas Knuckey, your servant, sir. Cousin to the Knuckeys of Truro, purveyors of fine perukes when nature has been ungenerous to gentlemen of position. Not that you would have need of my cousin's services, Mr Loveday. Hair of such robust quality must be the envy of your male acquaintances.' He clicked his fingers and two brandies were presented to them with remarkable speed. Knuckey raised his glass. 'Your good health, Mr Loveday, and to an enjoyable evening at the tables.'

'Sadly, that is a pleasure I must decline until I attend my bank on the morrow.'

'That would be a sad loss to us all. Would you consider me too forward, sir, upon such a short acquaintance, if I were to loan the funds for the game later? A man of your position should not be denied his pleasure. I find myself in the embarrassing position of also having arrived in town too late to call upon my bank. My horse lost a shoe and I had to walk the last two miles. I have a purse of one hundred pounds, which makes me nervous of pickpockets and cutpurses. Indeed, not only would it be an honour to accept your IOU for what to you must be a paltry amount, it would allow me to sleep easier knowing that my money is in safe hands.'

St John could not believe his good fortune. The call of the tables hammered in his brain. Then he recalled why he was in Bodmin. Certainly it was not to raise a loan for gaming, but to settle his debts. Yet if the game this night was all his companion had intimated, his winnings could stretch to a thousand or so guineas. That would keep his creditors off his back until the next harvest. Even so, he hesitated, 'Your offer is too generous, Mr Knuckey. I could not possibly accept such a loan.'

At that moment there was a stirring of heads from the far table and a man rose declaring loudly, 'For now the cards are against me, gentlemen. I will join some of you later when I must hope that Lady Luck will be more favourable.'

St John glared at the gambler, his face tight with anger as he recognised Tristan leaving the play.

Knuckey chuckled. 'He is not such an illustrious player as yourself, Mr Loveday. He lost several hundred pounds when I was at the table earlier and a thousand more when he played once before. He has a failing in that unlike yourself he is too reckless and bluffs too often. Some say he is a cousin of yours, Mr Loveday. If that is so, I fear you should warn him that when the stakes are high and his hand is a poor one, he sits absolutely still, not moving a muscle, not even blinking an eye.' Knuckey sidled closer and dropped his voice to a whisper. 'Some would say that was the stillness of a confidence trickster, but that could not be the case if he is some distant relative of yours.'

'He is no relative at all, Mr Knuckey,' St John brashly declared. The man had given him an insight into how to thrash Tristan at cards. After the humiliation of their meeting on the road, it was an irresistible challenge.

'It has been a pleasure meeting you, Mr Loveday. I will retire now to my room at the inn. I recognised some gentlemen who are leaving and will be going in my direction. I do not like being abroad on the street without company.' He nervously patted the inside of his jacket where a bulging purse was visible. 'I look forward to admiring your skill at the tables another time, Mr Loveday. I am only in the town for this one night.'

'Perhaps I have been too cautious, Mr Knuckey. You do appear overly concerned about the danger of cutpurses. You would be doing us both a service if you were to accept my IOU so that I could play tonight. It has been a pleasure meeting you and I feel you will bring me luck.'

Knuckey pulled the purse from his jacket with a relieved sigh. 'I will sleep much easier tonight, sir. It has been a beneficial meeting. I shall call upon you at the inn at midday tomorrow when you have had time to attend at your bank to repay my loan.' He laughed conspiratorially. 'Unless, as I suspect, you will be repaying me out of your winnings later this evening.'

Chapter Thirty-three

Tristan was the last man to join the gaming table. Eight men were to play, and he took the only empty seat, opposite his cousin. He greeted everyone individually and exchanged a witty remark. St John was the only one to ignore him.

'Gentlemen, have we come here to exchange inane pleasantries, or are we here to play?' St John scowled into his brandy glass. His discontent had carved deep lines around his mouth and brow and his fingers tapped an impatient tattoo upon the table.

Throughout the evening Tristan had kept a surreptitious eye on his cousin. So far St John had limited his drinking, but he noted that there was a brightness to the younger man's eyes: the fever that proclaimed the obsession that would overtake him once the game was underway. As the first of the cards were dealt, he kept his gaze on his cousin, knowing his scrutiny would undermine him. Years of living by his wits had taught Tristan how to take the measure of a man. Time had not favoured St John as it had Adam, and now no stranger would take them for twins, but assume that St John was the older brother by several years. His short hair was receding and his figure had thickened from his indolent nature. There was a looseness of flesh upon his jowls and a slackening of his lips: signs of the weak traits in his character.

At St John's rudeness, several of the players frowned in his direction. Tristan laughed. 'I am here to play. It is agreed that there are no limits to the stakes. I look forward to an interesting evening.'

St John surveyed the players. Of the seven others, four were strangers, while two he had played before and to those two he had

301

lost heavily. This would be a good night to win back his losses and also show Tristan who was the better man. A thorough trouncing would put his upstart cousin firmly in his place.

During the first hour of play the hands were won evenly between St John and Tristan, with a couple of good-size pots going to their companions. By midnight St John had won the last four hands from his cousin and his blood was fired beyond discretion as he relished his superiority and victory. The drink was flowing freely and the stakes were rising with each game. St John scarcely heeded when the four strangers threw in their cards and retired from the table. By now his hundred-pound stake had increased to twelve hundred pounds and his mind was fixed on the equally large pile in front of his cousin. The high stakes had drawn a dozen spectators to the game, and from behind St John's shoulder, Mr Knuckey praised his skill.

'The cards are with you tonight, Mr Loveday. I've never seen you play better,' Knuckey whispered, during a pause when cigars were passed round. He had decided to stay and watch the gaming. 'A few more games and you'll wipe the floor with your opponents.'

The press of bodies and the cigar smoke made the back parlour hot and stuffy. It was a heavy atmosphere. The players had removed their jackets and St John had loosened his stock. He had noted in several games where Tristan had lost that he sat absolutely motionless as Knuckey had intimated. With the confidence of that knowledge, he increased his stakes and won the next two hands.

As the remaining two players got up from the table, Tristan shrugged. 'The cards are kind to you tonight, cousin. I think I too will call it a night.'

'So you admit that you are no match for me?' St John challenged, his expression smug. 'How about one more hand? Double the stakes, or is that too much for your purse?'

There was a gasp from the spectators that increased the fever now racing through St John's blood.

'Well done, Mr Loveday. Lady Luck is surely with you,' Knuckey crowed in admiration.

Tristan eyed the money and IOUs piled on the table. 'How much do you wager?'

'Five thousand.'

'Very well.'

The cards were dealt and a hush fell over the room. Both men exchanged two cards and studied their hands. St John's cards were good but not the best, and he could feel sweat trickling down his shoulder blades. Tristan studied the fan of cards in his own hand, then snapped them into a pile and laid them face down on the table. His body had grown very still and his face was ironed of any expression.

'Let us make this more interesting,' he said. 'Double the stakes again.'

So far St John had only speculated with the hundred pounds loaned to him by Knuckey and had made a handsome profit. Though even that would barely clear his outstanding debts. But ten thousand pounds would settle all his debts and enable him to live in the style he chose without any curtailment to his gambling or pleasure. His heart quickened with excitement. He glanced again at his hand and then at Tristan, whose face and body were motionless as a statue. His cousin was bluffing. The pot was as good as his.

He snapped his fingers, and an inkwell and slip of paper were placed by his hand. He wrote the IOU with a flourish and tossed it into the centre of the table. Tristan did the same. Then, with a smug grin, St John revealed his cards. Every man watching held their breath as Tristan nonchalantly flipped his over.

'Bad luck, old fellow. It seems I am the better man.' Tristan rose and bowed to the spectators amidst a round of applause.

St John sat in stunned misery.

As Tristan left the room, he passed a purse of fifty guineas to Knuckey. 'You did a good job.'

Sleep eluded Tristan that night. He had expected to feel elation. Finally he had St John where he wanted him. His family would know him for the liar and blackguard he truly was. Even so, his triumph left a sour taste in Tristan's mouth. He had not set out to ruin his cousin, only seek justice. St John's arrogance and continued persecution had pushed Tristan's patience beyond his limits. Why should he show loyalty and mercy when none had been granted to him?

Through the dark hours of the night his thoughts kept returning to his past. He had never been able to escape the returning nightmares of the years he had spent in the most squalid poverty. They had robbed him of his innocence and trust in his fellow man. The night of the storm had shown Tristan that George Loveday regarded him as the black sheep of the family. His great-uncle had been harsh and unforgiving. He had blamed Tristan for the sins of Walter Loveday in deserting his family and choosing the road to perdition. He condemned Walter as a rakehell and wastrel steeped in depravity. George had also declared that while Tristan had adopted the veneer of a gentleman, nothing would erase the guttersnipe beneath. He would not listen to his great-nephew's explanation of those events. The favoured heir had ensured that he was heard first, and Tristan remained the perpetual outcast.

Even after so many years the pain of rejection cut sharply. Tristan had not wanted George Loveday's charity – he had wanted his acceptance. When it was obvious that he would never be so recognised, his crushed pride and heartache had driven him to run away. He had vowed that night that one day those who had turned their backs on him would learn the truth: that the heir to Trevowan was everything they despised. Thief, liar, indolent wastrel. Yet while Tristan had used St John's weaknesses against him, his cousin had been cunning enough until now to keep his baser nature a secret from his family.

Tristan had also vowed on the night that he had run away that he would never be poor or regarded as an inferior again. He took nothing with him but the few clothes he possessed, which were of good quality, and a few shillings that he had saved from money given him by either George or Edward Loveday during his time with the family. He was by then also equipped with an education that had taught him to read, write and have a good head for figures. He had learned enough French and Latin as a grounding for other languages, and been taught the manners and speech of a gentleman. The survival instincts of the gutter had given him a ruthless and opportunist streak. And his quick wits, good looks, charm and cunning were also the means for him to rise in the world as he intended.

He had walked to Falmouth and stowed away on a ship bound for St Malo. He had purchased a loaf and some cheese before creeping on to the ship at night to hide in the hold. He had learned that it would sail with the next tide. By good fortune no one had discovered his presence on board and he had jumped ship at the port after six days at sea. Even in the years before the Revolution began, unrest was stirring in France and he had been shocked at the plight of the poor. But in the ports trade was good and he had found work as a clerk and translator to a spice merchant, Jacques Fortin. The hours were long and the pay poor, but Tristan was interested in the money that could be made by buying exotic goods and exporting them to the rich cities of the world.

Jacques Fortin was in his fifties and a widower. Despite his wealth he lived frugally, with only one servant to run his household, and he never entertained. When Tristan had worked for him for three years, he was surprised to learn that Fortin had a daughter, being educated in a convent. Shortly after her sixteenth birthday, Emilie Fortin returned to her home. Fortin was determined that she would marry well. He was fiercely protective of her reputation, and Tristan had only seen her once in the six months since she had arrived. By then he had been promoted to head clerk, after he had proved to his employer his suspicions that the previous head clerk had been embezzling from him.

Three months later Fortin was attacked outside his shop and died within a week from a head wound. As head clerk Tristan attended upon Emilie on a weekly basis to inform her of the financial status of the company. From the first meeting he was aware that he had found favour in the young woman's eyes. What better wife to advance his fortune than a young, innocent, pretty heiress? He ruthlessly set out to woo her. All did not go smoothly. Emilie had been on the point of succumbing to his courtship when, to Tristan's dismay, her only other relative, the withered and irascible Aunt Claudine, appeared with all her baggage in St Malo. The old trout intended to act as chaperone to her niece, with the sole determination of protecting her from fortune-hunters. From their first meeting Aunt Claudine was suspicious of Tristan. Undaunted, he set out to charm the old harridan and within a month had won her over. Even so, Aunt Claudine refused to allow Emilie to marry until she was eighteen.

Tristan curbed his impatience at the delay and made plans about how to expand the business once he became its master. Finally they married, but Tristan became uneasy at the political situation in France. Food was scarce and the King and Queen were hated. He could taste rebellion in the air. Both Aunt Claudine and Emilie protested when he wanted to sell the business and leave France. Claudine he dispatched back to her cottage in Marseilles, but with the unrest in France growing he had been unable to find a buyer for the business. When Emilie informed him that she was carrying his child, he was shaken at the joy that possessed him. At last he would have his own family, the start of another dynasty of Lovedays. Leaving France to build his future elsewhere now became an obsession. With no buyer for the company, he stripped the warehouse of its goods and sent them to an agent in London to sell for him. The house he sold for a fraction of its true worth. Emilie was four months with child the day they set out to board a ship that would stop first in Jersey then sail on to Portsmouth. From there Tristan would sail to Cornwall. He had a beautiful and accomplished wife, a family on the way and, when his goods from the warehouse were sold, enough money to start any business he chose. He would show the Lovedays he was no longer a ne'er-do-well and guttersnipe but a man of position and fortune. Two chests of gold coins were also amongst their luggage that had been sent on ahead to the ship.

It was also the day that a riot broke out between the militia and starving citizens attempting to break into a flour warehouse. Tristan had been alerted by the angry shouting when they turned into a narrow street flanked by warehouses on the approach to the quay. It had all happened so quickly. What began as a minor disturbance changed drastically when a ragged man was clubbed to the ground and kicked by the militia. Then it had flared into a bloody and violent fight. The street was blocked ahead of them by the skirmish, and when Tristan turned to go back, a troop of armed horsemen were bearing down upon them, striking indiscriminately with their sabres at any in their way.

Tristan had pushed Emilie into a doorway, but in her terror she stumbled and fell. He raised her up and she clung to him, shaky and crying.

'Are you hurt?' he demanded.

'Get me out of here, my love. Get me to the ship.'

She stumbled several times as they headed towards the quay, and he scooped her into his arms, carrying her away from the danger.

As they approached the gangplank to the ship, the captain was waving at them, impatient for them to board.

'There's trouble in the town. If it spreads to the warehouses here the ship could be seized,' the bewhiskered captain bellowed. 'Hurry on board. We sail at once.'

Emilie was ashen and still trembling. 'Are you sure you do not need a physician to attend you?' Tristan insisted. 'We can find another passage.'

She shook her head. The sound of the rioting was getting louder, and musket shots were now being fired. Her voice rose with hysteria. 'Take me on board, Tristan. I can rest in our cabin. Please, take me away.'

Unbeknown to Tristan, when Emilie had fallen, her side had caught the edge of a step. They had been at sea an hour when the pains began. She miscarried as Jersey was sighted and she had bled to death before they moored at St Helier. Tristan ordered his luggage and his wife's body taken ashore. He abandoned his plans to travel to England; his wealth had no meaning without a family to build a dynasty.

It was not until the coffin was lowered into the cold ground that he realised how much he had come to love the sweet, innocent young woman he had married.

In his grief he spent three years travelling through Europe, until he eventually settled in Venice. For a time he sought oblivion pursuing the life of a libertine in the hedonistic city where pleasure and business were conducted with equal enthusiasm. Within a year most of his fortune had gone on gambling, courtesans and extravagant living. When he awoke in the middle of the night from a drunken haze, and found the courtesan he had left a masked ball with and her accomplice in the process of robbing him of all his valuables, he ran the accomplice through with his sword, though not fatally, and threw the whore out on to the streets.

The incident brought him to his senses. He was twenty-six and on the slippery path back to the gutter if he did not change his ways. He used the next two years in Venice to learn everything he could from the prosperous merchants, often by bribing their servants and clerks. Every luxury imaginable had been imported and exported from that glorious maritime port, and by both fair means and also the less than legitimate, he again began to prosper and recover his losses.

From Venice he returned to the Channel Islands, spending a year in Guernsey. He had been unable to face the larger island where his wife and child were buried. There he further increased his fortune, entering into a partnership with an agent who supplied contraband to the smugglers in England. The constant links with the West Country and Cornwall had drawn him back to his homeland. He was now a wealthy man and considered that with his new status and the passage of time a reconciliation could be effected with his family. When he landed in Fowey he learned that he had been branded a thief for stealing valuables from Trevowan. The news stunned him. He had taken nothing, and he knew that if anything had gone missing the night he ran away, the true culprit had deliberately blackened his name to escape punishment. By then George Loveday had been dead a year and Adam had been sent away from Trevowan to serve in the navy, while St John was beginning to earn a name for himself as a wastrel. What use to return to Trevowan and profess his innocence? They had judged and condemned him.

Wealth was the tool he believed would one day enable him to meet the Lovedays as not only their equal but their superior. Nothing less would salve his injured pride. His bank coffers might be full, but since leaving France he had accumulated no possessions. To be part of English society he needed a large estate and an impressive house, as well as a carriage, well-stocked stables and a dozen servants. Also a wife of impeccable lineage. He had not yet achieved the wealth to acquire all that, but he would by the time he next returned to these shores.

The first ship out of Fowey had been to Plymouth. From there he boarded a vessel for the West Indies. He stayed only a few months, having befriended a cousin of a plantation owner in Kingston who was shortly to return to his home town of Boston. Tristan was invited to join him. To be accepted by the elite of Boston society was an opportunity he could not refuse, and he proceeded to inveigle his way into the homes of the most influential people in the city.

A dozen years later there were occasions when Tristan had to pinch himself to believe his good fortune. Yet he also believed that it was good fortune carved from his own sharp wits and eye for a profitable investment.

In Boston he had fallen in love a second time, with a lovely young widow, Susannah Wynslow, who was not only blessed with a healthy fortune, but was from one of the foremost Boston families. Tristan had finally found the status and wealth he had desired. Yet still at the back of his mind was his need to return to England to parade his wealth and status to the family who had rejected him as a ne'er-do-well. However, with England now locked into a war with France, Susannah was a reluctant traveller and begged him to wait until peace was restored. As the war dragged on, she bore him a son, Walter. With a wife who adored him, a large mansion in Boston, and his business interests thriving, Tristan bided his time, never forgetting his vow to establish his home in England.

Then tragedy struck once again. Having been taught by Edward Loveday to sail, Tristan had never lost his love for the sea. Most of his adult life he had lived near it. He had bought himself a sixty-foot yacht, and to escape the heat of the summer would spend hours sailing the busy coastal waters around Boston. One afternoon a sudden squall blew up. With the lashing rain and choppy waves making sailing difficult, an inexperienced sailor rammed his yacht. The mast broke and she had capsized. Susannah and Walter drowned and Tristan could do nothing to save them.

In his grief, all his wealth and position meant nothing. He was consumed by a dark and destructive anger, driven by the wild blood of his ancestors, which had been too long suppressed by his quest to achieve respectability. Much of the following months was a drunken blur as he sought escape from his pain by whoring, gaming and fighting several duels. Gradually his American friends turned away from him and he realised that he had only been accepted because of Susannah's standing in the community. Most of his new acquaintances were parvenus and upstarts, all with the smell of adventurer and rakehell. They were easy pickings to bolster his fortune and he despised them all.

The old feelings of rejection returned. Again he felt an outcast, and a deep and terrible anger reignited in his breast. With nothing left to keep him in America, he sold all his business interests and the house in Boston and returned to England. The tragedy of the deaths of both of his wives and children seemed to underline the fact that family life was to be denied him.

On his arrival in England he paid informers to learn all they could about his family in the last twenty-three years. There had been many shocks, scandals and surprises. Not least Japhet's exploits and the twins' involvement with smugglers. St John's selfish and wastrel ways had been no less than he expected, but the existence of Tamasine Loveday had intrigued him and he had not had to dig too deeply to surmise that she was Edward Loveday's love-child. Now that had been a startling revelation. Meeting Georganna had been the greatest luck of all. He had immediately sensed her sadness, and he had met many men like Thomas in his travels. Though he had no real vendetta against Thomas, seducing his wife had been an instinctive and easy way to get back at one of his cousins. It had also given him more influence in furthering his association with Tamasine. And who could not fall prey to that young woman's vivacious spirit and unconventional charms? She had all the feisty Loveday qualities and none of their failings, and she had been vulnerable because of her past. That had formed an unspoken bond between them.

He had begun to hope that through Tamasine he would find acceptance. That dream had been brutally dashed by his cousins' recriminations at Beaucombe. Reflecting on those events had churned up the old rivalry. Adam had been angry, believing Tristan had somehow tricked his sister and that he could harm her reputation. St John's fury had been predictable, fed by fear of discovery of his lies and deceit. Tristan had not expected such a violent reaction to his homecoming. When the Lovedays had closed ranks, protective of their own and clearly believing his motives were dishonourable, his old wounds had reopened at their injustice. He had held some hope that Adam would at least listen to his side of the story once he learned that he was the customer who had saved the yard from ruin. When Adam had turned his back on him, that had seemed a double betrayal.

Then there had been Georganna's confession that she was carrying his child. He had set out to seduce her as a means to discredit his cousins, but that knowledge had changed his intentions. Although he did not love her, he had been prepared to make a life for Georganna and his child and raise the family he desired. Her rejection had been another blow to his pride. She had preferred marriage with a catamite to anything he could provide for her. If the Lovedays were determined to make him an outcast, then they would learn that he made a dangerous enemy.

Chapter Thirty-four

As a special treat for the older boys, Nathan and Bryn, Adam took them with him to call on a prospective customer for a brigantine who lived in Falmouth. He had hired a ketch to sail them there. They rounded the headland of St Mawes, guarded by the round-towered Tudor castle that perched on the promontory like a stack of giant cheeses, and tacked into the large tidal water of the River Fal estuary harbour, which consisted of the large central area of Carrick Roads, out of which branched several tidal creeks. Opposite St Mawes Castle on another headland was Pendennis Castle, with its tall square central keep.

'Both fortresses were built by Henry VIII against the threat of a French or Spanish invasion,' Adam remarked. 'Even at low tide there is a deep central channel which gives access to the port at all times, which is why it was chosen by the Post Office packet service for their overseas service.'

'There are a great variety of ships.' Nathan, who shared his father's passion for the sea, leaned against the ketch's side and pointed to two- and three-masted brigs, frigates and merchantmen moored alongside heavily armed men-of-war and sleek revenue cutters. The smaller luggers, sloops and ketches were used by fishermen or carried cargo along the coast.

Adam explained the differences in size and tonnage of the vessels to his son and noted that Bryn, who had been seasick for most of the voyage, gazed longingly at the quay with its tall grain store and warehouses and the tiled and thatched cottages spreading inland. He ruffled the boy's hair. The youth looked up at him and managed a weak smile.

'I must be a disappointment to you, Cap'n Loveday. I'm not much of a seaman.'

'It took me a while to get my sea legs. Hopefully, you will feel better on the voyage back to Fowey. And you are not a disappointment. The sea is not in everyone's blood.'

They stayed overnight in a respectable lodging house in the town and would sail back to Fowey after Adam's meeting the next morning. After they had breakfasted on devilled kidneys followed by smoked herring, Adam left the boys to explore the town.

'I should be finished with the customer by midday. Meet me back at the ketch by then so we do not miss the tide.' He gave both of them a handful of pennies. 'That's to buy a pasty if you are hungry, and I am sure you will find a shop in the town that sells sweetmeats. Stay on the main streets and don't go down any back alleys, get into any fights, or go off with any strange youth who entices you to see some strange sight. And stay together. The place is rife with pickpockets and rogues. Do I have your promise on that?'

'Yes, Papa.'

'Yes, Captain Loveday.'

The boys ran off. Adam trusted them to stay out of trouble. Though the port had its dangers, he and St John had been allowed to explore having been given similar warnings by their father.

After a couple of hours, their money spent, Bryn was bored. Nathan wanted to stay on the quayside and draw the different shapes and rigging of the ships. In the last year he had become interested in the workings of the shipyard and was showing the same skill and aptitude that Adam had done at his age. Bryn, although interested in the naval ships, was more fascinated by the other sights of the busy dock.

He sat on a pile of discarded sacking next to a crate of chickens that were to be loaded on a cargo ship larger than *Good Fortune*. For some time he watched the sailors rolling casks up the gangplanks to be stored in the hold, while others used pulleys to haul heavy crates over the side. Then the sound of a drum beating and pipes playing could be heard getting louder as whoever was playing them drew closer to the quay.

'C'mon, Nate. Let's go and see who's playing. It could be a travelling show with monkeys and wild animals.'

'It could be the King's men trying to trick a man into taking the King's shilling,' Nathan warned, trying to impress Bryn with his superior knowledge. 'You don't want to be taken by the pressgang.' He turned his head in the direction of the drumming. 'They could be coming down to the dock. Let me just finish this drawing, then we will go and see. I heard a church clock strike eleven. We have another hour before we must meet Papa.'

Nathan was immediately engrossed in his drawing, leaving a restless Bryn to amuse himself. The pipes and drum faded into the distance, the opportunity to witness some spectacle gone. Kicking a squashed orange that had fallen from one of the wicker baskets to be loaded, he wandered aimlessly through a maze of piled-up crates reading the destinations burned into the wood: Santander, Corunna, Lisbon, Gibraltar. He frowned. With the names came a tugging of memory, of heat scorching through clothing and an arid taste of dust. These flashes of dream-like recognition were coming more frequently, and often sparked the sensations of pain and darkness.

Then a harsh voice sounded from the direction of the ship – a voice with a cadence that chilled his blood and set his heart racing with terror. Instinctively he drew back, shielding his body with the crates. Through a gap he scanned the dock to locate the source of the voice. He caught a glimpse of Nathan some distance away, totally engrossed in his drawing and unaware of other events surrounding him. Then his eyes widened in horror. Further along the quayside stood a thin man of average height in beaver hat and greatcoat. Thick-sprouting black brows shadowed close-set eyes and a beak of a nose. A black goatee beard disguised thin turned-down lips and a prominent chin. Bryn shook uncontrollably. If the image was not enough, the man was striking the back and shoulders of his mute servant with the weighted end of his gold-topped walking cane. Memories crowded his mind. A woman's sobs. Angry shouts. Slamming doors. A child's scream of fear. Fear that was his own . . .

Bryn's ribs ached at the memory of that descending cane. A

name flashed into his mind. Ferdinand. Ferdinand was the name of the mute servant. The attacker was now shouting in anger. Terror gripped Bryn and he sank to the ground and covered his ears. The sound of his sobs was drowned by the noise of the shouted orders from masters and seamen, and the general bustle and melee of a busy port. For a long time he stayed hidden, until the hated voice was no longer audible, but still Bryn was too afraid to crawl from his hiding place. But he was no longer Bryn, was he? He was Xander, as his darling mother used to call him. Or rather he was Alexander Rufus Bryant.

Memories tumbled chaotically. His father had died when he was a baby. The beautiful manor house. His mother's remarriage and her unhappiness. The arguments. The tears. His stepfather, Eugene Mendoza Carforth, who was a brutal tyrant and the man on the dockside today. The arrival of Carforth's half-sister Arabella, who had spent her childhood with her family's Spanish relatives, but as Carforth's ward had now returned to England. Her tears and protests when a marriage was arranged against her wishes. Bryn sobbed harder, remembering the sudden death of his mother last year and the cold dark cellar where he had spent a month for disobeying his stepfather. Then had come the rescue by Arabella on a night when Eugene was away from the house, followed by their wild flight across England to find a passage that would take them to a cousin in Mexico, far away from their evil guardian.

His tears flowed faster. The last few days of their flight, when they feared they were being pursued, remained hazy to Bryn. But it must have been Arabella in the coach with him when it overturned. And all his mother's and step-aunt's jewels that had been stolen.

He tried to shut out the memories, but they clung like limpets, mocking the happiness he had found with the Lovedays. He did not want to remember. His mother was dead. Arabella was dead. He mourned them both. But Eugene Carforth was alive and his legal guardian. And Arabella had been convinced that her half-brother wanted Bryn dead so that he would become master of Bryn's father's estate.

Bryn was deeply scared. It was possible that Adam Loveday would never hand him back if he learned the truth. But the law was on the side of his legal guardian, not a stranger who had taken in a boy after a coach accident. And Adam Loveday was a man of honour and integrity. He would have no choice but to hand Bryn back to his guardian if Carforth so demanded, or he could face imprisonment himself.

Bryn did not want that to happen. He certainly did not want to return to his home and the dangers that awaited him. At eleven he was still a child, and too weak to fight the brutalities his stepfather could inflict upon him. But he would not always be a child. If he remained in Cornwall, he was safe and would grow up with a family he respected and who cared for him. When he became a man, he would confront his stepfather, win back his estate, and avenge his mother's death, for he was convinced that it had not been through natural causes but by the hand of Carforth.

He dried his eyes and calmed his breathing. There was only one certain way to escape his stepfather's clutches, and that was to keep secret his memories. He was happy to be Bryn Loveday until he came of age. How strange that young Joel, in choosing his name, had come so near to the truth. Bryn was similar to Bryant. His new identity still retained something of his true self.

He sat for a long time reflecting whether he could continue to keep this secret. He felt guilty that it would mean deceiving Adam and Senara Loveday, but what else could he do? He would never make the Lovedays regret taking him in, and one day, when he was master of his own inheritance, he would reward them.

The worried voice of Nathan calling his name made him stand up and dust down his clothing. After a hasty scan of the dock to ensure that his stepfather was nowhere in sight, he ran to join his friend. Adam was approaching the ketch, his step lighter than it had been for some weeks.

'That was a good morning's business. The man has placed an order for a brigantine,' Adam said. 'How was your morning, boys?'

Nathan showed his father his sketches, and Adam was lavish in his praise.

'What about you, Bryn?' he asked.

'I came to terms with my loss of memory, Captain Loveday. I have much to be grateful for in all you have done for me. I will never disappoint you, sir.'

'What has brought this on?' Adam laughed.

Bryn blushed and stumbled over his words in his attempt to hide his feelings of guilt at his deception. 'I just wanted to say that I could not have a better or more honourable man for my guardian.'

Adam ran his hand over the youth's head. 'I meant it when I said you would always have a place with us, Bryn. You have no need to fear on that score.'

Unable to control the emotion welling up, Bryn put his arms around his new guardian. Adam smiled down at both boys and placed his hands on their shoulders, making a silent vow that Bryn would never be judged an outsider and would be treated as an equal to his sons. The recent encounters with Tristan had been a salutary lesson about how good intentions could go wrong.

The morning after the disastrous gaming session, St John awoke with his brain murky and his head aching. With a sickly churning of foreboding gripping his gut, he attended the offices of Lancombe and Fairweather. His mood further deteriorated when he was kept cooling his heels for ten minutes before an officious-looking clerk ushered him into the inner office.

A bewhiskered lawyer wearing his wig and gown came from behind his desk to greet him. 'Mr Fairweather at your service, Mr Loveday.'

St John eyed him haughtily. 'And not before time. I have been kept waiting an unconscionable time.'

Mr Fairweather inclined his head in the briefest of bows. 'Your pardon, sir. I am of course your most humble servant. Do pray be seated.'

St John had dressed to impress in his newest gold-embroidered waistcoat, burgundy cut-away coat with pearl buttons and Italian leather top boots. He flipped his coat tails aside in the most imperious manner before seating himself in a leather high-backed chair. His hand rested negligently upon his gold-topped walking cane. The single sash window was closed tightly against the noise of the street outside and a sluggish fire burned in the grate. The room smelt of musty old parchment from the scrolls of dusty ribbon-tied papers piled on the floor.

Mr Fairweather coughed into his hand. 'There is a matter of some delicacy. The matter of several unpaid IOUs.'

Inwardly St John blanched, but he raised a brow as though incredulous and questioning. 'And why pray were they put into your hands, when they had but to be presented to me personally and they would immediately have been settled?'

'The sums are quite considerable.' Mr Fairweather remained obsequious.

'I shall attend upon my bank this instant. How much will settle these accounts?'

'Two and a half thousand guineas,' a clipped voice crisply informed him from the rear of the room. 'Plus of course the ten thousand pounds you owe me.'

St John shot from his chair and spun round, hatred contorting his features. 'So it's you? You'll get your damned money. Skulduggery was afoot last night.'

Tristan was leaning against the dark wood panelling beside the door, his arms crossed over his chest. He laughed coldly. 'Careful how you insult me. The moment of reckoning is upon you. Did you think I would forget your lies and deceit? You made me an outcast. The time has come for me to return the favour.'

'Go to hell!'

St John made to storm past his cousin to the door. Tristan barred his way. 'You will hear me out, unless you prefer that I call for a constable to arrest you for debt.'

'I said you would get your damned money,' St John bristled.

'There is not a banking house that will touch you. The IOUs are but the tip of the iceberg, are they not, St John? Once it is known you could not pay last night's wager, every creditor in the county will be pressing charges to recoup their losses.'

'Go to the devil! I am master of Trevowan. I honour my debts,' St John blustered. His face was a sickly grey above his high starched collar and the ruffles of his pristine stock.

'You have blundered through up until now.' Tristan's stare was icy as he gazed past St John to the lawyer. 'Mr Fairweather, would you kindly apprise my cousin as to the extent of indebtedness to myself?'

'I suggest that you be seated, Mr Loveday.' Fairweather nodded to St John. He picked up a leather document case and from it withdrew a sheaf of papers. When he spread them out across the

318

leather top of his desk, a sense of doom swept through St John. He recognised over a dozen other IOUs, his own signature on several loan documents, the contracts for the sale of two parcels of Trevowan land and the mortgage on the house.

'How are these in your possession?' His voice cracked.

'I have purchased them from the banks and the previous owners. They were eager to secure their money when I intimated that you were financially straitened.'

'You impeach my honour and will answer for it. Send your second to my room at the inn,' St John flung back.

Tristan laughed. 'If I had wanted to fight a duel over a matter of honour, I would have challenged you years ago for the treachery you perpetrated against me. I do not want you dead, cousin, and you would surely die, for there have been times when I have lived by the sword and pistol, whereas it is many years since you tested your skills.'

'You will not get away with this.'

Tristan grinned and spread his hands. 'I have done nothing wrong. Some would even see my actions as loyalty to a kinsman. A number of these creditors wanted their money some months ago. I have saved you from prison.'

'Then you know that to honour all these would make my family homeless.'

'As you made me homeless, my reputation reviled. But I am not so entirely heartless. I give you a month to raise the money before I foreclose.'

'Why do you not demand your pound of flesh into the bargain?' St John fumed.

'Thank you for reminding me,' Tristan drawled, regarding him through narrowed eyes. 'There is another condition. I want a written apology and a confession from you of what really took place that night on the beach. I want that now.'

'Never.'

Tristan turned to Mr Fairweather. 'Sir, kindly inform my cousin of the consequences of disregarding my request.'

The lawyer shuffled the papers uncomfortably. 'Mr Tristan Loveday would be within his rights to foreclose on the loans with immediate effect if the money is not repaid by the end of the day.

All these loans have been extended past their original repayment day.'

'And an extortionate rate of interest charged for the privilege,' St John flared.

'That is as may be, sir, but Mr Tristan Loveday is quite within his rights.' Mr Fairweather pulled a fresh piece of parchment from his desk, then took a quill from its stand in the inkwell and held it out to St John. 'I advise that you comply with Mr Tristan Loveday's request, sir.'

'I want advice from my own lawyer on these matters.'

Fairweather bowed respectfully. 'That is of course your prerogative, but his advice will be no different from mine.'

'And if I write this confession?' St John glared at his cousin. 'Do you intend to post it around the county?'

'I have been wronged by our family. I want them to know the truth and apologise. It need go no further.'

St John seemed to shrink in inches before Tristan's eyes. His face was deathly pale and his hands shook as though from the palsy. 'Why do you not just call me out and have done with it? That is the way gentlemen settle matters of honour.'

'I do not seek your death.'

'But this way my family will despise me.'

'They long ago accepted your faults, St John. I doubt their judgement will be as harsh upon you as it was upon me.'

'And the loans and debts? I need longer than a month to raise the money to pay them.'

'By giving you a month, I am offering you the second chance that you never gave me.' Tristan bent over the desk and opened the inkwell. 'Mr Fairweather will leave us while you write the truth of that night. And the document will be kept safe in my possession.'

St John knew when he was beaten. He still had a month to raise the money. His family would never turn their back upon him whilst he was master of Trevowan.

The long ride back to Trevowan was the loneliest and most agonising St John had ever undertaken. He had only his thoughts for company, and they were bleak indeed. The clear blue sky had brought a sharp frost and he pulled the collar of his caped greatcoat closer about his ears. He craved a warming drink of brandy but his hip flask was empty in his pocket. He had scorned to have it refilled before leaving Bodmin. Drink had been a major part of his downfall. He had decided to abstain from all alcohol and gaming. If only he could have found that wisdom and strength a year ago, how different everything would have been.

A groan of despair was torn from his chilled lips. Why had he not been satisfied with all he had inherited, a good wife and supportive family? He had failed everyone, not least his father, who had kept his trust in him to be a worthy master of Trevowan. His jealousy over Adam inheriting the shipyard had been based on his resentment that Adam had stolen part of his birthright. Yet St John would have hated running the yard. He had never been interested in shipbuilding and had no love for the sea. If he were to be honest, he would have sold the shipyard as soon as his debts began to mount, and that would have betrayed all that his father, grandfather and great-grandfather had worked to achieve. It galled him to admit it, but Adam had been a more deserving successor and the prestige of the yard had increased under his supervision.

His melancholy deepened. It would have been better had he drowned instead of being washed up on the beach at Porthleven. At least then there was still a chance the money could have been raised to save his family home. He recalled the madness of Izzy capering about the beach after she had found the silver buckle. She had so few expectations in life, but such joy in everything. He almost envied her. How different would his own life have been had he been so fully accepting of his fate? At the time he had been humbled that she had shared her good fortune in finding the buckle, which would have vastly improved her lot. She had seen his need as greater than hers and given him the money to buy a passage on a ship to return home. Once he was again lodged comfortably at Trevowan, he had not even thought to repay her, but had taken her generosity as his due.

Shame washed over him at his selfishness. It had been typical of many of his actions throughout his life, when he had thought of no one but himself. His mood darkened with every mile he travelled.

Night was almost upon him when he reached the crossroads that led to the shipyard. The evening star was bright in the clear sky and the moon when it rose would be two nights short of full and would clearly light the remainder of his journey. The cold had bitten into his bones, and having no wish to face the accusations of the womenfolk at yet another absence, he decided to eat at the Ship kiddley in the yard and warm himself with a hot toddy. He had not forgotten his earlier vow of abstinence. But one hot toddy would not make any difference.

Even in darkness the yard looked prosperous. Rush lights burned dimly in the windows of the cottages and the smell of woodsmoke drifted from the chimneys and formed pale clouds against the dark sky. A tall-masted ship was in the dry dock and the ribs of a large vessel were visible in the light of lanterns hanging outside the kiddley. It also looked as though another keel had been laid down. Inside the kiddley, men were singing a sea shanty to the accompaniment of a tin whistle.

Toby Jensen looked up when he entered and did not hide his surprise. 'Mr Loveday, this is unexpected. Your brother left the yard some hours past. Is aught amiss, sir?'

'No, Jensen. I am returning from Bodmin and the night is exceptionally cold. I thought to warm myself and take a hot toddy before I ride the last two miles to my home. Also I am tempted by the smell of your good wife's pasties.'

'Would it please you to come through to our own parlour, sir? The men are drinking to the laying down of the new keel.'

He shook his head and took a seat in a darkened corner. When he was recognised, the tin whistle fell silent and several men glanced curiously in his direction. 'Pray continue with your singing,' he said, 'I have no wish to intrude.'

As he ate his pasty and listened to the men's voices and coarse laughter, he felt alienated from this community, which had been such a large part of his father's world. If Edward or Adam had walked into the kiddley tonight, the men would have raised their tankards in welcome. For him there had only been suspicion in their eyes. He sipped his hot toddy and ordered another, then gestured to Jensen and threw several coins on the table. 'Give everyone a drink to toast the memory of my father.'

*

The moon had risen above the treetops when St John swung himself back into the saddle. He circled his gelding past the work sheds and forge and paused by the limewashed wall of his brother's and late father's office. Beyond the building the river inlet was silvered by the moonlight. He surveyed the outbuildings and school. The yard had virtually tripled in size since his days working here beside his father. He had until now regarded them as wasted years. But now tears stung the back of his eyes. They were treasured years, with Edward unendingly patient with his heir, who had no aptitude for woodwork or figures. Even then he had failed his father. Yet in the ghostly moonlight he did not feel his father's spirit cursing him. It was his own guilt that was the greatest burden to bear as he gave his horse its head and it picked up its pace towards its own stable.

It was late when St John reached Trevowan, and the women had all retired. That suited him. He could not face their recriminations. He took a candle up to the nursery and stood over his son's cradle. George Arthur was sleeping, but St John put the candle on a table and picked him up. He held him close, and in his sleep the boy's fingers curled around his own. When St John laid him back in the crib and covered him with his blanket, his own face was wet with tears. How would his son view the father who had wantonly gambled away his ancestral home and security? No doubt with hatred, for that would have been how St John would have reacted. He glanced briefly at Thea in her small bed. She was the image of Felicity and he felt a qualm that he had never loved the toddler as she deserved, always resenting that she was not the son he craved.

Retrieving his candle, he looked in briefly upon Rowena, who lay on her back with her arm thrown above her head, her fair hair spilling over the pillow. She was so like Meriel and could be just as calculating and demanding. She loved her father, but was it for himself or for all the good things he had provided for her? She would no doubt despise him for throwing all that away and was too spoilt to suffer without complaint any constraint upon the acquisitions she regarded as her right. Her mother had left him fast enough when a richer lover had enticed her away. Meriel had lied and cheated all her life. She had never loved him. He could not even be certain that Rowena was his child. Meriel had taunted him that Adam had been her lover before him, but she had chosen to marry

St John as he was the heir to Trevowan and Adam only a poorly paid lieutenant in the navy. Adam had denied her accusations, and out of pride St John had chosen to believe him. Rowena had always adored her Uncle Adam. No doubt she would now regard him with greater favour as the wealthier of the two brothers, and that would be a bitter pill for St John to swallow.

Finally, he opened the door to his wife's chamber. Felicity was turned on her side with her back to him. A significant omen for what was to come. He felt a moment's tenderness and put out his hand to touch the long braid of hair that lay over the sheet. It was soft and silken, her skin smooth and without blemish. In the early days of their marriage she had been an eager and ardent bedfellow. He had never loved or valued her as she deserved. She stirred in her sleep and mumbled his name. He pinched the flame from the candle with his fingers and drew back into the shadows, but his wife did not wake. For that he was grateful.

The moonlight streamed through the windows of the first-floor landing and hall as he retraced his steps downstairs to his study. He sat slumped at his desk, staring at the pale face in the portrait of his grandfather and seeking a solution to his woes. His guilt gouged him. He had failed Edward. Failed his wife. And God help him, he had bitterly failed his son. The boy would be penniless and homeless. He had even failed young Bryn, whom he had rescued, stealing the valuables that would have been his inheritance. Tristan had given him a month to find the money to save Trevowan. He faced the fact that had it been a year, he still could not succeed. The debts were too much to expect his family to help.

He rubbed his hand across his face, seeing only one honourable course left to him. He hoped fervently that one day George Arthur would forgive him for the way he had squandered his inheritance. Yet he could not forgive himself or bear to see the accusation that would one day surely shine in his son's eyes.

He took comfort from the thought that although Thomas and Adam had many responsibilities of their own, they would not fail his family. Adam would never allow those who had made Trevowan their home to be without a roof over their heads.

He drew the remaining coins from his pocket and placed them in a pile with a short note to Isaac Nance instructing that they were to be delivered to a woman called Izzy living on the beach at Porthleven and stating that she had saved his life when he was attacked.

He also wrote notes to his wife and to Adam. The hardest letter of all was to the son he had failed so lamentably. He told George Arthur that he loved him, asked for his forgiveness and warned him against the evils of gambling.

Those tasks completed, he went to the cabinet and took out the box of duelling pistols that had last been used by Captain William Loveday when he had killed his wife's lover. His hand was steady as he primed the powder and inserted the shot. Then, taking up the decanter of brandy that sat on the corner of his desk, he walked purposefully out of the house. His vow of abstinence had no meaning now.

Chapter Thirty-five

While St John had been facing his own nightmare in Bodmin, Georganna was also in the grip of terror. She had been in labour for two days and was convinced she was going to die. She was weak and exhausted, and to the horror of the midwife and the doctor who had also been summoned to attend her, she begged them to leave and give her a few moments alone with her husband.

'A birthing chamber is no place for a husband,' the lantern-jawed Dr Forsythe had protested. 'The child is ready to be born.'

'I must speak with my husband while I have strength,' Georganna gritted through clenched teeth during a lull in the pain. She had been pleading for an hour and become more distressed with each refusal. 'I am going to die. I must speak with him.'

'The child is merely slow in coming. You fear unnecessarily,' Dr Forsythe declared, his face florid beneath imperious side-whiskers.

'It is not slow; it is tearing me apart. Get Thomas. Get him now!' she screamed. 'Thomas! I need you. Thomas!'

The door burst open and Thomas glared at the shocked faces bent over his wife.

'Mr Mercer, I must insist you leave.' Dr Forsythe barred his way.

'Thomas, please.' Georganna held out her hand, her body and face wet with sweat. 'Come closer.'

The doctor and midwife retired to the far side of the room to grant the couple a brief moment of privacy. As soon as he was in reach Georganna gripped Thomas's hand with surprising strength, her voice hoarse with passion. 'Don't let my baby die. You must save it. The baby is innocent.'

'You must be strong, my dear. Were not Felicity and Hannah safely delivered of a son and a daughter recently?' Thomas stared down at the tortured woman and regretted the last months, when he had been so angry with her. When she had refused to reveal the name of the child's father, he had been furious and could barely tolerate her company. His mother had remonstrated at his neglect and he had used the building work at the theatre as an excuse to stay away from their home. Margaret Mercer had summoned him as soon as the labour began and he'd had no choice but to keep vigil at his mother's side throughout his wife's ordeal. As the hours had passed and Georganna's screams became louder, his anger at her betrayal had drained away. It had been impossible to hear her suffering and not be moved.

Throughout the long hours Margaret had sung Georganna's praises and Thomas was reminded of all that was good in her and the happier days they had shared. He could never repay his wife that their marriage had been the saving of Mercer's Bank. Had the bank failed and hundreds of people lost their money, Thomas would have carried that shame throughout his life. The scandal would have ended any chance he might have had of being a successful play-wright, for no one would come to see a play written by a man who had brought misery to so many lives. He owed Georganna his good name in more ways than one. If only she had not been so stubborn about revealing the father's name. Yet was that not also to protect Thomas and spare his reputation? A duel would cause scandal and speculation. It could be the ruin of his new playhouse.

Suddenly Georganna's eyes rounded in terror and a scream tore from her as her body arched.

'The child is coming.' The midwife elbowed Thomas aside. 'Push, my dear. Push with all the strength you can muster.'

'No!' The doctor intervened. 'There is a problem.'

His words halted Thomas, who was backing towards the door. Georganna had fallen back against the pillows apparently unconscious.

'Save my wife! You must save my wife,' Thomas demanded.

A deathly silence descended upon the room as the doctor bent over Georganna. Then the midwife lifted away from the bed a bloodied bundle. She stared sorrowfully at Thomas.

'I'm sorry, sir, the cord was around the baby's neck. It is stillborn. Ain't nothing we can do. It was a girl.'

There was a sob from Georganna, who had regained her wits and had heard the midwife's words. Her eyes were harrowed as she stared at her husband. 'Don't you dare say it is a blessing that she is dead. I wanted a child so much from the moment I first felt it move. I wanted someone I could shower with affection and who would love me unreservedly.'

Thomas shook his head and found there were tears on his cheeks. 'I am sorry, my dear. You must rest and regain your strength.'

'Better I had died than my child,' she moaned. Then her body again contorted in pain. 'Forgive me, Thomas, so that I can die in peace.'

'You are not going to die, madam,' Dr Forsythe said forcefully. 'That will be the afterbirth. Midwife, tend to her.'

'Ain't no afterbirth, Doctor.' There was excitement in the woman's voice. 'It's another baby. A twin. And this one's coming into the world with no fuss.'

Thomas stared in shocked fascination as another child was lifted from the mother. The midwife was beaming. 'Another daughter, sir. This one is alive.'

Thomas scarcely noticed the baby, his stare fixed upon the now unconscious form of his wife. Her face was whiter than the bed linen. He pulled a chair up to the side of the bed and stayed there with his head bowed, remembering all the happy times they had shared and the sacrifices this proud and intelligent woman had made for him. As he watched her weak and exhausted figure fighting for her life, he prayed fervently that she would not die.

Dick Nance, the gamekeeper at Trevowan, was patrolling the grounds an hour before dawn. A waist-high mist hung across the fields but the moon made his progress easy. He knew all the runs the poachers used for their rabbit traps and where a herd of deer sheltered in the wood behind the orchard. With the food shortages and the price of flour so high, poaching was on the increase. The Lovedays had always turned a blind eye to an occasional rabbit or fish taken from the streams, but in recent weeks it had become more serious and had to be stopped.

A single shot from the wood had him running with his blunderbuss at the ready. Half a dozen wood pigeons had been startled from their roost and flapped noisily overhead. Nance paused on the edge of the wood, his head cocked to one side, listening intently. His hand signalled his hound, Tyke, to lie motionless on the ground. There was no sound of stealthy footsteps, no telltale cracking of twigs to reveal where the poacher was working.

'Come out and show yourselves,' Dick shouted. 'Or it will be the worse for you.'

An eerie silence followed, broken only by the cry of a stoat. Nance sniffed the air for signs of human scent, his nose as sharp as any hound's. Another silent hand signal to Tyke had the hound criss-crossing through the undergrowth ahead of his master. A low growl turned Nance in the direction of a lightning-split oak, his gun cocked and ready to fire. Tyke was now making strange whimpering sounds, and then Nance saw the figure slumped at the base of the oak. A pistol shot to the side of the head was not a pretty sight, and blood and brains soaked the undergrowth. This was no shooting accident: the pistol was still gripped in his master's lifeless fingers.

Refusing to leave his wife's side as she maintained her fragile hold upon life, Thomas finally fell into a doze. He awoke with a start. Had he imagined it, or had Georganna whispered his name? The candle on the bedside table had burned low, the pale orange glow revealing the still figure in a lace nightcap and gown with the coverlet pulled up to the waist, her hands folded over her breast. Seeing her motionless, devoid of colour and the vibrancy that had been so endearing, he was again smitten with a sense of loss, of regret for what might have been.

He knelt on the floor beside the bed and took her hand in his. 'You asked for forgiveness, but I am the one who should beg you to forgive me all the wrongs you have suffered at my selfishness.' He kissed the hand and laid it against his cheek.

The fingers moved weakly, and when he looked into her face she had opened her eyes and was smiling. 'You were all I wanted and more, Thomas.'

Her voice showed her returning strength and he was humbled by her words. He blinked a tear of joy and relief from his eye that she had survived, his own voice strained with emotion. 'And you deserved so much better from me. Hush, my dear, you need to regain your strength.'

'You do not hate me?'

He brushed a tendril of damp hair from her brow. 'You faced and overcame your greatest fears. You are a woman to be admired. You must not torment yourself unnecessarily.'

Her eyes remained shadowed. 'I was such a fool, but I cannot regret the life I have been blessed and spared to create. I regret only that one was taken from me. That I never held her in my arms or kissed her cheek. I will never abandon my daughter.' Her grip tightened over his fingers as she fought for her child as valiantly as she had fought for her life. 'And if it means that we must now live apart, then I accept your judgement. Although it is not what I would wish.'

'I could not so dishonour you after all the sacrifices you have made for my family.'

'But can you accept the child as your own?'

'I can accept it as yours, and that is all that matters now. Have you a name for your daughter?'

'I would like Grace, if you do not object.'

'A fitting name.' He pressed her fingers again to his lips. 'Now rest, you will overtire yourself, my dear.'

He stood up, but as he stared down at her his smile faded and he could not stop himself asking, 'Twins run in the Loveday family. Was Tristan Loveday your lover?'

'In such thoughts lie madness and destruction. Grace is our miracle. A child died. Think only of Grace as God's gift. The Lord's second chance for us to have a family.'

When he did not respond, she added with heartfelt passion, 'Thomas, I hope Grace will be a blessing to you also. And it would please me greatly if Lucien would be her godfather. I would like us all to remain friends and things be again as they were between us.'

He bowed over her hand and once more raised it to his lips. 'As you will it, my dear. I owe you that much at least. A man such as I could not have a better helpmeet and wife.'

She smiled after her husband's departing figure. She knew him too well to believe that the matter of Grace's parentage would be easily laid to rest. And she was determined that their marriage would be fulfilling and rewarding for them both, and that most importantly Grace would never be tainted by the stigma of illegitimacy.

Adam had fought many sea battles and seen scores of bodies mutilated by grapeshot. When he had been warned by Dick Nance of the manner of St John's death he had thought himself prepared to view the body of his twin. Yet the sight of the corpse shook him to the core of his being. Ordering Nance to bring a cart to take the body back to Trevowan, he fell to his knees at his twin's side. Clearly this was no accident. The empty brandy decanter and the pistol still in his brother's hand were evidence of suicide. With a new son and everything to live for, what had driven him to such despair as to take his own life?

The depth of Adam's grief ploughed mercilessly through him. He took the linen stock from his neck and tenderly wrapped it around St John's wound to hide the grisly injury, then closed his brother's eyes. What had possessed him to kill himself? Sadly, Adam knew the cause must be rooted in his twin's gambling debts. But why had he not come to him? He would have given his last penny to save Trevowan and his brother from ruin. And how bad were these debts that St John would see his death as the only means of redeeming his honour? St John was selfish but he was also a fighter and had found the means to repay his debts in the past.

Adam wiped away the tears that streaked his face. Ever since he could remember, he had been at loggerheads with his twin. They had fought over everything imaginable, each trying to prove to the other that he was the stronger, faster, cleverer son. Natural rivalries when so much had been at stake, and the heart of it had always been Trevowan. All his life Adam had resented that because St John had been born a mere three minutes before him, his older brother would inherit the home Adam adored. That had been the main root of their rivalry – who was the more worthy heir to Trevowan. Yet beneath the rivalry had been the bond of twins driven by ambition and a hunger for adventure. They had never been identical either in appearance or nature. As the heir, St John had taken everything for granted and his expectations had been of a life of ease and luxury.

Adam had had to work for all he had achieved. They had never been like two halves of the same coin but rather the opposite sides of it, the head and the tail. Fashioned in the same mould but with two different identities bound by a common unit.

He hung his head and prayed for the soul of his brother. Already a tangible part of himself was cut adrift, and although they had fought and squabbled all their lives, Adam knew that he would mourn St John to the end of his days.

Dick Nance had returned with the wagon, and Adam lifted St John from the ground and placed him carefully on the wooden planks.

'You did right to come to me first, Nance. Take the body to the house. I do not want the women to see him until he has been laid out in a more fitting manner. Winnie Fraddon is discreet. She will lay him out. I want no gossip that this was more than a gun misfiring. I shall inform my womenfolk of the true manner of his death and then notify Sir Henry Traherne. As Justice of the Peace he must be informed. I trust I can count on your discretion?' He could trust Sir Henry to record death by a shooting accident. A suicide verdict meant the estate could become the property of the crown.

Nance nodded. 'It be a grievous day for Trevowan. You can rely on me, Mr Loveday.'

Chapter Thirty-six

The funeral was a quiet affair the next day, presided over by Joshua Loveday. St John was laid to rest in the Loveday vault at Penruan church. The family were in shock and gathered at Trevowan after the service. No amount of seclusion could stop the gossip spreading like wildfire through the community. It was two days before Christmas, and all family festivities had been cancelled. Felicity, who had shown great courage and dignity throughout the service, had retired to her room. Rowena had been sobbing hysterically and would only allow Senara to console her. They were in the young woman's chamber so that her tears did not unsettle the younger children. Since Adam and Senara's children had remained at Boscabel, Bridie had taken Charlotte and Rafe, who had become silent and withdrawn, to the nursery to play card games. Amelia and Elspeth were in the winter parlour with Japhet, Gwen and Peter, talking in hushed tones as to what could have driven St John to take his own life.

St John had appointed Adam and Joshua as executors and trustees of his will, and they were in the study with Mr Meredith, the family lawyer, who was the only non-family member to attend the service. Mr Meredith was reading the will, but had reached only as far as declaring Adam to be the appointed guardian of the estate and his twin's family when he was interrupted by the arrival of Mr Fairweather from Bodmin.

The lawyer bowed stiffly to the men. 'Gentlemen, my condolences upon your loss at this tragic time. I would not intrude upon your grief, but after learning of Mr St John Loveday's death, it was expedient that I inform you of the current state of Mr Loveday's affairs. They are pertinent to the future of the estate and may override any bequests in the deceased's will.'

Mr Meredith adjusted the spectacles that perched on the end of his nose and looked askance at Adam. His elderly figure was stooped with sadness, for he had served the family since the time of their grandfather.

'Then do pray inform us of the facts at your disposal, Mr Fairweather,' Adam replied. The sick dread that had settled over him since he had learned the manner of his twin's death threatened to unman him. Only the prospect of scandal and dishonourable consequences would have driven his brother to suicide. Adam drew a steadying breath, preparing to learn that the estate was more heavily mortgaged than any of them had believed.

Mr Fairweather cleared his throat. 'I act on behalf of a third party who is in possession of several loan agreements that have fallen due on behalf of the Trevowan estate. He also has in his possession a great many IOUs written by the deceased and which remain unpaid, and a mortgage upon the house.'

'How much do these amount to?' Adam demanded, his body already braced against receiving a weighty blow.

'It is my regretful duty to inform you that they are in excess of seventy thousand guineas. Mr St John Loveday has given my client a promissory note that if the money is not repaid by the first week in January, the house and estate will be relinquished in settlement.'

Adam shot to his feet, his face flushed with anger. 'I would have the name of your client who would strip us of our family home. And under what terms will he extend the payment date?'

There was a creak of floorboards behind him and Adam spun round as Tristan announced, 'I would not strip anyone of their home; indeed, my generosity over the last year has prevented me from foreclosing earlier. St John's incompetent estate management and excessive gambling have brought the family to ruin. At least this way Trevowan stays in the family.' His stare was chilling upon Adam. 'Though I suspect that you would rather have seen it burned to the ground than my ever being master here.'

Adam darted forward, his fist crashing into his cousin's jaw.

'Damn you, have you not brought enough shame to our family that you must now destroy us? Because of your underhand dealings St John is dead. You as good as killed him. Murderer!' He slammed a second blow into his cousin's gut, doubling him over.

Joshua grabbed Adam's arms and dragged him away. 'Enough, Adam! Fisticuffs is not the answer. There must be a way we can discuss this rationally.' He needed all his strength to hold Adam back and his voice was breathless as he demanded, 'Who are you, sir?'

Tristan bowed to Joshua. 'I am the grandson of your uncle Walter Loveday. Your servant, sir.'

'Good Lord, Tristan!' Joshua exclaimed. 'I did not recognise you. My nephew's death has robbed me of my wits. I do not know how you dare to show your face here.'

'What knavery did you perpetrate to cheat St John out of his inheritance?' Adam raged as he wrestled to be free of his uncle's hold.

'I see the old prejudices are still in place,' Tristan announced with haughty disdain.

'This anger will not serve anyone, Adam,' Joshua reasoned. 'This is a sorry business. And one that has shocked us all.'

'I did not seek St John's death.' Tristan ignored Adam and addressed Joshua. 'Mr Fairweather also has a document signed by St John that should be read by the family in private. I will not turn anyone who was dependent upon my cousin's hospitality from their home, although that door was slammed firmly in my face.' He bowed, his final stare challenging as it lingered upon Adam. 'Good day to you, gentlemen. I will take up residence at Trevowan at the end of next month.'

'Over my dead body,' Adam raged.

'If that is what it takes, so be it! I await your seconds calling upon mine.' Tristan spun on his heel and strolled from the room, adding, 'Though I warn you that the scandal a duel would unleash is far worse than St John gambling his inheritance away.'

Joshua tightened his hold on Adam as the younger man strained to rush after his cousin. 'You cannot fight the law, Adam. St John has lost everything.'

Mr Fairweather gathered together his papers and handed a sealed parchment to Joshua. 'This is the document signed by your nephew. Mr Adam Loveday would be wise to heed its contents before challenging my client.' Nervous at so much anger and tension, the lawyer scurried from the study.

Mr Meredith also bowed to the family and left.

Joshua released his nephew. 'This at least should be read before further judgement or decisions are made.'

'What difference can it make? I will sell Boscabel to pay St John's debts. I will never allow that knave to desecrate our family home.' Adam continued to rage.

'You would never raise the money in time.'

Adam acknowledged that his uncle was right. It would take months to sell Boscabel and raise the money to clear Trevowan of debt. In this Tristan had won.

Joshua broke the seal and scanned the few lines in St John's hand. His voice shook as he read.

I, St John Loveday, duly confess to the wrong perpetrated upon my cousin Tristan Loveday. He was innocent of the crimes of which he was accused. I was the one who stole from one of the dying on the beach on the night of the storm. Tristan fought with me to stop my actions. When Grandpapa discovered where we had been that night, I put the items into Tristan's coat and accused him of robbing the dead.

St John Loveday

'So Tristan was innocent,' Joshua proclaimed. 'He took no part in the abomination of murder and destruction caused by the wreckers that night. Sadly, St John had fewer scruples and compounded his betrayal by condemning your cousin. It is no wonder that Tristan hated him.'

'And now Tristan wants to destroy us all,' Adam fumed. His thoughts were reeling from this fresh shock. St John had kept up his lies for years. His twin had always been devious – but this . . . Adam shuddered. His old loyalty to his brother was still blaming Tristan for St John's death.

'If he wanted to destroy you, why did he commission the building of *Good Fortune*?' Joshua looked equally stunned by the confession. 'Without that order you would have had to close the yard.'

Adam was too angry to heed reason. 'He wanted to triumph over us all. He may now dress in fine clothes, but he still has the mentality of a guttersnipe. I will never forgive him for stealing Trevowan from us.'

'Your twin is the one who shamed our name. It was his weakness that caused his downfall,' Joshua said heavily. 'There have been many occasions when he lied to save his skin. Before St John became embroiled with the smugglers, your father suspected that certain objects of value had been pawned or sold by him to pay his debts. And certainly your Uncle William's legacy and his wife's jewels were far less than my expectation. Many of Lisette's jewels that should have been in her room were missing after her death. And when thwarted, St John had a vindictive streak. We all suspected that he tried to burn down Boscabel shortly after you moved in because he was jealous you would inherit the shipyard, which he considered to be his birthright.'

Adam digested this in silence. Everything Joshua said was true. St John had been capable of all that and more. Yet it did not lessen his anger at Tristan's treachery. 'St John lost Trevowan through selfishness and weakness. But Tristan was calculating and manipulative to achieve his ends. This proves that he never wanted to be part of our family. He was the viper in our breast.'

'And now we must inform the others of this catastrophe,' Joshua said heavily.

Felicity was asked to join them, but she kept her face hidden beneath the veil of her widow's weeds. Senara, who had given Rowena a sedative so the girl had fallen asleep, was also present. For some moments the news was received in stunned silence. Then Amelia began to weep into her hands. 'How could he so basely betray Edward?'

'Oh, the shame and humiliation,' Felicity gasped and fell into a swoon.

Elspeth banged her cane on the floor and stood up, anger bolstering her fortitude. 'So this is where family rivalry has brought us – to ruin! Tristan, the ne'er-do-well, is master of Trevowan.'

'The blackguard will answer for his treachery,' Japhet fumed.

'It is legally done.' Joshua held up his hands to calm their outbursts. 'If Tristan had not bought up St John's debts, then the estate would be declared bankrupt and the creditors would be swooping on it for any pickings they could claim. The result would be the same. Trevowan is lost to us. At least Tristan has spared us public disgrace.'

'How much is needed to buy back the debts?' Japhet demanded. 'Whatever I have is yours, Adam, to save Trevowan.'

'I appreciate your support, but it is not for you to sacrifice your dream, cousin,' Adam returned as he paced the room. 'Even the sale of Boscabel will not meet the debts, and the sale of my estate could place the yard in jeopardy. I cannot risk that when it is all we have left.'

Amelia was waving smelling salts under Felicity's nose, and as her wits returned, she groaned, 'Was the estate not entailed?'

'That is only to ensure it passes to a male heir; it does not save it from bankruptcy,' Adam stopped his pacing to reply.

'What is to happen to us?' Felicity wailed. 'I have only a small portion of money in trust to safeguard Charlotte's future. I have two other children and Rowena now to provide for.'

'To Tristan's credit, he has declared that no one is to be made homeless,' Joshua said.

'We will not take his charity so he can lord it over us,' Adam flared. 'I will provide for all our family.'

'Adam, you have four children of your own,' Amelia observed. 'I have a property in London I can return to and money enough to provide for Rafe. Felicity is welcome to live with me. And Elspeth . . .'

'But if you live in London, Rafe will become a stranger to us.' Senara voiced a deeper worry. 'It will divide the family further. Cornwall is the only home that Rowena has known. Her friends as well as family are here. As are your family and friends, Amelia.'

Their stepmother dabbed at her eyes. 'This has overset us all. I doubt I would now find the bustle and noise of London acceptable. I can afford to buy a house nearby, and would welcome the company of Elspeth, Felicity and the children.'

'Your offer is very kind,' Felicity sniffed, 'but I could not expect you to support us all. I still have a few investments in my name that should bring in an income of one hundred pounds a year, enough for us to live carefully.'

'Well, I have no intention of being driven from the home where I was born or giving up my mares,' Elspeth snapped. 'I am too old and too set in my ways.'

'You are welcome to live at Boscabel, Aunt Elspeth,' Adam stated.

'Or Tor Farm if it pleases you,' Japhet said, going to the side of the old woman. 'I would always value your expertise on the horses and there is room enough for you to stable your mares. Hannah could not have reared the foals without your help. I am indebted to you.'

'St John has much to answer for,' Adam raged.

'And he paid with his life,' Joshua reminded them. 'Now is the time for us to rebuild ours. Bricks and mortar do not make a family. It is unity and loyalty.'

'If only St John had confided in us the scale of his debts,' Peter said. 'There must have been some way we could all have helped.'

'St John guarded his secrets well,' Adam said with bitterness. 'As did we all in different ways. A secret is its own destructive force; even if taken to a deathbed it can cloud that person's whole life. I doubt any of us have been entirely innocent throughout our lives. We all have regrets and have made mistakes. It is the learning from them that is important. It is how we deal with the future that matters.'

'You cannot be suggesting that we allow Tristan to get away with his actions.' Japhet looked disbelieving.

'No. But unless we are to allow our wild blood to wreck what we have worked all our lifetimes to achieve, we must consider carefully. How would my father have dealt with this?'

Joshua nodded sagely, 'I would give much for Edward's wisdom now. If any lesson is to be learned, it is to be honest with ourselves and others.'

'I can never forgive Tristan,' Adam announced. 'By these actions he is and will always be an outcast from our family. But united we will go on to finer achievements and greatness.'

Japhet poured out glasses of Canary and handed them around. He raised his own glass. 'Ladies and gentlemen, a toast to ourselves and to triumphing over adversity. No one has succeeded in breaking our spirit. To our future success.'

Everyone raised their glasses, united and as one.

'To the Lovedays.'